PRAISE FOR THE NOVELS OF

EMILIE RICHARDS

"...intricate, seductive and a darned good read."
—*Publishers Weekly* on *Iron Lace*

"A fascinating tale of the tangled race relations
and complex history of Louisiana...this is a page-turner."
—*New Orleans Times-Picayune* on *Iron Lace*

"Emilie Richards makes a tale of class,
culture and color come alive with her emphasis on the
flavorful sights, sounds and languages of New Orleans."
—*Tallahassee Democrat* on *Iron Lace*

"Richards's ability to portray compelling characters
who grapple with challenging family issues is laudable,
and this well-crafted tale should score well
with fans of Luanne Rice and Kristin Hannah."
—*Publishers Weekly* starred review on *Fox River*

"Well-written, intricately plotted novel..."
—*Library Journal* on *Whiskey Island*

"A multifaceted charmer...
Richards's characters evince impressive depth...."
—*Publishers Weekly* on *Whiskey Island*

Beautiful Lies is "a romance in the best sense,
appealing to the reader's craving for exotic landscapes,
treacherous villains and family secrets...."
—*The Cleveland Plain Dealer*

"A multi-layered plot, vivid descriptions
and a keen sense of place and time."
—*Library Journal* on *Rising Tides*

IRON LACE

EMILIE RICHARDS

MIRA®

ISBN 1-55166-862-9

IRON LACE

Copyright © 1996 by Emilie Richards McGee.

MIRA and the Star Colophon are trademarks used under license and registered in Australia, New Zealand, Philippines, United States Patent and Trademark Office and in other countries.

Visit us at www.mirabooks.com

Printed in U.S.A.

ACKNOWLEDGMENTS

This book never would have been completed without the help of some special people. My thanks to the staffs of the New Orleans Public Library, Tulane University Library, the University of New Orleans Library and the Cuyahoga County Library in Bay Village, Ohio. Also thanks go to the staff of the New Orleans Collection, who enjoy researching even the most esoteric questions about their beautiful city.

Many thanks to two New Orleanians, the reverends Melanie Morel Sullivan and Albert D'Orlando, who over a period of years have shared with me their riveting personal stories about race relations and the civil rights movement in Louisiana.

I read so many wonderful books on New Orleans and South Louisiana that it's difficult to choose only a few to acknowledge here. The works of Lafcadio Hearn, Harnett Kane and Kate Chopin fueled my imagination. Works about the hurricane of 1893 by Dale Rogers and Loulan Pitre helped me ground my imagination in history, as did *Storyville* by Al Rose and *Satchmo* by Louis Armstrong. *Righteous Lives* by Kim Rogers gave me a greater understanding of those pivotal years when courageous African-Americans refused to sit at the back of the bus for even one more day.

Thanks to my agent Maureen Moran, who believed in this book from the beginning. Thanks to Damaris Rowland and Amy Moore, whose enthusiasm helped renew my own at different points on this journey. Thanks to my editor Leslie Wainger and MIRA's Dianne Moggy for their hard work and skillful guidance.

Personal thanks go to Karen Stone and Erica Spindler for their encouragement when this book was just a flicker in my imagination. And to Alison Hart, Jasmine Cresswell and Jan Powell who helped keep me on track as I struggled to bring that flicker to life. Many thanks to Karen Harper for her enthusiasm and support.

Most of all, thanks to my children, Shane, Jessie, Galen and Brendan, who did without mothering every now and then during the writing of this book. And most particularly to my husband, Michael, whose enthusiasm for New Orleans rivals my own, and whose enthusiasm for me never flags, even through the most difficult of times.

For Michael,
who has always believed in me and in this book.

CHAPTER 1

1965

Phillip Benedict was never easy to find. He had an efficiency apartment on New York's East Side and a room with a bed and hot plate in West Los Angeles. But when Phillip was in New Orleans, he shared quarters with Belinda Beauclaire.

Belinda had a place of her own, half of a run-down shotgun double with four rooms that lined up from front to back like the passenger cars on the *City of New Orleans.* She had painted those rooms the colors of jewels, amethyst and emerald, garnet and sapphire, and covered them with collages of fabric and photographs. Phillip had never been inside the shotgun when there weren't candles burning or incense from one of the botanicas on Rampart Street that sold goofer dust and John the Conqueror and whispered free advice on how to use them.

Belinda didn't believe in voodoo, but she liked it better than the Christian religions that had kept Negroes down since they stepped off the slave ships. She didn't like the term *Negroes,* either. *Negro* was all right if that other race wanted to call itself by the formal

Caucasian. But if that other race was white, then by God she was black, and certainly not colored, like something a little kid did on a boring rainy day. Phillip's mother agreed with her. It was just one of the ways Belinda and Nicky were compatible.

Belinda was a stunning woman, a kindergarten teacher with a fluid, loose-limbed walk, a slow smile and her own disturbing mixture of intelligence and sensuality. Everything about Belinda suited Phillip, and these days he found his way to New Orleans more and more often.

Early on a Saturday evening in February, Phillip left Belinda's house and locked the door behind him. Belinda had been gone since early morning, and he had spent the day hunched over his portable typewriter, punching keys with the fingers of one hand and swilling dark-roast coffee and chicory with the other. He was a freelance journalist, and unless he wanted the *free* to mean more than it should, he had to keep work hours like anybody else.

The sun had nearly reached the horizon, but he was surprised to find that the evening air was still warm and fragrant with the promise of spring. There were rain clouds forming, and the sunset was going to be spectacular.

He was not from New Orleans, had not masked for Mardi Gras as a child or attended the city's staunchly segregated schools. He had no memories of first cigarettes or first kisses to fill him with nostalgia, but every once in a while the city could still reach out and grab him, despite his best efforts to maintain a journalist's objectivity.

Curiosity could do the same. Today, curiosity, in the form of a telephone call, had grabbed and shaken him until he suspected that his good sense had been jarred loose. But, for better or worse, he was on his way to find out.

Phillip backed his car out of Belinda's drive and turned it toward the Garden District. In her brief call, Aurore Gerritsen had given him careful instructions on how to reach her home. He followed them now, as his mind dwelled on the remainder of their conversation.

Aurore Le Danois Gerritsen, majority stockholder of Gulf Coast Shipping, mother of State Senator Ferris Gerritsen and daughter of a family with blood as blue as Louisiana's fleur-de-lis, wanted him to write her biography.

The horizon was a glorious sun-washed gold by the time he parked just off Prytania Street. There had been room to park in front of Aurore Gerritsen's house—more than enough room, considering that her property could easily have accommodated the greater portion of a football field. But he wanted to experience the neighborhood, to understand the milieu that had helped to make her the woman she was.

There were more than enough clues along his two-block stroll. The houses he passed were a selection of Italianate, raised cottage and Greek Revival styles that had settled comfortably into the scenery a century before. Some deserved to be called mansions, while others were only homes for the well-to-do. Moss-draped live oaks as old as the Civil War creaked in the evening breeze, and magnolias waited patiently for the days in far-off May when their blossoms would perfume the city.

He glimpsed swimming pools and highly polished Cadillacs. Since it was carnival season, the coveted flag of Rex—flown only by the elite few who had been king of carnival—waved from two different balconies.

If any black people lived here, they were housekeepers and maids who fanned away the summer nights in airless attic rooms.

By the time Phillip reached Prytania, he was aware that his presence had been noticed. He was not dressed like a gardener or a house painter. He wore a dark suit and a conservative tie, and he was headed for Aurore Gerritsen's front gate.

"Hey, boy!"

Phillip considered ignoring the summons. Almost any other day, he would have. But this was research, too. He turned and gave the old man who had shouted to him a quick survey.

The man was pale and as gnarled as a cypress root. He wore a seersucker suit that was perfectly appropriate south of the Mason-Dixon line—but nowhere else on earth. He was leaning against an iron fence about fifteen yards away, in the nearest corner of the yard that bordered Mrs. Gerritsen's.

Phillip didn't respond to the man's beckoning hand. He spoke just loudly enough to be heard. "I assume you're talking to me."

The man pointed to another gate at the side of the house. "Deliveries in the back, nigger."

"Is that right? I'll remember that, in case I ever hire some white boy to run errands for me." Phillip opened the gate and walked through it, closing it carefully behind him. Then he strolled up the sidewalk and rang the front doorbell.

Aurore had had no appetite for dinner. In the dining room she had picked at fish and a stuffed mirliton, much as she had as a little girl. And, as then, she had been roundly scolded by a young woman who came to clear the table. It had long since occurred to her that life was a circle, the old and the young much closer on its vast circumference than she had once believed. She only hoped that she passed away before she was as helpless as an infant.

Dressed in a blue print dress and one strand of pearls, she waited now for Phillip Benedict in the front parlor. The room was not her favorite. Long ago she had furnished it with pieces from her childhood home, heavy, dark furniture from an era when tables and chairs were made to last forever—and, unfortunately, did. She had never been skilled at ridding herself of the encumbrances of the past.

The doorbell rang, and she gripped the arms of her chair. She had instructed Lily, her housekeeper, to show Phillip in, and she waited as calmly as she could while the seconds seemed to stretch into hours.

Lily appeared at last, followed by a tall man with calm, dark eyes that took the full measure of the room before they turned to her.

Words of greeting caught in her throat. She stood, though that was no simple feat. But she would not greet Phillip Benedict enthroned, like a grande dame in a bad costume drama.

"Mrs. Gerritsen?"

She held out her hand. He swallowed it with his. Dark and light.

Young and old. Strong and fragile. She was overwhelmed by the contrasts, and for a moment she thought about telling him that she had changed her mind. She could not go through with this.

He seemed to sense her confusion. He didn't smile—she doubted he smiled often. But he withdrew his hand and stood very still, giving her time to compose herself.

"I'm glad you could come," she said at last. "I've wanted to meet you for a long time."

"Have you?" He sounded doubtful.

"I've long admired your writing."

"That surprises me. I'm not well-known here."

"You're not well-known here because of what you choose to write about. This is a city that prides itself on...itself."

He seemed to relax a little. "If the rest of the world disappeared, New Orleans would hardly notice."

"Would you like coffee, Mr. Benedict? And my cook has promised dessert."

"I'm fine for now."

She wished he had said yes. She would have liked the time to get used to having him here. Much could be said over coffee that seemed silly without it.

"Then let's sit over there." She gestured to a sofa by the windows. "I'd like to get to know you a little before I tell you why I've asked you to come."

"An interview? Because I can tell you right now I don't want this job."

She smiled. "Not an interview. I'm absolutely sure I want you to be the one to write my story. And I hope you'll let me convince you." She saw curiosity as well as innate caution in his eyes, and she knew that she had hooked him. For the first time since he had arrived, she began to feel hopeful.

The sofa was uncomfortable, and she settled herself against a nest of pillows to make it more bearable. He settled himself at the far end of the sofa and sat forward, as if he planned to spring to his feet at any moment.

"Have you been in New Orleans long?" she asked.

"A matter of weeks." He faced her. "If you don't mind me asking a question at this point, how did you know I was here at all?"

"I've read your *Atlantic Monthly* articles, and your series on integration in *The New York Times*. As I said, I follow your work. So I know that your mother is Nicky Valentine and you visit here from time to time. When I began thinking about this project, I wished there was someone of your caliber who could write it up for me. And then I realized *you* might be able to. So I asked around..."

"And you found me?"

"It's really a very small town."

"I've discovered that."

She smiled. "You would have, by now. You weren't difficult to find. You've allied yourself with civil rights activists who make their presence known, even though you haven't been openly involved in any demonstrations yourself."

"I'm a journalist. I strive for objectivity."

"I see that."

"And nothing you've learned about me so far disturbs you?"

"No, it doesn't. It intrigues me."

"What would you like to know about me?"

"Tell me how you're enjoying your stay here."

He seemed to sift through possible answers. She already knew that he was not a man who would lie. He would be certain that whatever he said was exactly the truth. And sometimes the truth took time.

"I'll tell you a story," he said. "I took the streetcar yesterday, and though I didn't have to sit in the back, a woman got up and found another seat after I sat down across the aisle from her. I don't suppose you'd be surprised to learn she was white."

"No, I wouldn't."

"In the few minutes I've spent in the Garden District, I've already had an interesting encounter with your neighbor."

Aurore nodded. "I suppose Mr. Aucoine didn't mention that he and I haven't spoken in years, because we've found absolutely nothing to say to each other."

"There's another side to the city," Phillip said, obviously struggling to be fair. "Change is simmering in the air. You can smell potential everywhere you go."

"I'm glad to hear you say that."

"Why?"

She was startled, although she shouldn't have been. Nothing about talking to Phillip Benedict was going to be easy. The man had no easy inside him. "Because I want things to change."

"It won't benefit you," he said bluntly.

"You might be surprised what would benefit me."

He tapped his foot, and she knew he was anxious to get on with this. She purposely let him tap and took her time examining him. He was a handsome man, but that didn't surprise her, since she had seen his photograph more than once. Phillip Benedict had been on the front lines of the civil rights movement for so long that he had been caught on camera nearly as often as the people he was there to write about.

Photographs could capture the elegant set of his head, the strong, striking features, but they couldn't capture the vitality, the essence, of a man who rose above the crowd. She had hoped that he was the man she believed him to be. Now, watching him, she was sure.

She would have liked to stare longer, but she took pity on him. "I'm not going to keep you. Let me tell you what I have in mind, and we'll see if we can come to terms. First, I want you to understand that I know what an odd request this is. The world isn't holding its breath waiting for my biography to be published."

"I'm sure you've lived an interesting life."

"How lovely of you to be so tactful. But the truth is, we both know there's a limited market for the story of my life."

"How limited?"

"More than you've imagined. This is a private and very personal project. I have no intention of anyone besides the immediate members of my family having a copy of the manuscript when you've finished."

"That limits my royalties, wouldn't you say?"

"There will be no royalties. I'll pay you a set price." She paused. "You can set it yourself."

"I thought you were a businesswoman."

"I'm an *old* woman who wants this very badly."

"Why?"

"I think, when we've finished, you'll have your answer."

He didn't say no, but he didn't say yes, either. He examined her as if he could extract the answer by telepathy. "I'm going to be in and out of town for the next month or so. I'm covering the voter-registration activities in Alabama. How long do you think this will take?"

"I don't know. I tire easily. And I'm old. There's a lot to tell."

"From what you've told me so far, you could get the same results from plugging in a tape recorder."

"No, that's where you're wrong. I'll need your help. I couldn't tell this to a machine. I need someone with your intelligence and insight—"

"Look, Mrs. Gerritsen. You don't need me. I don't know why you called, and I don't know what this is really about, but I'm a black man. And by *any* standards in this town, including my own, that makes me the wrong man for this job."

"I do need you. I've read your interviews. You're unique. People tell you things they wouldn't tell anyone else. You know how to get the information they're withholding."

"Why would you pay me good money, then withhold information?"

"Because I've spent a good portion of my life living a lie, and sometimes I'm not even sure where the truth can be found."

He sighed and shook his head, but Aurore knew that he wasn't refusing to write her story. He had made a different decision, and already it annoyed him. "Five thousand dollars," he said at last. "And some kind of assurance there's a point to all this."

"I'll have the check for you at our next session."

He stood. "That will be tomorrow. The sooner we start..."

"The sooner we finish." She nodded, and stood, too. She wished she had her cane, but she hadn't wanted him to see her with it at first. She had wanted to appear stronger than she was.

She held out her hand, and he took it again. "Will ten be too late for you?" she asked.

"Ten will be fine."

"Then I'll look forward to tomorrow."

He nodded and said a polite goodbye. Then he was gone.

She counted the lies she had told him already. The biggest had been the last. She was not looking forward to tomorrow.

She was not looking forward to it at all.

CHAPTER 2

Phillip left the Garden District and turned north, toward Club Valentine, the jazz club that his mother had made famous. It was early, and Nicky was probably rehearsing. He wanted to talk to her, and he didn't want to wait until the club was crowded.

He parked several blocks from Basin Street and strode past rows of white frame houses. From porches and open windows, the Four Tops warred with the Supremes, and teenage girls in short, bright skirts frugged and watusied on the sidewalks. Someone was boiling crabs in an old sugar kettle in the middle of a driveway. The aroma reminded Phillip that he'd had too little to eat that day.

The club was a two-story building on the corner, with a cast-iron balcony overlooking the tree-lined street, and shuttered doors thrown open to catch the evening breeze. From the sidewalk, Phillip heard Nicky's voice rising above the street noises.

Inside, he waved to the bartender, who was busy doing inventory, and briefly scouted the front rooms for Jake Reynolds, his stepfather. When he didn't find Jake, he followed Nicky's singing to the back room. Her dress was red and tight, with a skirt that some people might have said was too short for a woman nearing sixty—although every man in the club would disagree.

He took a seat at the back of the room while she finished the song. Nicky Reynolds—whom the world knew as Nicky Valentine—had a voice that wrapped around the listener like a sable coat. She could wring from each note, each word, the regrets of a lifetime, the heat of tangled limbs on a summer night, the joys of discovering love.

He recognized the song as something of James Brown's, defining the term *soul,* which had just replaced *rhythm and blues* as a category on the charts. When Nicky sang, splinters of her soul rose up in her music. Phillip didn't know how anyone could see so clearly the problems and paradoxes of the world, but Nicky did. And when she was done singing, the audience always saw them a little better, too.

She spotted him just at the end of the last chorus, and she shook her finger in his direction. When she'd finished, she huddled with the band for a few minutes before she came down to join him.

"What are you doing here?"

He kissed her forehead, and he didn't have to bend far to do it. She was only a scant head shorter than his six foot two. "I wanted to talk to you. Do you have some time, or should I make an appointment?"

"I've always got time for you."

He looked around. The room was filling with employees preparing for a busy night. "Where can we go?"

"We could probably find a quiet corner in the bar. If you're hungry, there's a pot of red beans simmering."

"Great."

She led the way. "I don't think I'm going to like this conversation."

"What makes you say that?"

"Something about the way you said, `great.'"

"Don't go reading something into nothing."

She stopped. "Then it's nothing you want to talk about?"

"I didn't say that." He slung his arm around her shoulder and kissed her hair. "Listen to you giving me trouble already."

In the bar, he settled in a corner while Nicky went for food. She returned with bowls of red beans and rice, and half a loaf of French bread. The bartender brought them a pitcher of beer.

He waited until the first pangs of hunger disappeared before he told her his reason for coming. "I got a strange phone call today."

She ate on, clearly waiting for him to continue.

"Well?" he asked, when it was clear she wasn't going to comment. "You're not curious about it?"

Nicky tore off another piece of bread. "I never said I wasn't curious. I just know what kind of phone calls you get. Threats. Bribes. If you don't tell me about them, I can pretend you have a job that doesn't put you on the front lines every week or so."

Phillip switched easily to the French that had been his first language. He always did, when the emotional content of their conversations warmed. "Not every week or so," he said, with the accent of a native Parisian.

"Often enough to turn my hair gray."

"This wasn't a threat or a bribe. It was an offer. A job offer."

"So you'll be leaving again. Just don't tell me you're going to Vietnam." She didn't look up. Like any good New Orleanian, she used her bread to sop up the spicy remnants of the red beans.

"It's a job right here," he said in English. Phillip leaned forward and touched his mother's hand. His skin was shades darker than hers, but still lighter than that of the father he had never known. Once, in a newspaper article about Nicky's career, he had been described as toffee-colored and his mother as café au lait, and he had wondered why the skin of people of African descent was always compared to something to eat or drink. Since then, he'd toyed with the idea of describing whites as tapioca-hued or the color of applesauce, but discarded the notion as suicidal.

"I've been asked to write a biography," he said.

"Whose?"

"A woman named Aurore Gerritsen. Heard that name before?"

He had succeeded in making Nicky look at him. She narrowed her eyes and pondered the thirty-seven-year-old man who had once been a baby at her breast. "You're planning to waltz on over to White Folks' Acres and ply the richest woman in town with questions about her life? Who asked you to do this, anyway?"

"She did."

Nicky was too good at keeping her own secrets to let her surprise show. Her face was remarkably unlined for a woman her age. It didn't wrinkle now, nor did her hazel eyes narrow further. "I don't believe it."

"She called me herself, and I saw her right before I came here."

"Why'd she want to see you?"

"I thought maybe you could give me some insight."

Nicky leaned back in her chair, taking her hand with her. "I don't know the woman. And I've never heard her name mentioned in connection with any civil rights activities."

"I'll bet you know who her sons are, though," he said. "Or were."

"There's not a person of color in this city who doesn't know about them."

On the trip to Club Valentine, Phillip had considered and rejected half a dozen theories as to why Aurore Gerritsen had made her strange offer. She was an elegant old woman, white-haired and even-featured, with an expression in her pale blue eyes that was as warm and guileless as an old friend's. But he didn't believe a single thing she had told him. Not one word.

He had searched his mind for possible connections to the Gerritsen family, but he knew nothing about them that the rest of the city didn't know. Aurore Gerritsen had given birth to two sons. Her second, Ferris, was a state senator, well-known for his staunch segregationist views. The oldest son, Hugh, an activist Catholic priest, had been killed one year ago at a civil rights meeting in a parish south of New Orleans. The flamboyant ideological differences between the two brothers had made sensational newspaper copy after Father Gerritsen's murder.

"I just wondered if you knew something that I didn't," he said. "Do you think this is her way of siding with the dead son against the living? A rebellion? I write up her life story, and she hands it over to the senator with my name on the manuscript, in order to make some sort of statement?"

There were no answers in her eyes. "What do you think?"

"I think it's odd. Odd enough to make me want to know the truth."

"Are you looking for an excuse to stay in the city, Phillip Gerard? Is that what this is about?"

Phillip sat forward. "Go on. Come right out and say it."

She made an exaggerated face. "I think it's getting harder and harder for you to pack your bags. I think a certain kindergarten teacher snagged my baby boy but good, and every time he puts up a fight, she reels him in a little bit closer."

He laughed, in spite of himself. "Don't go getting your hopes up. Belinda's more independent than I am."

"You're saying that's possible?"

Phillip leaned over to kiss his mother's cheek. "Will you give this Gerritsen thing some thought? Let me know if something occurs to you?"

"Go write something and make me proud."

"You're already proud."

"Prouder, then."

He flashed the smile that had gotten him through doors few men of color had been allowed to open. Accepting, patient, the smile promised no demands. Most people fell under its spell before they noticed that the eyes above it were sharp with an awareness of life's ironies.

Nicky was sinfully proud of her son, but she had stopped telling him so the day she realized he was proud of himself—a feat not easy for a black man of the sixties to master. She stood at the front door and watched his retreat. At the end of the block, he turned and waved before he disappeared around the corner.

Flanking the street were huge magnolias spreading, leaf to leaf, like a string of botanical paper dolls. Every week Jake threatened to cut down the ones in front of Club Valentine, and every week Nicky threatened to leave him if he did. The magnolias partially blocked the street, and Jake wanted to know who was driving by and at exactly what speed. Nicky didn't even want to know that a street was there.

The sound of a car filtered through the trees; then the sound of another took its place. She knew that Jake had arrived, because the rattling engine of his Thunderbird needed a tune-up, and would continue needing one until it died in traffic and had to be towed.

He came up the sidewalk with his head bent to examine the flower beds lining the front. His expression was one she had seen on his father's face as he walked through his north Louisiana fields, worrying whether there would be too much rain, or not enough to grow his cotton and the vegetable garden that kept his large family fed.

"Hear it's supposed to shower tonight," she assured him.

Jake looked up. His smile always started in his eyes and worked its way slowly down to his lips. It was the first thing she had noticed about him. Everything else had seemed immaterial. "I'll set you to sprinkling if it doesn't," he said.

"That'll be the day." She waited until he was almost to the door before she walked toward him. Even now, after twenty years of marriage, she liked anticipating Jake's kiss.

He was tall and broad-shouldered, still straight and strong, despite a back that sometimes sent him to bed for a day. His hair was graying, but thick enough to stand out around his face like a warrior's helmet. She stood in his embrace and listened to the sound of thunder in the distance.

"Phillip tells me he might be staying around for a while," he said.

Nicky wondered how Phillip had managed to transfer that bit of knowledge already. "Did he? Did he tell you why?"

"Didn't get the chance. Car came up behind me, and I had to move on."

She moved away so that she could see his face. "Aurore Gerritsen asked him to write her biography."

"Gulf Coast Shipping Gerritsen?"

"That's the one."

"And he's going to do it?"

"He's going to start tomorrow."

Jake pulled her close again, and she only resisted for a moment. "I thought you'd be jumping for joy, Phillip staying around a while longer."

"They're not our kind of people, Jake."

"Well, that's for sure. Last time I looked, they were whiter than white."

She pulled away, but she kept her hand in his. "Ferris Gerritsen's the worst kind of racist."

"And what kind's that?"

"The kind that pretends it's not."

He squeezed her hand. "Phillip can take care of himself. And in the meantime, he'll be staying around. It's time he put down some roots, and there's no better place for him to do it."

She saw him glance toward the bar. He would check the inventory a second time. He always did. "We're going to have a full house tonight. Place is booked solid," she said.

"Booked solid every night."

She had thought they were done, but she found herself holding him there. "I want Phillip to stay, Jake. You know I do. I want him to have some roots. That's something I've never given him, never known how to. I just don't want him to make compromises. I don't want him fetching and carrying for some old woman who's trying to show the world what a liberal she is. What's he going to get from that?"

"A story?"

She was silent for a moment, then she shrugged. "Maybe. Maybe that's what it's all about. Maybe that's why he's considering it."

"Or maybe he's considering it because he's fallen in love and he needs an excuse to stay in town a while."

Music flowed through the bar from the back room, slow, smoky jazz from another decade. She recognized "It's Too Soon to

Know," one of Jake's favorites. She smiled. "Sometimes I think you believe all those foolish old songs I sing."

He dropped her hand, but only to cup her chin. "Sometimes I do."

Belinda was sitting on her side of the front porch when Phillip pulled into her driveway. Two neighborhood kids were sitting on the rail in front of her, leaning against a thick tapestry of jasmine vines that scrabbled to the roof. The older of the little girls was braiding the younger's hair.

"You're never going to need kids of your own," he said as he climbed the steps. "You've always got plenty of somebody else's."

"Best way to do it. That way I don't have to worry about taking care of some man, too."

Phillip wasn't sentimental. What sentiment had survived his childhood had been bled out of him, one drop at a time, in places like Birmingham and Montgomery. But something, some loose wire inside him, reconnected at the sight of Belinda.

She was wearing dark print harem pants and a fringed top that stopped short of her navel. Just weeks before, she had cut her hair nearly as short as a man's, and the effect was stunning. She had a long, regal neck, and an oval face accented by curly-lashed almond-shaped eyes. The radically short haircut brought the whole woman into view, the beauty, the pride.

The temper.

"You left coffee cups all over my desk, Phillip Benedict."

"I plead guilty." He leaned against the porch post. "What do you think I should do about it?"

"I think you ought to get yourself inside and clean up, that's what I think."

"You going to leave your little friends and come inside, too?"

"Amy, you done yet?" Belinda asked.

The oldest child, chubby-cheeked and sassy-eyed, giggled and slid down to the porch floor. "You gotta do what he say, Miss Belinda?"

"I never do what he says. You remember that."

"Then you're not going in?"

"Just 'cause I'm getting cold. You two scoot."

The little girls scampered off, skipping down the walkway, then along the curb. The oldest took the youngest's hand.

"Isn't it kind of late for them to be outside?" Phillip asked.

"They stay with their aunt at night while their mama cleans office buildings down on Canal. Aunt's got six kids of her own, and she has trouble keeping track. They'll be okay. Amy's an old lady at eight. But I'm going to follow behind them, just to be sure. You go on in." She got to her feet.

"You know every kid in the neighborhood, not just the ones that have been in your classes."

"Nah. But they all know me."

Phillip put his hand on her shoulder and stopped her before she could descend the steps. "Were you an old lady at eight?"

"I was an old lady at three."

"Come on, old lady. I'll go with you."

They walked hand in hand after the two little girls. New Orleans was a stoop-sitting kind of place, a place where the first puff of cool evening air was savored gratefully by the thousands of lungs that had waited patiently all day for it to arrive. Tonight, old people sat together reminiscing, and young people made their own memories, all in plain sight of their neighbors.

There was nothing special about Belinda's neighborhood. Some of the small houses were well cared for, with neatly trimmed lawns and fresh coats of paint. Others showed an absence of hope and energy. The worst example was a block and a half away, on a wide corner lot. They stood in front of it and watched Amy and her sister cross the street, scamper through yards and up to a porch overflowing with children.

"This is the saddest house on the street," Belinda said.

Phillip turned his attention to the house in question. "Why do you say that?"

"Because it's got the most potential, but it's been empty as long as

I've been living here. It used to be for sale. Probably still is, but nobody wants to do the work to put up another sign. There were squatters here last month, before the cops ran them off. But they'll be back. Rain'll pour in through the broken windows, and pretty soon the wood'll rot through. The city'll condemn it and take it down, and then there'll be a vacant lot here to dump trash on. And nobody'll build."

Phillip wasn't attached to houses. As long as he had a roof over his head, he was content. He never stayed anywhere long enough to care about more. But he imagined that Belinda's description of things to come was accurate, and it seemed a shame. The house had once been the finest on the block, two-story, with elaborate cast-iron grillwork defining wide double galleries.

"Whoever built this house had dreams," Belinda said.

"What do you mean?"

"See all that iron lace? You don't see much of that on this street. A woman built this house. A strong woman who knew what she wanted."

He put his arms around her and rested his chin against her ear. "You're guessing? Or do you know the history?"

"You just have to look at the house to know."

"Maybe it just takes a strong woman with a strong imagination to see it."

"It takes a strong woman to make dreams come true."

He thought of the strong woman he had met this evening. "I got the strangest phone call today."

She turned so she could see his face. "Did you?"

Thunder rolled across the sky, drowning out the possibility of a reply. As they stood there waiting for it to pass, the first raindrops began to fall. He tugged her hand, and they loped back toward her house.

On her porch, he shook his head and sent raindrops flying. Then he put his arms around her again.

"It looks like I might be staying around for a while."

"And just where do you think you'll be living if you do?"

"I was thinking about here. If you'll have me."

She didn't say yes, because she didn't have to. Phillip knew he was welcome. More was unspoken than spoken between them, but some things were perfectly clear.

"So tell me about that call," she said.

"I'll tell you about it inside."

"You do that, 'cause it's getting cold out here, and your arms aren't warm enough to take care of it."

"They're not?" He grinned down at her. "You're sure about that?" He lowered his head and nuzzled her cheek until she sighed in defeat. Her lips were soft against his.

There had been other women in his life. More than he could probably remember. But none of them had been as seductive as this one. As her body melted into his, he listened to the New Orleans rain, and he thought he might not mind listening to it for a while longer.

CHAPTER 3

Aurore chose the morning room for her first session with Phillip. The room was airy and open, warmed by sunlight and cooled by a soft breeze. There was a comfortable round table where they could sit, he with his notebook in hand and she with the one cup of real coffee she was allowed every day. As she spoke, she would hear birds outside the windows, and they would remind her that she was seventy-seven and the events she described had happened long ago.

She was ready by the time he arrived. She wore a comfortable lavender dress and no jewelry, hoping she could set a casual tone. But inside, she felt anything but casual.

When Phillip walked into the room, she was captivated once again by how handsome and confident he was. He wore a white shirt and a dark jacket, but no tie today, as if he planned to get right down to work and had no time to stand on ceremony. He carried a tape recorder, and held it up as he entered, as if in question.

"Yes," she said. "I think that's a good idea."

He seemed surprised that she hadn't put up a fight. "I'm glad. It will make things easier for me. But I'll still be taking notes."

"You can plug it in over here."

He crossed the room and began to set up the recorder. "I'll give you the tapes when I'm all finished."

That wouldn't be necessary, but she wasn't going to explain that now. "I've asked Lily to bring us a pot of coffee and a plate of her calas. Have you had them before?"

He was bent over the electrical outlet. "Don't think so."

"They're rice cakes. When I was a little girl they were sold in the Vieux Carré by women in bright *tignons* who carried them in woven willow baskets that they balanced on their heads. Sometimes I would shop at the French Market with our cook, and if I was particularly good, she would buy me one as a treat."

"It sounds like a real piece of old New Orleans."

"A piece I'm not really allowed to eat anymore, but sometimes Lily indulges me."

"Do you do that often?"

"What?"

"Break the rules that were made to protect you?"

She laughed. "As often as I can. At my age, there's very little to protect." When he straightened and looked at her, she added, "May I call you Phillip? It seems easier. And I'd like you to call me Aurore. Almost no one does anymore. Most of my close friends are already dead, and the next generation is so afraid I'll be offended without a title."

He didn't answer, he just smiled, as if she had asked the impossible and he was too polite to say so.

"Have you thought about how you'd like to start?" he asked.

She had thought of little else. She still wasn't sure. "Perhaps we can ease into it. Do you have questions you'd like to ask? Background? That sort of thing?"

"I'm a man with a million questions."

"Good. I'll try to be the woman with an answer or two."

Lily, dark-skinned, white-haired, and too thin to look as if she enjoyed her own cooking, arrived with a platter of golden brown calas dusted liberally with confectioner's sugar. She set them on the table and returned in a moment with a coffee service featuring a tall enameled pot, which she set on the table. "One," she told Aurore firmly. "And one cup of coffee. I'll be counting." She left with a swish of her white nylon uniform.

"She means it," Aurore said.

"Who hired who?"

"It's a draw. We suit each other. I don't listen to her, and she doesn't listen to me."

"Sort of like Mammy in *Gone with the Wind.*"

"Nothing like it. She does her job well, and I pay her well. We have nothing but respect for each other."

"And at the end of the day, she probably goes home to a street without a white face on it."

"If that's true, I suspect it's a tremendous relief, after taking care of me all day."

He settled himself across the table from her. She poured him coffee. The stream wavered in rhythm to the tremor of her hands. "How do you take it?"

"Black."

She smiled. "Segregation at the breakfast table, as well as everywhere else. I take mine white."

His smile was a reluctant ray of sunshine. "So, what do I know about you already?"

"Have a cala." She passed him a plate and a napkin, and edged the platter in his direction.

He helped himself. "I suspect you have something to prove here. That as your life winds to a close, you want to make a statement about who you were. And the statement is as important as your life story."

"And the statement is?"

"That you were different from others of your class. That for this time and this place, you were a liberal. Am I correct?"

"Absolutely not."

He worked on the cala, watching her as he did. "All right. What do I really know? Facts, not guesses."

This answer interested her immensely. She poured milk into her cup and stirred. "What *do* you know, Phillip?"

"Not much yet, since I haven't had time to do research. Gulf Coast Shipping is one of the city's oldest and most well-established companies. I believe it was your ancestors who started it, not your husband's, and that you were largely responsible for making it a million-dollar enterprise."

"That, like everything else, is only part of the truth. Henry kept our heads above water for the first years of our marriage." She laughed. "A good thing for a shipping company."

"Henry was your husband?"

"Yes."

"You had two children. Your youngest son is the state senator Ferris Gerritsen, and your oldest, Hugh, was a Catholic priest who was killed last year in Bonne Chance."

She wasn't smiling now. "Yes." She waited for him to say more about that, but he didn't.

"Do you have grandchildren?"

"A granddaughter. Her name is Dawn."

"Does she live nearby?"

"She's in England now, on an assignment. She's a journalist, too, a photojournalist."

"Oh? What's she covering?"

"British musical groups, I believe. She's in Liverpool."

He was jotting down notes. He hadn't turned on the tape recorder, as if he knew they were only marking time.

"Other living relatives?" he asked.

"Only some very distant ones that I haven't seen in decades."

"And that's about all I know." He looked up, squarely meeting her eyes. "Except that your son has consistently taken stands against integration, and he's popular with his constituents because of it. There's talk he may run for governor in the next race, and if he does, he'll probably win."

"That could happen. Or something might happen to prevent it."

"Would you prefer one over the other?"

"Yes."

"Which one?"

"The one that's best for Louisiana."

"And the hedging begins."

She nodded. "Perhaps that's because I don't want to talk about Ferris. I suppose it might seem as if he's the key to my asking you here. You might even believe that I'm trying to prove to the world that I'm not like my son. But that's not what this is about at all."

He tapped his pen against the stenographer's pad in front of him. "Okay," he said at last. "What is it about?"

"You haven't asked me anything about my parents."

"Is that where you'd like to start?"

She wanted to tell him that she didn't want to start at all, but that would require as much explanation as her life story. "No, I suppose it begins with my grandfather. His name was Antoine Friloux, and he was a Creole gentleman in the classic mold. With one exception. He was a talented businessman in a class that viewed work as something that others should do. Grandpère Antoine began Gulf Coast Shipping, although it was called Gulf Coast Steamship in those days. He was a rich man who became richer with every investment he made."

He waited for her to go on, and when she didn't, he turned on the tape recorder. "He was your mother's father?"

"Yes. Perhaps if he'd had a son, none of what I'm about to tell you would ever have happened."

Phillip settled back in his chair, propping his pad on the table's edge. "And why is that?"

But she didn't answer directly. As she had hoped, the story seemed to grow inside her, and she knew, for the first time, that she would be able to tell it all.

"There's something you need to know," she said.

"What's that?"

"In order to understand my story, you have to understand the story of a man named Raphael." She looked up at him and waited for his answer.

"And who was he?"

Again she didn't answer directly. "Our stories are entwined, mine and Raphael's. I can't tell one without the other."

"All right."

"Have you seen much of Louisiana, Phillip?"

He shook his head.

"At the very south of the state, there's a barrier island called Grand Isle. At the end of the last century, people of wealth used to go there to spend their summers. We went there when I was a child. A young child. My mother was...ill, and there was hope that the climate there would make her better."

"That seems like a good place to begin."

She met his eyes, but she didn't smile. "It is. Because everything else I'll tell you is connected to that summer in 1893."

CHAPTER 4

Louisiana Gulf Coast 1893

A man took a wife for children. A man took a mistress for pleasure. In the latter, Lucien Le Danois had been most fortunate. He had taken a mistress who could bestow such pleasure that the most demanding of Creole men, had they known, would have knelt at her feet. But as fate would have it, Marcelite Cantrelle was also more capable of bearing children than Lucien's wife, Claire.

A man merely looked at Marcelite and she grew heavy with new life, like the seed of the love vine, swollen with spring rain. Her body, wide-hipped and sturdy, was made for childbearing. Her breasts were a lush invitation to suckle and grow strong. Lucien knew well the mystical wonders of her flesh against his lips, the enticement of her earthy fragrance.

Marcelite had already borne him one child, a daughter brought into the world in a matter of hours, nourished on mother's milk and the freshest, sweetest fruits of the Gulf of Mexico. Angelle was a black-haired, laughing nymph, brown from the sun, like her black-haired mother. When Marcelite went down to the beach to mend nets, two-year-old Angelle knew how to dance away from the white-tipped waves. At home, as their house filled with the spicy scent of the day's catch cooking in the fireplace, she could climb the lone water oak outside their front door and, hidden among its moss-draped branches, call greetings to the fishermen who passed by.

Lucien attempted to think only of Angelle and Marcelite as he sailed across the Jump, the shallow pass that separated Grand Isle from Chénière Caminada. But, despite his best efforts, it was other faces that he saw.

The Jump separated more than two bodies of land. Earlier in the afternoon, he had said a stern farewell to his wild-eyed wife, and to Aurore, his only legitimate child. He could still feel Claire's fingers clawing at his arm as he pushed her away, still see the accusations in Aurore's pale eyes.

Why should he feel guilty? Hadn't he made the steamboat trip to Grand Isle well after the summer season had ended so that he could escort Claire and Aurore back to New Orleans? Hadn't he given Claire permission to stay these extra weeks, weeks she claimed to need in order to face the final months of her pregnancy?

As a husband, he could not be faulted. Perhaps their house in New Orleans was not as grand as the home she had once shared with her parents, but many men envied the large property he owned on Esplanade. Claire lacked for nothing.

And he had been patient. By all the saints, he had been patient as she lost baby after baby. A man could be outraged at a woman for less. He had watched and waited in silence as she failed to bring a son into the world to carry his name. Even now, she was pregnant again. Even now, he waited for the day when she would take to her bed and disappoint him once more.

For all Lucien's patience, Claire had given him nothing but one frail daughter whose skin was so translucent he could almost see her heartbeat. No one believed that five-year-old Aurore, their only child to be born alive, would live to adulthood.

So was he to blame if he took an afternoon for himself? He

had promised Marcelite a visit before he returned to New Orleans. Months would pass before he saw her again, months when he would dream of her body under his.

The wind suddenly filled his sail, the harsh sigh of a God impatient with his excuses. The small skiff bobbed closer to the shoreline, carried by the waves breaking against the sand. The tide was low. Lucien rolled up his trousers and took off his shoes, then swung himself overboard to drag the skiff to the beach.

In the distance, despite the afternoon's bursts of rain, he could see men in wide-brimmed hats offshore, casting circular throw nets. A cold front had come through, and the damp air was tinged with the pleasures of autumn. Two women, their homespun skirts dragging on the wet sand, piled storm-tossed driftwood to season for cooking and heating. Marcelite's pile was farther up the beach, stacked tall by her own hands and Raphael's.

Seven-year-old Raphael, Marcelite's son by a former liaison, was a good child, a help to his mother, a guardian and companion to his sister. He was as captivated by Angelle as Lucien was, and because of his enslavement to Lucien's daughter, Raphael had taken a special place in Lucien's heart.

Lucien scanned the beach, half expecting to find the boy hiding behind one of the woodpiles, in a game they often played. But Raphael was nowhere to be seen.

Lucien murmured polite greetings to the women before he made his way toward the village. The contrast between Chénière Caminada and Grand Isle was as wide as the pass that separated them. The large village on the chénière boasted over six hundred houses and bustled with the daily routines of its inhabitants. The fishermen and trappers of the chénière had large, close-knit families, and little contact with the outside world. Grand Isle was smaller, without a church or a resident justice of the peace. But in the summer months, Grand Isle swelled with the wealthy who escaped the punishing summers of the city and the fever that often came with the heat.

Lucien passed a small orange grove, its green-tinged fruit bending the branches into graceful arcs. Ahead, a group of frame houses set high on brick pillars lined the grassy path. As he passed, a group of women, chatting together and shelling crabs on the wide gallery of one house, called to him to get inside before it rained again. A small dog stepped into his path and sniffed his shoes, as if hoping to discover a story to share with a larger comrade asleep under the shelter of an overturned pirogue.

His destination was a leisurely fifteen-minute stroll away, past houses with vineyards and kitchen gardens. On Grand Isle, ridges of ancient, twisted oaks hindered every view, but here Lucien could see much of the village in one glance. The chénière natives had cut down their trees, to better feel the Gulf breezes on hot summer days.

He had come this way for the first time three years ago. He and a friend had sailed to the chénière from Grand Isle to buy a new fishing net as a gift for his friend's wife. The net was to be a decoration for an autumn soiree with a seaside theme.

On arrival, they had been directed to Marcelite Cantrelle's hut. Lucien had expected a toothless hag who would bargain ruthlessly. Instead, he had been enchanted to discover a dark-haired temptress who negotiated with such charm that by the time his friend had his net, he didn't even realize that he had spent twice the amount he had planned.

Lucien had gone back to see Marcelite often that first summer. He had found excuses at first—another net, advice on where he might have the most success fishing, a small gift for Raphael. But by the time August arrived, he and Marcelite had come to an unspoken understanding. He visited when he could, and brought her gifts and money. In exchange, she yielded her body exclusively to him. The arrangement suited them both.

Lucien had come this way many times, but he never failed to become aroused when he knew he would soon hold Marcelite in his arms. Now he rounded a bend, and her house came into view. Constructed of driftwood and thatched with palmetto, the house was as much a creation of local custom and culture as the woman who lived in it. In the distance, Lucien could see her, waiting in the shelter of the water oak. Her shirtwaist gleamed white against the weathered brown of the palmetto. He could see her hands sweep back and forth over a fishing net, tugging, straightening, tying, but her gaze was fixed on him.

When he drew nearer, she thrust the net aside and stood, but she didn't come to him. She wasn't a tall woman, but with her regal carriage and the proud tilt of her head, she gave the impression of height. She didn't straighten her skirts or allow her hands to fidget. She waited.

When they were face-to-face, he gave a little bow. *"Mademoiselle."*

"M'sieu," she replied, in the husky, staccato accent of the bayous. "Where are the children?"

She switched to English, since she knew he preferred it. "Angelle naps inside. Raphael explores."

"I didn't see him on the beach."

"He goes farther each day, looking for treasure."

"It's the influence of that old pirate Juan Rodriguez."

"Raphael seeks more than gold coins. He seeks a man to talk with."

Lucien heard no reproach in Marcelite's voice, but he felt it nonetheless. "He could do better than old Rodriguez."

"Juan is good to Raphael. The boy could listen to his stories forever."

Lucien propped one hand against the tree. The pose moved him closer to her. "And what could you do forever, *mon coeur?*"

She lifted her shoulders, and he watched the soft muslin collar glide along her neck. "Eat, *mais oui?* Sit in the shade and watch the herons catch their supper?"

"And what else?"

"I can think of nothing else I might want to do forever." She lowered her eyes until her lashes shadowed her sun-kissed cheeks. "But perhaps I can think of something I would like to do often."

His heart beat faster. He absorbed each detail of her, the way the light filtered through the branches and spangled her black hair, the tiny gold hoops at her earlobes, the strong curve of her nose, the sensuous curve of her lips.

Never more than at moments like this did he wish that time

would cease its steadfast march and leave him alone with Marcelite, secure and content in the life they had fashioned here together. She was a mixture of the diverse nationalities that had long claimed this marshy peninsula as their own, a spicy combination of this and that, much like the gumbo she often served him. It was her differences, as much as the things that made her like every woman, that compelled him to seek her out.

"I brought you a gift."

She lifted her eyes. "Did you? You've hidden it well."

"It's a small thing." He slid his hand inside his coat and drew out a rectangular package. "See what you think."

She took her time, letting her callused, capable fingers pluck at the strings with the patience and delicacy of a well-bred Creole maiden. When the gift was revealed, she stared at it without removing it from its wrappings.

"It's a folding fan," Lucien said. He took it and flicked it open, revealing embroidered red and gold roses on butter-soft leather. "The frame is violet wood. From France." He swept it under her nose so that she could enjoy the scent. "For when the breeze forgets to blow."

"And where, *M'sieu,* do I find the hand I need to use such a thing?"

He laughed. "Open the fan in the evenings, when your chores are finished. Sit on your little stool, right here, as darkness comes, and think of me."

"*Mais non*—it's the mosquitoes I'll think of."

He folded the fan and touched her cheek with the tip. "And you won't think of me? Not even a little?"

She examined him as a wife at the French Market might examine the day's catch. "Why should I?"

"Marcelite..." He moved closer. "Haven't you missed me?"

Her expression didn't change.

"Don't you like your gift?"

"My roof needs patching. My bed is damp. My house needs windows, a new door. I have no time to fan myself. I have no time to miss you. And now that I am with child again..."

He grabbed her arms. "What?"

"...I have less time than before."

"You're going to have a baby?"

"Where are your eyes?"

He let his gaze drop slowly, and he saw what he had missed. Despite her corset—which he knew she wore only for his pleasure—her waist was thicker. Her breasts, heavy and ripe, rebelled against the unaccustomed restraint and strained toward freedom.

"When?" he asked.

"In the spring. When the birds fly north."

All the implications ran swiftly through his mind. "A son?"

She lifted her shoulders again, and this time it was not her neck, but her breasts that he watched in fascination, to see if they would gain the freedom they so longed for.

"Do you want my son, Lucien? If I have your son, what will life hold for him?"

He thought of everything he had to offer. His home, his name, the money and social position that had come to him through his marriage to Claire Friloux, his stature as an officer of Gulf Coast Steamship. All this he had to give, but none of it could he offer Marcelite's child.

"What would you have me give him?" he asked.

"A house better than this one." She gestured behind her, toward the hut where they had spent so many pleasurable hours. "A lugger, so that he can earn his way in the world. Later, perhaps, a place in your business."

A son. Lucien felt his chest grow tight with longing. A son with Angelle's black hair and laughing brown eyes. A son grown strong on salt air and hard work, a son who could never carry his name, but who would carry some essence of him into the next generations. And perhaps, if fate decreed and Antoine Friloux, Claire's father, did not outlive Lucien, a son who might someday inherit part of his estate.

"You'll get your house," Lucien said. He touched her cheek again, but this time his fingertips weren't quite steady. "I promise to send a boat in the spring filled with lumber. Can you find men to build it?"

She nodded. Her eyes softened to the black of a moonlit bayou, her gaze flicked languidly over him. "Can you find a man to live in it with me sometimes, *hein?* A man to teach my son of the city?"

"Our son and our daughter."

"Maybe we should go inside and see our daughter now?"

He knew that Angelle always napped away the afternoon. They would see a child soundly sleeping, curled in a ball on a mattress stuffed with Spanish moss. From experience, he knew there would be more enticing things to view.

He followed Marcelite, then crossed the room and made the correct sounds of fatherly approval as he gazed at Angelle, asleep under the tied-back folds of a mosquito bar. His daughter lay just as he had imagined, her *cottonade* dress twisted high above her knees, her cheeks rosy. She clutched the doll he had bought at her birth, well used and loved now, no longer perfect like the dolls in Paris fashions that lined Aurore's room.

Finally he turned and watched Marcelite undress.

Her shirtwaist dropped to the crude wooden bench beside her bed, followed by her homespun skirt. She faced him in garments elaborate enough to suit Claire. He had given her the pink, lace-trimmed corset at the beginning of the summer, and it still looked as new as it had on that June day. Her chemise was snow-white, but the ribbon adorning it showed signs of wear. He told himself he must remember to buy her another.

She lifted her hands and began to uncoil her hair. It fell past her shoulders, past her waist. The airy room was pleasantly cool, but he could feel himself beginning to sweat.

She came to him without a word, holding out her hand for the straw hat he had already removed. He gave it to her and watched as she placed it carefully on the bench. He spread his coat while he waited, and when she returned he lifted his arms just enough so that she could push it off his shoulders.

Skilled and sure of herself, she took her time with the rest of his clothing. His eyelids drifted shut. He could feel the harsh whisper of her hands against his chest and arms, feel the damp breeze sifting through palmetto fronds to tease the beads forming on his forehead. Her hair brushed his face, and he savored the fragrance of the pomade she made from jasmine petals.

"You'll help me undress, too, *non?*"

He opened his eyes as she curved against him, lifting her hair so that he could find the strings of her corset. His fingers were heavy and uncoordinated as he struggled with the hooks. He felt her sigh as the corset came apart, but before she could move away, he cupped her breasts in his hands and felt them rest heavily against his palms.

"And the lugger for our son?" she asked, arching back against him. "A boat of his own, one he can fish from and sail to the city?"

Her bottom danced in a slow, sensuous rhythm against him, her breasts swayed in his hands. Lucien groaned. "You'll always have what you need, *mon coeur.* And so will your children. Always."

She turned slowly, and her legs spread to cradle him. He lifted her and moved toward the bed.

"The lugger?"

"More, if I can give it," he said as he fell with her to the mattress. "Trust me to take care of you. Trust me."

Aurore Le Danois was hiding from her mother. One noise, one breath sucked in too deeply, the whisper of one black stocking rubbing another, and she would give herself away.

As she watched, her mother crossed the room, returning from the gallery where she had rocked unceasingly for the past hour. She passed the little table that sheltered Aurore, but she didn't glance her way. At the doorway of her own bedroom, she raised her hand to her forehead and murmured something indistinguishable. Then she disappeared from sight.

Aurore waited, worried still. When she was certain forever had passed, she straightened one leg, biting her lip at the cramp that made it nearly impossible. When her mother didn't reappear, she slid back against the wall and stood.

She watched her mother every day, and knew her habits. Now she would sleep restlessly, moaning sometimes, like the wind that bent the trees outside their door. But not until Ti' Boo, Aurore's nursemaid, came back from her daily visit to her uncle's family would anyone think to check on Aurore. She was free, if she dared, to run outside and dance with the wind. She could play under the swiftly gathering storm clouds. And if the lightning came...

She clasped her hands. If the lightning came, she could watch it streak the dark sky and pry open the clouds. Rain would fall again, pure silver rain, as shiny as her bedroom mirror in New Orleans.

The wind beckoned. Leaves spun merrily, and many-hued petals of oleander flew light as angel wings through the air. Across the train tracks that ran in front of her, Aurore could see the empty cottages lining the other side of the clearing, and behind them, lowing mournful music, a small gathering of the sleepy-eyed cows who roamed the island.

The tracks were as empty as the houses. The tourist season was finished at the Krantz Place, and now the mule who pulled the tram car down to the beach twice each summer day was pastured behind the dining hall for a well-deserved rest.

She wished the season hadn't ended. In summer there were other children. Under the watchful eyes of Ti' Boo, she could romp and shout, and no one thought to tell her she must rest. No one remembered she was a frail, big-eyed child who took fever after too much excitement and sometimes couldn't draw a proper breath. In summer she waded in the Gulf, and collected shells and driftwood. She had learned to crab this year, and to float with her feet toward the waves. Next year, Ti' Boo promised, she would learn to swim.

She wanted to swim. She wanted to swim to the end of the Gulf, to the great water beyond, and never, never stop. She would leap high with the porpoises, and the sharks would not eat her. She was too thin, too pale, to interest sharks. Ti' Boo had told her so at the beginning of the summer, when she was still a little girl and frightened to get wet.

A gust of wind lifted a curl off her neck and plastered it against her cheek. She giggled and held out her arms to embrace her unseen playmate. In a moment she was under the oaks, whirling to the wind's rhythm. She scampered past the dining room. There hadn't been a shout from her cottage or any of the others. In the summer, fifty people would have seen her and asked questions. But now, on the last day of September, not even Mr. Krantz, who was such a large man he seemed to be everywhere, had spotted her.

She wanted to see the waves once more. Her family was leaving for New Orleans on Monday. Last night, her father, Lucien, had come from New Orleans to escort them home. And though they wouldn't go to church tomorrow, because Papa said that the chénière, where the church was located, wasn't a suitable place for his wife and child, her mother would pray in their cottage, and Aurore would be forced to stay inside.

Aurore knew that her father wouldn't discover her escape. Earlier in the afternoon, she had heard her mother and father arguing. Papa had wanted to go sailing, but Maman had begged him not to. M'sieu Placide Chighizola had warned her of an approaching storm, and she believed him. Hadn't he made her stronger with his herbs and diet? How could she believe he was wrong?

Aurore's father had scoffed, saying M'sieu Chighizola knew nothing. The old man's cures were voodoo, no better than the gris-gris bags carried by the blacks who still believed Marie Laveau, dead though she was, would save them from some imagined curse. His prediction of a storm was nonsense. Couldn't Claire feel the slight chill in the air? Every sailor knew a big storm never followed a cold front.

Aurore had watched her mother grow paler. Her father had grown paler, too. As she continued to plead with him, he had raised a hand, as if to strike her. Then he had turned and stalked away.

Aurore thought her father was the handsomest man in the world, but at that moment his face had been twisted into a horrifying carnival mask. She had seen his lips move under his luxuriant drooping mustache, and she had been afraid of the words he muttered.

Aurore had told Ti' Boo about the angry words. Ti' Boo had said that parents sometimes argued, and that once her mother had chased her father with a broom.

Aurore wished she was as old as Ti' Boo. To be twelve, and able to leave your parents for the summer to work as a nursemaid! True, Ti' Boo had to visit her aunt and uncle each day and submit to their questions, but Ti' Boo's life still seemed like freedom itself.

Someday Aurore would be twelve, too. She tried to imagine it, but she couldn't. To be twelve. To be free!

The waves seemed to call her, with their own promises of freedom. Her mind made up, she started toward the water, following the iron rails. In the distance, she saw the roofs of the bathhouses where she and her mother changed before entering the water. Far to one side there were other bathhouses for the men. Ti' Boo said that the men bathed without clothes, and that was why their houses were so far away. More than once, Aurore had tried to imagine such a thing.

As she reached the dunes and followed the track through them, she saw there were no fishermen today. Against the horizon, several boats with colorful triangular sails rode the angry waves, but no one fished in the surf.

She drew a sharp breath at the majesty of the waves. She was not foolish enough to get close. The waves ate into the shoreline hungrily, and they would eat a little girl, too. As she inched forward, the trunk of an ancient cypress, snatched by wind and water from some mysterious swamp, was flung against the sand, then snatched back.

She clasped her hands, as she had on the gallery. Far away, there was a silver flash, beyond the boats, beyond the waves. Light drifted down to the water between black thunderheads, as it did in the pictures of God's son rising toward heaven. She crossed herself quickly, then clasped her hands again.

"Ro-Ro!"

She whirled at the sound of Ti' Boo's voice. For a moment she hoped she could hide; then she knew it was useless. She could only fling herself into the waves, and she was afraid to do that.

Ti' Boo, her chubby face pink with exertion, came running through the dunes. "Ro-Ro!" She stopped and shook her finger at Aurore.

Aurore tried to look sorry. "I only wanted to see the beach once more, Ti' Boo. I wasn't going to go any closer. Truly."

"You scared me to death. My heart, it's stopped!" She clapped her hand over her chest.

"I didn't think you'd be back. I thought no one—"

"No one knows but me."

Aurore said a quick prayer of thanksgiving. "Don't tell! Please don't tell!"

Ti' Boo flung her arms out dramatically. "The wind, it could carry you away!"

"I was careful." Aurore took advantage of Ti' Boo's open arms to throw herself into them. She wrapped her arms around Ti' Boo's waist. "Don't tell, please?"

Reluctantly Ti' Boo stroked Aurore's long brown curls. "Silly *ti' oiseau*. I won't tell, but if we don't get back quick, someone'll find us here."

Aurore looked up at her friend. She thought Ti' Boo beautiful, with her cheerful round face and her straight black hair braided over her ears. "I don't want to go home. I want to stay here forever."

"Next summer, you come back, and I'll take care of you again."

"I wish you would come to New Orleans."

"*Non,* my home, it's on the b'you. What would my *maman* do without me, heh? Her with twelve to feed?"

Aurore brightened. "I could come with you to Bayou Lafourche. I could help."

Ti' Boo laughed. Aurore could feel the rumble against her ear. "And what would your *maman* do? Without her *ti' oiseau?*"

Aurore didn't think her mother would mind too much.

"Come on. Le's get back before anyone knows we went."

Aurore took one last look at the waves. She promised them she would be back next summer, too. Then she followed Ti' Boo through the dunes.

CHAPTER 5

Raphael Cantrelle stood high on a sand dune, one hand shading his eyes as he looked out to sea. In the distance there were pirate ships with billowing sails and masts so tall they speared the black clouds and carved a corsair's route to heaven.

They were coming for him.

Raphael felt inside the pocket of his pants. His hand stayed there a moment, savoring the feel of his tiny store of treasure. He had a section of rope, a chunk of bread and smoked fish wrapped and tied in a piece of cloth, a shard of glass finely polished by the sea, two shells, and a piece of driftwood shaped like a dagger. The pirates would be proud to have him on board. Jean Laffite himself would beg him to sail on the biggest and finest of the ships.

He would have to say no.

As he watched, the ships disappeared, one by one, until there was nothing left but a clouded stretch of sea and sky and two fishing boats coming into port. He recognized one of the *canotes,* with its red lateen sail and green body. It belonged to the father of Étienne Lafont, a boy his age with whom he played when Étienne could sneak away from his family.

Next to Juan Rodriguez, Étienne was his best friend. Étienne wanted to be a pirate, too, but Juan *was* a pirate. Juan could teach him everything he needed to learn until the day when his mother no longer needed him and Raphael would sail away with Dominique You and Nez Coupé. And if they really were dead, as Étienne insisted, then he could sail away with someone else.

He wanted to leave the chénière. He knew of no other place to live, had never even crossed the pass to Grand Isle. But he knew that somewhere there had to be a village where no woman would call his mother names, where no man would tell his children they couldn't play with him.

Only recently he had discovered that he was different from other boys. He was not the only child on the chénière without a father. From time to time, the Gulf waters took their toll, and boats washed in to shore, empty and battered by storms. But other fatherless children had families to see to their needs. Uncles and cousins, grandfathers and godfathers, brought them fish and game, milk and fresh vegetables from their gardens. Their mothers were welcomed into homes all through the village.

Raphael had learned from Étienne, just last week, that he had a family on the chénière, too, an uncle who was able to provide for Raphael's mother. But no one brought her fish or milk. She mended nets and washed clothes to buy the fish she didn't catch herself. Whatever else she needed, she bought with the coins she received from M'sieu Lucien or with the pretty gifts he gave her, traded to the storekeeper in the village, who sent them to New Orleans to be sold.

Étienne had taken Raphael to see his uncle's house. It was one of the finest on the peninsula. Anchored on a slight inland ridge, it rose high above the ground and the other houses surrounding it. Étienne had told him that the house was made of *bousillage-entre-poteaux,* and that it was so sturdy it would still be standing on Judgment Day.

Raphael had found his way there half a dozen times since. He had twice seen the man who was his uncle. Auguste Cantrelle was tall, twice as tall as Juan, with a chest as wide as a lugger's sail and curly dark hair like Raphael's own. The second time, Raphael had stepped out of the shadows. Auguste Cantrelle had looked at him; then, with an angry face, he had hurried away.

He hadn't asked his mother about the tall, tall man. Once he had asked her about his father, and she had told him that he had no father, that he had no family other than her and Angelle. After all, they were enough family for anyone, were they not?

Neither had he asked her about the boys who couldn't play with him, the mothers who shielded their children when he passed, the bad names they called softly after him. He had seen that some people spoke to his mother and some did not.

Raphael's hand slid into his pocket again, and this time he lifted out the packet of bread and fish. It had been some time since the noon church bell had tolled the Angelus. His belly told him it was time for food, but he didn't want to eat too early. His mother had told him to stay away this afternoon. M'sieu Lucien was coming to visit, so there was no hope of begging more bread from her. He wasn't supposed to go home until the sun was almost to the horizon, and if he disobeyed, he would go to bed hungrier than he was now.

He solved the problem by eating half the contents of the packet, then carefully retying the string and saving the rest of the rations for later. Feeling better, he went to find Juan.

Juan's house was far away, a long trip across the settlement, even though Raphael walked as fast as he could. Juan lived by himself in a house much like Raphael's own, but there were no neighbors to share his marshy land. When the twilight breeze blew from the direction of Juan's house, it always carried mosquitoes with it. He had asked Juan about them, and Juan had said that mosquitoes were kinder than people. Mosquitoes stung once or twice and took what they could, but people, they kept after you until every drop of blood was drained from your body.

Raphael had met the old man one morning outside Picciola's store. Raphael had been waiting in the shade for his mother, chasing chickens to pass the time, when he noticed Juan coming toward him. The old man had walked like a crab, with swift little steps that veered to one side until he stopped, straightened, then veered to the other.

Juan was small and bent with age, although he carried no cane. Instead of a hat, he'd worn a red scarf, knotted and tied over one ear. No one had spoken to him as he wobbled his way toward the store, but Raphael had seen people move to one side, as if they were determined not to get in his way.

There'd been little reason to worry. Juan had avoided them with even more determination, preferring to stumble into the shade, rather than take a chance on the crowded path. But Juan had misjudged, and his foot had become entangled in the roots of a chinaball tree. He would have fallen if Raphael hadn't sprung forward and braced him until he recovered his balance.

The old man's swarthy skin had flushed with embarrassment, but he'd mumbled a *merci*. Then he'd reached inside his pants and retrieved a small silver coin, pressing it into an astonished Raphael's hand before he started back toward the store.

On the way home, Raphael's mother had listened to his story, then taken the coin to keep with her own. In return, she'd told him that Juan Rodriguez was the son of a man who had sailed with Jean Laffite, and that some on the chénière believed Juan himself had sailed with pirates, too. Juan's mother had been a bayou girl, and at Juan's birth she had moved to the chénière to wait, always wait, for her husband to return from his journeys.

Raphael knew how hard his mother worked. There was little time for storytelling in her busy life, but on that rare day, with Juan's silver coin jingling happily in her pocket, she had told him about others who lived on the chénière.

The Barataria region, she'd said, had once been the haunt of pirates. Some of the people who lived here now were their descendants. He'd listened eagerly as she told more stories of the mélange of people who dwelled there, stories of people from Italy, Spain and Portugal, stories of people from Manilla and China who dried shrimp on tall platforms in Barataria Bay and danced over them until the shells fell off to be swept away by the currents. But it was Juan's story he'd begged to hear again. He had gone to sleep that night promising himself that the next stories he heard would be from Juan himself.

At first Raphael had been afraid to go to Juan's house alone. It was far from his own house, and Étienne had frightened him with stories about ghosts who haunted the marsh. But after a while he had found his way there.

Juan hadn't spoken to him that first day, or the next. But after Raphael had visited for a week, carrying fresh water in a bucket from the well and helping Juan weave more palmetto into the thatch of his house, Juan had finally begun to talk.

Now Raphael visited Juan every day he could. Sometimes the old man was out in his boat and Raphael returned home without seeing him. But on lucky days, Juan was sitting outside, ready to tell stories. Raphael lived on these tales of conquest as surely as he lived on the bread his mother baked in her mud oven.

Today, when Raphael arrived, Juan was nowhere in sight. His boats were there, however, both the pirogue that he used in the marsh behind his home and the skiff he sailed into the Gulf.

Raphael knocked on the door of Juan's hut, and when no one answered, he pushed it open a few inches to peer inside. The hut's interior was more primitive than Raphael's own. The floor was mud and the furniture nothing more than stumps of trees. There was a shrine in the corner, like the one Raphael's mother kept, but no statue of the Blessed Mother presided over the simple wooden cross and the stubs of two candles.

Raphael closed the door and backed away. From the distance, he heard a clap of thunder. He didn't want to be caught outside if the rain started again, but he knew better than to enter the hut without Juan's permission. Just as he was turning to run back toward the village, he saw the tall sedge beside Juan's house part in a rippling wave. As Raphael watched, terrified, the old man materialized in the mists rising from the marsh.

"Hey! 'Zat you, Raphael?"

Raphael swallowed hard. For a moment, his voice was locked in his throat, as if the ghosts he'd envisioned had wrapped their boneless fingers around his neck. He swallowed again, successfully. "I'z me."

"You don' see the storm comin', *cher?* You don' worry?"

Raphael shook his head and watched Juan stagger crab-like toward him. "It's jus' rain," he said bravely, like a good pirate.

"*Non. Mais,* I wish you was right."

"It's goin' away." Raphael squinted as Juan drew closer.

"She goes 'way, then she comes back. Boom! Like that!" Juan clapped his hands.

"How do you know?"

"Me, I seen it before. The gulls go; and the pelicans. The cows, they go up to the ridges."

"Why?"

"So they die slower."

Raphael took a step backward. "It's jus' rain."

"*Mais non, cher.* Is win', too. Big win'." He spread his hands wide. "Lights in the sky, this morning. I saw them lights. I know." Thunder sounded in the distance once more. He dropped his hands to his side, as if his point had been made for him. "*Hein?*"

"What can we do?"

Juan's expression didn't change. Slowly, he shook his head.

Raphael felt a thrill of alarm. He had experienced many storms in his seven years. He knew what it was like to be wet and miserable because his house leaked. But he could sense there was a difference between that and what Juan was saying. He tried to imagine a big wind blowing over the chénière. He couldn't.

"The win', she'll take your house." Juan turned toward his own house. "She'll take mine, too, that one, and twist it to little pieces."

Raphael thought of the few things he owned that weren't in his pocket. Most important was a pair of leather shoes that M'sieu Lucien had brought all the way from New Orleans. He seldom wore them, but now that he was old enough for short pants instead of the cotton dress he had worn until summer, the shoes were important. He couldn't let them blow away. School was to start the day after tomorrow, in a brand-new building that had just been erected. Although his mother hadn't yet promised he could go, he still held out hope. And he would need shoes.

There was also his rosary, and a tiny pirogue that he had whittled from a soft tree limb, along with a little man who sat in it. And there was Angelle's doll. That last thought made his eyes widen. "Angelle, will she blow away, too?"

"You mus' tell your *maman* to take you and Angelle to Picciola's store when the win', she start 'a blow. If she don'..." He shrugged.

Raphael nodded solemnly. "My *nonc,* Auguste Cantrelle, he has a big-big house."

"That one." He spat out the words. "He won' take you in."

Raphael thought about it, and decided Juan was right. "When does this storm come?"

"Who knows? Maybe soon, maybe later." Juan moved forward and cupped Raphael's chin in his hand. The old man stared at him long enough to make Raphael wish he could wiggle away. But he stood as still and tall as he could, and waited.

"Your papa, he was a good man." Juan dropped his hand. "You didn' know him, but me, I did. He was good, strong. *Les autres?* Those who say differen'?" He spat on the ground.

Raphael was affected by Juan's words. He wanted to ask more, but he was spellbound by the revelation that Juan had known his father. Suddenly he was no different from the other boys on the chénière. His father had been a good man.

"Come, I show you somethin'." Juan turned and started back the way he had come. Raphael was too excited by all he had heard to be frightened now of the marsh. He stumbled after Juan.

Juan parted the grasses, just like before. Raphael followed, noting their route as best he could. The path was both solid and liquid, and in places the sedge was taller than he was. He followed Juan's zigzag steps, glancing from time to time at a thicket of moss-draped trees in the distance.

They were almost at the ridge where three trees perched when Juan sank into water that came to the top of his boots. He turned and held out his hand to the boy. "You follow?"

Raphael looked at the water. He thought of what his mother would say when he returned with his pants wet and dirty. He thought of what Juan would say if he didn't continue. Juan, who had known his father. He stepped in and sank to his chest.

Juan nodded his approval, then started forward.

The mud oozed between Raphael's toes. His feet, as tough as shoe leather, still felt the prick of shells and roots. He thought of all the water creatures who could be lying in wait.

They were on land again in a minute. Juan held out his hand and lifted him up. "Wha' you hear?"

Raphael listened. The marsh was strangely silent. He frowned. "Nothin'"

"Tha's righ'." Juan started toward the trees. "Nothin'. What birds didn' leave, they listen, too. *N'est-ce pas?*"

"They listen for the wind?"

"Mais oui."

Raphael stared at the trees as they got closer. From a distance, he hadn't been able to tell that they were dead, but now he saw that they were mere skeletons of living trees, draped with moss like funeral shrouds. He didn't want to get any closer. The trees were dead, and he didn't want to think about them.

"Come, I show you somethin'," Juan said.

Raphael had little choice but to follow. As carefully as he had watched their route, he knew he might never find his way back to Juan's house or the village.

He followed two steps behind the old man, veering from side to side, just as Juan did. Juan stopped at the edge of the vague shadow cast by the middle tree. "Can you fin' the sun?"

Raphael thought that was a funny question, since the sun was well hidden by thick black clouds. But he squinted into the sky, then pointed at the spot where he thought the sun should be.

"Good," Juan said. "Remember." Juan took eight perfectly straight steps forward, then turned so that his shoulder faced the trees. He took eight more steps, also straight. Here the almost imperceptible shadows of two of the trees intersected. He turned again, at an angle to the third tree, and took eight more steps. Then he stopped and pointed to the ground. "Here."

Raphael ignored his fear of the trees and went to stand beside Juan. "What?"

"Here. You dig. Here."

"Dig?" Raphael looked down. The ground looked no different from that surrounding it. He looked up at Juan. "Why?"

Juan put his hands on Raphael's shoulders and pushed. "Go back. Try again, *hein?*"

Perplexed, Raphael turned and walked back to the edge of the shadow of the middle tree. When he faced the trees again, Juan had moved away. "Now," Juan said. "Again."

Raphael did everything Juan had done, even lengthening his steps so that they were as long as the old man's. He ended up in what he was certain was the same place.

"Non!" Juan came over to him and pushed him back to the spot where the shadows intersected, then turned him at a sharper angle. "Wha' d'you see?"

Raphael squinted. Far in the distance, exactly facing him, was a wide gap in the trees lining the horizon. He pointed. Juan nodded. "*Oui.* Now fin' the spot."

This time Raphael ended up where Juan wanted him.

Juan bent so that his face was only inches from the boy's. "You can fin', *hein?*"

"*Oui.*"

"If this win' takes me," Juan said, "you come back, you dig. You tell your *maman* to take you far 'way from this place, far 'way where no one knows you, no one knows your *papa. Vous comprenez?*"

Raphael *didn't* understand, exactly, but he knew he wanted to obey. Hadn't he dreamed of leaving the chénière himself?

"If this win' don' take me..." Juan shrugged. "Someday, somethin' will."

"What will you do when the wind comes?"

"I'll get in my boat."

"And sail away?"

The old man smiled. It was the first time Raphael had ever seen his expression change. *"Mais oui, cher.* An' sail away."

* * *

Lucien had stayed too long. Rain was falling by the time he made his way back to his boat, and dark clouds masked the fading daylight. The beach was deserted except for a small boy struggling to pull the boat farther ashore and out of the reach of the waves slithering toward its hull.

"Raphael!" Lucien hurried toward him, watching as the boy's thin arms strained with the weight. Affection filled him. "Don't worry, *mon fils,* I'm taking it back now, anyway."

Raphael straightened and turned. A smile gleamed white against his dark skin. "I was afraid it'd wash away."

"I wouldn't let that happen." Lucien ruffled Raphael's black curls. He had always thought Raphael a handsome enough boy, although he had the vaguely heathen look of some of the natives of the chénière and Grand Isle. Marcelite had told him that her family had come from Italy and Portugal, as well as France. Of Raphael's father she had said little, only that he had left her before the boy's birth, never to return. Lucien didn't care to know more. He tolerated Marcelite's past and even felt affection for her son. There was much he could overlook for what he received from her.

"You're leaving now?" Raphael asked. He licked his finger and held it up. "The win', she'll take you quick."

"You're right." Lucien ruffled the boy's curls once more, then dropped his hand. "Maybe quicker than I'd like."

"Juan Rodriguez says a big win' is coming." Raphael threw open his arms. "Big, like this. We'll all blow away."

The rain fell harder. Lucien had to bend to peer into Raphael's face. He saw excitement, but not one trace of fear. He suppressed a smile. "You mustn't believe everything the old man tells you, *mon fils.* It's too late in the year for a big storm. Don't worry your mother with stories. Promise?"

Raphael frowned. "Juan says if the big win' comes, we should go to Picciola's store."

"There's not going to be a big wind. I don't want you making your mother upset."

Raphael nodded, but his eyes were mutinous.

"Good." Lucien took off his shoes and socks and threw them in the boat, along with his hat. Then he rolled up his trousers. "I won't be back for a while. You must take good care of your mother while I'm gone."

Raphael nodded again.

"Come on and help me get the boat in." Lucien slung the rope over his shoulder. Then he started toward the water, dragging the boat behind him. He felt the thrust as Raphael lent his weight. Lucien climbed aboard and let the tide carry him out before raising the sail. He looked back and saw Raphael watching him. As the boy grew smaller and smaller, Lucien waved his last goodbye.

As the boat drew near to the opposite shore a short time later, a larger figure watched him. At first Lucien thought it was Mr. Krantz, assuring himself that his guest had returned safely from his sail, or perhaps one of his employees. The figure grew more familiar until he realized that the man who waited so patiently in the rain was Antoine Friloux, his father-in-law.

Apprehension gripped him. Antoine wasn't expected. Indeed, Lucien had left him only last night in New Orleans. Antoine must have come on a steamer he had hired himself.

But for what purpose? Antoine was not a man who relished physical discomfort. Yet now he stood in the steadily increasing rain. He made no move to assist Lucien as he waded in and pulled the boat to the beach; he just stood sternly, arms folded.

"Antoine?" Lucien shielded his eyes with his hand.

"Surprised, Lucien?"

Lucien moved closer. "Shouldn't I be?" He studied his father-in-law, trying to find a clue to his behavior. Antoine Friloux was a tall, slight man with the pale skin of his daughter and granddaughter. His dark hair and mustache were always perfectly trimmed, and his collar was always crisply starched. Even now, with rain dripping off his overcoat and hat, he looked distinguished.

"I've had certain surprises myself in the last few days," Antoine said.

"Is Claire—?"

Antoine waved away the question. "Claire is fine, as fine as a woman can be with a husband who plays her for a fool."

Lucien couldn't think of a response. He fell short of perfection, but what man didn't? He labored to provide all that a woman could desire. He performed his social obligations as a man of his standing was required to; in public and at home he displayed the good manners and breeding of his class. In what way had he harmed his wife?

"Do you know what I mean, Lucien?" Antoine asked.

Lucien glanced up at the sky. It was quickly growing darker. "Shall we discuss this under shelter?"

"I've taken the cottage nearest the dining room for the night. We can talk there."

Lucien nodded. He knew better than to show either irritation or dread. Antoine might be fifty, he might appear frail to one who didn't know him, but his appearance was deceptive. The reins of both his family and his business were tightly twisted around his spidery fingers. His slightest whim could effortlessly change the course of either.

Thunder boomed in the distance as they made their way along the track past the dining room to Antoine's cottage. Krantz filled the doorway of the dining room and nodded as they passed. Lucien was cold and wet enough to wish for either coffee or some of Krantz's excellent brandy, but he knew better than to stop.

The cottage, formerly a slave cabin, was simple, attractive in the summer, like all the others, with wisteria vines blanketing the gallery railing and beds of flowers scenting the air. Now, with the hotel nearly deserted and rain battering the shingled roof, the cottage looked as desolate as a much-sought-after belle when the last waltz of the ball has ended.

Both men took off their coats and shoes at the door. Someone had laid a fire in the fireplace, and Lucien went to stand in front of it. Antoine crossed to the table, where a decanter waited, and poured himself a drink. He didn't offer one to Lucien.

"Rather a poor afternoon for a sail, wouldn't you say?" Antoine asked, when his drink was half finished.

"It wasn't bad when I left. Then the time got away from me. When I realized the weather was worsening, it was too late to do more than bare my head to the rain."

"Did you consider stopping on the chénière to take shelter? I'm told the people there are quite hospitable."

"I didn't consider it. I knew Claire would be concerned if I didn't come back tonight."

"Quite the conscientious husband." Antoine toasted him with the remainder of his drink.

"What's this about, Antoine? I made the trip to Grand Isle at Claire's request. I saw nothing wrong in going sailing this afternoon as a small compensation."

"Small compensation?" Antoine laughed. "Oh, I think it was more than small, wasn't it? From what I've been told, when you visit Grand Isle, your compensation is abundant."

Lucien didn't like the direction of the conversation. There were certain things all men did, but rarely discussed. That Antoine would come so dangerously close to mentioning his son-in-law's mistress was unthinkable, the violation of a gentlemen's code. Lucien didn't know how Antoine had found out about Marcelite, but he didn't see how Antoine could fault him for taking pleasure whether he found it, not unless Claire was mistreated.

"All lives are made up of duty and occasional reward," Lucien said, when the silence had stretched too thin. "Mine is no different."

"No? And what happens when the reward becomes a duty, too?"

"I don't know what you mean."

"It's very simple, really." Antoine poured himself another drink. "Suppose something from which you take great pleasure becomes a burden. What do you do?"

"That would depend on what it was."

"Let's make it simpler, then. Suppose a man has a woman whom he loves. The woman is not his wife, but he has a wife and a duty to her. Now, let's say that he must leave this woman because, if he doesn't, he will lose everything he has worked his entire life to achieve."

Despite the fire, Lucien shuddered with a sudden chill.

"I see you begin to understand," Antoine said. "Let me proceed, then. So the woman, who was once a pleasure, is now a burden. Sadly, the woman is not the only burden. There are children, too. They, of course, are the reason he must leave the woman. The sanctity of his legitimate family cannot be breached. No chance can be taken that his bastards will inherit anything that belongs to the man, or his wife's family."

Lucien moved closer to the flames. There was no longer a point in denying anything, or in pretending that he didn't understand. He could save himself only with a promise, but as he made it, his voice sounded shaken, even to himself. "Marcelite Cantrelle's children will never inherit anything that belongs to the Friloux. You have my word on it."

"Your word? Of what worth is the word of a man who consorts with the whore of a slave?"

Lucien could feel color draining from his cheeks. He faced Antoine. "What?"

"You profess not to understand?"

"I don't know what you mean!"

"You've seen the whore's child, yet you've never seen the obvious?"

"Raphael?"

"Close your eyes and search his face in your mind. What do you find there?"

"Marcelite would have told me!"

"Not unless she's a fool." Antoine's lip curled in disgust. "Would she tell you that the boy's father was born into slavery, the son of a plantation owner and his house servant?"

He raised his hand to keep Lucien from interrupting. "Or would she tell you that when she became his lover, her own family drove her away to live alone and bear his child? And if you asked about her nigger, would she admit that he disappeared one night, never to be seen on the chénière again? Or that some say he was murdered by her brother?"

"No!"

"Yes," Antoine answered. He swished what was left of his second drink, but he didn't take his gaze from Lucien's face. "When a pleasure becomes a burden, there should be much thought about how a man rids himself of it."

Lucien stared at him, but his eyes were focused somewhere beyond Grand Isle.

"Neither your family nor mine has ever been touched by tainted blood. They can't be touched now," Antoine added, when Lucien didn't respond.

"Even if what you say about Raphael is true, my daughter's blood has no taint."

"Can you trust a woman who gives her body so easily? What blood runs through her own veins, do you suppose? The people on the chénière are pirates, smugglers, fishermen. Do they care if a tinge of color darkens their skin? No, they care if the next breeze blows, the next ship comes by, the next fish bites. Can you say for certain that your Angelle's blood is pure?"

Lucien turned paler still.

Shaking his head, Antoine set his drink down and moved toward the fire and Lucien. "I have watched my daughter fail to give you a healthy child. I am an old man. I may not live to see a grandchild who will grow to adulthood, but I have a brother, and he has children. I will not allow you to give everything I am, everything I have, to your bastards."

"They could not inherit, they—"

"They could inherit if you chose to make it so! And if Claire died, and you married this Marcelite, then they could inherit it all."

"That would never happen!"

"That *will* not happen." Antoine faced him. Their eyes were level. "I don't know how, Lucien, but you will end your relationship with this woman, and you will end it now. If you do not, I will destroy you. I will ruin your life in ways you have never dreamed of, but I will start by blackening your name in society and destroying you financially. When I am finished, you'll have nothing left to pass on to your bastard children."

"And Aurore? You would ruin her name along with mine?"

"I don't think Aurore will live long enough to be a consideration."

"Dear God..."

"A curious plea, under the circumstances." Antoine pulled his watch from his pocket and tipped it toward the flames. "Dinner is at seven. You should change."

"I need time to consider how best—"

"You have tomorrow. There will be no more time after that. We leave Monday morning for New Orleans, and when we do, you will leave behind all memories, all thoughts, of the chénière and your pleasures there. And if you don't?" He slid the watch back in his pocket. "Then you will know what it means to be sorry, and I will know what it means to be heartless. Perhaps you can spare us both those fates?"

CHAPTER 6

The church of Notre-Dame de Lourdes was Chénière Caminada's proudest possession, and the church's crowning glory was the massive silver bell that tolled the Angelus three times each day and called them to mass. On Sunday, Raphael counted its melodious notes. To his ears, there was no sweeter music.

His mother had told him the story of the bell. Years before, the people of the chénière had stopped their fishing, stopped their hunting and net-making, to build a church for God. And such a church it was. *Le bon Dieu* had looked down with favor, but he had been saddened that no bell rang out to the heavens, praising his name. So the priest had given a silver plate with his family coat of arms on it to be melted down, and the good people of the village had responded by donating all their gold and silver. In the dark of night, neighbor had watched neighbor steal outside on mysterious errands, and in the morning, shining doubloons and pirate treasure had been added to the collection.

When enough had been gathered, all the precious metal had been taken far away to be cast, and at last the bell had been lifted to the belfry to send its song over the peninsula.

Now the bell told Raphael that mass would begin soon. As always, his family would slip inside after the processional and leave before the benediction. Raphael did not understand why they didn't stay longer; he only knew that, although his mother did not make or mend nets on Sunday, it was a day much like others for her. They had no family to visit; they did not seek out friends. Sometimes they took walks along the beach, but they were invariably alone, unless M'sieu Lucien was visiting.

As always, the mass had begun when they took seats on the last bench. Raphael only half listened to the familiar words. Father Grimaud was a kind man who had once given him a piece of sugarcane. His voice was deep and resonant, and Raphael was sure that God himself spoke with less power. He watched as the few others who had ventured out moved forward to take communion, but neither he nor his mother followed their path.

When they left, the wind was blowing harder, and rain splashed at their feet. Raphael had not spoken to his mother of Juan's warning. Now he was torn between what Juan and M'sieu Lucien had told him. Despite his mother's cloak and the thin overcoat she had made him wear, they were quickly soaked. The wind plucked his mother's hair from the pins that bound it, sending it streaming wildly behind her.

At home, she sliced corn bread to dunk in thick cane syrup. They sat at the table and ate in silence, listening to the wind. Finally Raphael could be silent no more.

"Juan says a big win' comes, bigger than this. He says we can't stay here when it does."

His mother poured herself some of the strong black coffee she had brewed as the children ate. "Does he say when?"

"Non. But he says we must go to Picciola's store. Then M'sieu Lucien said I wasn't to worry you with Juan's stories."

"And did M'sieu Lucien think the wind would not worry me?" Marcelite wrapped her fingers around her cup for warmth.

Angelle stretched out her arms to Raphael, and he pulled her on his lap. She took the opportunity to finish off the rest of his syrup with the last crumbs of her corn bread. Her solid weight on his lap made him feel grown-up. He liked the scent of her curls, the touch of her chubby fingers against his cheek. Someday Angelle would be old enough to run as far as he did, and no one would tell her that she couldn't play with him. Already, when he told her about pirates and treasure chests, she listened attentively.

"Many would go to Picciola's," Marcelite said. "There would not be room for everyone."

"Angelle and I are small."

Marcelite didn't reply.

Raphael set Angelle on the floor when she began to squirm. She went to the driest corner of the hut to play with a toy that M'sieu Lucien had given her. He drank the small cup of milk his mother had poured him and waited.

"Father Grimaud would not turn us away," Marcelite said at last.

Raphael thought doubtfully of the long walk to the church. But the church was high off the ground, and much care had gone into building it. Surely, with God's help, it would stand.

Marcelite looked up at him and gave him one of her rare smiles. "You are a child, Raphael. You should not worry about these things." She held out her arms.

Shyly he circled the table and let her pull him to her. She smelled like jasmine and autumn rain. He laid his head against her breasts and vowed that even if he was a child, if the big wind came, he would get his mother and Angelle to safety..

The same dog who had sniffed Lucien's shoes yesterday crossed the path in front of him today. Tail tucked between its legs, it slunk toward a house with shuttered windows and began to howl.

Sailing to the chénière had been so difficult that now it was nearly three o'clock. As Lucien dragged his skiff to shore, he had noticed little that was unusual. The ebb tide had left small sea creatures and shells stranded in isolated pools, and a group of older children scavenged among them.

But as he neared the village, the sights no longer seemed as innocent. At every house he passed, there were women gathering everything they could carry and taking it inside. Even small children struggled under the burden of rubble that had once littered their yards. The men were outside, too, working to secure boats or make hasty repairs to houses, despite the fact that game birds often gathered on the ridges during storms and hunting on a day like this one would be a pleasure.

He hailed a young man with a cow tied to the end of a tattered rope. "What is everyone so worried about?" Thunder smothered his words, and he tried again, speaking slowly, since his own French differed so much from the patois spoken on the chénière.

The young man frowned, as if he resented having to point out the obvious. "There's a storm coming."

"But it's already October, and there's a low tide. The storm won't be a large one."

"You know this for a fact?"

"Then you believe differently?"

"God himself knows what kind of storm it will be. Me, I think I'll give him some help saving my cows."

Lucien thought of his return trip to Grand Isle. What if the man was right and the storm was a particularly bad one? What would Antoine do if he wasn't able to return in time for supper? The thought chilled him more than the rain seeping through his overcoat.

He moved faster along the path to Marcelite's and wondered how she would fare if the winds were high. Her house might be damaged, perhaps beyond repair. He thought of Angelle and realized she would suffer if the house leaked badly. But she was a strong child, and one drenching wouldn't harm her.

What would it do to her mother?

As he sailed from Grand Isle, he had considered and reconsidered how he would tell Marcelite that he was never coming back. She was not a submissive woman, nor a stupid one. Most of the people on the chénière had little or no education, but Marcelite spoke both French and English and read from her own prayer book. She was entirely capable of finding her way to New Orleans and confronting him with his bastard children.

He had promised her a house in the spring, and if she had a son, there was to be a lugger for him, as well. She would still demand these things, or more. And if Antoine discovered that Marcelite was still in Lucien's life, he would destroy him. Lucien had brought little more than a good name to his marriage. His finances were so intertwined with his father-in-law's that Antoine had ultimate control over them.

Despite the hours of pleasure she had given him, Lucien rued the day he had met Marcelite. The desire, the affection, he felt for her was nothing compared to the threat of losing everything that made him the man he was. Perhaps sometimes in New Orleans he had yearned for the simplicity, the warmth, of his life on the chénière, but never had he considered abandoning all that he possessed to live with Marcelite.

Now an answer to his troubles was thundering on the horizon. It was possible that the storm, if fierce enough, could work to his advantage. If she was frightened, Marcelite might realize how completely she was at the mercy of the elements. Anything he offered her afterward might seem a lavish gift.

For the first time since his talk with Antoine, he felt a ray of hope. The worsening storm could be an ally. He resolved not to tell her the purpose of his visit until the storm's end. Choosing the right moment could make the difference between success and failure, and failure was out of the question.

As he approached the hut, he noted a crazy quilt of driftwood patching the exterior. He imagined Marcelite, with Raphael's help, standing on a chair in the rain, trying to make the house watertight. It seemed she had already gotten a taste of what might await her when the storm expanded.

He paused at the door and tried to shake some of the rain from his overcoat and shoes, but it was useless.

"Marcelite!" He pushed the door open and peered inside. A lantern flickered, and he saw Marcelite and the two children across the room. He entered, pulling the door closed behind him.

"Lucien!" She leaped from her chair and crossed the room in three steps. He opened his arms and enfolded her. The children stared at him.

She spoke in French, not even attempting the English that she knew he preferred. "I thought you were back in New Orleans."

"I leave tomorrow. I hadn't intended to come here today, but when I saw the storm approaching..." He let his voice trail away.

She circled his waist and held him tighter. He felt her gratitude, and was distantly ashamed because of it. "You'll stay with us, then?" she asked.

"Until the storm is over."

"A storm killed my father. He and my uncles were out on the water. A storm blew up. Weeks later the boat drifted in to shore, full of rotten fish, fish you could smell across the whole chénière, but there were no men." She shuddered.

She had never told him anything about her past. Lucien held her and realized how frightened she must be.

Raphael got up from the bed where he and Angelle had been sitting. "M'sieu Lucien, if the storm gets much worse, we will go to the church."

"Don't be foolish! Soon the lightning and thunder will be closer. We'll be safer if we don't go anywhere. We'll do what we can to make the house tight, and ride out the storm here."

"But the wind!"

Lucien stared at Raphael. He saw that the boy's black curls weren't the innocent, silky curls of childhood; his skin wasn't brown from hours in the coastal sun. And his nose—how could Lucien not have seen how much stronger and broader it was than Marcelite's?

By all that was holy, the child had been like a son to him. How could he not have seen that Raphael was a quadroon? The signs of his mixed blood had been there all along, but Lucien had been too blinded by his infatuation with Marcelite.

He knew the penalties for such an error of judgment. Society sternly forbid any racial mixing. The color lines could not be breached, yet Marcelite had breached them in the most heinous of ways. And Lucien had lain with her repeatedly, indulged himself in her soft flesh whenever he could, without suspecting that another man to do so had been born a slave.

Now outrage filled him. "Am I to be ordered about by a child?"

Marcelite turned to her son and spoke so rapidly that Lucien missed much of what she said. But the essence of her message was clear when Raphael nodded reluctantly. The boy did not take his eyes off Lucien, however. Not for one second.

Marcelite turned back to Lucien. "He only tries to be of help."

"Make us coffee and something to eat. I'll see what needs to be done outside."

"Raphael can assist."

Lucien considered. The image of the boy wet and cold in the rain pleased him. "Yes, that would be good."

She spoke to Raphael again, but he refused to move.

"Raphael, if you want to help keep your mother and sister safe, then you'll come with me," Lucien said. He walked toward the doorway, then glanced behind him. "If you don't care..."

The child slumped at Lucien's words. Then Raphael followed Lucien out the door.

Raphael watched his mother pour Lucien another cup of coffee. He was chilled and hungry, but he knew that as long as M'sieu Lucien remained with them, his mother would tend to his needs first. Only yesterday he had wished that Lucien was his father, too. Now he was no longer certain. Was his own father watching from heaven, saddened?

Raphael pondered this as his mother bent and whispered something in Lucien's ear. Outside, the wind whistled louder, as if to keep Raphael from hearing what his mother said.

Angelle put her doll on his lap. It gazed blindly up at him, like old Leopold Perrin, who as a child had lost his sight during a fever. The doll's blue dress was tattered, but the silk was still finer than anything Raphael had seen. Once his mother had told him that in New Orleans some ladies wore nothing but silk, and some men, like M'sieu Lucien, rode everywhere in carriages pulled by shining, prancing horses.

Raphael didn't think that Lucien really wanted to be here. Usually he teased Raphael's mother and laughed with her. Today he sat quietly, as if he could think of nothing to laugh about. He had not lifted Angelle to his lap. He had not ruffled Raphael's curls or asked if he had dug for any pirate treasure.

Raphael didn't think he would have told him about Juan's mysterious instructions, even if he had been asked. Although Raphael didn't understand exactly why Juan had taken him into the swamp, he did know their trip was to remain a secret.

His mother ladled out two more bowls of crab gumbo and called the children to the table. Lucien stood and crossed the room as they sat down. He didn't open the door, but he peered through a crack next to the frame.

"The rain's coming down harder."

"Then come away from there," Marcelite said.

Raphael took his first spoonful of the gumbo. Usually it was thick with crab and okra and spicy enough to warm the coldest belly. Today his mother's thoughts had been elsewhere.

"Storms seem bigger here, don't they?" Lucien asked. "Like God's judgment. I think I would be frightened of them if I lived this close to the water."

"Then be happy you do not." Raphael's mother sliced hunks of bread for both children and set it in front of them.

"And helpless. I think I would feel helpless, too."

"There is only so much a person can do anywhere."

"Still, it's tempting fate, isn't it, to live where the wind can blow you away?"

Raphael stopped eating and watched his mother, but she didn't answer. She brushed the bread crumbs into her hand to store them in a can. Her hand did not seem steady to Raphael, and her lips were drawn in a straight line.

"We should go to the church," Raphael said.

Lucien turned away from the door. "What would you know about it?"

Raphael caught his mother's eye. She shook her head. He clamped his lips shut.

"You are nothing but a child," Lucien continued. "A child who's been too seldom disciplined."

"Raphael is a good boy," his mother said.

"You've said little about his father." Lucien started toward the table. "Was his father stubborn, too?"

Marcelite's eyes flicked to her son. "His father was many things."

"Would you say he was stubborn?"

"I would not have called him that."

"And what would you have called him?"

"Proud," she said, meeting his eyes. "Proud and brave, just as his son will be."

"Does your son have reason to be proud?"

"We'll speak of this no more."

"There are many things of which we haven't spoken." Lucien looked down at Raphael. "The boy's father is only one."

Whimpering, Angelle got down from her chair, clearly upset by the tone of their voices. The whimpering stopped when her bare feet touched the floor. She looked up at Raphael, her expression one of surprise. Then she sat on the planks of driftwood covered by woven palmetto mats and began to slide her hands back and forth.

Raphael looked down and saw nothing. He jumped from his chair and stood beside her. "The floor is wet," he said.

"It should be, with all the holes in this miserable place." Lucien stooped and felt the floor.

Marcelite stooped, too. "It's never been this wet. This is more than rain from the roof."

"It's blowing in the sides, too."

"It's coming in under the door." Raphael pointed. "Look."

"Raphael's right," his mother said. She straightened, then started for the door. "It's washing in underneath. What can this mean, Lucien?"

He muttered a curse in English. Raphael stepped far to one side, so as not to get in Lucien's way as he passed. At the door, Lucien stood behind Marcelite and peered outside. They were both silent for a moment. Unconcerned, Angelle began to dance her doll along the wet palmetto mat.

"The ground's covered with water," Marcelite said. "Covered, Lucien. I've never seen it like this."

"The rain's falling fast. The ground can't take it all in. When the rain slackens, the water will run off."

"It's never collected this way before."

"Every storm is different."

"*Mais oui,* and some are very big." Marcelite moved away from him and felt along the floor. Then she lifted a wet finger to her mouth and touched the tip with her tongue. "It tastes of salt!"

Lucien stared at her for a moment, then bent to perform the same act. When he straightened, his expression frightened Raphael. "Fetch my overcoat."

Marcelite hurried to the wooden peg and took it down. He snatched it away. "Stand away from the door," he said. "Raphael, help your mother close this when I'm gone."

Water poured into the room when he opened the door. He disappeared into the rain, and Marcelite and Raphael struggled to shut it behind him. Marcelite fastened it with a rope and peg.

"Light the candles on the shrine," Marcelite told Raphael. "Hurry. We must say a last prayer."

"*Maman,* the church—"

"It's already too late to travel that far. We'll have to find another refuge. But we must say our prayers first. Then we'll gather what we can." She spoke quietly, and he knew she was trying not to frighten Angelle. "You must be brave."

"Like my father?"

She brushed the back of her hand against his cheek. "There are many things I've never told you."

"Juan said my father was a good man."

"He was."

Raphael wanted to ask more, but his mother was already mov-

ing past him. "Light the candles," she repeated. "There will be time
to talk when we're safe and the storm is over."

They were finished with their prayers and their packing by the
time Lucien returned. The children were dressed in their wet out-
erwear, and Marcelite had already tied Raphael's small bundle to
his back. When she heard Lucien's summons at the door, she unfastened the peg. He brought the storm in with him.

"The tide's turned. I've brought my skiff. We're not safe here.
There are waves crashing over a good part of the peninsula. I lost
my footing on the beach and almost got dragged under. I saw a dog
swept out. Some boat sheds are gone."

"Where shall we go?"

"I passed a house set back from the shore. No one answered
when I knocked." He described the location of the house.

Marcelite nodded. "It belongs to Julien LeBlanc and his son.
They're probably at the oyster grounds."

"I don't want to try to go farther with the children. We'll go there.
I'm certain they'd give us shelter if they were home."

"I'm not so certain."

"Enough! That doesn't matter now."

"*Non.* You're right." Marcelite went to the bed and lifted her
bundle to her back, slipping her arms through two knots tied for
that purpose. She reached for her cloak and fastened it, then
stooped and held her arms open for Angelle.

"You and Angelle can ride in the skiff. Raphael and I will tow,
unless it grows too deep for him."

"That deep?"

"It grows deeper as we talk!"

Marcelite clasped Angelle to her and motioned for Raphael to
join them. He passed the shrine and paused to blow out the candles, but the wind blowing through the cracks had done it already.
He made the sign of the cross before he went to his mother's side.

The world outside was one he'd never seen. The sky was dark,
but flashes of lightning appeared one after the other, like sparks
trailing from a divine lantern. The wind threw him forward, and

only his mother's arm stopped him from landing in water up to his knees. Objects sailed by, dried branches of palmetto, a torn patch of sail. Over the thunder and the moaning of the wind he heard the sickly lowing of the island's cattle.

He took tiny steps toward the skiff that Lucien had guided almost to their door. His hand closed around the rope tied to the bow, and he no longer felt his mother's grip on his shoulder. He turned and watched as Lucien helped her into the boat. She grasped Angelle and wrapped her cloak around them both. Immediately the wind ripped it open.

Raphael held tightly to the rope and waited for Lucien. He heard a roar from the direction of the beach, and he imagined waves as tall as trees. They would be fierce, those waves, fierce enough to slam against his house and turn it back into driftwood. What had the people of the chénière done to anger the waves?

He felt a tug on the rope and saw that M'sieu Lucien had joined him. He wished they were already at Julien LeBlanc's.

They began to move. At first he stumbled frequently, but after a while he grew accustomed to the shoving wind and sucking water. He held tight to the rope until his hand cramped in place. As they made their way inland, the water was as deep as it had been at his house. He looked back once, but the rain was a solid curtain. He couldn't even see his mother's face.

There were others out in the storm. Men passed, towing boats larger than the skiff. At one house, two men were handing children into the arms of their mothers, who were already on board a large lugger. Raphael tried to imagine riding out the storm in the bowels of the fishing boat. He envied the children.

Someone shouted that Picciola's store would be a good place to wait out the storm, but Lucien didn't change course. They moved on, beyond the lugger, beyond houses, beyond trees bending low in the wind's path. A new sound rang out over the peninsula. The church bell was tolling erratically, as if it were being tossed slowly back and forth by the storm. *"La cloche! La cloche!"* he cried. But if M'sieu Lucien heard, he didn't answer.

Shivering with every step, he began to wish he could ride in the skiff. He had lost his bearings, and when they finally stopped in front of another house, he was surprised to realize that this was their destination. Water lapped at the pillars, but the rest appeared untouched. This house would ride the winds and laugh at the rain. Raphael said a quick prayer of thanksgiving.

Lucien dragged the skiff to the steps. The water wasn't as high here, and he waited until Marcelite and Angelle had climbed out before he pulled the boat to the railing and tied it there.

Marcelite helped both children up to the gallery, but the roof was little protection. The rain seemed to be falling from all sides. Angelle was crying. Raphael wanted to tell her that they were safe now, but he wasn't sure she would hear him over the storm. When Lucien joined them, he pounded on the front door. No one answered.

"We'll have to go in anyway!" he shouted.

Marcelite clasped Angelle tighter. "They aren't here. Their *canote*'s not in its place."

"Then we'll keep the house safe for them and pray they're out of the storm somewhere else."

In seconds, they were inside. For Raphael, the house was as much a surprise as the sudden end to the battering of rain and wind. The walls were as white inside as out, with ceilings that stretched high above even Lucien's head. There were mats on the floor made of cloth, and chairs covered with cloth, too. He wanted to run through the house and explore, but his mother took his arm. "I'll find something to dry us with. You take care of Angelle."

He slipped off his coat and the bundle tied to his back. Angelle wrapped her arms around him, and he patted her wet curls and whispered that she was safe now.

M'sieu Lucien lit a lantern that hung by the door; then he disappeared into the next room as Raphael's mother returned. She handed him a square of rough linen and used another to dry Angelle.

"We've chosen a good place," Lucien called from the back of the house. "This is well constructed, and there aren't many windows."

Angelle clung to her mother and sobbed. Marcelite lifted her and swayed gently back and forth until Lucien returned. "There's a bed in the back where the children can sleep," he said. "I left the lantern burning there."

"Angelle is exhausted." Marcelite held her closer.

Raphael protested. He wasn't tired; he wanted to stay awake and watch the storm. Now that he was no longer in it, it seemed the most exciting thing that had ever happened to him.

Lucien turned his back on them. "You will go to bed."

Marcelite put her hand on Raphael's shoulder. He knew what the hand was telling him, but he didn't want to give in so easily. "But I could help, *Maman.* I could watch to see if the water rises."

"You will watch from outside if you don't do as I say," Lucien said.

"You're not my father!"

Lucien whirled, and Raphael could see he was furious. "Of that, at least, I'm certain! It's not *my* blood that's made you what you are."

Marcelite clenched Raphael's shoulder and pulled him toward the back of the house. "Raphael, you'll go to bed. Someone must stay with Angelle, or she'll be frightened."

Raphael wanted to shout that he was glad now that M'sieu Lucien wasn't his father, but his courage deserted him. If he fought with Lucien, it would hurt his mother.

There was a bed finer than any he had ever seen in one of the two back rooms. Marcelite set Angelle on it and covered her with a quilt that had been folded neatly at the foot. Reluctantly Raphael climbed up and lay beside her, and Marcelite arranged the quilt to cover him, too.

"Rest now."

"When will the storm end?" he asked.

"Soon."

"Will our house still be there tomorrow?"

"I don't know. Pray that it will be."

"Why is M'sieu Lucien so angry with me today?"

Marcelite was silent.

"Maman?"

"M'sieu Lucien is worried about the storm. It only seems he is angry."

Raphael didn't believe her, but he couldn't tell her so.

"Take care of Angelle," she said. "Keep her warm." She leaned down and kissed his forehead, then she kissed Angelle, who was already sleeping. "In the morning the sun will be shining."

Outside the wind screamed, and through the window Raphael watched the skeletal branches of a chinaball tree claw the sky. He tried to imagine sunshine, but when his mother finally left and took the lantern, it was the storm he saw. Even when his eyes were closed.

CHAPTER 7

At home in New Orleans, Sunday was Aurore's favorite day, the only one when she was certain to be allowed to travel through the city. Because she was usually shielded from the ever-present threat of disease, the trip was her only view of life outside her house. Invariably she and her parents attended mass at the palatial Saint Louis Cathedral; then the family called at Grandpère Antoine's, where they were served an early dinner.

In contrast, summer Sundays at the Krantz Place were just one more day filled with wonder and possibility. Time drifted on the scented breeze of summer. Those who didn't attend mass on the chénière might observe a quiet hour or two in the morning, but the rest of the day was filled, like any other, with languid summer pursuits.

There were often dances on Sunday night in the *salon de danse,* half of the dining room, converted for that purpose in the afternoon. For a child alert enough to notice, there were smoldering looks exchanged on the dance floor between the young dandies of Bachelor's Row and the Creole beauties of Widow's Row, temptingly housed for the summer in cottages that faced each other. Sometimes there were recitals, sometimes games.

On this Sunday, however, there were no entertainments. Dressed in lace-trimmed white piqué, Aurore knelt with her mother and prayed for most of the morning. In the afternoon, as wind blew and rain fell, she lay in bed and stared at the ceiling while her mother napped. Her grandfather had arrived unexpectedly the previous afternoon, but she had seen little of him. Her father had gone sailing again, but not before there had been another argument with her mother.

Aurore's father had not returned by the time an early supper was served. Worried about both Lucien and the extraordinary pallor of her mother's face, Aurore picked at her food. No one spoke, but the wind whistled loudly, and sometimes the cottage shook with its power.

She went to bed early, glad to escape the dread in her mother's eyes. She fell asleep to the moaning of the wind. Once she awoke and thought she heard voices raised in anger, but she fell back asleep before she could tell whose they were.

The wind was much louder when Aurore felt arms lift her. It seemed she had just fallen asleep, and she didn't want to awaken. In her dreams, the house was quiet and she was safe.

The arms lifted her higher, and a tuneless whine chased away her dreams. She opened her eyes and stared into her mother's.

"We're going to the house of Ti' Boo's uncle. But you must be quiet," her mother whispered. "Grandpère Antoine believes we'll be safer here. He's asleep, and he mustn't know."

Aurore couldn't remember ever being held by her mother this way. Sleepily she touched her mother's cheek. It was wet with tears. "Ti' Boo will help you dress," her mother said. "But you must be quiet. Do you understand?"

"What's that noise?" Aurore whispered.

"The wind."

"Why are we going to Nonc Clebert's house?"

"He's taking Ti' Boo, and he says we must go, too."

Aurore wanted to prolong the moment. Her mother's arms were wrapped around her, as if she would take good care of this daughter she so seldom noticed. Aurore looked into eyes that were the pale blue of her own, eyes that for once were focused on her. She nodded.

Her mother set Aurore on the floor. Only then did the child see Ti' Boo across the room at the armoire, gathering clothes for her. "I'll be back," her mother whispered.

Aurore watched her go. Ti' Boo came to her side, but didn't speak. She helped Aurore dress. Aurore could feel Ti' Boo's impatience in the clumsiness of her movements. Then, when Aurore was ready, Ti' Boo took her hand and led her into the main room of the cottage. Nonc Clebert was beside the door. There was no lantern, but the room was illuminated by lightning that flashed so steadily Aurore could read his worried expression.

She no longer felt brave. The courage her mother's embrace had given her died. She began to sniff.

Ti' Boo pinched her. She put her mouth close to Aurore's ear. "If you cry, Ro-Ro," she said, "I'll pinch you harder!"

Aurore was so astonished by the pain, she forgot to sniff again. "Good," Ti' Boo whispered. "You must be a brave girl."

Aurore's mother came into the room, fastening a long cloak and bringing Aurore's. Without a word, she wrapped and tied it tightly at Aurore's neck. Then she took her hand.

"Where are you going?"

Aurore saw Grandpère Antoine in the doorway of the room that was usually her mother's. Her mother's hand trembled.

"I asked where you were going, Claire."

Aurore looked up and saw her mother's lips moving, but no sound emerged.

"You will go to bed," her grandfather said.

"No." Her mother gripped Aurore's hand harder. "No, I will not. I'm taking Aurore to Monsieur Boudreaux's house, Papa."

"You will not take the child anywhere."

"Come with us."

"You aren't well, Claire. You cannot make this decision."

"I've made it."

"I forbid it."

"You cannot." Claire clasped her daughter's hand tighter.

"Have you even glanced outside? If you go out now, you could be killed by a falling tree. I forbid it!"

"We should have gone hours ago, it's true. But you wouldn't allow it. Now we must take our chances, even if you don't approve." Claire began to move across the room, pulling Aurore beside her. She passed as far from her father as she could.

"My house, it's on a ridge farther from the shore," Nonc Clebert said. He was a small man, but wiry and strong. Aurore had visited his home twice with Ti' Boo, and she knew how quickly he could move. "It's protected by trees. We will pass the storm safely there." He stepped forward, as if to block Antoine from grabbing his daughter. "You would be welcome."

"I forbid you to take them with you!"

"I'm afraid I must."

Aurore watched her grandfather take several steps forward. Nonc Clebert turned to his side and raised a fist. Her grandfather seemed to grow smaller and older. He came no closer.

"My husband isn't with me," her mother said to her grandfather. "I don't even know if he's safe. Will you deprive me of my father, too?"

"This is folly. I'll not leave this cottage, Claire. Krantz has assured me we'll be safe here, and Krantz is a gentleman. If you must go, at least leave Aurore with me. She's too small to survive out there."

"She is my daughter. She comes with me."

"Every moment we wait will make it more dangerous," Nonc Clebert said.

"Aurore!" Grandpère Antoine held out his arms.

Aurore felt the pull between the two adults as surely as if each were holding a hand. Tears welled in her eyes and trickled down her cheeks. She looked toward the door, where Ti' Boo stood, and saw sympathy in her eyes. Then Ti' Boo held out her arms. Aurore wrenched herself away from her mother and flew to her friend.

"Papa, please come," her mother begged. "Please!"

"You are as crazy as your husband believes," he said sternly, "and as bad a mother. Now I understand why God does not send you more children!"

Aurore's mother made a sound like the moan of the wind. Then, wrapping her cloak tightly around her, she joined her daughter. Nonc Clebert turned and opened the door.

Then they were inside the storm.

Lucien had convinced himself that the storm, though fierce, would blow over quickly. Although the water was rising steadily, he still refused to consider that he might be in danger. But by the time Marcelite returned to the front of the house, the wind had strengthened, too. Carrying the lantern in one hand and lifting her wet skirts with the other, she joined him at the window overlooking the gallery. "It's growing worse."

"Nonsense. You're just frightened of storms. And who could blame you, living as you do?"

She set the lantern down. "But now, with your help, all that will change."

He didn't touch her. "When I go home after the storm, I won't be back again." He listened to her sharp indrawn breath. Even now, with an opportunity to tell the truth, Lucien couldn't bring himself to admit that his father-in-law had given him an ultimatum. "Does that surprise you? Haven't you always known that when I realized what race your son was, I would leave you?"

"My son is a small boy, a good boy. There's nothing else to know."

"Your son is a quadroon! His father was a slave. His mother is a whore!"

She faced him. "And what does that make you, Lucien? You've fathered two children by this whore, have you not?"

He struck her shoulder, and she staggered backward before he hauled her closer again and shook her. Despair welled inside him when he realized he didn't want to let her go, even though she had denied nothing. Even though his future depended on it.

"I can have nothing more to do with you! Don't you understand?" he shouted. The words were for both of them.

She struck at his arms until he shoved her away, and she fell against the windowsill. "Do you think I'll let you forget us so easily? I can't raise your children alone! We struggle for every mouthful of food. We shiver in the winter and suffer storms in the summer! To feed your daughter I sell your little trinkets! But in the spring I'll have another child to consider. I must have your help, and if you don't give it willingly, I'll be forced to take it from you!"

"And how will you go about that?"

"I'll go to New Orleans, and I'll tell everyone I see that Lucien Le Danois is the father of my children, a father who allows them to starve!"

He felt the color drain from his cheeks. "You wouldn't!"

"*Non?* Don't you think so? I have nothing but my children. I am dead to my family. I have no place here. I will go to New Orleans, and every day you will find me outside your fine mansion on Esplanade. Your wife and I will know each other well!"

He couldn't remember ever telling her where he lived. Yet she knew. She knew because she must have considered this possibility even before his announcement. He tried to curb his panic. "I never thought to leave you without money. I'll give you money. Some now, some later. You can find a better house. You won't have to suffer from storms like this one."

"Some now, some later?" She waved her hands to erase his words. "Do you think to buy me off so cheaply? A little here, a little there? Like an old family servant?"

"It's more than you deserve!"

"Perhaps so, but it is not what your children deserve, and for them, I will go to New Orleans!"

He saw his future in the unveiled fury in her eyes. He saw a life without stature, without money or any of the comforts it bought. He saw all the doors of the city closed tightly in his face. And, standing in the only door still open to him, he saw a woman who had not loved him enough to let him go.

"What must I pay for your silence?"

She was breathing fast, as if their fight had diminished the air in the room. She seemed to be planning as she spoke. "I no longer want to live at the mercy of every puff of wind. I want to take the children to New Orleans. I want money to take care of them and, later, enough to teach them a trade." She paused. "We would be near. You would always be welcome."

None of it was possible, yet he saw nothing to gain by telling her so. He couldn't give up all he possessed, and he knew that was exactly what he would be doing if he gave her what she demanded. Antoine would discover the truth before she and the children made the journey to the city.

"The storm makes us say these things." He moved closer to the window. "We're both uneasy. This isn't the time to talk."

"There is nothing more to say."

"Be reasonable, *mon coeur,* you're a woman without friends or funds. You can do nothing without my help."

"For years I've saved every bit of money I could. Someone will take me to New Orleans for what I can offer. If you think to leave after the storm and never see me again, you're mistaken. When the storm ends, I'll no longer have a home. I'll find a new one. Perhaps on Esplanade Avenue?"

"How can you threaten me, after all I've been to you?"

"The gull protects her nestlings from the hawk."

He saw her desperation. She would not be silenced by promises. In his world, she was a woman of no consequence, yet she was about to ruin his life.

A crash outside made her turn. She peered into the darkness. Lucien was grateful for the interruption. "What was that?"

"Someone's coming up the steps." She pointed.

"The LeBlancs?"

"I don't know."

He moved to one side to improve his view. More than half a dozen figures were struggling through the rain. In a flash of lightning he saw one stagger, blown to the opposite railing by the wind. An arm shot out to help; then the sky went dark.

Marcelite disappeared into the back of the house. She was returning with towels when the door flew open and a man appeared.

"Someone's already here!" he shouted behind him.

In moments, the entry was filled with people. Marcelite stepped forward as if the house belonged to her and helped the arrivals strip off their wet outer clothing and dry themselves. Lucien counted three men, two women and four children.

One of the women was sobbing. "Our house is gone," she said between sobs. "Everything is lost."

Lucien looked at the faces of the men, expecting to find that this was an exaggeration. Instead, her words were confirmed. "Your house is gone?"

One of the men nodded. "Collapsed."

"Is anyone hurt?" Marcelite asked.

A little girl extended an arm, as if to show an injury. One of the women snatched her from Marcelite's grasp, but Marcelite stepped forward so that the woman was forced to meet her eyes. "We're all neighbors, are we not? Especially now."

"Let her look," one of the men said.

The woman ignored him and held tightly to the child, but when Marcelite continued to wait, she finally dropped her hands. Marcelite murmured soothing words to the little girl as she wrapped a towel around her arm.

"How did you come here?" The first man to enter the room addressed himself to Lucien.

He explained. "I hope Monsieur LeBlanc will understand."

The man shrugged. "And if he doesn't? What's one man's fury next to that of the storm?"

"Was your house near the beach?"

"Not as near as some. And I built it myself. I bolted it into the ground!"

"Surely the worst will be over soon. Enough of your house may be standing so you can rebuild."

"Even now my house is driftwood for people on Grand Isle to pick off the beach. We thought to tow my boat to the trees in Leopold Perrin's yard, but the water swirled too quickly, and the wind was too strong. The storm isn't dying, *mon ami*. It's just playing with us."

Lucien glanced out the window. "No. Impossible."

"There was another storm." One of the other men joined them. He was old, the patriarch of the family, Lucien guessed, and his voice quavered from age and fatigue. "I was young. The winds raged and the water rose, but the worst of it passed over us here. Then, the next day and the next, when the skies were clear and the wind friendly, we saw bodies washing ashore, and pieces of houses. They were from L'Isle Dernière."

The younger man had obviously heard the story many times before. He seemed resigned. "If we're lucky, this one will turn that way, too. But no one lives on L'Isle Dernière now. If the storm is hungry for more than sand and palmetto, she'll come ashore here."

"She is coming," the old man said.

"How high has the water risen?" Lucien asked.

"It was up to the fourth step when we got here. It will be higher now. It's rising quickly."

"Someone else is here." One of the women pulled the door open, and more people entered on a blast of wind-driven rain. The two men left to talk to the newcomers. Marcelite passed close enough for Lucien to grab her arm.

"These men think the storm will worsen," he said.

"Will we be safe here?"

He thought about the old man's story, and the others he had heard before. Once, L'Isle Dernière had been a summer resort community, like Grand Isle. A dance had been held in the hotel ballroom during the storm, and the water had swept inside and carried the dancers away. Could he really be in danger? Had he been so sure of what he knew that he had refused to see the truth?

"There won't be a better opportunity to go somewhere else," she said. "If we're not safe here, we must leave now."

The door crashed open, and two more people entered. "These men know the chénière, and this is the house they've chosen," Lucien said. "What do I know that they don't?"

"Then I'm going to bring the children out here."

"No. Let them sleep."

Marcelite shrugged off his hand. "I want them with me."

The door slammed again, and a man entered carrying a young woman in his arms. The voices in the room fell silent until one of the men who was already inside took the woman from him. Everyone crowded around as he laid her on the floor.

Lucien saw that her face was as pale as death. An old woman, still wet and trembling herself, laid her head on the young woman's chest and pronounced her alive. Immediately others began to work on her, turning her on one side and pounding the water from her lungs. Someone brought a quilt.

Lucien approached the man who had carried her this far. His eyes were fixed on the scene before them. "How did it happen?"

For a moment, the young man seemed unable to speak. Other men gathered around, and this seemed to steady him. "Sophia fell. She was carrying little Rosina. They...slid under the water. When they sur—surfaced, they were far apart. I could only reach for one of them."

The house shook so hard that Lucien could feel the floor heave under his feet. The other men charged into action. One led the man who had just told his story to a chair, where he put his head in his hands and sobbed. Another lifted Sophia off the floor and carried her, wrapped in the quilt, to a rug in the parlor, where the women continued to tend her. Two others began to dismantle a table and fasten the boards over the window. Lucien watched his view of the world disappear.

The two men left to cover the few other windows in the house. Everyone seemed to have a mission, but Lucien was left alone. He couldn't see outside, but he could feel wind and water shake the house. He wondered how high the water had risen now.

Would the skiff be safe? It must already be in pieces. And if it was, he would have no escape if this house was destroyed. He wondered if he should go outside and secure it, perhaps even bring it up to the gallery. If the water rose that high, launching it would be the small matter of one push.

At the front door, he put on his overcoat, although as wet as it was, it provided no comfort. He explained his intention to one of the other men, who told him he was a fool to go back outside.

On the gallery, he realized the man was right. Before he could cross to the railing, the wind threw him against the front of the house. He dropped to his knees and crawled the distance, grabbing the railing to look below. The water was still rising. Had the house not been so high, it would have flooded already. The current was swift, and waves crashed in assault.

He saw the trunks of trees wash past, and something that looked like the section of a roof. One flash of lightning revealed the horns of a bull drowned in the rushing water. In the distance he thought he heard screaming over the roar of the wind. But one sound was unmistakable. The church bell pealed loudly and continuously, as if it were calling the people of Chénière Caminada to their own funeral mass.

Horrified, he dragged himself to the top step to look for the skiff. He spotted it during the next flash of light. The current had pinned it against a massive post, where it was temporarily protected. But any change in the wind could destroy it. He weighed his safety against that of the boat. Without the skiff, he might be helpless.

Helpless! He was filled with rage that his life was no longer his own. Marcelite and Antoine controlled his destiny. And now the storm was taking what was left of his future and twisting it to suit some demonic fancy.

Rage carried him into the water. Clinging to the porch railing, he lowered himself step by step until his feet touched the ground. The water was deeper than his knees, and miserably cold. Objects swirled in its depths. A tree eddied toward him, and he dived beneath it so that it would not pin him against a pillar. He surfaced and discovered that the current had already carried him beyond the skiff. He was completely exhausted by the time he fought his way back. He threw his arms over the stern and clung there, floating until he had regained some strength.

He thought he could feel the water rising beneath him. How

could it rise so quickly? What power did this storm possess that it could turn the tide and flood the land in hours?

For the first time, he thought about Claire and Aurore. Was the storm as bad on Grand Isle? The cottage where his family was staying was an old slave cabin, never fortified against this kind of wind. He and Claire had fought about Chighizola's prophecy. Had she found the courage to seek stronger shelter?

Something brushed against his chest, something soft and yielding. Horror gripped him. He couldn't force himself to investigate. He prayed the object would wash beyond him, but whatever it was wedged itself between his arm and the skiff. He tried to make his way around the boat, but the object seemed to follow him. Finally, he forced himself to look down. The body of a child—a girl, he guessed from the length of her hair—had snagged against the hull. Lightning flashed, and he could see her sightless eyes staring at him. Bile rose in his throat. He thrust himself away from the boat, and in seconds the current had ripped her loose and carried her away.

He struggled for a deep breath, but water filled his lungs. He floundered as more water closed over him, but as his panic grew, his hands closed on the skiff once more. He inched his way to the bow to begin the fight to get the skiff to the gallery.

The water had risen higher by the time he made his way back inside. A large family of refugees had found their way to the house. There were now twenty-five people inside.

After his immersion in the storm, the house seemed almost silent. Lucien scanned the room to locate Marcelite and the children, and found them in a corner. He took Angelle from her mother so that he could rock her against his chest. She was warm, and her eyes stared curiously into his. He saw only the dead child by the boat. When he could look at her no longer, he averted his eyes. Raphael was watching him.

He could feel nothing for the boy now except pity. He switched his gaze to Marcelite and acknowledged for the first time the strength that had helped her survive her disgrace. She would never give up easily. Tonight she would struggle for her family's survival. She would struggle until death.

She rose. "I'll get you some coffee. I've been saving a cup for you."

He stared after her. She was as much a part of him as the dreams he had each night. How could he have believed he could walk away? He closed his eyes, and the dead child stared back at him.

CHAPTER 8

Lucien had just finished his coffee when someone tapped him on the shoulder. Startled, he turned and saw the man whose house had collapsed. "The water has almost reached the gallery." He gestured toward the door. Lucien rose and joined the men gathered there. Time had passed, although he didn't know how much. Time now was a matter of rising water and strengthening wind. He struggled to follow the men's rapid, idiomatic French.

Their observations didn't surprise him. The storm would build even more. The worst moment would come later, when the winds changed and all the water covering the peninsula would rush back to the Gulf, taking whatever it could with it. There were arguments about how much damage might be done. Some believed if the water didn't rise above a certain height, they would be saved. Some believed they were already doomed.

"Is there another, better place to go?" Lucien asked.

The men stared at him as if he were crazy. "There is no place to go but into the belly of the storm." The man who'd spoken slashed his hand across the empty space before him in emphasis. The others murmured their agreement.

"What if there's a lull?" Lucien asked.

"There will be. Before hell is unleashed."

"And then, will you know the storm's intent?" another man asked. "Will you know where you will be safe and where you will not? Because if you know, *mon ami,* then perhaps you'll tell us?"

"I know nothing. I'm at your mercy."

"Then stay and help us prepare for when the water comes inside."

Lucien explained the plan to Marcelite and helped her get the children to the attic. They settled on a quilt in the corner, as far away from the window as possible. The window had been shuttered, but later it would have to be used to gauge the storm's progress. In the attic, the slash of rain and crashing drive of the wind made a wild, horrifying chorus. As children were led upstairs, they cried and clung to their mothers.

One of the men carried the unconscious Sophia upstairs and laid her gently on a rug someone else had brought up for her. Her husband knelt beside her and chafed her hands. Angelle put her head between Marcelite's breasts and covered her ears. Raphael, wide-eyed and silent, sat perfectly still, as if the noise had stripped away speech and movement.

Screams were audible here, along with the ceaseless clanging of the church bell. Lucien thought of those trapped outside, struggling to find their way to shelter. He had convinced himself that the child by the boat had been Rosina, Sophia's daughter, one child already known to be lost. Only one. Now, as he listened to the devil's own chorus, he knew more had died, and still more would die yet.

"The house is strong," he assured Marcelite. "It's holding well. We'll be safe."

Her lips moved, and he knew she was sending prayers to heaven. He left her and went back down the stairs. The men were taking turns watching the storm from a small section of the window that had been stripped of its cover.

His own turn came too soon. The world he saw was not the one he had left just hours before. His skiff was floating on the gallery. They were an island in a rushing river, and the river was alive. He shut his eyes, not wanting to examine too closely the objects sweeping by. He stepped back.

"People are dying," one of the men said. "We have to help."

There was a consensus that they must do what they could. Someone suggested they light a lantern in the attic window. Someone else proposed a human chain to rescue anyone who came close.

The man whose house had collapsed stepped forward. Lucien had learned he was Dupres Jambon and his father was Octave.

Dupres clapped his hand on Lucien's shoulder. "You unshutter the window upstairs and light a lantern. Ask one of the women to tend it. Then come down and stand guard. I'll prepare to be the first outside if I'm needed."

The house groaned, every joint tortured by the weight of the water pushing against it. The east side of the house was already bulging inward. "Do you think the house will hold?" Lucien asked.

"I'm taking my family to find better shelter when the calm comes," Dupres said. "You should leave, too. If the wind circles back from the west, this house will be in its path."

As he followed Dupres's instructions, Lucien considered his advice. If the calm came and the winds died, then the skiff could be rowed or pulled to a safer place. He was lucky that it was so small. A larger boat would be impossible to guide.

The question of where they might be safe filled his mind. Grand Isle had a high central ridge, with houses surrounded by century-old trees rooted deeply in the soil. The chénière had nothing comparable. They would have to choose a building, one as far from the shore as possible, and sturdily built.

He remembered Raphael's suggestion of the church, and at first he discarded it simply because it had come from the boy. But pride was a foolish emotion now. Mentally he calculated the distance, and the time it might take to get there. Certainly the building had been constructed by some of the most talented carpenters on Chénière Caminada. And beside it sat the presbytery, two stories, also well constructed. If either was standing, he would be given sanctuary there.

Water was pouring inside the house, gushing in spouts from holes the men had drilled in the floor to take advantage of the water's weight. With luck the water might stabilize the house, at least temporarily. Lucien could feel it rising toward his knees, but he kept watch at the shuttered window and gazed with mounting horror at the scene before him. Once he shouted to Dupres that someone was struggling toward the house, but before Dupres and the others could attempt a rescue, the struggle ended.

Slowly panic replaced horror. Was he to die here, among common fishermen? Was he to die unmourned, because those who might have mourned, would die as well? Was he to die without a son to bear his name?

The water rose to his waist and crept toward his chest. When there was nothing more to be done, he moved toward the stairs with the other men. One man stepped too close to one of the holes in the floor and was almost sucked beneath the house. Lucien felt carefully for each foothold, but by the time he reached the stairs, he was almost too frightened to climb them. The house groaned continuously, and cracks were opening between boards. If the wind heightened, if the storm sent a tidal wave crashing down on them, the house would break apart and throw all of them at the feet of God.

Upstairs, Marcelite clung to him. Women were wailing with the wind; children screamed and wept. Lucien held Marcelite and Angelle close. Even Raphael moved closer for comfort. The boy was trying to be brave, but his bottom lip trembled.

"Will Juan be safe?" he asked Lucien. "In his boat, will he be safe?"

Lucien couldn't find words to explain that everyone was going to die. He sat without speaking for what seemed like an eternity, waiting for the end.

"The water has stopped rising." One of the men who had been watching from the top of the stairs made the announcement.

Marcelite folded her hands and began to pray, her lips moving silently again. Lucien sat very still and listened intently to the wind. Was it his imagination, or was it losing strength? The house still rocked from both wind and waves, but was the battering less? He set

Angelle on her mother's lap and rose. The men were cautious, but some were optimistic. If the water rose no higher, if the wind died and gave the house a chance to settle, perhaps they had seen the worst.

Lucien caught Dupres Jambon's eye. Dupres shook his head. Clearly he didn't believe he would be safe in this house. "There is always a lull," Dupres told them. "And when the winds begin again, they will be stronger."

Lucien remained silent and tried to follow the arguments. His panic lessened. Had he not brought Marcelite and the children here? Had he not saved the skiff? He was alive because he had used his wits, and he could still use them to survive. He tried to piece together what he knew of hurricanes. There was usually a lull; then the wind changed direction. The lull could be long or short, but when it came, he must leave in the skiff.

Marcelite and the children watched him from the corner. He knew their fates might hang on his decision. He was strong enough to have a chance if the winds returned and caught him on his way to better shelter. But if Marcelite and the children were caught in the open, he might die trying to save them.

If they remained here, they might die, too.

Silently he cursed the God who was waiting for him to make the wrong choice. Marcelite seemed to sense his distress. "What's wrong?" she asked when he returned. "Are we lost?"

He told her the truth. "Are you willing to come?"

"Did you think to leave me behind?"

Her answer took him by surprise. He frowned. For the past hours, the storm had filled his mind, pushing everything else to the background. She had found the time to think of other things. "If you come, it must be your choice."

"I have already lived through hell." She met his eyes, and there was nothing inside her that she didn't invite him to see. "How different is the storm?"

He wondered how he could ever have believed she was a simple woman who needed him for love and guidance.

He listened to the others argue. The winds were definitely dying down, the water was receding. The world from the attic window was a scene from a nightmare, so terrible that the mind could not stretch wide enough to comprehend details. But the nightmare was ending. And until a new one began, there would be time to act.

When the winds were only those of any bad storm, Lucien crawled out the attic window onto what was left of the gallery roof. It sagged under his weight. He peered over the edge and saw that the skiff had floated away from the gallery. His best choice was to drop into the water as close as possible, then tie it where Marcelite and the children could be helped inside.

Dupres and three other men had already gone for the lugger they had left nearby. Lucien searched for them, but he could see only a short distance. The bell had never ceased its ringing. No longer tolling a funeral knell, the bell seeming to be ringing to lead him to safety.

He waited until he was certain the water wouldn't carry him away; then he swung himself over the roof and dropped into the waves. As before, the water was cold and turbulent, but deeper now, so that he couldn't stand. He battled as he had the first time, until he grasped the boat's side.

A huge gold moon lit the sky, as if to show what had been accomplished that night. Black clouds continued to blow across it, though with less fury. Lucien watched the current; it was still too swift to negotiate, but now he was sure that would change, too. He heard a shout, and from the west he saw a shape materializing in the darkness. He looked on as Dupres and the others brought the lugger toward the house.

When the lugger was secure, too, the men fought their way inside together. Upstairs, with little conversation, they gathered their families and what possessions they had. Octave passed out the last of the tools he had gathered. Lucien took a small ax to help break up logjams. Then, huddled together, they waited for the right moment to leave.

Lucien watched Marcelite with the children. She betrayed no fear, holding them close beside her, as if her strength alone could protect them from death. He envisioned her holding them that way forever.

The house began to shift, as if to find its balance again. Outside, the bell rang more clearly, as the screaming winds quieted. Dupres approached Lucien. "There's room on my lugger for everyone."

"I still think we'll take our chances in the skiff."

The two men wished each other well, then, with the others, went down the stairs for the last time and stationed themselves at intervals through the flooded house to help pass the women and children to the boats. Marcelite was the last woman down. She carried Raphael, and another of the men brought Angelle. Lucien left her to struggle with the boy, and held out his arms for his daughter. Then he led them to the gallery. Raphael held fast to a post as she scrambled into the skiff; then she reached for him and secured him on a seat. Lucien kissed Angelle's head, then handed her to Marcelite before he got into the boat himself.

"Hold tight!" he shouted. He reached for the rope, but he fumbled with the knot, suddenly uncertain, now that it was almost too late to turn back. The lull was a certainty, but the water still swirled with vicious intent, even though it was receding.

Behind him he could hear the other men shouting, and he turned to see the lugger launched from the gallery. The shorter men were hanging on to ropes, swimming beside it, but Dupres, taller than the others, seemed to be touching ground as he hauled the boat in the direction he had chosen.

Encouraged by their progress, Lucien unfastened the knot; then, as the water pushed the skiff toward the Gulf, he took up the oars and began to row. At first he made no headway, and panic gripped him. But little by little he began to see that they were moving toward the sound of the bell. He settled into the rhythm, pulling harder as he angled the boat between swells.

The world they passed through was terrible beyond his worst imaginings. Bodies swept past, both human and animal. Once he thought he saw a hand lift in supplication, but he was too far away to know for certain. Voices screamed from trees, from roofs drifting unanchored, from windows of the few houses still standing. He shut his eyes to the horror and rowed.

The farther they moved from the Gulf, the less he felt its pull. Once Lucien struck something with his oar, and hoped it was ground, but with his next pull he touched only water. Just as he was growing afraid that he didn't have the strength to keep up a steady pace, his oars struck something once more, then a third time. He stopped and lowered one into the water and touched bottom. He secured the oars before he climbed into the water. It rose to his chest, but he was able to retain his footing.

Each gust of wind was less than the one before. The clanging of the bell slowed. Marcelite shouted to him to watch out, and he hugged the hull as the wall of a house drifted by.

The church was still far away, but with every step they were drawing closer. Moments went by without the sound of the bell. Another skiff passed, and a man shouted something in their direction. The skiff was filled with passengers moving to a safer building, too.

The water inched downward to his waist. The lull had truly arrived now. The winds were quiet; golden moonlight warmed the terrifying landscape. He could almost have pretended the storm had been a dream, so suddenly had it ended. He wondered if the winds would come again, or if the stillness would last. He slowed his pace a little, stepping carefully, watching for landmarks, but it was as if the peninsula had been wiped clean and nothing he recognized remained.

He glanced behind him at the outline of Marcelite and the children and felt satisfaction that, at least in this, she depended on his goodwill. What choices did she have now? She was at the mercy of the storm, just as he was, and she needed his strength. What good were her threats, when her survival and her children's were linked so closely to his? He wondered if she would remember this moment when the storm was over.

There were more screams and shouts in the night, but he hadn't heard the bell for long minutes. Had it fallen at last, or was the wind so mild it could no longer lift the bell's weight? He had counted on the sound to guide him. Now he realized he could be off course, perhaps even heading into the marsh. Confused and exhausted, he stopped to rest.

"What is it, Lucien?"

He didn't have the breath to answer her.

"We must keep moving!"

He heard the fear in her voice, and his power to enhance it pleased him. He rested longer before he answered. "Must we? I don't know where to go."

"I'll guide you. Please, keep going!"

"How can you guide me? Can you see what I can't?"

"We aren't far. Listen! Hear the bell ringing?"

The bell sounded again, closer than he had imagined the church to be. The sound heartened him. He looped the rope around his waist and tied it before he began to move forward once more.

"We'll be there soon. Please, Lucien, don't stop again."

He felt a new surge of power. In this crisis Marcelite had no choice but to be all the things he had always believed her to be. Her very life depended on his whim. He turned his head to tell her so, and saw the most terrifying sight of his life.

Black clouds were massed to the west, made clearly visible now by slashing streaks of lightning. Thunder growled through the stillness, distant, but growing closer with every rumble. The wind picked up enough to ring the bell again, then again. As he watched, the clouds seemed to creep steadily closer, an army of death cloaked in black.

He turned and plunged forward, one hand on the rope still tied around his waist, one hand thrusting everything from his path. He couldn't gauge how much time was left to reach the church, but he knew it wasn't much. The lull had been just that. And behind it was a storm front so massive that what they had already lived through was as nothing.

He stumbled once, catching a foot on some unseen object, but he regained his balance and plunged on, jerking the skiff along behind him. The rain began again, lightly at first, then pelting him harder and harder. Lightning flashed so constantly that the midnight sky seemed lit by the sun. The shrieks of surviving animals who sensed death approaching merged with the fierce screaming of the wind. He plunged on, heedless now of anything except the bell.

At first he thought the flickering light in the distance was lightning. Only Marcelite's shout made him realize it was a lantern in the presbytery window. Something close to elation charged through him. He was almost to safety. The storm was closing in with all the fury of hell, but he still had time—precious little, but time nonetheless.

He plunged toward the light, letting it be his guide. The bell was pealing in rhythm with the frantic pounding of his heart. Only a little way to go now. Just yards to go.

He was almost on top of the remains of someone's house before he realized it was blocking his way. He jerked the skiff around, and for a moment he thought he had been in time, but the current pushed the skiff against the ruin and snagged the rope. He tugged, but it wouldn't give.

The sky was so light that he could see where the problem lay. The problem was a small one, easily taken care of.

"Throw me the ax!" he screamed, coming to the side of the boat. "For God's sake, the ax!"

He could clearly see the expression on Marcelite's face. She was terror-stricken, and Angelle was clinging to her, screaming. Only Raphael seemed capable of movement. He crawled along the bottom of the boat and brought the ax to the side. His eyes met Lucien's. Lucien saw terror there. Worse, much worse, he saw resignation.

Behind the boy, Lucien saw the storm rushing in, pushing a wall of water in front of it that was higher than anything still standing on the peninsula. A shout was torn from his own throat. He grabbed the ax and turned, heaving it frantically against the post that had snagged the rope. The post split. One more chop, only one, and the boat would be freed.

He turned back toward the storm and saw Raphael watching him. Rain plastered the boy's curls to his head and ran down his cheeks like a thousand tears. Behind Raphael he glimpsed Marcelite. In his power. Completely in his power now.

He brought the ax down once more, but not on the post. The rope tore free exactly where the ax had struck it. In seconds the weight of the skiff was gone. He whirled and saw it careening in the current, spinning farther and farther away from him. He heard screaming, and didn't know whose throat it had come from. In seconds the skiff was gone.

Head down, he turned back to the light in the presbytery window and, half swimming, half wading, fought his way there alone. Inside, he crawled up the stairs to the second story.

As the bell rang, a sobbing Father Grimaud welcomed and embraced him. The bell continued to ring until the only sound Lucien could hear was the bell. Louder than the screams of the dying. Louder than his own screams.

The bell rang, and even when it was finally silenced in the last hours of the storm, it still rang for Lucien's ears alone.

CHAPTER 9

There were eight little girls in Belinda's living room when Phillip returned from Aurore Gerritsen's house. He recognized Amy and her little sister, but the others were strangers to him. Each child had a sheet of newspaper spread out in front of her, with a lump of rust-colored modeling clay in the center.

Belinda stood at the opposite end of the narrow room, wearing a long, flowing robe of bright blue and green. A green turban bound her hair.

She flashed Phillip a wary smile, but otherwise ignored his entrance. Obviously she had just begun a lecture. "We don't know a whole lot about the people of Nok, 'cause African history's never been a big concern of the white man, but we do know that way back before the Romans and the Jews were fighting each other over the teachings of Jesus, about five hundred years before, in fact, the Nok people were sculpting statues of terra-cotta, kind of like that clay you've got in front of you there."

"When we be making something?" one of the little girls in the front asked.

"After you mind your manners and listen awhile. First, I want

one of you to come up and point out Nigeria on this map." Belinda
stooped and reached behind her, and when she straightened she
held up a large map of Africa.

No one stirred.

"None of you knows?"

Amy raised her hand. Belinda nodded, and Amy got up and went
to stand in front of her. She frowned, then poked her finger in the
center of the map.

Belinda didn't shake her head. "Amy's got the right idea. She's
real close. Thank you for trying, Amy. Are you proud of yourself?"

"I'm proud," Amy said.

"Good."

Amy went to sit back down.

Phillip watched the rest of the lesson unfold. The little girls giggled and whispered occasionally, but clearly Belinda had captured
their attention. For this afternoon, at least, they had become part
of a culture with an ancient and honorable heritage, and Belinda
was their role model.

"What do you think these people ate?" Belinda asked as the lesson wound to a close.

"Giraffes?" Amy's little sister asked shyly.

"Oooh... Now that'd be a long, tall meal, wouldn't it?" Belinda's
smile made it clear that she was glad the little girl had answered.
"But the truth is, we think they ate a lot of the things that you like,
things like beans and corn and yams, and they liked to season
them with lots of red pepper, just like we do here in New Orleans.
Fact is, some of your favorite foods came from Africa. They were
brought here by slaves who passed them on to the white masters.
When you're eating red beans and rice on Monday nights, you're
eating the same kind of thing the people of Nok ate. You're eating
African food, and don't you forget it."

"We won't forget it," they chimed together on cue.

"Now we're going to make statues, like the ones I talked about
before," Belinda said. "Archaeologists—that's people who study
civilizations from a long time ago—have found statues just this

high." She held her thumb and forefinger an inch apart. "And they've found some as big as real people. There are two things most of the statues have in common. First of all, they've got pierced ears. Second, their eyes are hollowed out. We don't know why. Not yet, anyhow. But when you make your statues today, I want you to try to make them like those Nok statues. Hollow eyes and pierced ears. I've got some pictures you can look at. Can you do it?"

"We can do it," they chorused.

"Then get busy. I'll help, and so will Phillip. You all know Phillip, don't you?"

Phillip immediately edged toward the door and escape, but eight little pairs of eyes stopped him.

He didn't like children, particularly. His experience with anyone under the age of ten was limited, and that was the way he had planned to keep it. But he had been thinking about children when he walked through the door—a boy named Raphael and a baby girl named Angelle. And their story, as well as Aurore's, was still with him.

He held up his hands. "Do these look like the hands of a man who knows anything about making statues?"

"Kids'll teach you everything you need to know," Belinda said.

He realized that more than eyes held him in place now. One of the littlest girls, her hair neatly sectioned and clipped with pink plastic barrettes, had clasped her arms around his waist. He was a captive.

An hour later, he had red clay embedded under every fingernail and a little girl wearing a dress meant for a larger child embedded on his lap. He had tried unsuccessfully to remove her half an hour before, but she was as tenacious as the woman teaching the class. Four feet away, Belinda was in the midst of promising the children an authentic Nige- rian meal at their next session.

"Now scoot," she said, clapping her hands. "And don't you forget what you learned here today. Some of you may even come from those Nok people. You can be proud of everything they did. Are you proud?"

"We're proud," they chorused.

The room cleared quickly. In a moment, nothing was left of the giggles and the whispers except eight little statues drying on Belinda's front windowsill.

Belinda put her hands on her hips and stared insolently at Phillip. "Well? Go ahead and say it."

"Say what?"

"Whatever you're thinking."

He didn't know what he was thinking. He hadn't known about Belinda's after-school classes. She hadn't discussed them with him, or asked for his advice. She hadn't even warned him.

Belinda stood in front of him, proud and indisputably magnificent. Phillip had been to Africa on assignment. He had interviewed African leaders, covered hideous tribal massacres, eaten from wooden bowls in tiny villages and silver plates in capital cities. He had lusted after dark-skinned women as beautiful as any in the universe. But he had never felt precisely what he was feeling now.

"What made you decide to do this?" he asked.

"You wouldn't understand."

"Try me."

"You don't know what it's like for these kids. You went to boarding school in Switzerland. You graduated from Yale. You write about civil rights, and sometimes somebody bars a door you want to waltz on through, but you don't know what it's like to be raised somewhere where nothing you ever do will be good enough."

"Because you're a Negro."

"Because you're black."

"Are you angry at me because my life's been different?"

She sighed, and some of the starch seemed to go out of her spine. "I'm not angry. You want the truth, I'm glad it was different for you. I'm glad it can be different for somebody. I just don't want you laughing at me, Phillip. I don't want you laughing at what I'm trying to do here, 'cause what I'm doing's important. These kids have a right to know who they are. Until they've got a past, they've got no future."

He stood and crossed to Belinda. The fabric of her robe was as fine as silk, and he savored it as he ran his fingertips up her arms.

"They ought to be teaching African history in schools. You shouldn't have to be doing it here, in your own home. But I'm glad you are."

She tossed her head. "You think there's any chance the school board would listen and let me teach it where it belongs? I got in trouble last week for playing jazz records while my babies were taking their rest time."

"You're trying to change the world. Do you really think anybody who's in charge now is going to like it?"

"Then you don't think this is silly?"

Belinda seemed oddly vulnerable at that moment. She was a woman of supreme confidence, but Phillip saw just how much his approval meant to her. "That's the last word I'd use." His hands slid to her shoulders, then to her neck. He cupped her face and kissed her.

She relaxed against him one inch at a time. Belinda was nearly thirty, and as independent as he was. Sometimes he thought it was a miracle that they had found each other. They were two souls who had never expected to find soul mates, yet here they were in each other's arms, with more between them than merely the promise of sexual fulfillment.

He understood the true beauty of the African robe when it pooled at her feet after only a little coaxing. His clothing was more difficult to remove, but he and Belinda proved themselves up to the challenge. Belinda wasn't a woman to be scooped off her feet and carried to bed. She led him there, and the movements of her slender, graceful body were a promise of the pleasure that was to come.

Their lovemaking had often been hot and hurried. Today it was a languid exploration of the curve of a breast, the taut muscles of a thigh, the levels of elation that a man and a woman could reach before they exploded in a frenzy of satisfaction.

When he held her tightly against him afterward, he thought about the seed he had spilled inside her, seed that would not fall on fertile ground since, as always, she had taken precautions. For the first time in his life, he wondered what it would be like to father a child.

"You're awful quiet," she said.

The words were not an indictment. Belinda seemed to have no

expectations of him. She was not a woman with hidden agendas. Phillip knew she was merely pointing out that if he wanted to talk, she was ready to listen.

He gathered her a little closer. The room was warm enough, but he didn't want to lose the intimacy of their lovemaking. "Do you want children of your own? You're so good with other people's."

"Not if it means raising them by myself."

"I guess you've seen a lot of that."

Her family had been poor, her education and independence hard-won. He knew Belinda spoke from experience and close observation.

"I used to think I wouldn't want them at all," she said. "Why should I bring a child into a world where he's a second-class citizen?"

"No child of yours would be anything less than first-class."

"What about you? Do you want children?"

"I don't live the kind of life where having them makes any sense."

She didn't question him further. She had never pushed him toward commitment. She lay relaxed and replete beside him, the give-and-take of her breath warm against his shoulder.

The talk of children made him think about something she had said earlier. Belinda believed that the girls she taught wouldn't have a real future unless they understood their past. His thoughts slid to Aurore Gerritsen, and he wondered if that was part of the reason she was telling him her story.

But by establishing the facts of her past, just whose future was Mrs. Gerritsen trying to assure? Her own? At her age, that seemed like an exercise in futility. Her son's? From what he knew about Ferris Gerritsen, it seemed unlikely.

"My session with Aurore Gerritsen didn't go the way I expected it to," he said after a while.

"No?"

He realized that he wanted to tell her what he'd heard. It was a weight in his chest that talking might ease. "Her story is nothing like I expected."

She pushed herself aloft so that she could see his face. "What kind of story is it?"

Phillip found himself repeating what he'd learned, drawing the picture of those few days in 1893, much the way Mrs. Gerritsen had. He had been surprised by the richness of detail. At first he had wondered if this was just a classic case of an old woman with a remarkable long-term memory. He had seen that before. People who couldn't remember what they'd had for lunch could still tell you every detail of the dress or suit they'd worn to a dance sixty years ago.

But as Mrs. Gerritsen continued, he had realized that the detail was forever imprinted in her mind because the story, even the parts of it that had happened to others, was so tragic. He had interviewed World War II veterans who remembered every shot that had been fired at them more than twenty years before, every blade of grass on the battlefield, every tragic moment their comrades had endured, and this was much the same.

Belinda was silent for some time after he finished. "Why?" she said at last. "Why did she tell you?"

"I have no idea."

"None?"

"I can only guess that she's trying to right a wrong. How she's going to do it is still a mystery to me. She's going to use this manuscript somehow, when it's finished."

"But why you? Why did she ask you to be the one to write it?"

"Guilt, I think. Her father cut that woman and her children loose and sent them to die in the storm primarily because of Raphael's race. That's what it all boiled down to. Maybe Mrs. Gerritsen likes the irony of telling a black man. Maybe she thinks some sort of justice has been done now."

"And that was all she told you?"

"More tomorrow." He turned to his side and smoothed her hair. He loved the way it felt, like velvet against her beautifully shaped head. "You didn't mind me telling you?"

"Mind?" She seemed perplexed.

He realized how seldom he had shared his work or any other part of himself with a woman—so seldom that afterward he'd had to seek reassurance. But inside, where it really mattered, he felt cleansed.

He wondered what it would feel like to lie here beside her when they were old, sharing the details of their days. "Thanks for listening," he said.

"I like listening to you."

And since she was a woman who never lied, he had to believe her.

Aurore had chosen the library for her second session with Phillip. The day was cloudy, and the view from the morning room was dismal. She'd had a small fire laid in the fireplace and the pale green drapes drawn to shut out the gloom. The Sheraton writing table in the corner had been readied for him.

They exchanged greetings when he arrived, and chatted comfortably as he set up his tape recorder.

"I think I'd rather sit over there," he said, pointing to the love seat beside the sofa where she'd made herself comfortable. I don't need a desk to take notes."

"That's fine." She was secretly pleased. She had enjoyed watching Phillip closely yesterday. He maintained a nearly impassive expression, but his eyes weren't as well schooled as he might like.

"I have some questions about what you told me yesterday," he said, after he had settled himself on the love seat.

"I assumed you would."

"I'll start with the obvious. How did you discover what your father had done?"

"It will be easier for me if I take it all in order."

"But you will get to that?"

"I'll get to everything. Eventually. If I ramble too much...be patient."

He laughed. She liked the sound of it so much that she wished he would do it again.

He flipped through his notes. "Then why don't you tell me what happened to you that night. Did you make it to Nonc Clebert's house?"

"Yes. We made it, but my mother miscarried during the height of the storm. The cabin at the Krantz Place where my grandfather had remained collapsed, and *Grandpère* was killed. We would have died, as well, had we stayed."

"I'm sorry." He wrote for a moment; then he looked up. "Is everything you've told me so far to be included in this manuscript? Is this something you really want your son and grandchild to know, or has it been background material? Something designed to show me the climate you grew up in?"

"It's to be included. Every bit of it. You'll see just why."

"All right." He looked down at his notes, riffling through them again, then up at her again. "It doesn't matter what I ask you, does it? You're going to tell this in your own way and time."

"You already know me well."

"Then shall we get to the next installment?"

She wished that he was less astute and that there had been more questions to cushion the moment when she had to begin again. She hadn't slept well last night after relating the story of the hurricane to him. She was afraid she was never going to sleep well again.

"I suppose the next part of this begins about twelve years later. Ti' Boo and I remained friends, you see, and I journeyed down Bayou Lafourche to see her married." Aurore closed her eyes, and she could almost see the densely shadowed bayou, with its solemn stretches of waving grasses and majestic birds, its vast acreages of sugarcane. She could smell the sickly-sweet scent of boiling sugar that still lingered in the air at the end of grinding season, hear the shouts from plantation and mill landings that had changed little since the Civil War.

She wished she were there again, and that she had her life to live over.

CHAPTER 10

Granted, it was odd for the heiress to one of New Orleans's finest steamship lines to travel to the bayou country on a *caboteur,* a peddler's boat. Odder still was the way Aurore had paid her fare.

The brooch in the captain's vest pocket had once belonged to Aurore's Tante Lydia, a woman who so resembled Aurore's father that feminine adornment of any sort had only emphasized the square jut of her jaw and the faint mustache brushing her perpetually clamped lips. Lydia had met her death two years ago, while crossing a Vieux Carré street. Sometimes a stiff neck and unswerving gaze were detriments, particularly when one of the new electric trolleys was only yards away.

Aurore had been ridding herself of her aunt's jewelry since the day she inherited it. Lucien saw to Aurore's needs. She had more clothes than she could fit into multiple armoires, more hats than she could wear in a month. But she did not have money to spend. Money, according to Lucien, was unnecessary for a young woman of good family. A Creole lady had only to ask for what she wanted—prettily, of course—and she would be rewarded with everything that was truly good for her.

The possibility that *not* having money could make it a consuming passion had never occurred to Lucien. Women in his social sphere had no consuming passions. They existed to embellish the lives of men. Since Aurore had never had the courage to openly dispute his views, she simply sold whatever she knew he wouldn't miss, or, as in the case of the captain of the merchant boat, she bartered. A brooch, in exchange for passage to and from Ti' Boo's home on Bayou Lafourche, hadn't seemed extravagant.

Now, as the levees glided slowly by, she leaned against the steamer's rail and envisioned the days to come.

At long last, Ti' Boo was getting married. At twenty-four, Ti' Boo had believed herself to be an old maid, *une vielle fille*. At the more proper age of eighteen, there had been an offer for her hand, but the boy had been fat and lazy, and Ti' Boo, envisioning a life of servitude, had refused him. Since then, there had been no more offers or opportunities to wangle them. Ti' Boo's mother had taken ill, and her care had fallen to Ti' Boo.

Now Ti' Boo's mother was stronger, and Ti' Boo's sisters were older. The widower Jules Guilbeau, a man with two small sons and enough land along the bayou to plant a little sugarcane and a little cotton, wanted Ti' Boo as his wife. And, despite the ten-year difference in their ages, Ti' Boo had agreed to marry him.

Aurore knew all this from Ti' Boo's letters. She had last seen Ti' Boo when she herself was only eleven and Ti' Boo a grown-up seventeen. Lucien had been on one of his many trips abroad, and Tante Lydia, who had moved into the house on Esplanade some years before to care for Aurore, had been away for the afternoon.

Perhaps if they had been at home, they would have discouraged Ti' Boo from visiting. The Acadian girl was, after all, nothing more than an unfortunate reminder of a summer Lucien wanted to forget. But Aurore had been the one to answer the door, and she had secretly treasured the afternoon.

Ti' Boo hadn't returned to New Orleans, but after that day, the two girls had corresponded. Their first letters had been carefully polite; then, later, as their confidence increased, the letters had turned emotional, filled with secret fears and longings. Over the years, Aurore and Ti' Boo had grown from child and nursemaid into true friends.

Lucien had been only peripherally aware of their correspondence. A woman's good breeding was most apparent in the precision of her penmanship and in her ability to gracefully turn a phrase. He encouraged Aurore to diligently practice the skills that would hasten her ascent into society. But when, after years of letters, Aurore asked permission to attend Ti' Boo's wedding, he had been astonished.

"A wedding in the bayous?" Lucien had risen from his favorite chair in the parlor, fingering the watch chain that stretched to his pocket. "You can't mean you want to do more than send a small gift to Térèse?"

"I'd like to attend." Aurore had not fidgeted. At seventeen, she knew the value of standing perfectly still when encountering her father. In many ways, Lucien was a mystery to her, but there was nothing mysterious about his ability to size up weakness. She didn't want to fuel the fires of a tirade.

"But why?"

She gave the answer she had carefully rehearsed. "I think a change would do me good. A little air, a little sunshine, and I'll be more eager for the next round of parties."

"There are other, better ways to take fresh air."

"But this would truly get me away from everything. Cleo could accompany me on the steamer, and once I'm there I'll be thoroughly chaperoned. Ti' Boo's family is very old-fashioned." She hazarded a smile. "The Acadians guard their daughters almost as closely as you guard yours."

"You find my devotion humorous?"

Aurore found nothing about her father humorous, but she would not demean him, as he had so often demeaned her. She was tied to Lucien by a myriad of emotions; that she didn't understand him detracted not at all from those feelings.

"I'm only trying to reassure you," she said. "I'll be well looked after, and when I return, I'll have stories to amuse you."

But the lure of stories had not been strong enough for Lucien to give his permission. The Acadians were peasants, the bayous mosquito-ridden and teeming with dangerous reptilian life. When she pointed out that years ago she had spent entire summers in south Louisiana, his lips had tightened to a parody of the departed Lydia's. The argument had been lost.

Now she was on her way to Ti' Boo's wedding, despite the fact that the trip had been forbidden. Lucien was on business in New York and Minnesota, and Cleo, the newest of a long line of housekeepers, had proved susceptible to bribery. If all went as planned, Aurore would arrive back in New Orleans before her father. If not, she would have to accept the consequences. There was little she truly wanted that Lucien could deny her as punishment. She only rarely had his attention, and never his love. How could he withdraw what he had never given her?

"Mademoiselle Le Danois?"

Aurore turned at the sound of the captain's voice. As New Orleans waltzed gracefully into the twentieth century, customs had changed. Now English was the language of commerce and French was the garnish. Aurore dreamed in a mixture of both, but she had grown accustomed to speaking English. The people of the bayous, like the captain, who was still a comparatively young man, had not yet made that adjustment.

She answered in French. "Are we almost there?"

He pulled at his mustache. "It shouldn't be much longer. The hyacinths make this trip slower each time I take it. Soon I'll be riding a mule through the middle of the bayou."

"How can anything so lovely be such a trial?"

His expression was frankly admiring. "To the contrary, anything lovely is always a trial, as I suspect your father has already learned."

She turned back to the water. Hyacinths, their lavender flowers stretching toward the sunlight, blanketed the water along the bayou's banks. They were invaders from the Orient, set free decades before by admirers who had never guessed the damage they might do. "Do you know my father, Captain Barker?"

"I know of him."

"I hope you won't make it a point to know him better."

"What? And begin our acquaintance by telling him that I helped his daughter run away?"

"I'm not running away. At least, not for long."

"I'm relieved. And I'll be more relieved if you tell me it's not a man you're running to."

She wondered if all men were so vain by nature that they assumed a woman would only run from the arms of one into those of another. "I'm going to a friend's wedding."

"This part of the bayou is remote, to say the least."

"Blessedly so."

"Then you're prepared for it to be primitive?"

"It's a shame you don't know my father. You would find him most agreeable." She listened to the sounds of the captain's retreat. The vista was changing, and she watched with interest.

She had boarded the peddler boat yesterday at dawn, not far from the foot of Saint Louis Street, near the sugar landing. The route along the Mississippi had been familiar, but after the canal had come the bayou. She had passed the day studying plantation houses. Some were collapsing, victims of changing economies and the lasting effects of the War between the States. Others reigned proudly over the surrounding fields, as if the days of white-suited planters and their hoopskirted daughters had never vanished.

Between the plantations were settlements of modest houses, and these interested Aurore most of all, because they were like the ones Ti' Boo had often described in her letters. She had been given plenty of time to examine them, since the boat stopped to trade at every one, which was why she had been forced to spend the night on a cot in one of its tiny cabins, under the shrewd watch of the captain's wife.

The houses were close together, strung like pearls along the bayou banks. Cows and mules were tethered here and there on the levee, and children romped under the occasional tree at the water's edge. These were the Acadian settlements, the homes of *les petits habitants,* the true heart of Bayou Lafourche.

Ti' Boo lived in one such settlement, Côte Boudreaux, a cluster of homes at the south end of the bayou, on land divided and sub-divided until little productive farmland along the levee was left for any one family.

But what did that matter, Ti' Boo had asked in one of her letters? How much did one man need? Only enough to feed his loved ones, to grow a little cane to trade for things he couldn't produce, to save a little extra to benefit the church.

A little extra. Aurore thought of all she possessed, and all she did not. Ti' Boo's life seemed as exotic as a Parsi's or a Hottentot's.

The churning paddle wheels slowed as one of the floating bridges, pulled from bank to bank by a wire cable, passed in front of them. She looked ahead as a new group of houses, their long galleries whitewashed or painted in weathered pastels, came into view. There were people waving from the landing.

"Côte Boudreaux," the captain said from behind her. "It looks as if you have friends here."

Aurore waved back. Her reception committee was too far away for her to make out faces, but she guessed the woman in the very front, dressed in blue, must be Ti' Boo.

Ti' Boo. She swallowed an odd lump in her throat. She would never see her friend, or even receive a letter from her, without memories of the night in October, twelve years before, when Ti' Boo's uncle had swept her from the cabin at the Krantz Place to the safety of his home in a grove of ancient water oaks.

The sloshing of the paddle wheels slowly died, and the steamer drifted to the landing. Now Aurore could see Ti' Boo's face, framed by the old-fashioned cloth sunbonnet, or *garde-soleil,* she wore.

"Ro-Ro!"

Aurore went to the side and waited until she could disembark. Then she was in Ti' Boo's arms.

"You can't be bigger than me!" Ti' Boo thrust Aurore away to stare. "You can't be!"

"Now I'll have to nursemaid you." Aurore stared at her friend, hungry for every small detail. Ti' Boo was shorter than she was by several inches. She was no longer plump, but her figure was pleasingly feminine, and her skin was as smooth and rosy as it had been in her childhood.

"But you are so fashionable. *Très chic,*" Ti' Boo said, shaking her head in awe.

Aurore had chosen to travel in her simplest linen suit, decorated with only the most modest braid trim. On her head she wore a plain straw sailor's hat with trailing ribbons. But nothing she owned was as simple as Ti' Boo's jacket dress of Atakapas *cottonade.* "Too fashionable," she said, fanning herself with her hand. "And forever uncomfortable."

"I think you're beautiful."

For a moment, Aurore felt as shy as she had as a child.

Ti' Boo grabbed Aurore's hand and pulled her toward the people gathered at the edge of the dock. "Come meet my family. With the wedding so close, not all of them could come. I was working in the garden when I heard that the boat had been sighted."

Aurore was quickly surrounded. She was introduced to Ti' Boo's father, Valcour, four of her younger brothers, and a sister, Minette, who was a taller, slimmer version of her older sibling.

Valcour ordered the boys to go on board and bring Aurore's trunk and assorted luggage back to the house. With Ti' Boo's arm tucked lovingly around hers and Minette close at her heels, Aurore waved goodbye to the captain and his solemn-faced wife, who had joined him on deck.

A dirt road ran beside the levee. On the opposite side of the road sat houses spaced so closely together that a good shout from one of the wide front galleries would receive an answer from neighbors on either side. Hounds slept in the shadows, barely lifting their heads to acknowledge the parade of young ladies, but the galleries and yards teemed with humans who were not so oblivious.

Ti' Boo stopped at every house, proudly introducing Aurore to cousins, aunts and uncles, godparents and ordinary neighbors whose place in the Boudreaux family hierarchy seemed as assured as any blood relatives. Over and over again Aurore was examined and pronounced acceptable in bayou French that wasn't always clear to her.

What was clear was the excitement her visit had created. She was a city woman, a New Orleans Creole, who had come this distance to witness a friend's wedding. Surely she was different somehow from the others of her class. Who among these bayou residents had heard of a woman like Aurore traveling this long, difficult distance without even a friend or relative to watch over her? Ti' Boo must have been a good friend to have a good friend like this.

"My father doesn't know I've come," Aurore told Ti' Boo, when they were between houses and nearing Ti' Boo's own. The parade had lengthened. A trail of giggling, barefooted girls in loose cotton smocks and bonnets followed several yards behind.

"Will he be angry when he discovers you've gone?"

"I hope he never discovers it." Aurore threaded her fingers through Ti' Boo's. Her friend's hands were rough, testifying to hours of scrubbing clothes and hoeing in the kitchen garden. "But if he does?" She shrugged. "He has no other children, and no hope of ever having more. Whatever else he sees when he looks at me, he also sees his only hope of immortality."

"That's no way to speak of your papa." There was no force behind Ti' Boo's words; rather, she sounded sad that Aurore was compelled to say these things, things that were all too true.

"While I'm here, let's just pretend I don't have a father. Pretend I'm your..." Aurore cast around for the right concept. "Your sister."

"Sister? Me, I already have sisters. Too many sisters. A cousin? From New Orleans?"

"A cousin." Aurore smiled. "Your dearest cousin. So, cousin, when do I meet Jules Guilbeau?"

Ti' Boo pulled her to the side to escape a passing wagon drawn by a team of sturdy horses. "He's visiting tonight. You'll meet him then."

"Is he handsome? Truly handsome?"

"Handsome? Oh, so handsome! In truth, he has only a few faults. One leg is higher than the other, so he walks with a cane. He has no teeth of his own, but he's promised to send to Donaldsonville for some before the wedding. His hair is too long, so he ties it on top of his head in a Chinaman's knot to cover the bare patches."

"Ti' Boo!"

Ti' Boo laughed and squeezed Aurore's hand. "You will see for yourself, *chère*."

"He is the handsomest old man in the village," Minette said.

Ti' Boo slapped at her. "He is not old, merely well seasoned. The young men who court you are like gumbo without pepper or salt."

"The young men who court me are too many to count."

Aurore listened to the two sisters teasing each other as they approached the Boudreaux home. Although it was fall, and late afternoon, the sun devoured her shoulders and neck through the stiff cloth of her dress. Dust stirred by the wagon mingled with the steam of swampland and bayou so that the air felt gritty in her lungs. Even the short walk was beginning to tire her.

Minette lowered her voice. "Who's that driving the wagon, Ti' Boo?"

Aurore looked ahead. The wagon had stopped up the road at the house just beyond Ti' Boo's. As they watched, a young man leaped to the ground and secured the horses to a fence rail. An older man followed at a more measured pace.

The wagon was filled with lumber, rough-sawed boards that looked as if they had come straight from the mill. The young man shouldered several and slid them from the wagon; the older man grabbed the ends, and the two started through the gate.

"Étienne Terrebonne," Ti' Boo said. "And his father, Faustin. Faustin has a mill in the swamps. Étienne is his only child."

"That's Étienne?" Minette's eyes widened. "*T'es sûr de la?*"

"I'm certain," Ti' Boo said. "When you saw him last, you were still playing *faire la statue* on the levee with your friends. You weren't interested in young men."

Minette rolled her eyes. "Was there ever such a time?"

Aurore laughed along with Ti' Boo. If she'd worried that coming here might not be worth the price of her father's anger, that worry had nearly disappeared.

The laughter caught in her throat as Faustin Terrebonne stumbled and the boards that had been balanced on his shoulder swung toward the limb of a tree in the center of the yard. For a moment, there was only the slap of wood against the tree; then the air was filled with a fierce buzzing.

"A hornet's nest." Ti' Boo pointed. "Look, he's shaken up a hornet's nest."

Aurore gauged the distance. Already the hornets had targeted their closest victims. Faustin leaped from foot to foot, slapping and cursing. Étienne, under attack himself, grabbed for his father's hand, as if to pull him away.

The rest unfolded slowly, like a clock badly in need of winding. One of the horses reared, a new and captive target for the angry insects. His mate heaved from side to side. In their distress, they tore the fencepost from the ground, and it followed behind them, along with a portion of the fence, clanging against the wheels as the wagon plunged down the road toward the place where Aurore and the others stood.

"Quick! Out of the way!"

Instinctively Aurore leaped to one side, bringing Ti' Boo with her. Behind them, Minette and two of the little girls who had been trailing them remained in the road, mesmerized by the sight of the approaching horses.

"Minette!" Ti' Boo started back for her sister, but Minette, suddenly aware of the danger, made a dash for the side of the road. She collided with Aurore, who was shouting and running toward the little girls. For a moment they were a tangle of arms and legs; then Aurore freed herself and leaped toward the shrieking children.

Behind her she could hear more screams, the clanging of the fencepost against the wagon wheels, the harsh breathing of the horses and the wild sound of their hooves against the hard-packed earth. She despaired of reaching the little girls in time. They were incapable of movement, so frightened by the sight of the horses bearing down on them that they were rooted to their places.

Any moment she expected to be trampled to the ground. She couldn't spare a second to see how close the horses were; she could only run faster, despite the impediment of her long skirt.

She heard a shout. The air behind her seemed to thicken with the strong smell and heat of horseflesh. She dived for the two children, her arms spread wide, and knocked them sprawling into the ditch along the roadside. Only then did she have time to scream.

She was gasping for another breath, another scream, when arms encircled her.

"Ro-Ro, are you all right?"

She was. She realized it in that moment. She didn't know why, and she didn't know how, but she was all right. And the two little girls sobbing in the ditch beside her were all right, too.

She sat up and scanned the road. Étienne Terrebonne was hanging like an anchor from the harnesses of the horses. Their eyes were wild, but as Aurore stood, the horses calmed as Étienne muttered to them in deep, unintelligible French.

"Étienne grabbed them," Ti' Boo confirmed. "I've never seen anyone move faster, except maybe you."

A woman sprinted up the road, her long white apron billowing to the side. She grabbed one of the little girls and kissed her on the cheeks and forehead before she hauled the child to her feet to shake her. Another woman appeared to repeat much the same drama with the other child. Then, after several excited renditions of the story, profuse thank-yous to Aurore and to Étienne, who was still anchoring the horses, the mothers dragged their bawling daughters away.

Aurore dusted off her dress and retrieved her hat, which had flown from her head. Her hands weren't quite steady. Only minutes into her stay in the village, and she was already a heroine. In the retelling, her simple act had already assumed mythic proportions. She had risked her life for the two little girls. Assured of death and yet unafraid, she had thrown herself on top of the children.

Étienne turned. The horses were now completely under the spell of his voice. Sweat gleamed on his forehead, and an angry welt on his cheek confirmed his encounter with the hornets.

"You're all right, then?" he asked.

"Fine. What about you?"

He smiled, as if he found the question amusing. His teeth were white against his tanned skin, and his dark eyes flashed with humor. "A runaway horse is a small thing here. Two? Two small things."

His voice was resonant, a musical baritone. Aurore was accustomed to listening to the voices of young men; she wasn't accustomed to finding them so pleasing.

She smiled, too. "Well, it's no small thing anywhere to dive at them and risk your life. I don't know if I would have gotten out of the way in time if you hadn't stopped them."

"It would have been a shame to see such a lovely young woman trampled."

Ti' Boo stepped forward. "Étienne, you haven't even been introduced. *T'as du goût.*"

The phrase was a bayou one, unfamiliar to Aurore. But she knew enough to understand that Étienne had been chastised for being too forward. "I think our introduction is only missing a name or two," Aurore said. She extended her hand. "I'm Aurore Le Danois, from New Orleans." She waited for his response.

There was the briefest hesitation. She guessed that his hands were dirty and he didn't want to dirty hers. "Étienne Terrebonne," he said, clasping her hand, then dropping it quickly. "From New Orleans?"

"I've come for Ti' Boo's wedding."

"She's known Ti' Boo since she was a child," Minette said, insinuating herself into the conversation. "And have we been introduced?"

Étienne turned politely. "Maybe not. I don't often come this way." He made a quick, old-world bow.

A rapid-fire explosion of French cut off more conversation. Faustin, limping and muttering, joined them. He looked nothing like his son, who was tall and lithe. Faustin was a small man, stocky and bent from years of hard labor. "Them bees have settled down. Let's get rid of this wood so I can go, Étienne."

Étienne frowned and touched a series of welts on his father's neck, but Faustin slapped his hand away. "Come on, let's get this done."

Étienne gave another quick bow, then began to turn the horses. The women stepped out of the way of the wagon and watched from the side of the road until Étienne and his father were busy setting the fencepost and rails back in place.

"You can get the stars out of your eyes right now," Ti' Boo told her sister. "*Maman* would never let you go to a man from the back of Lafourche, especially not Étienne. He and his father live alone, and they have little."

"It would almost be worth living in the swamps."

Aurore knew only vaguely of swamps or of the kind of poverty that Ti' Boo was hinting about. But after even a brief introduction to Étienne, she thought that Minette might be right. At seventeen, Aurore was already much sought after by the young men of New Orleans society. She was a rare combination of pure Creole bloodlines and substantial wealth that appealed to both the impoverished Creole gentry and the canny American opportunists.

But never in her forays into society had she come across a man quite like Étienne Terrebonne, a man who balanced charm and strength as easily as he balanced cypress boards from his father's mill.

CHAPTER 11

Jules Guilbeau had a full set of God-given teeth and a thick head of silvering hair. He was broad-shouldered and svelte, and when Ti' Boo was in the room, his affectionate dark-eyed gaze never left her for a moment. In the days since Aurore's arrival, more than one woman had confided that Jules's first wife had been sickly, a complainer who had depended on the goodwill of her *maman* and sisters to see that her chores were finished and her children tended. Ti' Boo would better suit such a man as Jules, a man worthy of devotion and sacrifice.

Aurore had never fully understood devotion or sacrifice. Now, on Ti' Boo's wedding day, she understood it better. Life on Bayou Lafourche was more difficult than she had imagined. Even the youngest Boudreaux child understood that his work was important for the family's survival.

As an honored guest, Aurore wasn't expected to contribute to the well-ordered family system, but Ti' Boo's *maman*, Clothilde, a woman with her oldest daughter's intelligence and instincts, had understood Aurore's longing to be included. She had found plenty for Aurore to do, jobs that needed few skills other than those Aurore had come with.

Her needlework had been in high demand. She had sewn buttons and hems, embroidered rosettes on a nightdress for Ti' Boo's trousseau and initials on half a dozen handkerchiefs. Ti' Boo, whose own needlework was extraordinary, had made her wedding dress, ivory silk with a scalloped lace yoke, from fabric sent weeks before by Aurore as her wedding gift to the bride. With Aurore in residence, the two women tucked, adjusted and gossiped unceasingly until the dress was perfect.

Some of the other preparations were less artistic. With dozens of wedding guests expected, the feast was to be lavish. Women had gathered every morning to help. At times it seemed that any woman who had ever passed within one hundred yards of the Boudreaux house was expected to come and lend a hand.

After the first day, Aurore had given up trying to remember names. She shelled and chopped nuts on the wide gallery with dark-haired, dark-eyed women who quickly got over the novelty of her presence and giggled when she winced at the squeals and squawks of the animals being slaughtered behind the house.

The men were just as busy. After the butchering, they came to dress the meat and to trade boasts and stories. Café noir, dark coffee freshly roasted and ground by Clothilde, flowed as freely as the muddy water of Bayou Lafourche. After twilight, home-brewed whiskey flowed, as well.

On the morning of Ti' Boo's wedding, the excitement reached a fever pitch. Outside, Valcour, with the help of his sons and brothers, roasted a dozen small pigs. In the kitchen at the back of the house, Clothilde supervised a work crew. Aurore had peeked in twice to see the progress. Gallons of shrimp, crabs and crawfish waited in barrels of cool water to be boiled with red pepper and herbs. Spicy jambalaya, a fragrant mixture of rice, vegetables and sausage, steamed in roasting pans. Duck gumbo, made from a closely guarded recipe of Clothilde's, bubbled enticingly in a cast-iron kettle.

The girls' bedroom, tiny and crowded under ordinary circumstances, was a riot of colorful dresses and noise.

"You're sure you didn't break any thread when you were fixing the wedding dress?" Minette asked Aurore. "Very sure?"

"I don't think so," Aurore said. She shooed away a tiny cousin who was edging closer and closer to the dress in question.

"And there were no knots in the thread?"

"The dress looks beautiful. Perfect. Ti' Boo will be the most beautiful bride ever. What could be the problem?" Aurore cocked her head in question.

All the girls in the room giggled in unison. "You don't know?" Minette asked.

Aurore fell to the nearest bed, a simple moss-stuffed mattress, and tucked her feet beneath her. "Tell me."

"If the thread for a wedding dress is broken, it means the marriage will end in sorrow. If there's a knot, there will be trouble!"

"Then this marriage is sure to be happy."

"Mine will be the same," Minette confided. "I already have a serious suitor. Did you know?"

"Already?"

"I'm nearly sixteen. *Maman* was married at sixteen, *Mémère* at fifteen."

"Only one suitor, then? And you want to marry him?"

"*Mais non!* After he comes to the house, I sweep it right away, to sweep away his love."

Aurore tried not to smile. "And does that work?"

"I think so, yes. He comes less often now."

"He comes less often," Ti' Boo said, entering the room to chase out all the younger children, "because you are so rude to him."

"That, too," Minette agreed cheerfully.

"Do you love another man?" Aurore asked. "Is that why you're rude?"

"I've seen the face of my husband-to-be in our well! Now I have only to wait for him to court me."

"In the well?"

"I don't think you're learning anything you need to know in New Orleans," Minette said.

"If you look in a well at noon, and you're lucky," Ti' Boo explained, "you'll see the face of your intended."

"Did you?"

"Me, I saw nothing, and when I leaned over to search harder, I nearly fell in."

"It's almost noon!" Minette clapped her hands. "Aurore must try."

"But I don't want to get married," Aurore said. Silence fell—an extraordinary event in the Boudreaux household.

Aurore wondered how she could explain. She had never seen a happy marriage, except, perhaps, in her brief sojourn here. By society's standards, Ti' Boo's parents were poor, and despite Clothilde's poor health, they both worked unceasingly. But they were seldom cross with their children or each other, and when they had a few minutes that didn't have to be parceled out to someone or something else, they spent it together. Aurore had seen them touch hands when passing; she had heard their contented murmurs late at night.

In contrast, there was the marriage of her own parents. It had ceased to resemble a marriage many years ago. "I don't think of marriage as you do," she tried to explain. "Look what it did to my mother."

Ti' Boo sat on the bed beside her and took Aurore's hand. "I haven't asked before, because I was afraid it would make you sad. Is Madame Le Danois any better?"

Aurore considered a lie, but the truth was a burden better shared. "I was allowed to see her six months ago. She sat at the window and murmured lists of names, like a new mother choosing what to call her baby. Boys' names, of course."

Ti' Boo's hand tightened spasmodically around Aurore's. "And you think marriage did this to her?"

"She worked so hard to please my father and hers. I don't think she ever thought about what she wanted, except on the night of the hurricane. After that, she blamed herself for *Grandpère*'s death. His name is prominent on the list she repeats."

"But she pleaded with him to leave Krantz's."

"Yes. I remember." Aurore stroked Ti' Boo's hand. She also remembered the terrible, ceaseless screaming of the wind, the miscarriage her mother had suffered that night, the horror of learning that her grandfather had been killed in the collapse of the cottage he had believed to be safe. "I didn't come to Côte Boudreaux to convince you not to get married. But there's no hope I could marry for love. How could I tell if a man wanted me, and not my money or my name?"

She was afraid to speak a worse possibility out loud. What if she mistakenly married a man like her father, a man who viewed women as ornaments, or brood mares? What if she ended up in a locked hospital room, endlessly repeating the names of babies she hadn't been able to bring into the world alive?

"Ro-Ro, do you think I marry for love?" Ti' Boo said. "I make marriage with Jules to care for his children and give birth to my own. I marry him to have a home that's mine."

"You marry him to have a man to warm your bed," Minette said. "And because he makes you laugh."

"You're too young to speak of such things!"

"Do you love him, Ti' Boo?" Aurore asked.

"I won't mind growing old with him."

Minette rolled her eyes. "He'll grow old before you."

Ti' Boo jumped to her feet and started after her sister. "I'll grow old sitting here listening to your chatter. Enough!"

Aurore didn't have much time to think about their conversation as the day progressed. She spent the rest of the morning on the gallery, helping Ti' Boo's weeping *nainaine* put the finishing touches on the traditional paper flowers for the church. In the early afternoon, Aurore arranged Ti' Boo's hair. The task had fallen to her after a great deal of consultation. It was decided that only Ro-Ro would know the latest styles and have the good taste not to make Ti' Boo look like a china doll.

While Ti' Boo sat on a chair before her, Aurore brushed the shining mass of waves, silky and soft from a rainwater wash the night before. She parted it in the middle, then pushed it forward before she doubled it back to the crown and twisted it into a perfect Psyche knot. Carefully she freed tiny wisps from the sides and curled them around her fingers.

"Jules is a good man," Ti' Boo said, as if their conversation of the morning had never been interrupted. "I want children of my own, and I love his children already."

"They'll be very lucky to have you as their *maman*."

"Don't you want children, Ro-Ro?"

Aurore did want children. But she was afraid she knew the choices she faced. A loveless marriage and much-loved children, or no marriage and no children at all. She told Ti' Boo something she had never told anyone. "I don't know, but if I ever do have children, I'll be like *your* mother, not mine. I'll give them my life. I won't let anything separate us. Not illness or misfortune. Nothing. Not ever."

Ti' Boo took Aurore's hand and placed it against her cheek. "You'll be a good mother, too."

When it seemed as if the day had stretched to the breaking point, Clothilde arrived to tell Ti' Boo it was time to dress. Like Ti' Boo's *nainaine,* Clothilde wept, and like other Acadian mothers before her, she threatened not to attend the wedding because it would be too sad to witness. Aurore wondered if Acadian mothers were unhappy because they were losing their daughters or because they knew what awaited them in their married lives.

Clothilde threatened, but in the end she dressed in her Sunday best and climbed into the buggy. Ti' Boo, resplendent in her dress and long veil, with her mother and father beside her, took the long ride to the church at the head of a lengthy procession. Aurore, in pale green batiste and a discreetly feathered hat, was escorted by a Boudreaux aunt and uncle.

The small church was lit by gentle, lingering sunshine. Despite a tradition that real flowers were a show of vanity, the paper flowers had been supplemented with bright blossoms from family gardens. Ti' Boo walked down the aisle to the smiles and sobs of the people who loved her best, and Aurore shed her own sentimental tears.

There were no tears after the last words were said. Ti' Boo and a formal Jules, dressed in black, climbed into his buggy to lead the race back home. The Boudreaux and Guilbeau men, who had been models of propriety, raucously fired shotguns into the air.

At home, all unnecessary furniture had been stacked against the wall to make space on the floor for the *bal de noce,* the traditional wedding dance that was to begin later in the evening. Tables had been set under the trees for the feast, and honored matrons took their places in line to serve the wedding guests.

Aurore wasn't hungry. Throughout the day she had sampled tidbits, until her appetite was gone. Since the meal was to be served one sitting at a time, she was happy to wait.

To the mournful cadences of a lone fiddler, she stepped out on the gallery. As she had promised her father, the Boudreaux had been as strict with her as with their own daughters. She had been watched and kept from any compromising behaviors. Her virtue was assured; at home she would resume the life of a New Orleans debutante, and nothing on the surface would be changed.

But *she* was changed. The days at Ti' Boo's house had awakened memories of childhood summers on the Gulf, of warm, scented afternoons at the Krantz's Place, when her mother had sat on a cottage gallery and watched her play with the other summering children. She had recalled what it felt like to be wanted, to be part of a community of people who cared whether she was happy.

No one watched her now. Clothilde was splendidly occupied as overseer of the feast, and Ti' Boo's aunts were in the serving line. Holding her skirt with one hand and her hat with the other, she crossed the buggy-lined road to stroll along the levee.

Geese flew across the twilight sky, and on the opposite bank of the bayou a heron skimmed the water, searching for its final meal of the day. From somewhere up the bayou she heard the whistle of a steamboat. She would start her journey home in the morning. Ti' Boo and her new husband would spend tonight at an aunt's, and tomorrow they would lay paper flowers on the graves of their closest departed relatives before returning to Jules's home. Ti' Boo would begin her new life as Aurore returned to her old one.

She was so immersed in that thought that she came within yards of a solitary figure before she realized she was no longer alone.

"Mam'selle Le Danois." The man swept off his straw hat, and gave a little bow. With some relief, she recognized Étienne Terrebonne.

"Étienne." She glanced behind her and saw just how far she had strayed. "Clothilde will be furious with me for coming out here alone."

"You're not alone anymore."

"If she knew that, she'd be even more furious."

"Then better run back home before she finds out."

She laughed. "No, I think I'm safe. She's well occupied for the moment. Ti' Boo was married today. Did you know?"

"I'll be at the *bal de noce.* I'm staying overnight at their neighbor's house to build a new room."

"Then you're a carpenter?"

"And a trapper, a fisherman, a moss picker. An Acadian. Have you learned what that means?"

"It means hard work." She crossed her arms and stood beside him to stare at the bayou. Something more than surprise flickered inside her. She was aware of the differences that separated them, but there was also an awareness of similarities unexplored. She could almost believe he knew what it felt like to yearn for what he'd never had. She wondered at her own sentimentality. Étienne was a stranger, one she wouldn't see again after tonight.

"Your life in New Orleans must be very different," he said.

"It's boring in comparison. Much more formal. Both more and less are expected."

"And you don't always want to do what's expected?"

"Oh, I'm more rebellious than you can guess. I'm not supposed to be here at all. I'm supposed to be at home, dutifully searching for a husband. If my father knew I had come to Ti' Boo's wedding..."

"Your father didn't approve?"

"There's little about me he approves of."

"Then we have that in common."

She turned so she could see him. "Do we? But you work with your father, don't you?"

"Faustin Terrebonne is not my father, not really."

His profile was strongly masculine, a bold statement against the orange streaked sky. She admired the hook of his nose, the carefully etched width of his lips. His hair curled back from his ears, emphasizing the proud set of his head. "Then who is your father?"

"My real name is Étienne Lafont. I was born in Caminadaville, on Chénière Caminada. Do you know it?"

Her pulse quickened. The coincidence was extraordinary. "Better than you might think. I was on Grand Isle when the hurricane that destroyed the chénière struck the coast."

"Grand Isle wasn't hit so hard."

She couldn't let him make light of what she had suffered. "Maybe not. But if Ti' Boo's uncle hadn't rescued my mother and me and taken us to his home, I would have died, too."

He didn't look at her. "Nearly a thousand died on the chénière. All my family was killed. I was washed away by the wave that destroyed our house, and thrown against the remains of someone's skiff. I clung to it until the worst of the storm died. Somehow I managed to heave myself onto what was left of it before I passed out. When I regained consciousness, I was in a cabin in the swamps. Faustin had been taking supplies to the few survivors. Apparently the skiff washed into the marsh. He found me four days after the hurricane ended."

"God spared you for something, Étienne."

"That's what Zelma, Faustin's wife, always said. I caught a fever before I could recover and hovered near death for weeks. When I regained consciousness, I learned I was an orphan. Zelma swore that I had been delivered to her because she had never been able to have children of her own. She nursed me back to health. She was truly a second mother to me."

"Was, Étienne?"

"She died at Eastertime."

Aurore hugged herself for warmth. She felt bonded to him by the horror they had shared. "But Faustin isn't a father to you?"

"He's an old man. His life has been a bitter disappointment. Is your father disappointed by life, too? Or is he only strict and old-fashioned?"

"My father has everything, but nothing he ever wanted. He was nearly killed in the hurricane himself. He was out sailing when it blew in, but he found shelter on the chénière, in a church presbytery. He never speaks of it, but even now, when he hears the tolling of a bell, he turns pale."

Étienne was silent. She was silent, too, thinking of that time. "I should get back to the house," she said at last.

"Will you save a dance for me?"

"Yes, I'd like that."

She turned and started back. Halfway there, she looked over her shoulder. Étienne was still staring at the bayou.

Aurore ate dinner sandwiched between two of Ti' Boo's cousins, who made sure she tried a bit of this and that until the laces on her corset nearly popped. Afterward, the fiddler fell silent and everyone gathered around as an uncle of Valcour's gave the *adresse aux mariés,* a kindly lecture on the meaning of marriage. There were sly jokes about Jules's age, and the fact that by now he could give the address himself, but no one seemed to doubt that Ti' Boo had made an excellent match.

The music started again. This time the fiddler, who had moved inside, was joined by his brother. A third man played the accordion. Fiddles were common, but an accordion, an instrument that could coax poignant emotion from a mere dance tune, was thought to be a miracle.

Like any well-bred girl of her time, Aurore had been introduced to all the classics. She could play some of the Chopin Études and more than half of Mendelssohn's "Songs without Words" on her father's Steinway, shipped from New York the very week that Tante Lydia decided her musical education should begin. But this music was as different from the classics as it was from the whistles, horns and cigar-box fiddles of the spasm bands that sometimes performed in front of New Orleans's theaters and saloons.

The fiddlers sawed at the heartstrings of their audience as surely as they sawed at their instruments. And the man on the accordion, a handsome young rake with sorrowful eyes, wailed haunting French verses that told of centuries of oppression, of loved ones left behind and families forever parted by the Acadian exile from Nova Scotia.

"Do you like our songs?"

Aurore turned to see that Étienne was standing behind her. "I hope they won't all be so sad."

"Not all. But as a people we choose not to forget the wrongs that were done us."

He sounded so serious that she had to question him. "Why not? What good can it do for you to remain in the past?"

"The past has made us strong. We came to the bayous with nothing, and now they belong to us. The Germans, the Spanish, the Americans, all came to make the bayous theirs, and soon we turned them into Acadians."

"So you owe your strength to misfortune? You as a person must be stronger than most, Étienne."

"Stronger?" He shrugged. "More determined? *Oui.*"

"Determined to do what?"

"Find my own place in the world."

She considered that, along with the unique character of their conversation. Certainly, Étienne's past must have affected his need to establish himself in the world, but she was surprised he had admitted as much out loud. In her experience, men seldom admitted to having feelings at all.

"Where will that place be?" she asked.

"Not here."

She wondered why, but before she could find out, she saw that Minette was signaling from across the room. She realized that talking to Étienne where the men were congregating must be a breach of etiquette.

She skirted the edges of what was now a dance floor, arriving on the other side just in time for the wedding march. Ti' Boo, who appeared flustered but determined, walked around and around the room, her hand clasped in that of her new husband. The family followed close behind. When the march ended, the little band swung into a waltz. The floor cleared quickly, and Ti' Boo and Jules were left to dance alone.

"It's been a perfect wedding," Minette said, coming to stand beside Aurore. "But mine will be more perfect."

Aurore watched Ti' Boo whirl around the floor, clasped closely to Jules's chest. Ti' Boo had always seemed older than her years, and now, despite the ten years that separated her from Jules, she looked every bit his equal. He gazed fondly down at her, and Aurore felt relief, or something very much like it, fill her. "I think they'll be happy," she said. "He cares for her."

"I think he always has. I think he wanted to marry Ti' Boo when he was a young man, but he was too old for her, and he would have had to wait too many years to win my papa's approval."

"Really?"

Minette giggled; the sound was slightly higher-pitched than silver striking crystal. "Does it matter?"

"Oh, you see romance everywhere."

"I saw you talking to Étienne Terrebonne. I've discovered he has a reputation."

"Does he?"

"He's a fighter. They say there's no man for a hundred miles or more who can fight like Étienne."

Aurore tried to determine from Minette's tone whether this was considered a good thing. Not too many years had passed since hot-blooded New Orleans gentlemen had routinely dueled for honor under the massive live oaks of what was now City Park. She wondered if Étienne fought for honor, too. Perhaps it was a way to make up for what was lacking in his life.

"They say he cut off a man's ear when the man insulted his father," Minette said.

"I don't believe it." Aurore looked across the room and found Étienne. He was standing among some of the other men, but there was a space surrounding him, out of either respect or fear; she couldn't be sure which. "He seems kind to me." She searched for a better word. "Understanding."

"I'll tell you something else. He has an education, even though he comes from the back of Lafourche. His mother, she was taught by the nuns in Donaldsonville, and then she was a teacher, too, before she married. It's said she taught him everything she knew, but only when his father was gone from home or asleep from too much whiskey. Faustin doesn't believe a man should read."

"That seems a pity."

"Étienne's the most handsome man here, don't you think?"

Aurore found that difficult to answer. *Handsome* was inaccurate. Some of the other men had features that were more refined, more purely French. But did she measure Étienne by those standards, or by the ones that gave her own eyes pleasure? "He's easy to look at," she said.

"I think he could hold a woman and make her feel passion."

"It wasn't Étienne's face you saw in the well, was it?"

"*Mais non.* Sadly not." Minette didn't sound sad at all. She sounded young and thoroughly enchanted with herself. Aurore felt a surge of affection. "Then show me your young man."

Aurore murmured her approval when Minette finally pointed out the youth she believed would be her intended. Then she commiserated when couples began to join Ti' Boo and Jules in their waltz and Minette's secret love asked another girl to dance. Finally she watched as Minette was swept away in the arms of an uncle.

"May I have this waltz?"

She had been so busy soothing Minette that she was surprised to find that Étienne was standing before her. "I'm not sure I dance exactly the way you do," she warned him. "The music and the step are a little different."

"You'll learn quickly."

She took his hand. His was rough, steady and warm, the hand of a man who does hard labor and loses nothing of his self-respect along the way. He held her at a proper distance and began to waltz her slowly around the room. His hand was even warmer at her waist, and his widespread fingers rested comfortably against her hip. Face-to-face with him, she could analyze exactly what it was about him that she found most appealing. She decided it was his eyes. They were dark, like a winter night when even the occasional glimmer of starlight is an excuse for hope.

"Did you really cut off a man's ear?" she asked.

Étienne smiled at her. She noted that something inside her seemed connected to his smile. Something had responded, and pleasantly. "So you've already learned how stories can be augmented here," he said.

"Was that one...augmented?"

"*Ah, oui.* It was only part of an ear."

She stumbled, but caught herself. "Which part?"

"The part he didn't need. I left the part he hears with."

Despite herself, she laughed. "May I ask why?"

"Why I did it? Or why I didn't carve off more?"

The music ended. They stood together, waiting for the next song. Since the waltz had begun with Ti' Boo and Jules on the floor alone, they had not yet had an entire dance. "Why do you fight at all? Aren't there better ways to settle matters?"

"Some men fight for lack of anything better to do. Some fight to avenge old wrongs. Some, new ones."

"And you?"

"All and none."

She wondered if she should be afraid of this man. He had risked his own life to save her, but he was also a man too comfortable with violence. He was watching her, as if aware of her thoughts. His gaze was unflinching, but she knew, without understanding how, that he expected her to turn away. She stood her ground. "Well, you're not fighting now."

The music began again, a song that was faster-paced and humorous. In a moment she was in Étienne's arms once more and they were whirling around the floor in a polka. She had to concentrate on her feet. By the time she had mastered the step, the dance had ended. He returned her to the appropriate side of the room and made a polite bow. "Thank you," she said.

"*Pas de quoi.*" He started to leave.

"Étienne?"

He turned back.

"I hope you find everything you're looking for."

He seemed surprised. "And you."

Aurore was swept up for the next dance by an elderly Guilbeau cousin, and then by an endless line of young and old men who wanted the opportunity to dance with Ti' Boo's Creole *ami.* Her older partners instructed her in the traditional Acadian *contredanses,* and she two-stepped with the younger. She passed Ti' Boo time and time again. Ti' Boo danced with every man on the bayou, and Minette danced with nearly as many.

As the evening wore on, she watched for Étienne. Once she saw him partnering a young woman in a square dance, but the rest of the time she didn't see him in the room.

During a temporary lull in the music, she was sipping punch and gazing discreetly through the crowd when Minette approached her. "It's too exciting," Minette whispered. "There's going to be a fight behind the house. Beside the stables."

"What is anybody doing out there this time of night?"

"Fighting the roosters."

Aurore knew cock-fighting was common in the area. Indeed, it was common enough in New Orleans, despite efforts to put a halt to it. Albert, Ti' Boo's youngest brother, had taken her to the barn to see Valcour's prize bird, a shiny-feathered red rooster who had valiantly attacked the sides of his cage when Aurore leaned over to peer at him. But she hadn't known that a fight would be acceptable entertainment at a wedding dance.

"Is it just roosters that are going to fight, or people?" she asked.

"Most certainly people. And I know how we can see it."

Aurore wasn't sure she wanted to. On the other hand, she wasn't sure she wanted to miss something so delightfully forbidden. Tomorrow she would be home again, and life wouldn't be nearly as entertaining.

"I will tell *Maman* that we're going to help Tante Grace in the kitchen, and we will, for a little while." Minette measured an inch with her thumb and forefinger. "Then we'll tell Tante Grace that we are taking the last of the cakes back to the house, and we will...but we'll store them by the cistern first, until we've seen the fight."

"And no one will suspect?"

"Not even if they talk to each other about it. We will have done exactly what we said, with just a little lie in the middle."

Aurore knew that Clothilde would be loudly unhappy if she discovered what was planned. But Minette added a further enticement.

"I think Étienne Terrebonne will fight," she whispered, so softly that Aurore had to strain to hear her. "There is a man outside who once vowed to punish Étienne's father for a slight. Faustin isn't here, but his son is."

"How do you know all this?"

Minette's eyes widened. "Me, I listen."

Minette's plan went exactly as described. Fifteen minutes later, Aurore found herself skulking quietly through the cool evening mist toward the stable where the horses and the mule were kept. The cakes, lavishly iced and studded with pecans, were safely hidden on a covered ledge of the cistern.

The cockfight was easy to find. There was flickering light from a campfire to guide their way, along with muffled shouts and curses. Minette had agreed that they wouldn't get close enough to be seen. Instead, they would stay in the shadows, behind the willows that provided shade for the stableyard.

They picked their way silently through the darkness until they had moved as close as they dared. From this distance they could make out the faces nearest the flames. The crowd was small, and most of the men were unfamiliar to Aurore. No more than ten stood around a sawdust-layered ring to watch the birds fight. Their stance was relaxed, and their cheers were good-natured. If the birds hadn't been slaughtering each other in the midst of them, Aurore would have thought it was just another example of Acadian men passing a good time together.

She found Étienne at the edge of the circle, standing slightly apart from the others. He seemed uninterested in the spectacle in front of him, but Aurore imagined that he, like the others, had wagered on the outcome of the fight. She swallowed as the shrieking of the birds grew louder, then squeezed her eyes shut as one of the men stepped forward to lift a dying bird from the ground and hold it up for the others to see.

There were more cheers than curses now; apparently most of the men knew how to judge a winner. But one man wasn't pleased that his bird had lost. He took off his hat and beat it against his leg. In the moonlight, his bald head gleamed like polished marble as he stepped forward to grab the rooster from the man's hands and fling it into the surrounding crowd.

The rooster landed at Étienne's feet.

"Ah, Vic. *Quoi y'a?* You still haven't learned to lose?" Étienne asked. "*Ça c'est malheureux.* You lose so often, too."

The men grew silent. Aurore judged that Étienne was only a few years older than she, but here on Lafourche he was considered a man. No one would rise to his defense.

"What's you doing here, 'Tienne?" Vic asked. He was a tall man, but not as tall as Étienne. As he moved closer, his shadow fell across Étienne's feet. "This is a sport for Acadians. You...you was found in the marshes, where the *loup-garou* prowls. And your papa, he's another *loup-garou.* He plows his land by day, and at night he does his hoodoo when the moon is full, like tonight. That's why he's not here. Either that, or him, he's afraid to come, afraid of me!"

Étienne stood nonchalantly as Vic beat his chest in a parody of victory. "My papa is afraid he'll hurt you, Vic," he said, when Vic had finished. "Like he did last time. You can't risk more scars, can you? Too many scars and there won't be any real skin holding you together."

The men laughed. Vic visibly bristled. "You afraid like your papa, 'Tienne?" He sent his hat sailing to the edge of the ring where the roosters had fought. "Me, I'm a man. And you?" He pulled a large handkerchief out of his pocket and waved it in Étienne's face.

"*Grand rond!*" one of the men shouted.

"What's going on?" Aurore whispered as the men circled Étienne and Vic. She turned. Minette looked as properly awed as a Creole maiden at her first opera.

"It's the *bataille au mouchoir.* They each have to hold a corner of the handkerchief and fight until one of them drops it."

As a child, Aurore had played far less deadly games with handkerchiefs. "How can they fight and hold it, too?"

"They'll fight with knives."

"Knives!"

"Shhhh..."

Aurore stepped forward, forgetful now that she was supposed to remain in the shadows. She couldn't believe that the men would really use such a small excuse to hack each other to bits. But as she watched, metal flashed in the firelight. Crouching in a fighter's stance, Étienne grabbed a corner of the handkerchief with his left hand. He flipped his knife into the air and gripped the handle with a flourish as it fell toward the earth.

"I'm ready, *mon ami,*" he said.

Aurore wanted to scream. Nothing had ever seemed more absurd. A man called another a name, and suddenly they were about to kill each other. The cockfight had been civilized by comparison. The cocks had been bred for nothing less.

Vic seemed to reconsider; then, without warning, he shifted his weight and sprang. Étienne was ready. He twisted and easily dodged the lunge. As Vic fought to regain his footing, Étienne pricked his shoulder. "You bleed like a pig in a *boucherie!*"

"He could have injured him more." Minette tried to pull Aurore back into the shadows, but Aurore refused to move. "He's trying not to kill him."

Aurore was hardly reassured. Even if what Minette said was true, Vic seemed to have no such reservations. Clearly, he was bent on murder. He lunged again, and again Étienne dodged. This time he gouged Vic's forearm. "Be careful you don't end up on a spit like that pig," Étienne said.

Vic spun and came at Étienne from a different angle. As if he had easily anticipated this new attack, Étienne blocked Vic's arm with his own. Then, with his knife aimed at Vic's chest, he drove it home, slashing off the buttons of Vic's shirt. With an angry cry, Vic fell against him, but each time he tried to wound Étienne, Étienne was somewhere else. Étienne took a swipe at Vic's sleeve, and the fabric hung by threads. He took another, and blood flowed from a long cut along Vic's neck.

Vic screamed in fury and lunged again, this time catching Étienne's arm. Cloth ripped, but no blood appeared. Aurore covered her mouth in horror.

Étienne stepped to one side, as if to avoid another clash with Vic's knife. In triumph, Vic bent toward him, his knife raised, but Étienne easily dodged his blow. This time Vic fell to the ground, still clutching the handkerchief's corner, and his knife flew out of his hand. He rolled onto his back and saw that Étienne was leaning over him, his knife poised over his heart.

Étienne crouched low, bringing the knife closer and closer. Vic stared his hatred at Étienne, but he didn't drop the handkerchief.

Étienne drew the blade across the cloth, severing the handkerchief from end to end, so that each man was left holding a piece. "You have courage, Vic. I don't kill a brave man."

There was a murmur from the circle. Heads nodded; one man gave a weak cheer. Vic looked at the cloth in his hand, then at Étienne's face. Slowly he stuffed what was left of his handkerchief back in his pocket.

Étienne straightened and looked directly at Aurore, who had continued to stand in plain view. He smiled a little and gave a slight bow, but even from a distance, even with only the flickering firelight to illuminate his face, she knew he felt no triumph.

CHAPTER 12

Aurore Le Danois was gone. That morning, amid a flurry of good-byes, she had boarded the merchant's battered flat-bottomed steamer and disappeared up the bayou. Disappeared from Côte Boudreaux, perhaps, but not, Étienne vowed, from his life.

Étienne drove his last nail into the last board of the room he had agreed to build for Valcour's neighbor. Nestor Johnson had been kind to him. He was old, with married sons who saw no need for another room on their father's house, so Nestor had hired Étienne. He needed a room, a quiet room away from the family that still lived at home, the garrulous wife, the son who wasn't right in his head, the two daughters who had yet to marry. A room to think in. Did Étienne understand?

Étienne understood. Sometimes thinking was all a man had.

The basic structure was finished now. It still needed a roof, but Nestor thought his son could manage that. Shingles on a roof, one laid over another in rows, this was simple enough.

Étienne put away his tools. Nestor was on the gallery, repairing a fishing net on a bench in the shade. As always, when

Étienne saw someone at this simple task—one he himself had done many times—his insides knotted strangely.

"I'm done now." He climbed the steps. "It's all finished."

"Even faster than I hoped." Nestor jerked his head to the side. "The money's in that can over there."

Étienne went to the corner, picked out a layer of fishing weights on the top and pocketed the amount they had agreed on. Then he buried the rest under the fishing weights again and set the can on the floor. "Where'd you get all this money, Nestor?"

"My wife's egg money. I take a little here, a little there, she don' notice. She's the reason I need the room." Étienne held out his hand, and Nestor stood to shake it. "You going back home now, 'Tienne?"

"Going down the bayou first."

"Far?"

"Far as I can go."

"What's to do down there? Nothing there anymore."

"I was from there once. From the chénière."

"Nobody much left. Nobody but ghosts on the chénière."

"Maybe I'll talk to those ghosts, find out some things."

"You can take my skiff, you want."

Étienne considered the offer. He had his pirogue, hewn from a single cypress log. But Nestor's skiff would get him to his destination quicker, before he could change his mind. "You sure?" he asked.

"What do I need with it? I've got a room now. Don' need to go out on the water when I get tired of talk."

"A room without a roof," Étienne reminded.

"It's got a door and a lock?" Nestor asked.

"Yeah."

"And windows?"

"No windows."

Nestor sat down again and picked up his net. "Like I tol' you, 'Tienne—me, I've got everything a man needs."

The sun had started to sink before Étienne reached his destination. The long trip had been tiring, even for a man used to navigating Lafourche's waters.

The house he had come to see was smaller than he remembered. Where once it had been flanked by oaks, now it stood alone except for the tangled brush hiding the gallery foundation. Creeper edged along windows that had once been outlined by green shutters.

He remembered the shutters well. He remembered that they had been drawn the last time he stood in the shadows and stared at the house. It was strange, the things he remembered. Twisted oaks, green shutters and the face of a man. An angry face.

The house appeared to be deserted. The door hung from one hinge. A section of the roof was missing; Étienne wondered what storm had sent it sailing. The storm that had killed his family? Or one of those that had come later, one of those that had driven more of the coastal residents up into the bayous? It hardly mattered. Whatever storm had torn at the house, uprooted its trees and taken its roof, that storm had done its job well enough.

Like the rest of the chénière, like the barren land that stretched to the water, this house was inhabited only by ghosts.

"Qui c'est là?" Étienne had just turned away when the voice called after him. He whirled and faced the house again. A man stood on the gallery—not a tall man, though he had seemed that way to a small boy. *"Fous le camp!"*

Étienne wondered if he should do as the man insisted, go away and never return. He could feel his future balanced between the choices expected of him and the choices he expected of himself. The man walked to the edge of the gallery and shaded his eyes with his hand. He was dressed in worn trousers. His hair, curly and streaked with silver, needed cutting.

"Are you Auguste Cantrelle?" Étienne asked.

Auguste jumped off the gallery—the steps were missing. He approached Étienne warily. "And if I am?"

"I've traveled from Lafourche just to find you."

"So? For what purpose?"

"To send you to hell."

Auguste stopped several yards away. "Who are you?"

"Don't you know?"

"Whoever you are, go away. I want no company."

"Not even that of your nephew?"

Auguste swallowed visibly, as if his throat had suddenly closed, but when he spoke, his voice betrayed no emotion. "I have no nephew," he said. "I'm a man without family."

"You're a man who could have sheltered your family in this house. Instead, you left them to die."

"I have no family! I had no family. I'm a man alone."

"*Non,* Nonc Auguste. You are the same man who came to the swamps, who stood over a child's bed when he was sick with fever. You're the same man who told Faustin and Zelma Terrebonne that the child was Étienne Lafont, and that you had buried his family after the storm, buried them with your own hands."

Auguste narrowed his eyes. He moved closer, but he moved slowly, carefully, the way a man moves during a fight. "So, you are Étienne Lafont. *Oui,* I buried your family. All but you. You and I have only that in common. Nothing more."

Étienne reached for his knife. He held it in front of him; then, without taking his eyes off Auguste, he touched it to his wrist without flinching. He could feel the blood flowing, warm and sticky against his skin. He held up his arm. "We have this in common, *nonc.*"

"Go back from where you came, boy! There's nothing here, no one here for you."

"Why did you tell the Terrebonnes that I was Étienne? Were you certain that he wouldn't float in from some raft on the Gulf, like me? Did you bury him, too, Nonc Auguste?"

"You are Étienne Lafont!"

"I am Raphael Cantrelle!" The words freed something inside him, something as powerful as hatred or love, something that resonated so sharply that for a moment he couldn't breathe.

"*Non!* Raphael Cantrelle died in the hurricane. He was buried beside his mother and sister. I saw their grave with my own eyes before it was covered. A stranger from New Orleans buried my sister and her children, the man she flaunted before all the villagers like the whore she was!"

Raphael advanced slowly. For the first time since the storm, he could think of himself as Raphael, and for the first time he let himself feel the blood of his mother, his sister, flowing through his veins as surely as it flowed down his arm. "I have heard stories about you, nonc, even in Lafourche. You *made* my mother a whore, when you killed my father and left her with nothing!"

Auguste retreated. "Go back to the bayous! You are Étienne Lafont. Raphael Cantrelle was the child of a whore and her lover. You are Étienne Lafont, an orphan from a good family. The past matters not. Remember who you've become."

"I have become a man without a soul." Raphael advanced, the knife still carefully balanced in his hand. "Perhaps we have that in common, too?"

"I would not want to fight you. I would not want to kill you!"

"*Non?* It was easy to kill my father, wasn't it? And easy to sentence my mother and sister to death? I escaped your sentence once, but only by the grace of *le bon Dieu*. Now I've returned, Nonc Auguste."

Auguste gave up all pretense. "*Imbécile!* When I learned that the Terrebonnes had found a boy that matched your description, I went to their camp to see for myself if you were still alive. The boy that was buried with your mother, there was no way to truly identify him. Others were sure, but I was not. When I saw you were still alive, I could have brought you back here and ended your life myself. But I didn't. I told the Terrebonnes you were someone else, someone I was sure had died. I gave you new life!"

"But you see, *nonc,* unfortunately, I long for my old one."

"*Non!* Do you know what you are? You don't, do you?" Auguste halted his retreat. Despite the knife in Raphael's hand, he spat on the ground at his feet. "You are the bastard son of a mulatto, a man who believed he was good enough to bed my sister! You're a quadroon, and the truth is written on your features for anyone who looks hard enough for it. You've only passed for white because I gave you a name that no one would question. No one would dare accuse the Lafonts of having tainted blood."

But they *had* accused him. Raphael remembered too well. There had been taunts as he grew up with the bayou children, insults and innuendos. *Ah, Étienne, your skin is so dark, one would think you got tanned in the womb. Ah, Étienne, your hair is so curly, it's like the wool of that old nigger down on Cross Bayou.*

"Does my blood look tainted to you?" Raphael asked. He thrust his arm in his uncle's face. "Your blood, *nonc,* does it look any different than mine?"

"Why did you come here?"

"Why did you let me live?"

Auguste drew in a breath. Raphael could hear it wheeze through his lungs. Sweat dotted Auguste's brow, even though evening was coming and, with it, cooler air. Raphael listened to him fight for another breath, then another. Up close he could see that his uncle's skin had an unhealthy golden tinge. "Because there had been too much death," Auguste said.

"Such grand sentiment." Raphael gripped the knife harder.

"I will fight you," Auguste said. "No matter what you see now, or think you see, I will fight you if you come closer."

Raphael didn't move. "Do you dream of Marcelite sometimes? Do you dream of your sister? Do you wonder if God is waiting for you to die so that he can punish you for your sins against her?"

"I have no dreams! The sin was not mine!"

Raphael looked deep in Auguste's eyes and knew he lied. "Your dreams are full of her!" The knife was warm in his hand, slippery because his palm was sweating. "Which is worse, do you suppose, death or dreams?"

"Go home, Raphael. Be Étienne Lafont and make a life for yourself. That was the best I could give your mother."

"It was nothing!" Raphael stepped back. "Because I am not Étienne Lafont. I am Raphael Cantrelle, the son of good parents, and the nephew of a man who will burn in hell for all eternity."

Sweat dripped from Auguste's brow. "Leave me in peace. I am a sick man. Leave me to die in peace."

"Pray God it will be long and slow, so you will have time for a million prayers. Pray God the first things you see after you finally close your eyes are the smiling faces of my mother and father."

Raphael took one step backward, then another, but his gaze never left Auguste's. Finally, when Auguste's gaze wavered, Raphael Cantrelle turned and walked away.

The marsh where Juan's hut had stood twelve years before was deserted. Latanier and other brush grew in ragged clumps, obscuring any signs that the area had ever been inhabited. Raphael looked in vain for Juan's well or the foundation of his mud oven. But the hurricane had destroyed all landmarks, and the memories of a seven-year-old boy could hardly be trusted.

He had brought corn bread and cold beans with him, and he settled down at the marsh's edge to eat. Soon the mosquitoes would come, and although he had brought a mosquito bar, canvas and blankets, he knew the night would be a long one.

When the stars came out, he was still wide-awake. He had made a small fire, as much to drive away ghosts as insects and marsh creatures. The wind moaned through the three-cornered grass, and somewhere not far away a bull alligator called for a mate. The marsh was alive with melodious croaking, with the hoots of screech owls and the rustling of nocturnal predators.

The marsh was alive, but the chénière was dead. Only a few structures remained, and most of the valiant survivors who had tried to build again had finally gone away for good. He had visited the cemetery. The hurricane victims had been buried in mass graves, graves in a land where water lapped at bodies in the earth until one day the remains washed away. There had been no markers to tell where his mother and sister lay. He had knelt in the cemetery, even knowing that they were somewhere else, and choked out a prayer, because he knew that his mother would have wished it. But he had no faith that God had heard his voice.

Now he closed his eyes. He saw a woman's face, but not his mother's. The woman was younger, her hair the sleek, soft hue of a fox's pelt, and her eyes were the lavender blue of the water hyacinth. She smiled gently at him as he fell asleep, and it was Aurore's face he saw again just before he awoke in the morning.

As the sun turned the chénière a rosy gold, he continued his search for signs of Juan's hut. He ranged the marsh's edge, aware that the tide could have changed the ground into marsh itself. Finally he pulled on the boots that he used when picking moss and waded at the water's edge.

He almost missed the well. It had been built above the ground, a structure made from timber, mud and moss. The mud and moss had disintegrated with time, but a rotted timber crunched against his boots as he waded. He stooped and parted the grasses. The outline of the well was just visible. He calculated the position of Juan's hut. It had been somewhere to his left, and behind it was the watery path to the ridge.

He was much taller now, but the water was still deeper than he remembered. He guessed where the house had been. Finally he gazed in the direction where the moss-draped oaks had once stood, and saw a nearly empty horizon. But the ridge, now almost level with the water, was still there. Shrubs that needed solid ground at their roots peeked above the sedge, and something—the broken trunk of a tree, perhaps—rose against the sky.

He tied his supplies on his back and started toward the ridge. The mud sucked at his boots and slowed his pace. He had never felt so alone. He knew the swamps around Faustin's house, a ramshackle structure on stilts that had withstood generations of storms and rising waters. He knew those swamps and their attendant marshes, and even when he was trapping or running a trotline alone, he knew his absence would be noted if he didn't return. But no one would ever guess he was here.

He wasn't frightened. How could a man be frightened, when he had lived through the murderous fury of a hurricane? How could he ever be frightened again, when absolute terror had once filled every space in his body? He remembered the moment when he had lost his mother and sister, and the moment when the skiff had exploded into a hundred pieces. He remembered the instant when he could no longer cling to consciousness and the world had dissolved into darkness.

Less clear were the memories of waking with Zelma Terrebonne standing over him. At first he had believed her to be his mother. He had felt her stroking hand, cool against his forehead. He had smelled the strong odor of peppermint oil, used to combat fever, and tasted the sweetness of honey and elderberries against his lips. Then he had opened his eyes and known that his mother was dead.

He hadn't been able to speak. Perhaps he hadn't wanted to, afraid of what he would be told if he asked questions. Perhaps the fever had thickened and slowed his tongue. When he next awoke, Auguste Cantrelle had been standing by his bedside, intoning his new name. He had known the truth. He hadn't been strong enough to make himself understood, but his thoughts had been clear.

By the time the fever was gone and he was strong enough to speak, he had become Étienne Lafont. Not in his mind. He had never forgotten his real identity. But outwardly he had become Étienne, the laughing, bright-eyed friend of his childhood. He was no longer a child, and his friend was no longer alive. But he had pretended. He had known, without quite understanding why, that to be Étienne was safe. To be Raphael Cantrelle, son of a woman scorned by her family, by an entire village and by the lover who had cut her adrift to die, was not safe at all.

The mud sucked at his boots, but he kept moving. Finally, the water deepened, and he half swam, half waded, to the ridge.

He rested on solid ground and stared at the splintered trunk of a tree that had once been a flourishing cypress. He was surprised that even this much of it had survived. Twelve years before, the tree had already been dead.

There had been two more trees, and now they were gone. In twelve years, much wind had blown, and at every high tide water had washed over the ridge. There was a good chance no sign of the other trees would ever be found, but he had hours to look for roots, for cypress knobs and suspicious depressions in the soft earth. He untied his pack and made a small fire from driftwood to roast a fish he had caught and cleaned the night before. Then, after a handful of shriveled grapes from a chénière vineyard gone wild, he began his search.

The sun had risen in the sky when he finally paused to reflect on what he had found. The tree that still stood was probably the middle one of the three. Beside it, far to the left, Raphael had found a honeycomb of roots and rootlets not far under the soil. The ground was spongier there, as if the small hollows around the roots had caused the earth to shift.

On the other side of the remaining tree, and far behind it, he had found cypress knobs. Cypress was as impervious as stone, and the knobs could have been left by a lumbering foray into the marsh a century ago. But they were important in helping him tell where to start his journey.

He sat back on his heels and watched the remaining trunk as the sun rose. The shadow was nearly twice as long as the trunk itself, distorted, but clearly defined. The shadow slanted far to the right. As the sun rose higher, it slanted still farther.

Finally the sun was in the correct place in the sky. He rose and realized that his hands were trembling. He went to stand in a direct line with the shadow, but far from its end, where he thought the shadow of the entire tree would have ended. Then he took eight steps forward. Eight steps. He remembered the number clearly. It had mattered so much to him that Juan be pleased.

He turned, and his shoulder faced the emaciated tree trunk. He took eight more steps. Here the shadows of the two trees would merge—if the trees still existed. Using the trunk as a guide, he tried to imagine a tree growing where he had found the roots. He adjusted his position a little; then he turned again and stared at the horizon. Once there had been a gap in a line of trees in the distance. Now all the trees were gone.

He closed his eyes and tried to imagine the horizon as it had once been. Desolation filled him. Missing the right spot by an inch was as bad as missing it by a mile. He could dig and dig and never find a thing. And what was he looking for? The memories of a man who had probably perished in the storm? Items that might have had meaning for Juan, but would be useless to him?

He searched his own memory, imagining the horizon. The gap had been to the left. He opened his eyes and adjusted his position again; then he paced off eight more steps. He marked the spot with driftwood and went back for his shovel. It sank willingly into the shell-studded soil, until there was a sizable hole, several feet deep and wide.

Juan had not told him how deep to dig, but Raphael imagined that whatever he was looking for was neither too deep nor too near the surface. The ground was still firm at this level, but if he dug much farther he would find water. He dug another foot, then sat back on his heels to consider his next move.

He decided to pace off the distance again. He followed the same plan as before, calculating feet and angles with the help of the tree trunk. This time he ended up a short distance from his first hole. A new hole brought the same result as the first. He spent the rest of the afternoon carving a ditch between them. By the time it was clear there was nothing to be found, he was exhausted, and disappointment was a heavy weight inside him.

There could be many reasons for his failure. His calculations could be wrong; his memory could be faulty. Crazy old Juan might never have buried anything here in the first place. Or Juan might have survived the hurricane, come back for his treasure and sailed away, never to return to the chénière. What, after all, had been left for him to return to?

Raphael rested beside the ditch, his head on his knees. Gulls cawed in the distance, and the salt-tinged air was nostalgia in his lungs. He was hungry, and if he wanted to eat tonight he had to forage for food. He could dig for weeks, and even if something lay waiting for him beneath the earth, he could still miss it. He gazed at the tree trunk, then pivoted and gazed at the horizon, where trees had once stood.

He shook his head. Perhaps there had never been trees there. Perhaps Juan's treasure was a childhood dream, one he had held on to for comfort in the years after his mother's death. Hadn't he held on to others? He had told himself that life here had been good. That if his mother had lived, she would have made a comfortable place for them here, that people would have seen that he was a good boy and learned to be kind to him.

Now he knew what a dream that had been. No one who knew his father's race would ever be kind to him. He had been set apart. He had been destined, like all people of mixed blood, to belong nowhere. Either he lived a lie as Étienne Terrebonne, or he doomed himself to a future of isolation, misfortune and bigotry. And was he any different from what he had been yesterday? Wasn't he the same man, no matter what the race of his father?

There were colored men on the bayous, men who spoke French with Acadian accents, men who fished and trapped and went to the dances, the *fais-dodos,* in their own communities, just like their white neighbors. They were accepted—in their place. If they didn't get ideas about being better than they were supposed to be, if they didn't look at white women or act surly with white men, if they understood their lot and kept to themselves.

But he would never be accepted. He had lived as a white man, danced with white women. He had been educated by his adoptive mother, who had wanted something more for him than life in the swamps. He had overstepped all bounds. Now, if he ever told the truth, he might not have a future at all.

But even if he stayed silent, the truth might be told. Auguste had said it was written on his features. Zelma had explained the swarthy hue of his skin as chénière blood. The mix of nationalities here had been more varied than on the bayous. Surely Étienne had Italian blood, or Portuguese. Perhaps someone in his family had come from the Canary Islands, like the many who lived in Saint Bernard Parish. But Zelma was no longer alive to fend off questions, and Faustin did not care enough.

The horizon didn't change as he stared at it. No trees grew there, not even in his imagination. He saw a blank stretch of sky, the sun moving slowly toward the water. Soon it would be night. There was nothing more he could do here today.

He was standing to go when something caught his eye. In this direction, there were trees. Not as many as he remembered, but trees. And between two clumps of them was a noticeable gap. He frowned and stared, trying desperately to remember, to recall a day twelve years before when he had been frightened of ghost trees and shrouds of Spanish moss. If this was the direction he had been told to face, then somehow he had forgotten Juan's instructions. He tensed, trying to force a different memory, but he could remember only the instructions he had repeated to himself every night for the past twelve years.

Perhaps the problem was not the instructions, or his memories of them. He spun to peer at the tree trunk, then the patch of soft earth where another tree had stood. His calculations had been based on the trunk serving as the middle tree, but maybe the cypress knobs had not belonged to the third tree. Maybe the third tree was to the left, not the right, and the trunk was not the middle tree at all.

He was excited now. He walked toward the area where the third tree could have been. The ground was marshy. The third tree had stood on solid ground when he came here with Juan, but land and water frequently changed places. Hadn't he found Juan's well in the water? He waded in his bare feet, moving only inches farther out every time he turned. Just when he was certain the search was futile, he stumbled. Something snagged at his toes. He knelt and felt the ground with his hands. He found the almost imperceptible stump of a tree.

He stood and imagined the angle of this tree's shadow. Once it had been a tall, stately cypress. Just past noon, its shadow would have extended back toward solid ground. He imagined the place where the shadow of the other tree might have ended. He marked the stump with a branch. Then he returned to the place where the shadows might have touched. He turned toward the gap in the trees on the horizon and took eight careful steps.

He was standing twenty yards from the ditch he had dug. He was almost at the water's edge now. He remembered that the water had been much farther away when he was seven. But so much had changed. So very much.

He marked the place, then went back for his shovel. He had just enough time to dig one hole before he would be forced to return to his camp. He dug a hole one foot wide and one foot deep. The sun continued its descent. He gauged that he had one more hour until dark, and dug faster. Now he was forced to choose between breadth and depth. There would be time tomorrow for both, but not tonight.

He chose breadth, assuming that the tides had carved away some of the soil on top of the ridge. Whatever Juan had buried would be closer to the surface now. His shovel dipped, and he lifted and tossed the dirt behind him. The rhythm of digging no longer soothed him. He was tired, discouraged, aching. He wanted only to eat, to sleep, to forget. But he thrust the shovel into the widening hole again and again.

The shovel hit something solid.

He was so exhausted that for a moment he thought only that he had hit a root, a chunk of buried driftwood, a portion of someone's wind-tossed skiff or lugger. He thrust the shovel into the hole again, and again it wouldn't penetrate.

This time he knelt and dug away what dirt he could with his fingers. He followed the outline of the object. It was flat and square. He scrubbed the top until his fingertips were raw. Then, standing, he wedged the shovel in the side of the hole and pried.

The object was a metal box, about one foot square and deep. He removed it from the hole with trembling hands. Juan *had* hidden something, and he hadn't lived to come back for it. He felt a stab of sympathy for the old man who had befriended him, a man who had known his father and spoken well of him. Juan had indeed sailed away forever.

He wiped the box with his shirttail. A rusted padlock hung from one side, sealing the box tightly shut. With the aid of the shovel and a piece of iron-hard driftwood, it was a small matter to force it apart.

He sprawled on the ground with the box on his lap. It wasn't often that a man held dreams in his hands. He could open the box and find nothing more than letters or photographs, another man's dreams.

Or he could open it and find his own.

The sun was nearly gone before he pried open the rusted lid.

The flaming colors of sunset revealed dreams that were too splendid for a man awake.

CHAPTER 13

The mirror beside Lucien's office door proved his worst suspicions. He was paler than he had been yesterday. Paler, with the faintest hint of blue about his lips, as if his blood, pumped by a heart that frequently faltered, could no longer defy gravity's pull.

He turned away and gazed out the window overlooking the wharf recently built for the Gulf Coast Steamship Line. The wharf was the finest monument to his tenure as president, sleek and efficient, like the SS *Danish Dowager,* the newest of the company's ships. In Antoine's time the wharves had been so inadequate and the charges so high that some shipping interests had begun to find different routes for their cargo. Antoine hadn't had the foresight to realize that a port in trouble meant that a shipping company based there was in trouble, too.

But what could one expect from a man who had resisted logic and convention when he threatened his own son-in-law? A man whose sanctimonious visit to Grand Isle had brought about his own death?

Antoine's death. The death of Marcelite Cantrelle. The deaths of her son, daughter and unborn child.

The scene outside the window blurred. Lucien's heart lurched painfully. When the Gulf Coast office building had been constructed after Antoine's death, Lucien had specified that the walls were to be extra thick and the windows small. He hadn't wanted city noises to find their way inside. But there were no walls thick enough to keep out the noises of the river, the whistles of the tugboats, the bells.

There was a bell sounding somewhere in the distance now. A man never realized how many bells there were until they began to toll away his final days.

He fumbled for the back of his desk chair and sat, dropping his head between his knees. He managed a deep breath, then another. How could it be that at the beginning of a new century, an age of amazing progress, there was still nothing that could be done about a heart that wouldn't beat properly?

He had journeyed north nearly a year ago, to New York and Minnesota, unsuccessfully searching for a cure. No one in New Orleans except his personal physician knew the extent of his illness. Even Aurore had no idea. Luckily, she hadn't asked questions about the trip, even though it had stretched into weeks. He imagined that a rigorous schedule of dances and parties had kept her too busy to worry. She had never been home when he telephoned. He had returned to find her social schedule full, just as he had hoped.

The bell continued to toll. Lucien sat up and reached inside his desk drawer for a letter. He laid it carefully against his chest and willed his heart to beat steadily again. He murmured some of the text of the letter, a soothing French litany he knew by memory.

" 'You are not guilty, my son. You must lay aside this burden and take up your life. There was nothing more you could have done to save those poor souls lost in your skiff. So many people, hundreds upon hundreds, died that night. Can a father blame himself because his newborn son was ripped from his loving arms, or a mother because her daughters were safely nestled in the room of a house that collapsed? These were acts of God, acts that could not have been changed.' "

Lucien fell silent. As he had many times before, he told himself that Father Grimaud was correct. He could not have changed the events that occurred the night of the hurricane. He had seen truth in the form of a giant wall of water. And had he known that Antoine would die that night, making Marcelite and the children's death a terrible irony, nothing would have been different. Nothing.

"Papa?"

Lucien sat up straighter, and thrust the letter from Father Grimaud into the drawer. He couldn't stand with his heart still squeezing painfully in his chest, but he nodded at Aurore, who stood in the doorway, and gestured for her to take a chair.

"I know you don't like me to come here," she said, as soon as she had seated herself.

"But you come anyway."

"The riverfront is just too interesting. I can't seem to stay away."

She sounded so much like the young Claire Friloux that for the briefest moment Lucien wondered if he had been cast back in time. But no, the woman sitting beside his desk was Aurore, Claire's only surviving child. Her voice was like her mother's, but her hair was a shade lighter, her eyes a paler blue. Claire, at eighteen, had been rosy-cheeked and robust, with a wicked, throbbing laugh that made men yearn for her. He, the victor, had discovered how quickly that laughter could be extinguished.

Aurore was dressed in a dark tailored suit that made her thin features even plainer and a blouse of ivory lace that provided no contrast to her complexion. He recognized the hat that perched on top of her thick roll of hair. He had selected it himself. Bird-of-paradise plumes drooped artfully over one side of her face, a coquettish touch for a young woman who had too little of the coquette about her.

"There must be more important ways for you to spend your time," he said.

She smiled, but the smile did nothing to light up her face. "Papa, if I'm to provide you with an heir to Gulf Coast, don't you think I should occasionally see what happens here?"

"It will be enough that your husband sees."

Her gaze didn't falter. "And if there is no husband?"

His heart lurched painfully. The morning was still pleasantly cool for April, but he could feel a fine sheen of perspiration dampening his shirt. "Don't talk nonsense."

"Nonsense? I haven't met a man I want to marry."

"You're like all young women today. You expect love and forget duty. When you realize what's expected of you, you'll find a dozen suitable men."

"A dozen?" For just a moment, there was a gleam in her eye that hinted at hidden vitality. "Perhaps that's too much to hope for, when I can't even seem to find one."

Lucien wanted her to leave. The problem of his daughter and Gulf Coast Steamship was one he had gone over and over in his head since the surgeon in Minnesota had warned him that the days left to him were few. "What exactly do you want to see?"

This time, there was more than a hint of vitality. Her eyes blazed a more brilliant blue. "Will you give me a tour of the new dock?"

"I haven't the time." He stood. "And I see no point, but if you must see the wharf, then I'll have someone else show you."

She stood, too. "I'd rather you did."

Lately it had been hard to dismiss her. "I've explained I'm too busy."

"Papa, are you feeling well?"

Lucien wasn't pleased that she had noticed a difference in him. "Of course."

"It's just that you seem tired recently. And I think you're afraid the walk will tire you more."

"That's foolish. Not another word about it to anyone! There are plenty of people who would be upset if they thought my health was suffering."

She didn't flinch. "Why?"

"Because I've just made a huge investment in the *Dowager,* and in building that dock. *I* built it, not the dock board. I invested in our long-term future by improving the port, just like some of the other steamship companies have done. And I've loaned the dock board money for further improvements."

"I still don't understand."

"The money had to come from somewhere."

"And so you borrowed it in order to lend it?"

He was surprised she had understood. "In a sense. I borrowed it from myself, from other investments and property."

"And will the commissioners pay you back eventually? Or do you own the dock now?"

"Gulf Coast has sole use. We'll be paid back by credits on revenue."

"With interest?"

She was leaning toward him, completely occupied by their conversation. He couldn't recall ever having seen her so animated. "No. The board wasn't authorized to pay interest. We can only hope the company will benefit in the long run."

"But the short run might be difficult?"

"Not if we have a good year. Not if the improvement of the terminal here pays off immediately, the way I expect it to."

"I think I see why rumors that you're ill might create problems. Everything is very carefully balanced, isn't it?"

"Yes." He frowned, realizing for the first time that he had discussed the situation with her as if it were something she needed to know. "But I don't want to burden you with my business dealings. This is far too complex for you to think about."

"Oh, it's not a burden." She smiled; it was a very different smile from the one he had noted earlier. This time, her face was altered until she could no longer be considered plain. "But you've conveniently gotten me off the subject of your health."

"I told you, I'm well."

"So you did."

Lucien wanted nothing so much as to sit down again. He considered who to send with Aurore as an escort. His secretary had a gentleman's manners, but he was no match for the stevedores and screwmen. Aurore needed an escort who would command authority and still treat her with the proper deference.

"Wait here. If you really insist on this, I'll find someone who can give you a tour."

"I really insist," she said pleasantly. "Yes, I think I must insist, Papa."

Once again she sounded like her mother, but this time Lucien noted an underlying strength he had never heard in Claire's voice. Lucien was filled with the disquieting notion that for eighteen years he had badly underestimated his daughter.

Aurore prowled her father's office while she waited for his return. If she had designed this building, she would have placed it as close to the water as possible; then she would have created long windows that could be thrown wide-open, so that the smells and sounds of the river seeped inside the room.

She had always loved everything about the riverfront: the sight of cotton bales stacked like the building blocks of a snow king's castle, the warehouses filled with bags of aromatic coffee beans from exotic South American countries. She loved the chants of men unloading the ships, the mule bells and shrieking locomotive steam horns, the odors of creosote and freshly milled lumber, the smoke of coal fires. There was nothing in her life that compared to the thrill she felt on the rare occasions when she came here.

She thought of Ti' Boo and the days they had spent together on Bayou Lafourche. Ti' Boo was going to have a baby. Her letters were fewer now, but when she wrote she sounded happy. Jules was a considerate husband and a hard worker. No, Ti' Boo did not feel like a muskrat caught in a trap. And the baby she carried—a girl, she hoped—made up for the things that weren't good, the disease that had ruined Jules's meager sugarcane crop, the flood that had washed away their kitchen garden.

Aurore remembered that she had felt alive in Bayou Lafourche. But afterward she had come home to an empty house and an empty life. There were other young women in New Orleans who reveled in the social whirl of the city, particularly the carnival season, with its luncheons and dances, its dinners and formal balls. But she wasn't one of them. Perhaps if her father had agreed to let her attend college she might have been happier. But Lucien hadn't seen a need for more education. The Newcomb College set, with their bloomers and their emphasis on exercise, had seemed unwomanly to him.

She looked out her father's miserly window and envied the men below, all engaged in backbreaking labor. The stevedores unloading tons of bananas might have to worry about hidden tarantulas or poisonous green snakes that had survived the long voyage, but at least they were free when work was finished to do whatever they chose and go wherever they wanted. In contrast, she had to fight for every breath, every idea, every dream.

The office door opened, and she turned at the sound of her father's footsteps. She stood very still and stared at the man who had entered with him.

"Aurore, this is Étienne Terrebonne, our new traffic manager."

She made the appropriate response, but her eyes never left those of the man standing beside her father. He was dressed in a classically styled blue suit, but there was nothing dandified about him. He looked as masculine in the suit, with its starched white shirt and striped four-in-hand scarf, as he had in rough Atakapas *cottonade*.

"I understand you want a tour?" he asked in excellent, barely accented English.

Relief and curiosity warred inside her. Étienne hadn't pointed out that this was their second introduction. She still considered it something of a miracle that Lucien had never learned of her trip to Côte Boudreaux. "Yes, I'd like a tour very much," she said. "You'll be my guide?"

"If you'll allow me." He gave a slight bow.

"Absolutely. It should be fascinating." She smiled politely, exactly as expected.

"Étienne, I don't want Miss Le Danois to have any unfortunate encounters," Lucien said.

"I've already sent word that I'll be showing her the dock."

"Good." Lucien turned. "Aurore."

She had been dismissed, and she was delighted. She didn't speak again until they were outside in the roadway. Étienne took her arm and pulled her closer to the building. A wagon loaded with bags of coffee passed. He didn't drop her arm immediately. They stood together in the shadows and stared at each other.

"Hello again," he said finally.

"You must have some things you'd like to tell me."

"What would you like to know?"

"Everything."

"Everything, and a tour of the terminal, too?"

"We could do the tour another time."

He smiled for the first time since they had been reintroduced. A year had passed, but she recognized the effect of that smile. A familiar connection had been established. "I told you I was going to find my place in the world," he said.

"But you never mentioned it would be here, in the middle of my father's business."

"I didn't know."

"And the clothes?" She stepped back a little to view him better. "The perfect English?"

"The English was far from perfect when I came, but I learn quickly. As for the clothes..." He shrugged. "Do they matter?"

"I'd say they matter a lot. If you dressed as you did on the bayou, my father might have hired you to unload his ships, but not to manage anything."

"Exactly."

"Now tell me the truth. Why did you decide to come here?"

"My father died, and afterward I discovered that he'd stored away a sizable amount of money. So I used it to come to New Orleans. I wanted to learn the shipping business. It seemed like a perfect choice."

"When was this?"

"Not too long after we met."

He began to walk toward the dock, and she joined him. They crossed an area where track was being laid for the new Public Belt Railroad, then passed through an alleyway in a huge stave yard. The barrel staves—among the main products that Gulf Coast exported to Europe—were used in wine-producing countries where wood was scarce. Sometimes she wondered if there were any trees left in the northern states.

"I'm sorry about your father," she said.

"Thank you."

"But why the shipping business? And why Gulf Coast?"

"What business in New Orleans doesn't have to do with shipping? And I'm used to the water, so the railroads held no interest for me. Why do we lay miles and miles of track, when we have a river running through the middle of this country? They tell me it used to be so crowded a man could walk for miles just by stepping from one steamboat to another."

"That's how it was when I was a child." She moved to one side and waited as a rat ran from one pile of staves to another.

"We shouldn't have come this way. Your shoes are getting muddy."

"The purpose of shoes." She lifted her skirt a little higher. "I envy you working here every day."

"Do you?" He sounded skeptical.

"Don't tell me you're one of those men who thinks a woman is only interested in what she wears?"

"Then you're on this tour because you really want to see what's here?"

"Why else would I be communing with rats and mud?" He was walking faster now, as if he wanted to finish the tour quickly. "When you went to work for my father, did you connect our names?"

"I didn't start out working for him. My first job was to collect wharfage from the boats along a certain route."

"How did you move from that to this?"

"One day I was too late. A boat left before I could collect. I learned one of your father's steamers was on its way upriver, so I offered to unload in Baton Rouge if they would take me with them. When I got there, I found the boat and collected the toll, and then I unloaded a thousand bunches of bananas."

"And how did you get back home?"

He lowered his voice conspiratorially. "I hopped on a barge

going downriver, and spent the night on a cotton bale. I got back just in time to collect my fares the next morning."

She laughed. "But you still haven't said how you got this job."

"Your father heard the story and approached me. He said he was looking for someone resourceful and hardworking."

"And did you know that Lucien Le Danois was my father?"

He hesitated. "I suspected. But it's not something I could discuss, particularly when I would never have met you if you hadn't escaped to the bayous without telling your father."

"Then you know a secret about me. And I know one about you."

He stopped and faced her. "Do you?"

"Certainly. I know your past."

"Do you?" he repeated.

"Yes. You're Étienne the knife-wielding Acadian from the back of Lafourche."

"And what shall we do with these secrets?"

"Guard them carefully."

"Carefully?" His eyes were opaque, as if he had already started to guard secrets. "Is that necessary? You don't come to the riverfront often. And your father doesn't show an inclination to invite me for dinner. I doubt our paths will cross often."

He asked questions as if they weren't questions at all. Perhaps it was easier that way, because then he could deny his own intentions if the answer wasn't to his liking. But Aurore wasn't fooled. He wanted to know if he would see her again. Even as he pointed out the differences between them, the worlds that separated them, he wanted to see her again.

"I think I'll be coming to the riverfront often," she said. "My father has no sons. One day Gulf Coast will be mine."

"Then we'll have to agree to watch out for each other."

"Yes." She searched the face she had once found so appealing. A year later, it was even more so, stronger and more mature. "Yes, we'll have to agree."

"Maybe that won't be too difficult."

"Perhaps not." She forgot to smile. She stared at him and measured this man against others. She had no illusions that knowing Étienne Terrebonne would ever be easy. But she thought that it might be worth whatever difficulty it created.

Finally he turned away. "I'll tell you about the wharves. Before the dock board assumed control, they were privately managed. Originally what structures there were along the riverbanks were built of wood, but now our sheds are made of steel. We can berth two steamers here, and more down at the next dock, with permission. When the *Danish Dowager* is launched, there'll be room for her on our wharf."

"That's a day I want to see."

His glance was approving. "We're equipped with electric conveyors operated by fifteen-horsepower motors. They were installed with lifting and lowering devices to adapt to the water level of the river."

She walked beside him and listened with interest. But most interesting were the things that had already been said..

There were days during the summer when Lucien was certain each breath was his last. There was no relief from the heat. It seared his lungs and clutched at his heart. He slept sitting up— when he slept at all—in a chair beside his bedroom window. By lamplight he wrote letters to Father Grimaud.

He went to the office in the mornings, but rarely stayed past noon. The heat seemed worse on the riverfront, as if the Mississippi trapped the highest temperatures in its murky depths. He avoided the Pickwick Club, formerly his refuge, afraid that his increasingly gaunt appearance would start rumors. Sometimes he traveled the necessary miles to the outfitting pier where the *Danish Dowager* was being completed, but most afternoons he simply made excuses and went home.

By October, the temperatures had dropped enough to give Lucien some relief, but the summer had sapped his interest in Gulf Coast. His steamships continued to glide in and out of port, bringing bananas from Costa Rica and coffee from Brazil, carrying cotton to Italy, timber products to France and grain to England. Loading and unloading was easier and more efficient, but there was still less movement on the river than he had hoped to see.

At least he had good men working to improve Gulf Coast's revenues. Karl, his secretary, could be counted on to protect the company's interests when Lucien wasn't in the office. His operating manager, Tim Gilhooley, a veteran prizefighter who had reached his peak in the last century—along with the city's enthusiasm for the sport—could still crack a head or two if it was called for, or slip a bottle of Kentucky's finest bourbon to any man who needed a gentler touch.

Then there was Étienne Terrebonne. Étienne had impressed Lucien from the start. He was obviously a young man of good upbringing, even if he came from the nether regions of Bayou Lafourche. His skin was too dark, his heritage too obviously Latin, but he dressed well and had a good education. Most important, he was not afraid of hard work.

At times, Étienne seemed like a man possessed. He had learned more about shipping in the months he had been with the company than most of Lucien's employees knew after years. He had been promoted twice, most recently to traffic manager. Under Tim's watchful guidance, Étienne was in charge of trade.

Étienne wouldn't have progressed so quickly under ordinary circumstances, but Lucien no longer had years to carefully assess and train his associates. Where once he had expected to ease Aurore's husband into the company, now he was forced to find alternatives. She had no serious suitors on the horizon.

Aurore was as sought after as any of the young women who attended performances at the French Opera House. She was visited in their family box by young men as often as any of her friends. She had wealth and name. Lucien had been a duke in the court of Proteus, and the young Claire had been the queen of Comus. In New Orleans, a place in the best carnival organizations was a serious matter. The crowned heads of Europe received only a trifle more admiration—and not from the residents of the Crescent City.

So Aurore was New Orleans royalty, with the added bonus of being the heiress to a great New Orleans steamship line. There should have been multiple offers of marriage, but Aurore had discouraged them. Never before had he allowed her to resist his plans for her life. But the year was 1906, and even the sternest patriarch couldn't force a woman to marry against her wishes.

Faced with a heart that struggled to beat and a willful daughter, Lucien had been forced to look for a man with the youth, intelligence and ambition necessary to provide leadership for Gulf Coast when he was gone. Étienne was his top candidate. An offer of stock, a promise of Tim's job upon Tim's retirement, a glimpse of the prestige that could be his if he made Gulf Coast his life's work, and Lucien believed that Étienne would commit himself to the company.

One afternoon in late October, Lucien was preparing to leave the office. He had stayed longer than usual to go over some figures Étienne had given him. As always, everything seemed in perfect order. He was gathering his gloves and hat when there was a knock at his door. He called an invitation to enter, hoping it would mean only a short delay. His housekeeper had promised him an early supper of soft-shell crabs fresh from the French Market.

"Mr. Le Danois." Étienne waited politely in the doorway.

Lucien motioned him inside. "I went over the papers. Everything's in order. You're doing an excellent job."

"Thank you. Do you have any thoughts on the new insurance plan I suggested?"

"Gulf Coast has always done business with Fargrave-Crane. I hesitate to make changes now."

"I can understand that, sir. I only thought you might be interested in saving a considerable amount of money."

There had been a time when Lucien wouldn't have considered Étienne's suggestion. There was an unwritten code among the owners and management of the larger companies on the riverfront. The men all moved in the same social and political circles. They demanded loyalty, even if sometimes it was costly. In return, they supported each other by looking the other way when times were difficult. Often a personal guarantee for funds was as good as money in a bank vault.

But Étienne was not bound by the ethics of the inner circle. With Tim's consent, he had entertained estimates from new insurance companies after discovering the large sum that Gulf Coast paid to insure its fleet and cargo. Lucien had only allowed the search to progress because he was concerned about finances. He was sure he had been correct in building the new facility and in making a substantial loan to the dock board. He was sure that the SS *Danish Dowager,* Gulf Coast's newest and largest ship, had been a good decision. But his own progressive outlook had put operating revenue at a premium.

He decided to take a gamble. "Have Tim thoroughly check out Jacelle and Sons. Then we'll discuss it again."

"Yes, sir."

"Are you enjoying your work here, Étienne?"

"Very much."

"Are you finding time for a personal life, too? I don't want you to exhaust yourself. There must be hundreds of young women who would be happy to show you the pleasures of the city."

"I'll remember that, sir."

Étienne smiled, and Lucien read all the easy confidence of youth on his face. The smile made Lucien feel older and closer to death. He envied Étienne the years ahead of him. "Do you miss your home? I know you said your family is gone, but don't you sometimes wish you could go back?"

"Yes." Étienne was no longer smiling. "But as a boy I used to long for this day. Now I'm determined to make the most of it."

"So you were always ambitious." Lucien pulled on his gloves. "Generally I've found Acadians to be an easily satisfied lot. Why are you so different?"

"Different? Or unfortunate? Who's to say that devotion to achieving my goals won't ruin me?"

"I was different, too." Lucien didn't know why he suddenly felt so inclined to share his story with Étienne, but there was something compelling about the young man's barely leashed vitality, his dark-eyed intensity.

"How so?"

"How many Creole families held on to their fortunes?" He didn't wait for an answer. Both men knew that the Creoles of New Orleans were a dying breed. Many of the old names existed still, but they had been grafted onto sturdier, more resilient stock.

"And do you know why not?" he continued. "Because they didn't believe in work. Even my father-in-law, Antoine Friloux, found it distasteful, if necessary. The war destroyed most of our Creole families. They didn't know how to take the little that was left and make something out of it. But I did. And now I control an empire, because hard work didn't repel me."

"An example for any man to follow," Étienne said.

"You're young." Lucien allowed himself a sigh. "You still have so much to learn. I always hoped to have a son of my own to teach someday."

Étienne didn't reply. Obviously he respected a dream unrealized.

"Don't stay here all night," Lucien said. "Go home and have a good meal. I'll see you in the morning."

"Thank you, sir."

Lucien nodded his goodbye. In the carriage, he closed his eyes and let the peaceful clack of the wheels on the granite-block roadway soothe him to sleep.

Étienne watched Lucien's carriage weave through the riverfront traffic. His driver was an elderly Negro who had been with the family since before Aurore's birth. She had told Étienne that she was very fond of the old man, Fantome, who had often lied gallantly for her when she had disobeyed her father. Étienne didn't know where the name had come from, or if it had any relation to the one he had been born with, but Fantome was indeed a phantom. He existed in the shadows of Lucien and Aurore's life, a tall, stiffly formal specter who gazed at Étienne with knowing eyes.

Étienne had seen the same recognition in the eyes of the Creoles of color who dwelled in the Vieux Carré. The *gens de couleur* were a class to themselves. Free a century before the Emancipation Proclamation, some of them had owned slaves and large properties themselves, but the war had not improved their position. Where once they had been a respected part of society, now, in the twentieth century, their rights and privileges had been eroded. Still, they kept to themselves, mixing as infrequently as possible with black or white.

These handsome, cultured hybrids from another century knew Étienne's heritage at a glance, as sensitive to the width of a lip, the arc of a nose, as they were to the slights that befell them every day. They understood why a man of color would choose to be white if he could pass. Many of their brothers or sisters had made that choice. They made no comments in their dealings with him, but he saw their thoughts. If they knew his lineage, then it was only a matter of time before others suspected. Étienne was playing a dangerous game.

But no one had any idea *how* dangerous. Étienne stared out the window until Lucien's carriage was no longer in sight. Years ago, hatred had become the sole purpose of Étienne's existence. Now, the actual sight of Lucien Le Danois made his heart beat faster, his breath come quicker. Sometimes his hands trembled and he couldn't trust his voice or expression.

He remembered their reunion a year ago. He had been afraid that Lucien would know him, afraid and yet hopeful. If Lucien had recognized him, then Étienne could have sought immediate, if imperfect, retribution. But there hadn't been so much as a flutter of recognition. Lucien had so thoroughly dismissed the child he had sent into the hurricane to die that he hadn't seen Raphael's face written on a stranger's. _Lucien wasn't haunted by uncertainty. He wasn't haunted by guilt. And he didn't suspect he was haunted by a ghost who would one day steal everything he held dear.

A noise sounded behind him. Étienne composed himself before he turned. Aurore crossed the room and held out her hand. "He's gone, isn't he? I saw the carriage and hid in a doorway. I thought he'd be gone long before this."

"Others may not be gone." Étienne took her hand.

"I'll tell them I'm just here to see my father, and so sad to have missed him."

"If you insist on meeting me, we'll have to find a better place to do it."

"*I* insist?" She tossed her head. Her eyes were as blue as the patch of sky outside Lucien's window. "Aren't you the man who suggested I might like to go for a ride in the country tonight?"

"How do you get away, Aurore? Aren't you missed when you meet me like this?"

She moved closer. "Am I missed when I can't make our meetings?"

In the months he had been secretly meeting Aurore, Étienne had searched to find something of Lucien in his daughter. But the woman gazing at him with longing seemed unscathed by her parentage, as genuinely warm as her father was cold. "Yes," he said. He reached out and ran the backs of his fingers down her cheek.

"I lie." Her eyelids fluttered shut. "I lie, and I give Cleo gifts so she won't be inclined to see if I'm telling the truth. And I have friends who lie for me. They think our trysts are wonderfully romantic."

"And what do you think?"

"I think they could be even more so."

His awareness of her was heightened. The late-afternoon sunlight turned her complexion to pearl. She was as young as a child and as old as a woman. He bent and brushed his lips over hers. He felt her shudder, and he pulled her closer. This time, he searched her mouth to discover which she was. She sank against him like a woman, her soft breasts pressing over her corset and against his chest. The heat of their bodies infused the space between them until there was only a sudden pulsing of blood and breath mingled with breath.

"Étienne." She was the first to pull away, flustered and clearly unsure of herself. She opened her eyes. "Somebody might come in."

"So they might."

"You look pleased with the thought."

"I'm pleased we're going to be together this evening."

"Can we leave now?"

"I'll go first and wait for you behind the coffee shed. I've ordered a carriage to meet us around the corner."

Her eyes sparkled. "And you really think we can get away without being seen?"

"Depend on it." He lifted her hand and kissed it without taking his eyes from hers. "Don't leave right away."

"I won't."

Outside, he started for the coffee shed, secure that she would follow. Unknowingly, Aurore had led him to New Orleans and her father. Now she led him down a new path, a route to ruining Lucien of which the child Raphael had never dreamed.

He had thought to destroy Lucien Le Danois by taking everything he had built. But destroying a man's business was small punishment for murder. Now the man the world called Étienne was presented with an even greater opportunity.

He could destroy Lucien's daughter and, with her, Lucien's claim on the future.

CHAPTER 14

The SS *Danish Dowager* was to be the flagship of a new fleet. She was a luxury craft designed to carry passengers, as well as cargo. Lucien thought of the *Dowager* and the other ships that would follow as living memorials. Le Danois translated as *The Danish.* The next ship was to be the *Danish Diva,* the next the *Danish Dancer.*

Aurore had learned that the company's board of directors was less than enthusiastic about the *Dowager.* The expenses were huge. Nothing was too good for Lucien. The *Dowager* was to be the finest ship operating out of the port. Though she had been built and launched in New York, Lucien had insisted that she be finished in New Orleans so that he could oversee all the interior work. He had made periodic inspections at the outfitting pier. Once, distressed by the pale gold chosen for the grand saloon, he had insisted that all the paint be thrown overboard so it wouldn't be used elsewhere on the ship.

The *Dowager*'s route had been carefully planned. In the winter tourist season she would travel between Havana and New Orleans; for the remainder of the year her destination would be New York. She was 412 feet long and fifty feet abeam. She was to carry a crew of over one hundred and just as many passengers, and she was to travel at a speed of sixteen knots.

Compared to the monumental Atlantic ocean liners of the Cunard and Hamburg-America lines, she was not a large ship, but she was just as luxurious. Aurore had asked repeatedly to see the work in progress, but her father had brushed aside her requests. Like a small child with a toy he didn't want to share, he had even begrudged the board of directors their right to a tour and made excuses not to be present for it. If Lucien had gotten his way, Aurore wouldn't have seen the ship until it was completed.

But Lucien could no longer control Aurore.

In December, just before Christmastime, Aurore waited in the shadows fifty yards from the ship. The day had been pleasantly warm, but the evening was growing chilly. She held her cape shut, but the wind danced beneath it. Fantome had driven her here; tight-lipped and eagle-eyed, he waited not far away, in her father's carriage. He had promised not to tell Lucien, but she felt his disapproval even at a distance. It would be even greater when he saw whom she was meeting.

She heard footsteps and withdrew farther into the shadows. The riverfront was dangerous at night. Nearby Decatur Street was lined with bars and sailors' dens. In an effort to clean up the city, the city fathers had established boundaries for a red-light district, but crime couldn't be contained so easily. The riverfront was removed from the district, but the river drew its own brand of sinners. Wharf rats were said to live under the wharves, thieves who slit sacks through the gaps between the widespread planks and neatly drained their contents.

A man came into view, cutting a striking figure against the winter sky. "Étienne." Relieved, she started forward. "I'm glad it's you."

"Why didn't you wait in the carriage?"

"I was afraid I might miss you."

"You might have missed me entirely, if someone else had found you here." He stepped into the shadows, and she went into his arms, as naturally as she had for months.

His lips were warm against hers, and familiar. But familiarity

was as exciting as curiosity once had been. Now she could anticipate each kiss and know exactly how his lips would feel.

She lived for these stolen moments, moments that were growing increasingly dangerous. Lucien had questioned her twice about
her whereabouts on afternoons when she had been with Étienne.
He was at home more often now, as if his suspicions were aroused.
When he was with her, he encouraged her to tell him about her
days, and he listened carefully to her responses.

Once, Lucien's attention would have meant everything to her.
Every minute he spent with her had been the axis around which her
world revolved. Now his attention added weight to her guilt. It was
harder to go against him when he seemed so genuinely concerned for
her welfare. It was harder, perhaps, but more necessary, because for
the first time in her life, she had found a man whose attention mattered more.

Étienne moved just far enough away to see her face. "Are you
ready to board?"

"You're certain no one will come after us?"

"I've made arrangements. No one will bother us."

She slipped her arm through his.

The ship's watchman appeared on the deck when they approached; without a word, he let down a temporary gangway. They
boarded, and with a tip of his hat he departed. Étienne pulled up
the plank again, and they were alone.

"It's ours until ten," Étienne said. "Then he'll be back."

"Ours." She liked the sound of that.

"What shall we do first? Shall we dine? Dance? Have a tour?"

She had come for the last. Since they were the only people on
board, the others were impossible. "A tour." She whirled, and her
cape flew around her. "Definitely a tour."

He held out his arm. She took it, snuggling against the wind.
"Where shall we start?" she asked.

"We'll start with a lantern. There's no electricity while she's at
dock." They walked along the deck. She could envision it crowded

with chairs and the colorful clothing of passengers. It had recently been varnished, and the smell added a pleasant tang to the air.

Étienne found and lit a lantern. "Let's start on the boat deck, while the sun is setting." He led her up a stairway with brass railings that squealed as her hand dragged across them. At the top, he watched as she ran to the side to look out on the river.

"Look, there's a tug passing."

He came to stand beside her. "Your father's spared nothing. This deck will be equipped with a dozen lifeboats."

"Why? The *Dowager* won't go down. I know ships wreck, but not ships like this. It's a new era."

"You forget about acts of God."

Aurore chose to ignore the act of God she and Étienne had both endured as children. "The newspapers have talked of nothing but Mount Vesuvius and the San Francisco earthquake since spring, but that was land and this is water. How could a ship as perfect as this one go down? I refuse to believe it."

"Your father says the same thing, but even he sees the need for lifeboats."

"My father has faith in his ships because he can build to his own specifications. He thinks if he spends a fortune he can bend anything to his will. But he doesn't have faith in the river or the Gulf, because nothing he can do will tame them."

"Eads tamed the river when he built the South Pass jetties."

Until 1874, large ships hadn't been able to pass through the shallow mouth of the Mississippi. James Eads, a remarkably capable engineer, had been so certain that he could use the river's own current to carve a deeper pass that he agreed to absorb the expense if his plan wasn't successful.

"Eads didn't tame the river," Aurore said. "He catered to her whims. In return, she allows us to pass through her mouth into the Gulf. It's a favor she grants us."

"She?"

She tossed her head, and soft curls bounced engagingly against her cheeks. "Of course. The river is a woman."

"On the riverfront they call the Mississippi Old Man River."

She turned her back to the water and leaned against the railing so that she could see his face better. "A woman gives life."

He raised a brow. "A man has something to do with it."

"Most men don't seem to remember that. But even so, it's the woman who nurtures her child and nourishes it, the way this river nurtures and nourishes us. She responds to the seasons, the phases of the moon, rising and falling, and always carrying with her the gift of life. How could she be anything but female?"

"The river also floods and destroys everything in its path."

"Woman is capable of that, as well."

"Man is the destroyer."

"Woman is every bit as mighty, as commanding, as this river, when she's forced to be."

His expression was inscrutable. "How do you know? What have you ever been forced to destroy?"

"It's a mistake to think that a woman's feelings are less powerful than a man's, Étienne."

"All her feelings?" He touched her cheek.

She could feel each separate fingertip against her skin. When Étienne touched her, she felt as if something had been completed, as if something that had always been missing had now been returned to her. She closed her eyes and kissed his palm. "All," she said.

Hand in hand with her, he showed her the bridge, equipped with the most modern technology, and the crew's quarters. They stared down through stained-glass skylights to the smoking and drawing rooms below. As the sun dipped behind the horizon, they went down to the promenade deck and patiently strolled the circumference of the ship.

The smoking room was luxurious, with ornately carved walnut paneling, burgundy carpeting and comfortable leather chairs. Tables were set up for dominoes or a rowdier game of cards, and a bar extended along one side to cater to a gentleman's whim. Beside the drawing room, in the center of the deck, was a small writing room for ladies, with gilded mirrors on the walls and delicately carved plaster ornaments adorning the ceilings.

"If I was traveling on this ship, I would adjourn here every day and write you a sad, sad letter," she said, dragging a gloved fingertip along the surface of a Queen Anne secretary.

"What makes you think I'd let you come on board alone?"

Her voice grew softer. "Wouldn't you?"

He moved closer. "And have you so far away? A letter wouldn't be good enough, Aurore. Not even a sad, sad letter."

She was afraid to believe what she saw in his eyes. She had yearned for love all her life, even as she had grown accustomed to living without it. Now she couldn't think of anything else. Her waking moments were filled with thoughts of Étienne; her dreams were the same. She lived for the hours they spent together.

"I wouldn't want to leave you behind," she said. "But what a scandal we'd cause if we took a room together."

"Not if we married."

She looked down at the secretary. "What a scandal we'd cause if we married."

He lifted her chin. "Would the pleasures be worth it?"

"My father has plans for my life. He'd be furious if I married you."

"I'm good enough to work closely with him, but not good enough to marry his daughter?"

"No," she said honestly. "But those are his thoughts. Not mine."

"And what are yours?"

She looked away. "Do you understand that if we married, my father would do everything in his power to leave me penniless? Even the law couldn't protect me. He would give away everything, just to be sure I received nothing after his death."

"Do you really believe that?"

"I've never claimed to understand my father, but I do know he expects total obedience from me. He'd crush us both if I strayed too far from his plans."

He dropped his hand. "Then why are you here? To pass a little time? To stray just a little?"

"Why are you here?" she countered. "Did you think you might better your prospects by seducing the daughter of your employer and making an advantageous marriage?"

She expected him to turn away; most men would have. But Étienne didn't. "I'm here because I want you."

"Even without my money or my name? Even without a single share of Gulf Coast Steamship stock?"

"I've never wanted your name! And I have money of my own."

She had held herself erect throughout their exchange. Now she sagged a little. "Then why do you want me?"

"The first time I saw you, I knew you were going to be mine."

"There are more beautiful women, cleverer women."

"None of them is Aurore Le Danois." He took her hands and clasped them in his own. "But tell me if I'm wasting my time. If you're bound by what your father thinks or says, then you have to tell me now."

"He's your employer."

"There are other shipping companies on the river. Other companies in other places."

"You would give up what you've worked so hard to achieve?"

"My goals aren't as narrow as you seem to think." He pulled her closer. Their faces were only inches apart. "I've never expected to stay at Gulf Coast forever."

She gave herself up to a kiss that said more than words ever could. With his arms around her, she felt surrounded by his warmth and strength. She had never thought of love as a refuge, but now she escaped into the world he was creating. For the first time, she really allowed herself to imagine a life with Étienne, a life far from the demands of her father.

His lips moved over hers, insisting with passionate grace that she had nothing to fear and everything to anticipate. She swayed against him and wished that her clothes weren't a barrier to the hard pleasures of his body.

"I have more to show you," he said at last.

Her breath was coming quickly. She had learned the joys of intimate kisses, of tongue dancing with tongue and hearts beating together. "You've already shown me so much."

He took her hand. Hers was trembling, and his was not much steadier.

He led her to the stairs and down to the saloon deck. She had forgotten about the tour, but he pulled her into the grand saloon and left her by the door. "Wait here."

She didn't know what to expect; she hadn't known what to expect since the day Étienne had walked into her father's office. A small flame flickered in the corner, then another. As she watched, the darkness turned gradually lighter, until she could see dozens of candles set against huge mirrors. She clapped her hands as Étienne circled the room. When he had finished, he joined her and held out his hand. She let him lead her to a table in the center.

"Mademoiselle Le Danois." He gestured to the table. "Your host requests the pleasure of your company at his table tonight."

The room was an enormous octagon, a fairy-tale ballroom with a vaulted ceiling that rose two decks. Between the many mirrors were beautifully rendered figures from Greek mythology. She recognized Apollo and his twin sister, Artemis.

A balcony circled the room a floor above them, and tall windows behind it let in the soft glow of moonlight. The table Étienne had chosen was one of more than twenty, octagonal, like the room. Although the others were bare, theirs was covered with fine linen and set with china adorned with spidery letters: intersecting Ds, the insignia of the Danish Line.

Pale golden roses bloomed in crystal at the table's center, and sterling shone beside the plates. "Étienne?"

"Mademoiselle." He pulled out her chair. She let him seat her. Before she could ask another question, he disappeared into the shadows at one side of the room. She had eaten a light meal, because she hadn't expected to eat again. But now she realized she was famished.

He returned with a silver platter. As she watched, he lifted a dome and displayed two small, glistening roast ducks. He set the platter on the table and disappeared again. When he had finally returned for the last time, the table held a salad of colorful vegetables cut into thin strips and dressed with a pungent sauce, a dish of fragrant oyster dressing, spinach garnished with hard-boiled eggs, and a fruit compote with its own pitcher of heavy cream.

"How did you arrange this?" she asked.

He seated himself beside her. "It's better not to ask."

"It's wonderful. You're a magician." She spread her hands to encompass the room. "And this is truly magic."

"Shall I carve?"

"Please." She watched as he expertly sliced one of the ducks. She passed her plate, and he presented the tender fowl to her on a slice of toast. Together they served up the remainder of the meal, passing and receiving plates. Her eyes rarely left his. They ate, and although she knew the food had been prepared by a talented, if mysterious, chef, she hardly tasted a bite.

The candlelight flickered in Étienne's eyes. He had taken off his hat, and his hair brushed his forehead in a way that made her want to test its curl with her fingers. She watched the planes of his face shift and change in the soft light. She could imagine watching him this way forever. Until tonight, she had not dared to imagine watching him grow older, to imagine children they might have together.

He smiled, and she saw possession in his eyes. It was not the careless ownership she saw in her father's. It was darker and more intimate. It hinted at secrets, at whispered words exchanged in candlelit rooms, at kisses more passionate than those they had exchanged.

Étienne pushed his chair back and stood when she had finished. "Is *Mademoiselle* ready to dance?"

"Can the magician produce an orchestra?" She stood, too.

"The magician can produce music."

She watched him vanish into the shadows again, but this time her eyes were more accustomed to the darkness. She could see him stooping at a table on the far side of the room; then a man's voice began to sing. She clasped her hands. "A gramophone. Étienne, you think of everything."

He returned. "May I have this dance?"

"I'm not sure you're on my card for this one." She pretended to check, holding the imaginary card up to the candlelight. "You are at that."

He took her in his arms. They waltzed between tables to the strains of "Let Me Call You Sweetheart." The gramophone scratched at the words and distorted the melody, but she was as entranced by the sound as if it were a full orchestra.

She closed her eyes and let him guide her between the tables. He had a sure sense of rhythm, and waltzing with him was like floating. He pulled her closer, and she could feel his signals—turn, two, three, turn again—through her whole body.

He left her for a moment when the song had slowed to nothing, then returned to take her in his arms for a Strauss waltz that continued long after silence filled the room. By the third waltz she was no longer thinking about the music, only about the delicious freedom of standing so close to him. When he kissed her, she wasn't surprised. They waltzed on, slowing their steps until they were no longer dancing at all.

She clung to him, too aware that their evening was ending. She didn't want to let him go. She had found love, and she never wanted to live without it again.

"Aurore." He held her tighter and rested his cheek against her hair.

"I don't know when I can get away again," she said finally, moving away to see his face. "My father seems suspicious. He couldn't avoid attending a meeting tonight, but most nights he stays home and expects my company."

"We'll find a way." He framed her face with his hands. His eyes burned with emotion. "Shall I show you another room in the time that's left? One you haven't seen?"

"Yes." She didn't ask where.

The cabin to which he led her was on the promenade deck. It was the largest and most luxurious on board, a muted blue-and-green suite with its own connecting bath. The bed was wide and soft, dressed in fresh linens. Moonlight floated in from a wide window.

She didn't pretend that this was a stop on the tour. It was the end of one thing and the beginning of something else. She knew so little about love, but she did know that when love appeared it was to be held close and cherished.

Étienne didn't touch her. He stood in the doorway with the lantern as she wandered the room. She parted the lace curtains and looked out over the river. "I've always been alone," she said. "I think you have been, too. How do we learn what we need to know to be together?"

"We teach each other," he said.

"Will you begin?"

"Only...if you're sure."

She faced him. "I love you, Étienne. I think I have for months. Would I be here if I didn't?"

He came forward and set the lantern on the vanity, but he still didn't take her in his arms. "Do you say that easily?"

"Are you asking if I've said it to other men?" She rested her hands on his shoulders and looked for answers in his eyes. "There's never been a reason to."

He seemed to struggle with himself. "This will change your life," he said at last.

"I hope so." She rose on tiptoe and tested her mouth against his. "Dear Lord, I hope so," she whispered against his lips.

His arms came around her, and he crushed her against him. Her body curved into his, as pliant as her will. She helped him find the hooks and buttons of her dress, the ivory pins in her hair. She slid his coat from his shoulders and smoothed away his shirt. She learned the feel of his bare chest, the mysteries of a heart beating against hers, the heated slide of his lips against her breasts.

On the bed, she let him teach her the secrets she had never expected to learn. She took him into her body and gave herself in return. And when at last he held her quietly in his arms, she knew that he had been right.

Her life had changed forever.

CHAPTER 15

By the time carnival had New Orleans in its whirlwind grip, Aurore had little doubt she was carrying Étienne's child.

For once Cleo, the housekeeper who had few opinions that couldn't be bought, gave her opinion for free. Yes, Aurore's friend, whose monthly bleeding had stopped and whose stomach was tormented by the smells of horse droppings in the street, was surely *enceinte*. Cleo knew how the friend could be rid of the unwanted burden. Horrified by the diagnosis *and* the remedy, Aurore escaped to ponder both.

Her room looked over the back garden, where something was almost always in bloom. Ephraim, the gardener, and his crew dug up flowers on schedule and replaced them. She had always hated those mornings when the old, spent plants were ripped from the ground and callously tossed in a pile, their tired leaves and blossoms shriveling in the sun until they were carted away.

Today, as mockingbirds sailed back and forth from magnolia to magnolia, the old man and his crew replaced asparagus fern and tiny white snowdrops with pale lavender pansies. Tulips nodded in the row behind, on the verge of bursting into scarlet glory. When they had finished blooming, they would end up in the gardener's cart, too, because their life cycle couldn't be sustained in the Louisiana climate.

Aurore was flushed. She could feel heat pulsing against her skin and beading on her forehead, but she didn't dare open her window. The sounds of Ephraim ripping the snowdrops from the soil would make her worse. Then she wouldn't be able to control the bile rising in her throat, the sick rumble of her stomach. She drew the curtains closed.

A child.

She hadn't wanted children. What did she know of caring for a child, of cuddling a baby on her lap or smothering it with kisses? How did a mother listen patiently to a child's innocent prattlings? What did she say in response?

She was carrying a child. Étienne's child. She wondered how she could tell him. Despite everything, thinking about him pumped an errant giddiness through her veins. Étienne, whose dark eyes found all her secret thoughts, whose slender, clever hands knew all her secret desires. She had never imagined that love could be like this, that she would ever believe there was only one man for every woman.

But Étienne was that one man. Until her monthly bleeding had ceased, she had thought of nothing but him. She had lied repeatedly to be with him. She had risked her good name and freely given her virginity. She had traded security for love. And, despite everything, she would do it all again.

When she was with Étienne, the sheer glory of his touch was enough to make her give up everything. She had found she was weaker than she had dreamed, but stronger, too. Love was worth any risk. She had tried her entire life to earn Lucien's love, and she had failed. She had done nothing to earn Étienne's, yet he'd given it without asking anything in return.

She wandered the room, afraid to be still. Lucien had firm ideas about his daughter's room. There was nothing of substance inside the four walls, nothing that spoke of strength or courage. Everything could be destroyed with the sweep of a hand. But Aurore had learned she was nothing like the dainty Louis XIV furniture, the Staffordshire shepherdess on the mantel, the Brussels lace that hung in airy folds from her tester bed.

She was carrying a child, and even as nausea roiled inside her she knew she would carry this child safely into infancy. The pale little girl who sometimes gasped and fainted had changed into a strong woman. Her body would surround and cushion the baby growing inside her. She was not Claire. A cycle would be completed. Neither man nor nature itself would interrupt that cycle until it was time for the child to be born.

"Étienne." The name gave her courage. She felt it on her lips and in her heart. He hadn't known love, either. He had nearly said as much, and she had guessed the rest. Like her, he had been raised alone. There had been no children in his life to smother with affection. But together they would learn how.

She forced herself to imagine her father's reaction. She fell to the bed and closed her eyes. It wasn't a lack of courage that made her heart pound faster. She lived what was to come so that, when it did, she would be strong enough to face it.

It was late afternoon when she rose from the bed and went to the armoire to choose another dress. A sour smell rose from the basin where she had vomited. But the legs she stood on didn't buckle, and the hands that sorted through tea gowns and walking costumes were steady.

Étienne was almost afraid to believe that everything he had worked for was within his grasp. He had spent the years on Bayou Lafourche dreaming of revenge. But even after he had come to New Orleans and the moment was closer, he hadn't known how to ruin Lucien. He had assumed that finding a way would take years. He would have to gain Lucien's trust and favor first, then slowly, carefully, work his way into a position of importance, where some plan would present itself.

Instead, he had caught Lucien's eye immediately. Through no calculation of his own, he had come into Gulf Coast Steamship at

a crucial juncture in its history. Expansion had made an old man
out of Lucien, and he'd seen the need for young blood.

Étienne's rise had been a series of talent and accidents. He had
the correct combination of youth, energy and intelligence. His
background and education appeared good enough not to raise suspicions about his character, and lowly enough not to raise suspicions about his motivation or ambitions.

Now Étienne was on the verge of taking his revenge. Years
hadn't elapsed; ideas and methods hadn't been traded in for better ones. The vehicle for Lucien's destruction had been so clear
that at first Étienne feared it was too easy. He had gone over and
over it in his mind, rehearsed it, sorted through the consequences, but still revenge remained simple. Long ago he had
pieced together Lucien's motivation for setting the skiff free. The
details were murky, and might remain so, but Étienne was sure
that Lucien had murdered his mother and sister because their existence had begun to threaten him. Whether the threat had been
to Lucien's reputation or his assets was a small matter. Now
Étienne was in a position to destroy both.

One evening, he sat in his small apartment, staring at the photograph Aurore had given him. She was dressed in the white gown
in which she had made her debut, with rows of lace accentuating
her breasts. Her hair was pulled high off her forehead, with one
long curl resting on a bare shoulder. Her eyes sparkled, as if her
thoughts were tantalizing.

Aurore's was not a face best captured in repose. She was beautiful only when she moved, talked, laughed. Love, and the confidence that came with it, had changed her. Now her skin glowed. Her
features were more animated; she smiled more often. In bed, where
it was impossible for her to hide her feelings, she was capable of a
passion the woman in the photograph could never imagine.

Étienne felt the cool metal frame, the glass protecting the image.
The flesh-and-blood woman was warm, and a familiar yearning
stole over him as he stared at her face. In the past weeks, he had

given up pretending that he had seduced Aurore to avenge his family. There was nothing of Lucien in his daughter. She had suffered at her father's hands. Not as his mother and Angelle had, but she had lived through a painful, loveless childhood and sacrificed her own yearnings on the altar of Lucien's selfishness.

Now, after years of seeking Lucien's love, she had given up all hope of it. She had come to Étienne with no promises, come like a starving child grateful for any crumb he offered. And what had started as a quest for revenge had turned into a fierce need to have and protect her always.

A knock interrupted his thoughts. He laid the photograph in his desk drawer and opened the door to find the real woman. She fell into his arms before he could close the door behind her.

"What are you doing here?" he asked. "I thought we decided it wasn't safe for you to come here." He clutched her tightly. She was trembling against him.

"It seemed safer than the office."

He touched her hair, drawn back from her face with a spray of seed pearls and white silk roses. His hand settled there, and he dug his fingers into it. "Safer, maybe, but still not safe. Does your father know you're out?"

"I waited until after he'd gone upstairs. I'm supposed to be at a party tonight, and I was afraid he might attend with me but he didn't come back down. I don't think he's feeling well." She raised her face to his. "But what he thinks doesn't matter anymore, Étienne."

He cupped her chin and searched her eyes. "Come in and sit down. I'll get you some coffee. You're freezing."

She turned paler. "No. I can't drink coffee."

He frowned. "Tea, then?"

Something wavered in her eyes. A failure of resolve, perhaps. She drew back a little. "All right."

He led her to a love seat and left her there. In the kitchen, he put the kettle on to boil and searched for tea. When he had a tray ready, he set it on the table in front of her. "Are you feeling better?"

"Yes. It's warm in here."

He noted that she had removed her wrap. Her gown was mauve, trimmed with pearls and roses to match those in her hair, and her skin was the translucent white of the pearls. He poured the tea, even though it hadn't had enough time to steep properly, and added three sugar lumps to her cup. He handed it to her, despite her protests. "Drink."

She sipped. Little by little he watched color returning to her cheeks. "Now tell me what's wrong," he said, when she had finished. "Has your father found out about us?"

She shook her head. "No, but he will."

He waited for her to go on. She looked tormented. "Has he ordered you to marry someone else? Is he sending you away?"

She shook her head. Fear began to nibble at him. He wondered if Lucien had discovered his identity. Had he told Aurore the full story? Even as he worried, he discounted that possibility. Lucien could never tell anyone what he had done the night of the hurricane. But he might tell an altered version, one that absolved him of all blame.

"Has your father upset you?" he asked.

"No. Not my father." She set down her cup. "It's us."

Fear devoured him. She had changed her mind. So close to making a final commitment, she had realized what she would be giving up. In moments of passion, he had promised to care for her, to someday give her as rich and full a life as she would be forced to abandon in New Orleans. But the fear of losing everything had overwhelmed her. She didn't want him anymore.

As if she saw his fear, she shook her head wildly. "No, Étienne. I still love you." She clasped his hand. "More than ever. But I'm afraid..."

"Of what?" he demanded. "In heaven's name, tell me, Aurore!"

"I'm going to have your baby."

The possibility hadn't occurred to him. Perhaps in the first moments of their lovemaking on the *Dowager,* before he realized that taking her virginity was not an act of revenge so much as one of love, he had thought to get her pregnant. Perhaps he had imagined the look on Lucien's face when he learned that Raphael Cantrelle had planted his seed, the seed of a man of mixed blood, in his only daughter. But the thought, if he'd had it at all, had been fleeting.

And it hadn't recurred. Not until now. "A baby." He felt her hands stiffen around his. He covered them and brought them to his lips. "Are you certain?"

"As certain as a woman can be without seeing a doctor."

"Are you well?"

"No!" She looked away. "I'm frightened, Étienne. What will happen now?"

A grand denouement. A drama brought to its close. He squeezed his eyes shut. A vision of Lucien's face stretched across his eyelids. Lucien, as pale, as tormented, as his daughter.

He opened his eyes. "That's easy. We'll get married. And we'll move away, to New York or the Great Lakes. We'll make a home and a life together, and we won't look back."

"A home and a life." Her voice trembled. "Are you sure?"

"How can you believe otherwise?"

"I won't be allowed to bring anything with me except our child and the clothes on my back."

He saw Lucien's handiwork as clearly as he had on the night a small skiff was set free to tumble into the face of a hurricane. She believed she was worth nothing, just as she had been conscientiously taught. "You'll bring everything. You'll bring yourself. I don't want anything else."

"Oh, Étienne." A teardrop ran down her cheek. "I can work to help us get started. There's not much I know how to do, but my French is perfect. I could tutor young ladies—"

He put a finger to her lips. "Hush. You have nothing to worry about. We won't be poor. Far from it. I told you I had an inheritance from my father, but I've never told you what it was."

"You don't have to. It's not my concern."

"It soon will be. We should get married immediately." He stood. "Wait here."

She was sitting in exactly the same position when he returned. She looked lost and frightened, but fear was only a thin veneer. She was a woman who would get through this trial, and every other foisted on her. Behind the shadowed eyes was a woman who would persevere.

He sat beside her and placed a wooden box on her lap, although he knew the weight would make her uncomfortable. "Before you open this, you should know that you're looking at dreams."

Her hand smoothed over the satin wood. "Dreams?"

"A young boy's, a young man's." He watched her stroke the wood. "An old man's, too."

"Your father's?"

He had been thinking of Juan, but now he thought of the man, the slave's son, he had never known. "I'm sure my father had dreams for his son, though I never knew them."

"And he left you this?"

"Yes." He covered her hand and lifted the lid on the box.

"My God." She stared at the contents, transfixed. "Étienne..." She fell silent.

He knew each of the pieces as well as he knew the bitterness in his heart. "Touch whatever you like."

"*Like?* What a funny word." Still, she didn't move.

He broke the spell, reaching for a strand of rubies. He dragged it across her cheek, and they warmed her skin. "These suit you."

There was little jewelry inside the box. The man responsible for the cache, probably an ancestor of Juan's, had not been sentimental. Étienne guessed that when the booty was divided, he had chosen mostly gold and silver coins as his share. Or perhaps Juan himself, or others who had once possessed the treasure, had sold off everything else. Now there remained only the necklace, a pair of emerald-and-diamond earrings, a ruby-and-sapphire ring.

And the cross, executed in purest silver.

Aurore lifted the cross. It shone in the cradle of her lap. "I've never seen anything so beautiful."

"I haven't been able to make myself sell it."

She laid it carefully in the box, against a wealth of gold doubloons. "How and where?" she asked. "These aren't the usual family heirlooms."

"Pirate treasure."

"Dear God."

"Very dear." He scooped up a handful of coins and let them dribble through his fingers. "I can only guess where it came from, Aurore. There was a parade of Spanish ships that carried treasure back and forth from the New World to the Old. Some of them are known to have gone down in Louisiana waters. Some were taken by pirates."

"But how did your father—?"

He told her a story he thought she would believe. "When my father found me in the marsh, the hurricane had also churned the earth nearby. Trees lay uprooted. As he was carrying me to his pirogue, he saw a chest that the storm had uncovered. Inside was this."

"And he never spent it? Never tried to make your lives better? Your work easier?"

"I think he knew treasure couldn't change him into someone else. And he was a miserly man. Perhaps he was waiting to spend it one day when he was old. He told me where he had hidden it just before he closed his eyes for the last time."

"But Étienne, once it belonged to someone."

His lips quirked in a half smile. "But to whom? The Spanish who pillaged the Aztecs? The Mayans? Should I return it to them, do you think?"

She closed her eyes. "How much—?"

"I don't know. Some of the coins are very old. They'll be worth more to collectors than they're worth for their gold. I don't know if a price could even be put on the cross."

He lifted the chest from her lap. Her eyes were still closed, and she was still too pale. "There is no one this belongs to more than it belongs to us." He touched her cheek at the same moment he kissed her. The kiss was gentle and undemanding. He wanted nothing except color in her cheeks.

"I'll be marrying a rich man," she said as she opened her eyes.

"Rich? Maybe not. But this can be parlayed into real wealth, Aurore. We can start a business together. We have the means to do it."

"Then why, with all this, have you been working for my father?"

"Because money is nothing without experience. And the things I had to learn couldn't be taught in classrooms."

She seemed to believe him. She nodded. "But this still won't make my father accept you as his son-in-law."

"I don't want his acceptance. I want his daughter."

"She's yours." The color he had hoped for flooded her cheeks. "She was yours before this." She swept her hand toward the treasure. "And she will be yours after. She'll be yours forever!"

He clasped her to him. He tried not to think of anything except the woman in his arms. But, despite himself, he thought of Lucien, and what Lucien would say.

"I don't want you to tell your father," he said, against her hair. "He'll attempt to stop us. We'll arrange a place and time to meet. I'll have tickets for the train. We'll leave Louisiana, and we'll never look back."

She turned her face to his. He saw both sorrow and hope in her eyes. But as he kissed her, the sorrow disappeared.

CHAPTER 16

On Lundi Gras, Rex, costumed as a French monarch of happier times, arrived at the riverfront on his royal yacht and paraded to Gallier Hall. Crowds lined the streets to cheer the king of carnival in his gold-and-white carriage. The city simmered with excitement as the clock ticked off the hours to Mardi Gras. By evening, when the Proteus parade was to begin, anticipation seeped through every street, from the palatial mansions of Saint Charles Avenue to the crowded shacks of Freetown in Algiers.

Up until the hour before Proteus was to appear, mothers worked on hampers of food to share with friends who lived on Tuesday's parade route. Children designed and redesigned costumes, sewing bits of ribbon and small silver bells to cheap cambric and sateen. Then a flood of humanity spilled from houses all over the city and headed downtown to Canal Street.

Aurore pushed her way through the good-natured crowds, swimming against the tide. In the streets the shrill honk of automobile horns blended with the screeches of horses. On one corner a small boy waved a carnival bulletin and pleaded for a dime. She had no use for it, but she bought one as a defense against fellow vendors at every corner. She was halfway to the riverfront before she realized that she was carrying a last colorful souvenir of her life in New Orleans. In days to come, she might look at the beautifully rendered lithographs of each float in the Proteus parade and dream she was home again.

Except that now home would be wherever Étienne planned for them to live. Afraid that her father might learn the truth before they were safely away, she hadn't asked their destination. She was willing to turn her back on Lucien, but not to lie.

The crowds thinned. Far away she heard the music of a brass band. Then, as she neared the river, the sounds faded.

Carnival, with its relentless preoccupation with social status, its numbing regard for the most ephemeral of human values, would be easy to put behind her. She had never experienced carnival from the streets, never scrambled for a place on the parade route or worn a daring costume of her own creation. She wouldn't miss what she had never really known.

The river was another matter. As she hurried toward it, she could smell its mysterious scent. Odors mingled into an essence as encompassing as the fog rising toward the darkening sky. The river was running faster and higher now, in anticipation of spring. Tears burned her eyes. She wasn't sorry to be leaving New Orleans, because she was leaving with Étienne. But she hoped that someday, somewhere, she would know the river again.

She walked faster, because it was growing late. She was to meet Étienne that evening at the train station. They had chosen this night because her father would be occupied with the parade and the ball to follow. It would be late before Lucien realized she was not among the young women in the call-out section. By then Aurore would be gone. But first she had one last goodbye.

As she neared the water, she schooled herself not to be disappointed. She had tried to get word to Ti' Boo that she was leaving New Orleans. She had entrusted a letter to the same captain who had taken her to Côte Boudreaux, and she had telephoned a relative of Ti' Boo's in Napoleonville. She had asked Ti' Boo to meet her here, but she hadn't gotten a response.

Aurore didn't know if Ti' Boo had never gotten word, or if she had been forbidden to come. She was now the mother of a two-month-old infant, a healthy girl she had named Pelichere. Travel from Bayou Lafourche could be difficult, and it wasn't unusual for an Acadian woman to stay forever in the confines of her small village. But Ti' Boo had come to New Orleans once, on an uncle's oyster lugger, and Aurore had prayed she could come once more.

She turned left and headed for Picayune Pier, near the French Market, where she hoped they would meet. Luggers docked here and unloaded fish, oysters and fresh vegetables from the bayous and lakes of the south, and in the daytime a mélange of men of all colors and races sailed in and out on boats with square sails.

At twilight the pier was not as enchanting. Every shadow menaced; every stranger was a potential enemy. She hurried until she was close enough to read the names of boats. Canvas tents covered cargo and blocked her view. She knew that men lived on their luggers; some had no other homes. Gazing at the crowded decks, she wondered if she had asked Ti' Boo for the impossible.

She was debating whether to turn back when she saw a small figure unfold aft of one of the canvas tents. "Ro-Ro!"

She covered her mouth with her hands and watched as Ti' Boo maneuvered past the cargo on her uncle's lugger. Then she made a leap that would have done justice to longer legs and landed on the planks beside the water. In a moment they were in each other's arms.

"I can't believe you came!" Aurore hugged her tighter. "How did you manage?"

"I couldn't let you go, not without seeing you."

Aurore buried her face in Ti' Boo's hair. She realized that she had needed a portion of Ti' Boo's courage to move forward with her life.

"Ti' Boo!"

Aurore looked up and saw Jules on the deck of the lugger.

"Over here." Ti' Boo waved. "He wouldn't let me come, not without him," she told Aurore. "He thinks to keep me and Peli safe."

"Is he angry?"

"Angry?" Ti' Boo laughed. "I treat him too good."

Jules joined them. His hair had turned grayer, but he was clearly a man who improved with age. He greeted Aurore, then went to examine the lugger's moorings so that they could talk.

"But where's the baby?" Aurore asked.

"Asleep on the cot beside my *nonc.*" She inclined her head toward the boat. "She'll be awake soon enough. You can see her then."

Aurore had a thousand questions to ask, questions about marriage, childbirth and motherhood. She hadn't told Ti' Boo why she was leaving New Orleans, afraid to put the reason on paper. Now she couldn't hold it inside any longer. "Ti' Boo, I'm getting married," she said.

If Ti' Boo was surprised, she didn't show it. "Does your father know?"

Aurore shook her head. "He would disapprove. You know the man. It's Étienne Terrebonne from Lafourche. He came here to work for my father."

"Étienne." Ti' Boo's face was inscrutable. "But why?"

"Because I love him."

"And that matters more than what your father will say?"

"I'll never know what my father says. We're leaving tonight. We'll be married out of state."

"Ro-Ro..." Ti' Boo shook her head. "You can't escape what you are. Neither you or...Étienne."

"We can try." Aurore took her arm. "Please, let's walk."

"Jules will follow," Ti' Boo warned.

"Good. Then we'll be safe."

They strolled arm in arm, and Ti' Boo questioned Aurore about her plans. "But to be married without family," Ti' Boo said. "How you must ache."

"I've never had family." Aurore squeezed her arm. "You know that better than anyone."

"And your *maman?*"

"She doesn't even know me anymore, and Papa forbids me to see her. Even the nuns who watch over her say she seems happiest when she's left to herself."

"Poor Ro-Ro."

"No. Not anymore. Now I have someone who loves me, Ti' Boo." She flung out an arm, as if to encompass the whole world. "You don't know what it's like after all these years!"

Ti' Boo made a comforting sound.

"I just had to see you once more before we leave. I don't know if we'll ever see each other again," Aurore said. "I know it was hard to come, but it means so much to me. By tomorrow my father will know."

"He'll try to find you."

"I don't think so. He'll cut me out of his life."

"And leave you with nothing."

For a moment, Aurore felt a pang at that thought. Her father had never thought her capable of learning Gulf Coast's affairs. But she had always hoped that someday she would have a place in the company, no matter how modest. There had been women in business in the city. One had inherited a daily newspaper and managed it until her death. There was even some precedent for women working on the river. Several had been noted riverboat captains, and one still worked as a pilot.

She was no less capable. She was as intelligent, as enthusiastic, as any man, and she had hoped to prove that to her father one day. Now, with the *Dowager,* the Le Danois tribute to the future, completed and docked at Gulf Coast's own wharf, it was a difficult dream to abandon.

"I don't need Gulf Coast." She gathered courage from saying it. "Étienne and I will build a life together. Maybe someday we'll have our own shipping company."

"How well do you know him?"

"How well did you know Jules?"

"But others knew Jules. My family has known his family always. We are distant cousins. There was nothing about Jules that was unknown."

"And you've known Étienne, Ti' Boo. Is there anything about him that would cause you worry?" Aurore expected the obvious answer. When Ti' Boo said nothing, she frowned and stopped. In the distance, she could hear a band, and what sounded like the booming of fireworks or cannonballs. The parade had begun.

"Ti' Boo?"

"You know how he came to live with Faustin and Zelma Terrebonne. When he was ill, he was identified by a man from Chénière Caminada." Ti' Boo crossed herself as she said the name.

"I know."

"It's said the man became a hermit after the storm. *Il a pas tout.*" She touched her head to indicate that the man was crazy. "There are those who wonder if he told the truth."

"About what, Ti' Boo? What are you trying to say?"

Ti' Boo looked away. "There are those who wonder if Étienne...if Étienne was a child of mixed blood."

Aurore stared at her.

"My *maman* told me the story after my wedding. She thought it wasn't for my ears before. Faustin began to suspect after Étienne had lived with him for some time. He grew bitter and silent. He began to drink. Zelma wouldn't allow him to send Étienne away to an asylum for orphans."

"But why? What reason did he have for such a terrible suspicion?"

"Nothing more than Étienne's face."

Aurore closed her eyes and saw the face of her beloved, the face that danced through her dreams. "No." She opened her eyes. "No, if Étienne had Negro blood, I would have seen it. I live with Negroes in a way you never have, Ti' Boo. They surround me. I see them on the levee, I see them in my kitchen, my carriage house, my garden. I see light-skinned and dark-skinned, and some so white they could pass if they weren't carefully watched."

"And some who *have* passed, Ro-Ro." Ti' Boo looked away. "It's a terrible thing when a man must pretend he is something he's not. It could be more terrible for a woman who loved him. Especially if there were children."

Aurore had planned to tell Ti' Boo about the baby she carried. Now she couldn't find the courage. "You're wrong. I would have known. My father would have known!"

"Do you think it's so easy to tell? We're taught to see only what we expect. If we notice the unexpected, explanations, even the poorest ones, satisfy us. The people of the chénière came from many different places. Perhaps the lines weren't as strictly drawn there. Perhaps Étienne is the child of such a merger. You must consider this."

Aurore drew away from her friend. "No. I refuse."

"What do you refuse? To consider? Or to care? Because each is different, *n'est-ce pas?* For one, you pretend there is no question. For the other, you admit to the question and disregard the answer."

"I thought you were my friend."

"I think, perhaps, I'm the only real friend you have."

Aurore couldn't answer. Misery welled up inside her. She was angry at Ti' Boo, but along with anger had come suspicion. She tried to thrust it away, but it remained. She could feel the coarse texture of Étienne's hair, see the spread of his cheekbones, the width of his nose, the hue of his skin. The things she had loved most about his face were now evidence against him.

"We never have to speak of this again," Ti' Boo said softly. "If you can say you don't care, then I won't care for you."

"Ti' Boo!" There was a burst of French behind them. Jules gestured and pointed downriver. He spoke so quickly and in such a heavy patois that at first Aurore couldn't follow his words. Then she saw the glow in the sky. At almost the same moment, she heard the blast of horns and bells along the river.

"Fire." She understood, and wished she hadn't. Fire was a dreaded event. The port had *Samson,* a tug fireboat, always on guard. But once a fire began, it was difficult to end it without substantial loss of property. Large ships lay on the river bottom, the victim of flames less impressive than these.

She struggled to gauge where the flames might have originated. Denial made her calculate and recalculate, but when she was finished, she knew the fire was near Gulf Coast's wharf.

She began to run. She heard Jules and Ti' Boo calling her; then she heard their footsteps following. The Gulf Coast wharf was far away, but the air already seemed tainted with smoke. She ran faster. She forgot about Étienne and Ti' Boo's suspicions. She could think only of Gulf Coast and her father.

Lucien allowed Fantome to place his coat over his shoulders; then he waved the old man away so that he could examine himself in the mirror. "Get the carriage."

Fantome left as silently as he had come. Lucien continued to stare at his own reflection. He was still imposing in formal clothes, and now that the weather was better, his health had improved. Or maybe it was the impending launch of the *Dowager.* She sat at Gulf Coast's own wharf, a testimonial to everything Lucien had achieved. Tonight he could almost believe the doctors were wrong.

He remained careful of his health. He had refused to ride on a Proteus float, and he had intended to find an excuse not to attend the buffet supper at the Opera House or the ball afterward. But at the last minute he had changed his mind. He wanted to scrutinize Aurore's dancing partners.

There was a certain aura about a woman in love, a look, an essence; he believed that Aurore had succumbed at last. After careful analysis, he'd decided the young man was Baptiste Armstrong, the son of a cotton broker whose New Orleans roots went back the requisite number of generations. Lucien wouldn't have chosen Baptiste, who lived off his father's largess and made only occasional forays into the business world. But, with his impeccable background, he was acceptable. Lucien intended to speak to Charles Armstrong that night. Between them, he hoped, they could control and shape Baptiste until he was the son-in-law Lucien had always hoped for.

Of course, there was the possibility that Baptiste was not Aurore's *ami*. Lucien had questioned Aurore and carefully watched her for the past weeks. But she was canny and secretive, and though it irritated him that she hadn't confided her choice, he had developed a grudging admiration for her. He had deduced Baptiste's identity from the gossip of Claire's old friends, so there was still the possibility that Aurore might surprise him.

He found himself looking forward to the evening.

"Monsieur Le Danois?"

He turned and frowned. He hadn't expected to see Fantome again until he stepped into the carriage.

"Monsieur Terrebonne is here. He says he must see you."

Lucien pulled out his watch and squinted at the time. The buffet was due to be served soon. "Show him in, and hurry."

Étienne entered the room, carrying his hat. Lucien nodded curtly. His watch remained in his hand.

"My apologies," Étienne said. "But you know I wouldn't have come if it weren't an emergency."

Unaccountably, Lucien grew more annoyed. He searched for the source of his feelings, and realized it was that Étienne didn't seem sorry at all. "What is it?"

"Something I think you must see."

"I don't have time. I'm due at the Opera House."

"Sir, I truly think this must take precedence."

Lucien saw a young man in his best years, a strong, handsome man with eyes that brimmed with emotion. Something besides annoyance stabbed at him. He felt the first flutter of unease, and with it the speeding of his heart. "Just tell me what's wrong."

"I have to show you. We'll have to go to the office."

Lucien knew instinctively that Étienne would not be budged. He felt some of the same admiration that in the past weeks he had felt for Aurore. He thrust his watch back into his pocket. "Very well. But you presume too much, Terrebonne."

"I think you'll see the reason," Étienne said.

Lucien measured Étienne's deference, and didn't like his calculations. But he was powerless. If he went to the Opera House, he would wonder all night what disaster might be brewing. "Fantome will take us."

"Yes, sir." Étienne politely stepped aside and waited for Lucien to precede him. Lucien walked out into the hallway. He was strangely aware that his back was to Étienne. His heart began to speed faster, and even though he told himself that he had nothing to fear, his hands began to sweat.

The Gulf Coast building was silent, musty and dark. The sudden glare of artificial light did little to warm it. Étienne paid no attention to his surroundings or to his own speeding pulse as he closed and locked the front door behind them. Lucien had sent Fantome to the Opera House to give his regrets. They were truly alone.

"Suppose you show me whatever's so important that I'm missing my supper because of it," Lucien said.

"Everything is upstairs." Étienne stepped aside, and Lucien climbed the steps, stopping near the middle to rest. In his months at Gulf Coast, Étienne had watched Lucien's health deteriorate. Lucien thought he had hidden his lack of breath, the sweat that sometimes dotted his brow even in the coldest weather, the blue tinge of his complexion. But Étienne had seen illness claim him, and he had silently rejoiced. He wanted a slow, agonizing death for the man who had killed his family.

At the office door, a panting Lucien stepped aside to let Étienne turn on this light, too. Then he moved inside and took the chair closest to the doorway. His own office, one door away, was obviously too far. "Whatever it is, you can show me while I sit here."

"Certainly." Étienne went to the oak filing cabinets along the wall and withdrew a folder. He presented it to Lucien with a mock bow.

Lucien frowned, but he didn't reprimand Étienne. He shuffled through the papers inside, then held them out. "I see nothing here that demands my attention. These are just our copies of the insurance papers on the *Dowager.*"

"Perhaps you'd better look at the signature."

Lucien dropped the papers on the desk and began to go through them again. "I still don't see a problem."

"I suppose you might not see the difficulty," Étienne said. "Since you don't know George Jacelle's signature at a glance. But I can assure you that this—" he pointed at the signature at the bottom of one of the papers "—isn't it."

"What are you saying?"

"What you're holding in your hands is a forgery. George Jacelle never signed that document, because he was told that you had decided to let Fargrave-Crane insure the *Dowager.*"

Lucien still didn't seem to comprehend what Étienne was saying. Étienne felt a surge of power rush through him. He had moments to savor Lucien's fall, to watch it slowly unfold.

"M'sieu Lucien," he said. "May I call you that again?"

"Again?" Lucien looked momentarily dazed.

"Yes. I used to call you M'sieu Lucien. A long time ago. Don't you remember?"

"What are you talking about?" Lucien's uncertainty gave way to anger. "I don't know what you're talking about. Signatures I know nothing about, and now this gibberish!"

"You've always disliked the feeling of not being able to take hold of a situation, haven't you? There's so little that's out of your grasp. Even fate."

Lucien tried to stand, but Étienne put his hand on Lucien's shoulder and pushed him back into the chair. "What's wrong, *M'sieu?* Have you grown so feeble I'll have to take command?"

"As of this moment, you no longer work here!"

"As of this moment, I no longer need to." Étienne leaned closer. "Look at me, *M'sieu.* Look carefully, and tell me what you see."

"A madman," Lucien said, but his eyes betrayed fear.

"Nothing so predictable. If I were mad, you might be able to soothe me and escape. But I'm the one who'll escape and leave you here to make sense of what's left of your life."

"You're truly mad!"

"Look closer. And think of a small boy named Raphael."

Lucien's eyes widened. Étienne saw denial there, then a deepening fear. "Raphael?" he whispered.

"Come back from the dead." Raphael smiled. He could be Raphael now, Raphael forever. "Not Étienne. Never Étienne again. Haven't you always wished you could have known me as an adult? For a time, you were like a father to me."

"I buried Raphael myself!"

"Apparently you didn't."

Lucien tried to stand once more, but this time it was his own body that betrayed him.

"I suppose you'll want to know about my mother and sister," Raphael said. "It's too bad, isn't it, that they can't be here for our reunion? But you *did* bury them. In a grave along with dozens of others, and you didn't even stay to erect a headstone. Marcelite Cantrelle, beloved mistress of Lucien Le Danois. And Angelle Cantrelle. Beloved daughter."

Lucien rested his head in his hands.

"There are details you're probably curious about," Raphael continued. "You've probably wondered how my mother and sister died? I'll tell you. After you cut the tow rope, our boat rushed out toward the Gulf. You saw that much yourself before you sought shelter. We were on the crest of a wave when Angelle was pulled from *Maman*'s arms by the wind and thrown into the water. *Maman* dived from the skiff after her. She never reached her. They didn't even die together."

Lucien's words were barely audible. "What is it you want?"

"Nothing I don't have already." Raphael took the papers and walked to the window to look out over the river. He knew that Lucien wouldn't find the courage to leave until he had found a way to silence him. Lucien still didn't understand.

The room was very quiet. Raphael stared toward the river. He knew the time to the minute; he had checked it repeatedly on their journey here. When the room was rocked by the sound of an explosion, he didn't remain at the window to see the results. He turned.

"What was that?" Lucien asked. His head jerked away from his hands. His eyes were wild, and growing wilder.

"That was the sound of vengeance, *M'sieu.*"

The syllables Lucien strung together had no meaning. Raphael shook his head. "She was a beautiful ship. Too beautiful to be yours."

Lucien managed to stand and find his way to the window. The river was spouting flames. He couldn't form words.

"The *Dowager,*" Raphael confirmed. "And now do you understand about the signature?" When Lucien moaned, he continued. "You put me in charge of the paperwork to insure the *Dowager.* I was to have it prepared by Jacelle and Sons. And you took care of your obligations to Fargrave-Crane by allowing them to insure the rest of your fleet. That way you thought you could save money and save face. You even stopped attending social gatherings or business meetings where the subject might be raised again."

Lucien was finally coherent. "You bastard!"

"You signed the new documents and dispatched me to carry them to Jacelle and Sons. Instead, I carried regrets that you had changed your mind and would continue on with Fargrave-Crane. Then I forged Jacelle's signature on our copies of the documents. I told him that pressing his case would only antagonize you. If he hoped for Gulf Coast's patronage, he should show gentlemanly restraint and wait until I informed him another bid was welcome. George Jacelle is a gentleman."

Lucien turned, as if to run. Perhaps he had hopes of saving something of the ship that had been the culmination of his career, but Raphael's next words stopped him.

"Now the *Dowager* has no insurance, and neither do the goods piled at the riverfront. It will be interesting to see if there's anything left of your wharf when this is over."

Lucien stumbled and grasped the nearest chair.

Raphael shook his head. "I was surprised to discover how vulnerable you are. I've examined the company's books until I understand them perfectly. You insisted Gulf Coast borrow more money than it could hope to take in for some time. You believed your investments would eventually take root and flourish. You gambled, but the odds were in your favor. Until now."

Bells began to sound along the river. Flames shot several stories into the air. The watchman and his hirelings had done their job well.

Lucien covered his ears, as if the warning bells were the final horror. "I may be ruined," he said, "but I'll take you down with me! I'll tell the authorities what you've told me!"

"Proof?" Mockingly Raphael held out the papers to Lucien, then he ripped them in half, and in half once more, before he put them inside his coat pocket. Lucien still covered his ears. Raphael spoke louder. "And I don't think you'd tell the authorities everything I've told you, would you? If they question me, I'll share the rest of the story with them, the way I've shared it with you."

"Do you think something that happened sixteen years ago would matter to them?"

"I think stories persist. They can ruin a man's good name, and sometimes that's all a man has left."

"You bastard. You should have died in the hurricane. You were meant to! Why didn't you?"

"That's plain, isn't it? I survived to avenge my mother and sister."

The room was growing warmer. Raphael didn't expect the Gulf Coast offices to go up in flames. The wharf and the *Dowager* were distant enough that there was a good chance the office would be spared. But cotton bales were highly flammable, and the nearest warehouse was piled high with them. The stave yard, packed tight with creosoted lumber, was directly across from them. With the right combination of wind and mismanagement of the fire, the building could ignite. "You should know the rest."

Lucien pitched to his knees. He began to gasp for breath. Raphael folded his arms and watched; his expression never changed. "I'll tell you quickly, while you're alive to hear it all. Your daughter's pregnant, and the child is mine. We're leaving the city tonight. You've lost both your daughters, *M'sieu,* and ensured that your lineage will be forever mixed with mine. My only regret is that I've tainted my own bloodlines."

"You lie!" Lucien gasped out the words. "You're lying!"

"Ask yourself if I'm lying tomorrow, when you wake up and discover Aurore's gone. Better yet, ask yourself if I'm lying tonight, when you read the letter she's asked Cleo to put on your pillow. She's worth a hundred of you. And because I'm not completely heartless, I'll leave you with a little hope. I love your daughter, because there's *nothing* of you inside her. I'll care for her as you never have. I'll promise not to see you in any of our children. And we'll have many, *M'sieu.* Many, many children to carry on the Le Danois heritage."

Now the riverfront was a screaming confusion of noise. There were shouts and the sounds of running feet. Horses whinnied in confusion. Fire was as dreaded here as anywhere. It had nearly destroyed San Francisco and Chicago, and more than a hundred years ago had almost destroyed New Orleans itself. But the streets near the river received heavy abuse and were still some of the worst in the city. Despite every effort, it would take time to maneuver fire engines into place.

The flames from the *Dowager* leaped higher. Raphael couldn't see clearly, but he thought the flames were licking at the dock. Gulf Coast Steamship was going up in smoke before his eyes. He waited for the thrill of elation. He had done everything he'd intended. The small boy who had lain awake each night and plotted revenge had achieved it. His mother and sister could lie quietly in the arms of God.

And Lucien could burn in the depths of a hell on earth.

He didn't know how much time had passed before he looked at Lucien again. He was collapsed on the floor now, the color of the ashes drifting in the air. He was breathing, his fingers digging ineffectually in the rug beneath him. But there was nothing he could do except lie there and face his own destiny.

"I'll leave you to find your way out," Raphael said. "I'd advise you to leave as quickly as you can. This building will probably be safe, but even that's not certain. Nothing's certain in this life, is it? There are always surprises in store."

He started toward the door, but he wanted one more glimpse of Lucien. He had yet to feel the thrill of victory. In the doorway, he turned and saw that Lucien was still, except for the slight rise and fall of his overcoat. He waited for joy to fill him, but he was as empty inside as he had been before he fell in love with Lucien's daughter.

Aurore. He turned away for good. No matter his feelings or lack of them, his past was behind him. He had no doubt that Lucien would rally or that Fantome would return in time to help him. Lucien had survived worse. Now Raphael had just enough time to get to the train station, where he had already deposited his bags. Aurore would see the smoke and worry, but he would reassure her. Then, when they were safely on board, he would relive his success, and at last know satisfaction.

He took the stairs three at a time and unlocked the door. As he had expected, the air was thick with ashes. He heard the clatter of a fire wagon and the shouts of men on the riverfront.

He felt a searing blast of heat as he stepped outside. He hadn't expected that. The wind, which had played softly throughout the afternoon, had picked up. Now it was fanning the flames. He didn't have time to investigate, but a part of him insisted, even if it meant that he would have to run all the way to Rampart.

The fire mesmerized him. He moved in the direction of the river, through the stave yard and along the same path where he had once led Aurore. The smoke grew thicker and more menacing with every step. Closer to the river, he saw why. The dock was on fire now, but it was the spectacle of the burning ship that held his attention. Never had he seen anything like it. Outlined in flames, the SS *Danish Dowager* was already just a shell of what she had once been. The little fire tug, *Samson,* was gamely trying to relieve the *Dowager*'s agony, but the attempt was hopeless.

He had his revenge. It writhed in the water in front of him. As he stared, the sight merged in his mind with another boat, a small, frail skiff with three terrified passengers. He felt the skiff buck beneath him, felt the rough wood of a seat against his clinging hands. He shut his eyes, but the moment became clearer. Over the roar of wind, he heard his mother scream. He squeezed his eyelids tighter, but he saw his sister's body hurtle through the air, to disappear under a wave that was taller than an oak tree. He reached for his mother, but she shook off his hands and disappeared into the water after her daughter.

He had clung to the seat for time unending. Just the way he had clung to his hatred for Lucien Le Danois. Just the way he had clung to his determination to seek revenge.

Raphael opened his eyes and realized it was not elation he felt, but despair. He had prayed and schemed for this moment, yet now that it was his, he knew his prayers had been blasphemy. In one terrible moment of panic and selfishness, Lucien had condemned his lover and his daughter to death. Raphael's moments had been many, moments calculated and hoarded, moments that had multiplied into years dedicated to destruction and hatred. And none of it could bring back his mother and sister.

"Aurore!" He turned and began to run back toward Gulf Coast and the street that would lead him to Rampart. For the first time he knew what he ran from, and what he ran toward. There was nothing he could do about the holocaust he left behind, but he could protect Lucien's daughter from what lay ahead. She must never know what had transpired here. She must never know his part in her family's destruction.

He paused for breath beside Gulf Coast. He could feel the wind at his back, strong gusts that swirled smoke and skipped burning debris along the ground. Something stung his neck, and he brushed a live cinder to the walk. Whirling, he saw a glow in the stave yard. As he watched, the glow deepened. The lumber, impregnated with flammable chemicals, would go up quickly.

The Gulf Coast building would be destroyed. Even as he heard the clatter of more engines, he knew they would be too late. He looked for Lucien's carriage, but Fantome was either late returning or had found it impossible to get through.

Lucien was upstairs, and it was only a matter of time before the building collapsed around him. There was time to rescue him, to find someone who would be certain he was taken out of the area. There was time, but was there reason?

He moved toward the door, then stopped, torn between old hatreds and new revelations. He saw Aurore's face in his mind and knew he couldn't live with her if he took this final, fatal plunge into revenge. He had flung wide the door and started inside when he heard a shout.

"Étienne!" As if his thoughts had conjured her, she appeared through the smoke, coughing and choking. "Étienne!"

Two people materialized behind her. He recognized Ti' Boo and Jules from Lafourche. His heart began to speed. Aurore fell into his arms. "What are you doing here?" He pushed her away and grasped her shoulders. "What are you doing?"

"I—we saw the fire. It's the *Dowager,* Étienne!"

He saw that she was sobbing. Fear gripped him. "There's nothing to be done about it now!"

"And the dock. Étienne, the dock! Everything my father built. Gone."

"It doesn't matter. We have to get out of here now. The office is going to go up, too. The wind's blowing this way!" As if to illustrate his words, there was a roar from the stave yard. What had been a glow was now visible flames.

"We have to save what we can! Anything we can!"

"We can't carry anything worth saving, Aurore." He tried to push her toward Jules, but she wouldn't budge.

"We have to try!"

"No! We have to get out of here. Jules, take her. Start toward Rampart Street. I'll follow in a few minutes. I have to be sure no one is inside."

"Inside?" Aurore still refused to move.

"Aurore, you have to go. Now!" He couldn't think of anything that might start her on the way except part of the truth. "Your father was here. I told him we were leaving the city together.

He was furious. I don't know if he left the building afterward. I have to see, but you can't go. He can't see you again, not if you have any hope of leaving with me!"

Her eyes widened, and he knew he would always remember her this way, face pale with shock, eyes wide with tears streaming from them. "My father?"

"Aurore, go!" He succeeded in pushing her towards Jules. "Jules, take her now, and get her out of here. If Lucien is still here, I'll be sure he's safe before I follow."

"No, I have to see for myself!" She resisted Jules's grip, and before either man could stop her, she dashed for the stairs.

Raphael followed, and he could hear footsteps behind him. He prayed that Lucien was gone, that somehow he'd rallied and left the building when Raphael was at the riverfront. But even as he prayed, he knew what they would find.

Aurore shoved the door open and flew across the room. "Papa!" Lucien was exactly where Raphael had left him. He groaned at the sound of his daughter's voice. She flung herself to the ground and grasped his shoulder to try to turn him onto his back. "Help me, Étienne!"

Raphael knelt beside her and took her hands. "I'll get him out of here, Aurore. You've got to leave. You can't stay. If you want to leave with me, you must go now!"

She shook off his hands. "I can't leave him! Papa!" Jules joined her, and between them they turned Lucien to his back. His eyelids fluttered open, but he didn't speak. "Papa!"

Something knotted inside Raphael. "If you stay, he'll never allow you to marry me. Jules will get him to safety for us. But your father knows about us now. We have to leave. I'm sorry, but you've got to make a choice!"

"How can you ask me to choose?" Tears streamed down her cheeks. "He's my father. He may be dying!"

"He's not!" But even as he said the words, he saw that Lucien's face was a death mask. Every breath that wracked his body took him one step closer.

"Aurore." Lucien's voice was so soft that for a moment Raphael wasn't sure he had heard it.

"Papa." Aurore drew his head to her lap. She put her face as close to his as she could. "We'll get you out of here," she said. "I'll stay with you. You're going to be fine."

"Étienne..."

She lifted her head. "He's calling you," she said.

Lucien's eyes rolled back in his head, and his hands fluttered wildly. "Aurore."

"What, Papa? Étienne's here, too. What is it?"

"He's...a bastard."

She drew in a sharp breath. "Papa, don't worry about any of that now. We'll have time to talk about my future later." Her hands fluttered helplessly over his cheeks. "Papa, dear Papa, don't worry. I'll stay with you."

"He's a...bastard. His father was a...slave. Your baby...have to get rid of it. He did this to you...to get even with me.... Set fire to the *Dowager.*"

She gave a sharp cry. "You don't know what you're saying, Papa. You don't know!"

"I know." Lucien struggled, as if to sit up. "You're my child...only child." He grabbed her hands; his clenched spasmodically. "Revenge. That's all. A madman. If you love me, get rid of..."

Her sobs were audible now, wrenching cries that shivered through Raphael with the same intensity as Lucien's words. "He doesn't know what he's saying, Aurore," he said. "He's sicker than I thought. And he would say anything to make you leave me."

"Papa!" she cried. She lowered her face to his. "Étienne is a good man! He loves me."

"No. He hates...me. Wanted revenge. Told me about the baby. Was here when the *Dowager* exploded. Told me he'd done it. His blood...mixed, Aurore. Never loved you. He wanted to leave us with...nothing. Forged papers...in his coat. No insurance." He struggled to sit up again, then fell back into her lap.

She was sobbing so hard she couldn't speak. Raphael reached for her, but she shook him off.

"My daughter," Lucien said. "Loved you. Wanted...everything for you. Don't go...Aurore. Stay. Salvage what you can...Gulf Coast. Do what you..." His lips stopped moving, and his eyes stared straight ahead.

"No!" She shook him. "Papa! No!"

From somewhere in the shadows, Raphael heard a woman's keening. He had forgotten Ti' Boo's presence. He lifted his head and saw horror reflected in Jules's eyes. Jules knelt and edged Lucien's body away from his daughter's. Raphael grabbed for Aurore, to shield her.

"No!" She turned her face to his. "No! Not until you tell me what he meant!" She stared at him.

He was empty, and he couldn't find words to answer her.

"No!" She shut her eyes and threw her head back and screamed. "No! It's true! What he said is true!"

He found his voice on the edges of her scream. "There's more, Aurore. More than he said. I love you. That was never a lie. And I want you and our baby!"

"Did you start the fire?"

He stared at her.

"Did you, Étienne?" She pounded his chest. "Did you?"

"You can't understand. Not unless you know it all!"

"Did you? Answer me?"

He couldn't.

"You did!" She drew back in horror. "And the other? Your father was a slave? Your blood is—"

He waited for her to say the word. When she couldn't even say it, he knew that all his hopes had been foolish, and all his dreams of love had been for nothing.

He stared at her, and for the first time he saw Lucien in Lucien's daughter.

"My father was a good man," he said. "You'll never be able to say the same."

"No!" She came at him again, fists bunched, but he grabbed her hands.

"Have you forgotten you carry my child?" he asked. "The grand-child of a slave." He gave a bitter laugh. "You carry the child of a man you've already learned to hate! And you'll hate the child, too, won't you? You'll pass on your father's hatred and pride to another generation. You'll teach our child to hate himself, the way you hate me now!"

"I won't raise your child!" She spat at him. "I won't have your child!"

He shoved her away. "You'd commit a mortal sin because your father told you to? You would kill your own baby?"

"This child shouldn't be born!" she screamed.

"Ro-Ro!" Ti' Boo stepped out of the shadows. "You don't know what you're saying! Come away now."

Jules bent to help her up, but Aurore shook him off. "I won't have your child, Étienne! I won't!"

"You will have it, and you'll give it to me!" He reached for her, and when Jules tried to intervene, he hit him. Jules stumbled backward.

"I will never give you anything!" she screamed.

"The child will be mine."

"Never." Her voice dropped, but it shook with intensity. "If you try to claim it, I'll go to the authorities. I'll tell them you were responsible for destroying the *Dowager.* I'll find out about the forgery my father spoke of, and I'll see it comes to rest at your door."

"Ro-Ro." Ti' Boo took her arm. "We have to get out of here. The fire's coming closer." She pointed to the window.

"And if you try," Raphael said, "then I'll tell them that Aurore Le Danois carries my child out of wedlock, and that she's nothing more than a woman scorned and hoping for revenge. There's not a shred of proof I had anything to do with the fire."

"Ti' Boo and Jules heard you admit it!"

"No. I never admitted it."

She whirled to search their faces and saw the truth. Ti' Boo shook her head and took Aurore in her arms. "We must go. Now, Ro-Ro. Jules will bring your father. But we must get out of here now!" She began to drag Aurore toward the door.

"No!" Aurore threw her head back and wailed. "No!"

Raphael watched Jules struggle with Lucien's body. He stepped back as Jules stumbled; then he watched them disappear through the door to the stairs.

"No!"

He heard Aurore's cry once more, and it echoed through the void inside him.

CHAPTER 17

The convent infirmary had bare walls and a tile floor scrubbed clean each morning and evening by a postulant who moved back and forth on her hands and knees, her white robe fluttering about her. Sister Marie Baptiste had told Aurore not to speak to the postulant, not even to ask her name. Aurore had lain in silent agony each time and struggled not to inhale the fumes of the disinfectant.

She had no doubt that this was part of her penance for bearing a child out of wedlock. Five months ago the sisters had taken her in because she had paid them well and because they had been persuaded it was their Christian duty. They had given her a room, meals and endless hours of contemplation, but there had been no attempt to ease her suffering when labor finally commenced yesterday. This was something Aurore must undergo alone, and if she felt great pain, that was so much the better. Was not woman's lot to atone for the sins of Eve? And was not Aurore's particular lot to labor for days to bring this child into the world, a child she must then give away?

Aurore squeezed her eyelids tight and wished for death. The pain was unrelenting. There were no moments when she could escape into sleep. She had lost track of time, and there were no windows in the room to help her gauge. She had been forbidden to eat or drink as she labored, so there were no meals to mark the hours. The sisters who checked on her came and went without speaking, and when she begged for reassurance, they only told her that the baby was not yet ready to come.

Étienne had done this to her. He had taken her virginity, her wealth, her father, and her youth. He had left her with his child and marked it with his blood, so that even if Aurore had wanted it, she couldn't keep it. Now she struggled in agony to bring into the world one more life that would have to be lived behind unimaginable barriers.

Unless the child showed no signs of its heritage.

Sweat poured onto the sheets, and despite the last sister's warning, she kicked off the blanket that covered her. Under the best of circumstances, the windowless room would have been unbearable. In August, it was a hell of temperatures and humidity so high that water hung in the air to choke her if she cried out.

Months ago, Cleo had taken her to another room, not a room with clean white walls and a scrubbed floor, but a room with roaches that sailed like small birds from corner to corner and cobwebs that hung from ropes of herbs festooning the rafters. She had lain on another bed and smelled an abortionist's evil stench. And she had learned that no matter how much money she had paid, no matter how much she hated Étienne Terrebonne, she could not go through with killing his unborn child.

Instead, she had turned to God. She had come to the convent and promised that after the baby's birth she would don the mothlike robes of a postulant and dedicate what was left of her life to cleansing her soul.

She had believed the last might be possible, but now, after hours of agony, she knew differently. She would never be free from hatred. Prayers and endless good works would change nothing. She hated Étienne Terrebonne. She would never forgive him. And if cleansing her soul meant she must forgive, then she would die uncleansed and unrepentant.

The door opened. She could not suppress a groan. The sisters were competent and thorough. They took no notice of her cries or protests, going about their business as if she were an animal in the field. She wanted to believe their presence meant the end was near, but she was afraid it was only time for another agonizing examination.

"Ro-Ro?"

She opened her eyes and saw Ti' Boo's face. For a moment, she thought she imagined it. "Ti'—?"

"Don't try to talk. It's all right now. I'll stay with you."

"How—?" Pain knifed through her, and she struggled against it.

"Shhh... Don't fight so. The pain, you make it worse when you fight."

"I can't—" A scream escaped, despite the sisters' stern warnings that she was not to indulge in self-pity.

"Take a deep breath and squeeze my hand." Ti' Boo grabbed hers and held it tight. "Someone's coming to look at you soon. Sister Mathilde got a message to me this morning. I made her promise she would, when your time came."

Aurore grabbed Ti' Boo's hand as another contraction peaked. Ti' Boo had arranged Aurore's stay in the convent through her parish priest. The small brick building was on a secluded bayou, and it housed a strict, cloistered order of French-speaking nuns with few resources and even less hope for expansion. But it was close enough to Côte Boudreaux that Ti' Boo had been able to visit twice, and far enough from New Orleans that Aurore had been confident Étienne could not track her there.

"Étienne. Have you seen Étienne?"

"He won't find you. Ro-Ro, squeeze harder."

"He wants this child!"

"He wants nothing but to make you unhappy."

Tears streamed down her face and mixed with drops of perspiration. "He...has succeeded."

Ti' Boo wiped her forehead with a handkerchief. "I've found a home for the baby. A place he'll never find it."

"Do they know... Do they know..." She couldn't make herself finish the sentence. Did the family know the child wasn't white? That its father had only passed for white until discovered? Even the thought sent deep shame through her.

"They are light-skinned people of color who live on the Delta," Ti' Boo said. "They can't have children, and want to raise this one."

Aurore had a thousand questions. She hated this child's father with the intensity with which she had once loved him. For a time, she had hated the child, too. She still hated the child's race, if for no other reason than that it was not her own. She could escape to the North with her baby and hope that its racial heritage would never be detected. But whose face would she see looking back from the cradle? What excuses would she make as the child matured and questions were raised?

And what kind of mother could Aurore Le Danois, once the heiress to Gulf Coast Steamship, be to the grandchild of a slave?

She rested a little, trying to draw strength from somewhere to survive the next pain. "Are they...good people?"

"Of course. Would I send your child to bad?"

"What...what if the child looks white? Wouldn't it be better...a white family?"

"It's better that the child be what it is, Ro-Ro." She murmured something low.

Aurore heard her. "Blood will tell." She sobbed out the last word.

"There have been enough lies."

Aurore knew the life to which they were dooming her child. She knew the plight of Negroes, no matter how light their skin, although she had never given it more than a passing thought. She had always been surrounded by them, nurtured and attended and advised, but she had never imagined herself tied to them in any way. Now she was to give birth to one.

And would her child suffer the humiliation of always serving and submitting to the white man and woman? Would her child forever ride in the back of a streetcar, say its rosary in the back of a church, have no voice in politics and little or nothing to say about its future? Her child, a Le Danois, no matter what the hue of its skin, the texture of its hair. Her child.

"They are good people, happy people," Ti' Boo assured her. "They will raise your child to be good and happy, too."

"That's not enough!" She gripped Ti' Boo's hand. In the same moment, she felt an overwhelming urge to expel the child from her body. "No!"

"What is it?" Ti' Boo leaned over her, saw her expression, and guessed. "I'm going to get Sister Marie Baptiste. I'll be back, Ro-Ro. I'll be right back!"

"No!" Aurore had prayed for nothing more than this. Now she was paralyzed by fear. Until this moment, she had been able to protect her son or daughter from what lay ahead. She had felt the child grow inside her, felt her own concern grow until it overshadowed the hatred she felt for Étienne. Now she could protect it no longer.

She felt another urge to bear down, and even as she struggled against it, she knew there was nothing she could do. The baby would become the son or daughter of light-skinned strangers on the Delta. The child would be lost to her forever. She would never be allowed to protect it from a world that wished it had never been born.

"No!" But even as she screamed her final protest, the child began to emerge.

Clarissa lay quietly in the basket that the sisters had provided for her. She had cried little since her birth twelve hours ago, and she had rarely slept. She lay with her eyes open and her fists and legs waving spasmodically, as if to challenge the air she had only recently begun to breathe.

Aurore bent over her, defying the orders of Sister Marie Baptiste, who had told her not to get up or hold the infant. Clarissa was to be brought to her at regular intervals to nurse, then she was to be put back into the basket. Aurore wasn't to look at her as she held her; she was not to attach herself to the child in any way.

Clarissa was the most beautiful baby Aurore had ever seen. Her eyes were an indeterminate color, a hazy, smoky hue that would not be brown like her father's or blue like her mother's. Her skin was light, though it might darken with time, but it was not the rose-tinged white of Aurore's. It had a warm golden tone, as if she had already been kissed by the sun. Her head was covered by a mop of brown curls, soft as a duckling's down.

Aurore carefully lifted her new daughter and cradled her in her arms. Clarissa gazed somewhere in the direction of Aurore's face. Aurore held her tighter. "What do you see, Clarissa? The woman who tried to kill you? The woman who doomed you to a shack on the Delta and a job in a white woman's kitchen?"

But even as she stared at her daughter, she knew the last would never be possible. With a mother's wisdom, she saw that Clarissa was going to be beautiful, remarkable—and therefore dangerous—in the tradition of many women of mixed blood. No white woman was going to allow her in the kitchen or any other part of her house.

Tears ran down Aurore's cheeks. "Do you see the woman who wants to take you and fly away to some land where nothing matters except that you're her beloved daughter?"

Aurore realized she was crying. She didn't know how she could have tears left. She lifted Clarissa to her shoulder and cradled her there. Slowly she began to rock back and forth.

She heard a noise in the doorway, but she didn't turn.

"You were told not to hold the child."

Finally she did turn. Sister Marie Baptiste, covered in sweltering black, stood in the doorway. Sister Marie Baptiste, who was to have control over every minute of the rest of her life, whose every whim would be Aurore's cross to bear until one of them met God face-to-face.

"This is my child," Aurore said softly. "In two weeks I will never see her again. Are you so heartless, so empty of human feeling, that you have no pity left?"

Sister Marie Baptiste didn't answer. She dissolved into the darkness and left Aurore to wonder about the years ahead.

* * *

They had been given two weeks together, because it was deemed best for the child's health that she be nursed that long by her mother. Aurore's breasts had rapidly filled with milk, and each time Clarissa murmured, Aurore felt them tighten and throb unbearably until Clarissa began to suck.

She told Clarissa all the stories of her childhood. Of Ti' Boo and the hurricane, of her *grandpère* Antoine, of her father and the proud steamship company that had been her heritage. She tried once to assure her daughter that she had been conceived in love, but the words caught in her throat. The night on the *Dowager,* other nights afterward, were the memories of another woman.

Ti' Boo came again at the beginning of the second week, bringing Pelichere, who at eight months could negotiate Aurore's tiny, airless room on her hands and knees. Aurore knew that Ti' Boo meant to cheer her, but the presence of the two Guilbeau females, most content when they were only a short distance from each other, filled Aurore with despair. Ti' Boo thought she knew the sorrow Aurore would feel when Clarissa was taken from her. But she had no idea how distraught Aurore felt already.

Nor did she know the hatred Aurore felt for Clarissa's father. Each day she hated him more; each moment she grew closer to his child, she found herself wishing harder for revenge. His heritage separated her from her child. He had destroyed her future, and now it was to be spent behind the suffocating walls of a convent, with only the torpid waters of a bayou to remind her of the river her family had ruled and the life that had been taken from her.

Only one glimmer of light pierced the darkness of those weeks, Étienne's vow that he would raise their child. Aurore had stayed in New Orleans long enough to see her father buried and to be certain that Tim Gilhooley had the legal authority to salvage what he could from the catastrophe that had befallen Gulf Coast. Then she had begun a circuitous journey to the convent, crossing and recrossing her own path until anyone who followed would be hopelessly lost.

If Étienne knew where she was, he would have appeared by now. His absence was proof that she had bested him. He would never see their daughter, much less have a voice in her future. She only wished that she could face him and tell him that in this, if nothing else, she had won.

On the evening before Clarissa was to be taken to the Delta, Aurore prepared herself for prayers in the chapel. Tomorrow she would give up her child. Next week, in a ceremony as old as the order itself, she would give up her freedom. She wanted to pray for understanding, to beg that the poison draining through her would one day abate.

She had prayers to say for Clarissa, too. She would say them each day for the rest of her life. Blessed Jesus, let Clarissa find peace and happiness. Blessed Mary, watch over her always. Blessed Father, let my daughter know that her mother loved her and did the best she could.

Clarissa was asleep when Aurore left their room. Aurore had just nursed her daughter, rocking her slowly afterward until her tiny eyes closed. Compline had ended. Since her confrontation with Sister Marie Baptiste, no one had demanded her attendance at scheduled devotions. But she knew that when Clarissa was gone, the demands would begin and never diminish.

The convent halls were empty and silent. The sisters had gone to their cells. She tried not to imagine what went on behind their doors, the prayers, the scourging. In time, perhaps, the endless rituals would bring her peace.

She covered her head with a scarf before she entered the chapel, tucking in all wisps of hair. For a moment, rebellion flared, and she wondered why the tyrant God who had allowed her to bring a child into the world only to give it away would be offended by a bare head. But she quickly stifled the feeling. It was she who was to blame, not God. She had lain with a man out of wedlock; sending Clarissa away was her punishment.

She dipped her fingers in the holy-water font and made the sign of the cross before she genuflected. The altar was illuminated by the vigil light. Head reverently bowed, she started toward the front.

She knelt at the railing, her head still bowed. She had so many prayers, so many sins for which to ask forgiveness. She crossed herself and folded her hands. Only then did she look at the altar. At first she saw nothing unusual there. It was starkly simple, covered with clean white linen and adorned with polished silver. The convent was a poor one, the order not well endowed. For the most part, the sisters were from poor bayou families who could provide little as a dowry. The linen had been patched by an expert seamstress, and the silver was only plate.

None of that mattered. God was present here, just as present as in the mightiest cathedral. He was present here to give her courage to face what she must and strength to live with her decision. She believed in his power, just as she feared that the poison inside her had extinguished his voice.

She lowered her eyes, but as she did, a flash of silver in the soft light caused her to raise them again. She stared at the cross, placed squarely in the altar's center. It was not the one that had been there yesterday. She had seen this cross once before, had held it in her hands. It was solid silver, ornate, handcrafted in the Spanish style. She had last seen it on the night a man opened a chest of pirate treasure and promised her a new and perfect life.

Étienne came the next morning. She was waiting for him beside Clarissa's basket. Clarissa was asleep, but she found her fist and sucked on it from time to time, a substitute for the mother who had gently removed her from her breast.

Sister Marie Baptiste escorted Étienne into her room. That morning she had answered Aurore's questions about the man who had donated the priceless cross in memory of his departed mother. Aurore had told her that if the man returned and asked to see her, she would meet with him.

Sister Marie Baptiste left, and Aurore met his gaze.

"We have a daughter," he said.

"I have a daughter. I share nothing with you."

"I told you I would come for her."

"Yes."

"Did you really believe you could escape?"

"There seems to be no end to my stupidity."

"Sister Marie Baptiste says you'll soon take vows."

"Sister Marie Baptiste is wrong. I've discovered that even God can't help me escape you and the evil you've wrought." She examined his face. It was unchanged. She wondered what she had thought she would see.

"And our daughter?"

"Ti' Boo has found a family who will take her and raise her as their own. My father is dead, and my life is ruined. Can you find it in your heart not to take vengeance on my daughter, too?"

"She's my child. You refuse to raise her. I will."

"And if I had said I would keep her, would I have known a moment's peace from you?"

He shrugged.

She had a thousand questions screaming inside her. But Étienne had as many lies as she had questions, and she knew there was no hope now of ever hearing the truth.

"Where will you take her?" she asked. She heard her voice break.

"Where she will be cared for."

"I want to know more than that. I want to know where!"

"Back to New Orleans."

There had been no charges filed. After hearing her accusations, Tim had advised her not to implicate Étienne, in order to save her own good name—if that was still possible. There was no reason Étienne couldn't stay in New Orleans. Except one.

"If you stay in the city," she said, "I'll be sure that your life isn't worth living."

His smile chilled her. "How do you intend to accomplish that?"

"Any way I can."

He looked down at their child for the first time; then he touched a soft curl. "I'll have to give her a name, won't I?"

"Her name is Clarissa. In honor of my mother. She was baptized by that name!"

He looked back at her. She knew there were tears in her eyes, and she hated herself for them. Nothing flickered in his, and she knew he would not allow her even this small concession. "If you punish me, Aurore, you will punish our daughter."

She knew she had been defeated. She closed her eyes without looking at the baby again. "Take her and be damned!"

When she opened her eyes, the room was empty.

CHAPTER 18

"I never misled you, Phillip. I never said this story would be easy to listen to."

Phillip didn't answer. He packed up his notebook and pens. He had already unplugged the tape recorder and secured the cord.

Aurore turned away from the window where she had been staring at the rain that had fallen throughout the day. "I imagine you have some feelings about what I've told you so far."

"I'm not here to have feelings. I'm here to get the facts of your life on paper. If those are the facts, then those are the facts."

"I gave away my child. My own child. To a man I had every reason to despise."

"Yes. So you've said." Phillip got to his feet. He didn't know what else to do. He didn't want to stay in the library another moment. The fire that had gently removed the chill from the air seemed to have removed the air, as well. He wanted to loosen the collar of his shirt. He wanted to inhale the fresh air of February, to stand quietly in the winter rain and feel it wash his face and hands.

Aurore waited until he had gathered his things and started toward the door before she spoke again. "Will you be back tomorrow?"

He paused. There was really no question of whether he would return. He would see this through to the end; he had given his word. But the fact that she'd asked said everything about the guilt that she'd lived with for so long. He was her confessor, and she was searching for absolution. She had chosen a black man because her crime had been against a black child.

"I'll be back, if that's what you want," he said, without turning.

"It is."

He reached the doorway, and she spoke again. "Phillip, I'd rather you didn't tell anyone what I've told you. Not until you've heard it all."

He looked over his shoulder. "What will hearing the rest of it change?"

"The truth is always more than the sum of its parts. I've lived a long life. Don't judge me entirely on what you've heard today." She held up her hand as he started to speak. "And, yes, I know that you're not being paid to judge me. I also know that you will. How could you not?"

He nodded, although it was less in agreement than in goodbye.

The New Orleans streets were wet and slick. Nicky had given Phillip a car to use while he was in town, a beige compact that was so innocuous he didn't know which American auto giant had produced it. At well below the speed limit, he dodged pedestrians and drivers who, like the city itself, seemed to exist on brief adrenaline highs.

He found a parking spot on North Rampart not far from Club Valentine. Despite a light sprinkle, he took his time. As he turned onto Basin Street, the Iberville Housing Project stretched as far as he could see. It was the second oldest project in the nation, built of red brick and adorned with front stoops and balconies. The architects had understood the lifestyles of the people to be housed there and refused to kowtow to the Washington bureaucrats who complained of frivolity.

Basin was a short, inconsequential street, although it hadn't always been so. Once it had marked one of the boundaries of Storyville, the city's official red-light district. Storyville, irreverently and unofficially named after Alderman Sidney Story, who had proposed it, had been set aside in 1897 to ensure that prostitution wouldn't flourish in other parts of town. Straitlaced women and poker-faced men had cried out against sanctioning prostitution, but a greater number had sighed with relief. Finally, if they chose, they could avoid that section of town that was given over to vice and pretend that the streets of New Orleans were respectable.

The district had flourished until 1917. At the beginning, more than two thousand prostitutes worked within its boundaries, and thousands more lived off its bounty. Storyville property was the most expensive in the city and considered the best investment. Fortunes were made by dignified scions of society, who might not patronize the houses, but had no qualms about buying and renting them.

Storyville, with its razzmatazz, its honky-tonks, still existed in living memory, although not in reality. Like a monster that devoured history to sustain itself, the Iberville Housing Project had swallowed Storyville whole.

Phillip knew very little about his mother's childhood. He knew that she had lived on Basin Street, and that a timeline placed her here somewhere near the end of Storyville's heyday. She had only rarely talked about those days, and never in any depth. She had no living relatives. She had been raised by her grandfather, a jazz pianist named Clarence Valentine, who had died in Paris soon after Phillip was born. She and Phillip had been a unit of two, and later, of course, Jake had become a welcome addition.

Phillip hadn't spent many hours puzzling over an absence of family. He had been schooled with wealthy Europeans who knew their servants better than their parents. He had never known his own father, who had left Nicky before Phillip's birth, and in the months he spent with Nicky, the musicians in her bands had become surrogate uncles and grandfathers. He had never lacked for spoiling or discipline.

Now he wanted to know more. Aurore Gerritsen's story had whetted his interest in his own history. For the first time, he felt rootless, like an exotic orchid that had been grown without soil. Perhaps his intensifying relationship with Belinda had made him aware of the shallow nature of his life. Perhaps Belinda's desire to be connected to her African past had affected him, too. But his kinsmen in this country, the descendants of men and women who had been ripped from their families and thrown into the crowded holds of ships, had found it hard through the centuries to reestablish their family trees.

He was no different.

This time, when he walked through the front door of the club, Nicky wasn't rehearsing. It was early, and chairs were still overturned on tables. Most of the lights were off, but the spicy scent of boiling seafood wafted from the kitchen. Best of all, Nicky sat in a well-lit corner, her feet propped high, riffling through papers. She looked up and smiled as he approached. "I'm not used to having you around so much," she said. "It gives me the best feeling to see you walk through that door."

He kissed her cheek before he took a free chair. "What are you doing?"

"This and that." She swept her hand toward the table. "Bills. Music. Menus. It's never dull."

"Where's Jake? I thought he took care of bills and menus."

"He went north for a few days. His sister's sick. You remember Lottie?"

Phillip nodded. When Jake and Nicky married, an entire extended family had come with the deal. Jake was one of ten children.

"Looks like she's going to be all right, but he wanted to see his folks, anyway. We're going back up there together next month."

"What's it like having all those people fussing around you?"

"Why don't you come with us and find out sometime?"

"You need reinforcements?"

"They're good people. They produced Jake, didn't they? There's just so many of them."

"Didn't you have all kinds of people swarming around you when you were a kid?"

"It was different."

He settled back in his chair, pleased that they had gotten to the point of his visit so quickly. "Tell me about it. You hardly ever talk about your past."

"Seems like you'd be getting enough of people's pasts these days without listening to mine. How's the interview going, anyway?"

"It's made me aware of just how little I know about my own history."

"There's not much to tell."

"You don't remember your mother at all?"

"She died when I was born."

"And your father?"

"Died when I was young."

"What about relatives?"

"Not a one that I ever met."

"And you don't know anything about your family?"

"I've told you about my grandfather. The rest of my family were the people who helped raise me along the way. They were all the family I needed. I never missed the other kind."

Nicky's answers were familiar to Phillip. They were the same answers she had always given him. She had always been generous with information about her life after his birth, but her early years were a mystery.

"You really don't like talking about this, do you?"

She looked up from a sheet of music. "I can't talk about what I don't remember."

"Do you remember anything about being a child here on Basin Street?"

"Not much. I can't even tell you how old I was when we moved away. But I was still young. I remember missing the music. There was always music on Basin Street."

"There wasn't music where you moved to?"

She looked past him, as if she were trying to remember. "There were music lessons." She looked back at him. "My father paid for them. Funny, the things that stand out in a little kid's head."

"Then your father was still alive?"

"Yes."

"Do you remember when he died?"

She hesitated just an instant too long. "No."

Nicky was almost compulsively honest. The only punishments Phillip remembered receiving as a child had been for telling lies. Now, for the first time he could recall, Nicky herself was lying. Whatever pieces of the truth she remembered, she didn't want to share them with him.

"Sometimes I feel like I didn't come from anywhere at all," he said. "Like I sprang from the air. If I have children, what will I tell them?"

She lifted a brow. "Are you going to have children?"

"I don't know."

"But you're thinking about it?"

"Right now I'm thinking about the past, not the future."

"I would help if I could."

This time Phillip knew she was being honest. For reasons he didn't understand, Nicky couldn't tell him more.

"Were my grandparents good people?" he asked. "Do you remember that much?"

"I really don't know anything about my mother. But my father was a good man. He would have been proud of you."

He thought carefully about his response. "Well, if you're ever ready to tell me more, I'm ready to hear it."

She didn't deny that there was more. She reached across the table and placed her hand on his. "Why don't you bring Belinda by one of these nights? I'll reserve a table up front."

"I'd like that."

"You've got family all around you, Phillip. It's not who you come from, but who's standing right beside you, that counts most. Remember that."

Phillip had been gone for an hour when Nicky finally put her papers away. She had accomplished little after his visit. He had done something she had believed impossible. He had made her remember.

Early in her life, she had learned not to look behind her. She suspected she was that kind of person naturally. She had been a carefree child who moved from one experience to the next without worrying about what had come before. Her world had been filled with color and music, with women who fussed over her and men who gave her money just because she was pretty.

In later years, looking back had been too painful, so she had kept her eyes forward. She had done the things she needed to in order to survive, and she hadn't regretted any of them.

But sometimes, when she least expected it, a memory crept in. A song, the scent of magnolias in May, a humid summer night, and she was back in the district.

She rose and went to stand at the front door. The sky was beginning to darken, and down the street the small children who had crowded the Iberville sidewalks—or banquettes, as the native-born New Orleanians called them—were beginning to be replaced by older children, children just on the verge of becoming adults, children who, even if they didn't yet realize it, were trying to discover who they were.

Her son was thirty-seven, long a man. But, like the children across the street, he needed to discover himself. She had given Phillip everything she could, but she had not given him what he needed now, not even the fragments of truth about her past that she remembered. There was no foundation and no sense of continuity to Phillip's life. And if he was going to continue on from here, if he was going to build a family of his own, he needed to know where he fit.

She walked slowly down the street, her arms crossed in front of her. The city of New Orleans had done its best to erase all signs of Storyville. For a time, even Basin Street, synonymous with the district itself, had been renamed North Saratoga, and not until the forties, when the memory of what had gone on here had acquired new luster, had the name been changed back. But by then there had been little else that was fit to save.

It was an accident that Club Valentine was on Basin Street. Years ago, when she and Jake decided to settle here and open a nightclub, they had looked at all manner of property, and the location they chose had been the best available to them.

But now she wondered if it was an accident at all. Had childhood memories, so long suppressed, surfaced as she had considered the building? Had nostalgia colored a decision that at the time had seemed merely practical?

She stared at the other side of the street. She didn't know exactly where on Basin Street the Magnolia Palace, her childhood home, had stood. She supposed there might be a record at City Hall, but it was of no consequence anymore. Identical two-story redbrick buildings sprawled in every direction. There was nothing left of the Magnolia Palace.

Nothing except her memories.

CHAPTER 19

New Orleans 1913

When Violet moaned, she sounded like the low note on Manuel Perez's trumpet. Violet was a tiny woman who waltzed through the dogwood parlor in short ruffled dresses, shiny buckle shoes and no underdrawers. If a man knew just how to bend his head and squint as Violet glided across the room, he could glimpse in the patent-leather reflection the pleasures that awaited him.

But this morning it was Violet's moan, her musical baritone moan, that held Nicolette's attention.

"How long's she gonna keep it up?" Nicolette whispered. "She's gotta have air, don't she?"

"The way that man's pumping his man-thing into her, he's blowing her up like a balloon. She won't need no air for a long, long time."

Nicolette tilted her head and frowned. Although she wasn't yet six, she had already begun to read and do simple arithmetic. What little she knew of science she had learned from watching the world around her. She thought her friend Fanny was wrong. "No, look there. She breathed. She stopped moaning, and she breathed!" Her voice rose. "I heard her!"

"Shhh..."

But it was already too late. Nicolette felt a hand at the back of her neck, a hand that rarely touched her. Fear magnified all her senses. She was acutely aware of the sharp tang of floor wax, the musty, mingled odors of body powder, tobacco and sweat that always lingered in the house. She felt the agonizing tug of a curl trapped in her father's stern grip and the imprint of his fingers against her throat. As he dragged her away from Violet's door, she could hear the thunder of Fanny's footsteps fading down the hallway.

"What are you doing here?"

Tears sprang to her eyes. She was afraid to speak.

"Nicolette?"

"Listening," she whimpered. "I wasn't hurting nothing."

"Are you supposed to be here?"

She tried to shake her head, but his grip tightened. "No." Tears began to run down her cheeks.

"Have I told you not to come up here?" The curl was suddenly freed, springing against her neck where his hand had just been. "Look at me."

She turned slowly and saw how angry he was. She knew, having seen and compared him to the hundreds of men who strutted or staggered down Basin Street, that Rafe Cantrelle was the handsomest man in New Orleans. But when he was angry, he terrified her. She tried to look at him, but her eyes kept turning to the ground.

"Suppose you tell me why you decided to come anyway?"

She was too frightened to answer. She scuffed her bare toes along the edge of the Persian carpet. The moaning stopped in Violet's room, and the hall was very quiet. She waited for her father to hit her. She was no stranger to violence. Sometimes the men who visited the Magnolia Palace to sample the pleasures of the city's most beautiful octoroons thought the greatest pleasure was to leave a woman bruised or bleeding.

"Did Fanny put you up to this?" he demanded.

"No. I wanted to see if Violet would fix my hair." She peeked at her father from under her lashes. "That's all. I didn't think Violet would be 'taining this early. I didn't, Mr. Rafe." She reached into the pocket of her pinafore and retrieved calas, rice cakes folded neatly in a linen napkin. "I was bringing her something to eat, so's she'd help me."

"That's no excuse."

The carpet was patterned, with a bloodred border that was a shade lighter than the wallpaper. Nicolette hooked her toes under one edge and felt the cool, smooth wood beneath it. "I been up a long time." She risked another glance at his face. "I got lonely."

"You are not to come up here. Do you understand me?"

For just a moment, she wondered what would happen if she said no. Would he hit her then? She thought he wanted to. He always looked as if he wanted to, although he never had. Sometimes she wondered how it would feel if he did. Sometimes it seemed it would be better. "I know," she said.

"Go on, then."

She started after Fanny, who had long since disappeared. At the stairs, she turned for a quick look at her father. He was standing exactly where she had left him, staring at her.

She found Fanny cowering in the butler's pantry, behind sacks of rice. "Come out now," she coaxed. When Fanny refused, she began to sing the words. "Come out, come out," she sang. "Come out from behind there."

"Mr. Rafe's gonna get me for sure."

"Mr. Rafe went away," Nicolette lied.

Fanny peeked around the rice sacks. "There's a mouse in here, I seen it."

"Where?" Nicolette squeezed in beside her.

"In here." Fanny began to dig between baskets of onions. "What'd Mr. Rafe do?"

"He told me not to go up the stairs again."

"Oh."

"I like it up the stairs," Nicolette said.

Fanny began to lob onions into the corner behind the baskets. "You won't listen."

Nicolette didn't bother to answer. She would go up again, of course, as soon as she knew her father was gone—which he usually was. During the day, up the stairs was the best part of the house. Violet and Dora, Emma and Florence, all her favorite people lived there. They had mirrors on all four walls of their rooms and armoires filled with dresses covered with feathers and things that shimmered under the red Venetian lamps in the Azalea parlor. Violet let Nicolette dress up in any clothes she liked. Sometimes they dressed alike and pretended they were sisters.

Fanny's efforts were rewarded with a terrified squeak. The mouse scurried over Nicolette's foot and disappeared behind a basket of peppers. "Caroline finds that mouse," Nicolette said, "she'll chop it into bitty little pieces."

Fanny had lost interest now that the mouse was out of easy reach. "Go see who's out there."

Nicolette obliged. She peeked through the wooden slats. "Nobody." Fanny gave her a shove, and Nicolette opened the door.

The kitchen was steamy-hot and smelled of coffee. Early in the morning, Nicolette had watched Caroline grind the beans. Under Caroline's supervision, she had poured the boiling water over them herself, a little at a time, until there was enough for Caroline to take a demitasse to Mr. Rafe. When she returned, she'd heated her big iron skillet and fried the calas, made from yesterday's rice.

Now Caroline was at the market with Arthur, the butler and carriage man, but a stockpot of scraps bubbled enticingly on the back burner. Except for the duchess, the women in the house didn't rise until late afternoon, but when they did, there was always a big meal waiting for them. While they slept, Fanny's mother, Lettie Sue, and two maids carefully scrubbed away signs of last night's trade, rings on the duchess's prized furniture, overflowing cigar trays, mud or worse on the carpets. The house was as quiet as it would ever be.

"Your papa's as mean a man as I ever saw," Fanny said.

"Is he?" Nicolette thought that was interesting.

"He's got devil eyes."

Nicolette had never seen the devil, but she thought he must be a sight, if his eyes were like Rafe's. Nicolette could hardly wait until she knew things like Fanny did. Of course, she wasn't sure Fanny knew a lot, just because she was older. It might be because she didn't live in the district. She lived back of town, in a place called the Battlefield, one streetcar ride away. She even went to school with her brothers and sisters when she wasn't at the Palace helping her mother. She didn't like school, but she told Nicolette stories about it, just to make her jealous.

Voices drifted in from the hallway. Nicolette recognized the growl of her father's. The woman's was unmistakable, too. "Duchess's up," she said.

"You lied. Mr. Rafe's still here."

"Hide if you want." Nicolette went out the door and stood on the side porch, where she was screened by a vine Caroline had planted at carnival time. Shiny green mirlitons hung from it now, heavy and ripe for the picking. In a few minutes, she saw her father walk past alone.

She stayed where she was and watched Basin Street begin to crank up for the day. From a saloon up the line, she could hear music, brass and piano and the faint, faint warble of a woman's voice. A horse-drawn wagon rattled as it rode slowly over the pockmarked street, and the driver, a withered old man with skin as dark as Caroline's stove, shouted that he had blackberries to sell. Almost immediately his cries were drowned by the shrill steam whistle of a train pulling into the station.

Three women in wide feathered hats, inhabitants of another district residence, strolled down the banquette, arm in arm. They weren't cheap crib girls. Nicolette knew the difference. The crib girls didn't dress like ladies. Some of them lived back of town and just came into the district to work, often sharing a rented room with another girl so it could be used day and night.

The crib girls didn't need fine clothes. From what Nicolette could tell, most of the time they didn't need clothes at all. She had seen them nearly naked in their doorways on Iberville and Conti, talking low and dirty to every man who passed by. They weren't like the women at Magnolia Palace, who took their clothes off upstairs, and then only for gentlemen.

"He gone?" Fanny asked from the doorway.

"Gone."

"Good!" Fanny streaked past her, turned at the steps and started toward the stableyard. Nicolette followed at a run. The summer sun bit into her arms and bare legs. She wasn't supposed to be running wild outside. The duchess had told her so more times than Nicolette had numbers to count with. But the duchess never tried to stop her.

The duchess wasn't really a duchess. She was plain old Marietta Ardoin, and she hadn't been called *Duchess* until she moved to Basin Street. There was a countess on Basin Street, too, Countess Willie Piazza, who also had an octoroon house. But since Magnolia Palace was better than the countess's house, anyone could see why Marietta called herself a duchess now.

Sometimes Nicolette wished the duchess would talk to her the way she talked to Violet. What Violet did was important. Nicolette wondered if she grew up one day and entertained in a room next to Violet's, if the duchess would talk to her then.

Tony Pete, in a red flannel undershirt with a suspender hanging down, was in the stables, shoveling out the stalls. Nicolette flung herself at his legs, and the shovel clanged against bricks as it fell from his hands.

"What you think you're doin', Nickel gal?" he shouted. But he wasn't mad. Tony Pete was never mad at her.

"Fanny and me wanna ride!"

"Can't ride now. None of that. And don't go bawlin', or the duchess'll be out here with one of those whips of Flo's, only she'll be usin' it on me!"

"I wanna ride!"

"Can't ride now!"

Nicolette could tell he was going to let her. Tony Pete could never turn anybody down. All the women used him for errands. At twelve,

Tony Pete already knew what drugstore on Bienville sold cocaine over the counter and what newsboys sold marijuana cigarettes, three for a dime. He kept a tab and collected his tips on Sundays, when the duchess paid the women their third of the take. If somebody couldn't pay, he'd wait for his money without making too much of a fuss.

"I'll help you shovel," Nicolette said. "After!"

"Sure you will. Those puny little arms of yours couldn't haul enough shit to stuff a thimble."

"Please?" Nicolette clasped her hands in front of her and tilted her head, like Violet always did when she was trying to get a man up to her room. "I'll be good to you, Tony Pete."

"You're too young to be good for a thing, Nickel." He ruffled her hair, a wild mass of curls that fell past her shoulders. "Awright. One ride apiece. Just one, and only if the duchess ain't watchin'."

"She's sleeping," Nicolette said.

"Ain't! You lying!" Fanny said. The two girls amicably argued the point while Tony Pete put a bridle on the duchess's carriage horse, Trooper, an old bay mare who rarely saw duty.

Nicolette watched him scout the yard before he led Trooper outside. No one was about, and even if someone saw them from the house, it was too early and too hot to make much of a fuss. "Youngest first," he said, clasping his hands to give Nicolette a boost.

Nicolette saw Fanny pout. She had a wide, pretty mouth—along with long, curling eyelashes—that she already knew how to use to her advantage. Nicolette thought Fanny might be sweet on Tony Pete. He was a fine young sport when he was dressed in his best pressed trousers, strutting down the street with his thumbs in his pockets and his fingers pointing right and left.

"You can be first next time," Nicolette promised. She didn't like to disturb the delicate balance of her relationship with Fanny. Fanny was older, but Nicolette's father owned the Magnolia Palace. Most of the time, that made them even.

Up on the mare's back, she bounced with excitement. Her days were filled with activity, but a ride on Trooper was always one of the high points. Someday she would have horses of her own, dozens of them, and she would ride like this, just bare legs against her horse's flanks, through streets she had never seen before.

Tony Pete was taking her for her final turn around the yard when Trooper's unexpected whinny was answered by another horse. She looked toward the house and saw a carriage parked in the drive. In the evening, buggies and automobiles crowded Basin Street, and the narrow drive was often snarled by traffic. But at this time of day, activity was unusual.

By the time Tony Pete had helped her dismount, she had decided to check out the visitor. She straightened her pin- afore and combed her fingers through her tangled hair. If the visitor was a gentleman caller, he might give her money to carry a message. The prettier she looked, the more money she would get.

Nicolette liked to do errands for the gentlemen who visited the house, because they always gave her coins or candy, even whiskey-soaked kisses on her cheeks. She knew she was a favorite. When her father wasn't there, she served wine in the parlor in her best dress, and sometimes she recited poems that Violet taught her. She didn't understand all the words, but she did understand that she had better not say them in front of Mr. Rafe.

She knew she had better not sing the songs that Clarence Valentine taught her, either. Not that there was anything wrong with those words—at least, she didn't think there was. But she was not supposed to go into the parlors when the gentlemen were there, and that meant she wasn't supposed to know the words to Clarence's songs. She had figured that out on her own, and she was glad. Mr. Rafe was one of the few people who didn't like her—the duchess was one of the others—and she didn't want to make him even madder, if she could help it.

She walked along the grass edging the drive until she had to cross the oyster shells. Her feet were tough, but she didn't like the way the shells crunched under them. The duchess talked about laying bricks on the drive instead, but she never had. The duchess talked about a lot of things.

The carriage was closed up, which seemed strange on such a

hot morning. If Nicolette had a carriage, she would open it up to the air, stick her head out the side and let the breeze cool her skin. The old man sitting on the open front seat stared as she approached. She smiled at him, smiled Violet's most winning smile, but he didn't smile back. The carriage looked as old as the man, and just as battered by time.

"I can take a message," she said, in her most grown-up voice. "I can do just about anything."

He didn't answer, but he stopped staring. He looked away, as if the sight of her pained him somehow. As she waited, he tapped on the carriage wall. She wondered what she should do next. Then the door opened.

A woman sat by herself inside. Nicolette's smile faltered. Men were unfailingly generous with her, but women were a different story. They held on to their money the way Tony Pete held on to Trooper's reins when he led her around the yard. They might fix her hair or let her dress up in their clothes, but money was something else entirely.

The woman stared at her. Nicolette was suddenly aware that her face was dirty and her dress was sticking to her thighs. She stepped closer anyway.

"Lady?" Nicolette curtsied; it was an affectation that always made the gentlemen laugh. "Can I help you?"

The woman nodded. Her lips moved, but no words emerged. She cleared her throat. "Can you come over here?"

"Sure." Nicolette ambled closer, craning her neck to peer into the carriage. The lady was older than Violet, but younger than the duchess. She was a white lady, with soft brown hair and eyes so pale a blue they reminded Nicolette of a cloudy sky.

"Would you like to sit in here with me?"

Nicolette frowned, until she remembered that she looked like a monkey when she did. Violet had showed her once in the mirror. "Is it hot?"

"Not very."

"Okay." She sprang up onto the running board with enthusiasm.

In a moment she was seated across from the lady, who was looking her over very carefully.

"My face is dirty," Nicolette said. "I washed it, though. Yesterday."

"You...have a beautiful face."

"Violet says men'll pay a lot for me."

The woman dug her fingertips into the seat. "Who is Violet?"

"My best friend." Nicolette considered that. "No, Clarence is my best friend."

"And who's Clarence?"

"He plays the piano in the dogwood parlor. He sings, too. Professor Clarence Valentine. You heard of him?"

"No."

"He can play anything. Two steps. Rags. Jass. Sometimes he sings the blues. But just late at night, when the gentlemen are gone. Do you sing?"

"No."

"White folks don't—least, not very well. Clarence said so."

"Do you sing?"

"I do," she said proudly. "Clarence says I got just enough nigger blood to make me sing real pretty."

The woman had no answer for that.

"What's you doing here?" Nicolette asked.

"I brought you something."

"Me?" Nicolette looked puzzled. "Why?" She reconsidered before the woman could respond. The question wasn't in her own best interests. "*Merci.* See? I can speak French. All the women at the Magnolia Palace got to speak French, 'cause some of the men want to hear it. There's a house up the street called a French house. You been there? They don't speak French, though. They do French things."

"How do you know what they do there, Nicolette?"

"You know my name?"

The woman nodded. "Yes."

"How come?"

"I knew your mother."

Nicolette forgot about monkey faces and mirrors. She frowned. "I don't got a mother."

"I know. But once you did, and I knew her. And I know that today's your sixth birthday."

"Nobody told me about any birthday." She was puzzled.

"They must have forgotten." The woman drew a small box from beneath her skirts. It was wrapped in silver paper with a white silk ribbon. "This is your birthday present."

"You sure?"

"Absolutely." The woman reached across the space between them and took Nicolette's hand. Her hand was as soft as Violet's, but it trembled.

"Will you open it now?" She put the box on Nicolette's lap.

"Sure." Nicolette tore into the paper. When she lifted up the top, a gold locket lay on soft cotton. "Mine?"

"Yes. But, Nicolette, this must be a secret."

Nicolette's eyes brightened. "A secret?"

"Yes, dearest. You mustn't tell anyone. Especially your father."

"Why?"

"He would be unhappy with me." The woman's voice caught for a moment. Nicolette decided that maybe she had the croup. Once Nicolette had gotten a bad cough, and the duchess had made her drink wine with a candle melted in it.

"Has he told you anything about your mother?" the woman asked.

Nicolette fingered the locket "I don't got a mother."

The woman sat back. "He hasn't, then. He was very unhappy when your mother went away."

"She died."

"Yes. When she went away to heaven. He wouldn't want to be reminded of her. And this locket was hers."

"My mother's?"

"Yes."

Nicolette held up the heart, dangling it on the gold chain. It was simple, nothing like the jewelry the women in the house wore, but six tiny diamonds set among etched roses sparkled in the sunlight. "Was she pretty?"

"Oh, not as pretty as you are. But she loved you. Very much. And she didn't want to leave you."

Nicolette slipped the locket over her curls. It tangled, but she managed to free it without the woman's help. "Then she shouldn't have gone and died," Nicolette said.

"Sometimes things don't turn out the way we plan, dearest."

"I don't need a mother, anyway. I got Violet and Clarence."

"And your father?"

Nicolette didn't know what to say about that. She shrugged. "And Mr. Rafe."

"You call him that?"

"Everybody calls him Mr. Rafe."

"Is he good to you, Nicolette?"

Nicolette was perplexed. She had never really considered that. "Does he ever hurt you?"

Nicolette shook her head. "He'll like me better when I'm not so much trouble." She heard tapping. The woman did, too, Nicolette saw her glance at the side of the carriage.

"Do you remember what I said about hiding the locket?" the woman asked. "You must hide it, or your father will be angry at both of us."

Nicolette tried to pry the locket open.

The woman reached over and spread it wide. "See how it's done?"

"There's nothing inside."

"Someday you can put a photograph in there."

The tapping sounded again. This time louder.

"You'd better go now," the woman said. But even as the words passed her lips, she reached across the seat to hold Nicolette there.

"Will you come back?" Nicolette asked. She had decided that the lady was pretty, even though she didn't smile much. And she was nice. Nicolette wouldn't mind seeing her again, especially if she brought another present.

"I want to. But if your father finds me here, he'll be very angry."

"Do you live in the district?"

"No."

"You work here?"

"No!"

"Then I guess I won't see you again." Nicolette pushed the door open and started to stand.

"May I hug you?" the woman asked. "For your mother?"

"I guess."

She reached for Nicolette and pulled her onto her lap for a hug. Nicolette was surprised at the ferocity of it, but she circled the woman's neck and hugged her back.

"Remember, don't tell your father," the woman whispered. She tucked the locket inside Nicolette's dress so that it wasn't visible.

"I like secrets."

"Goodbye, dearest."

Nicolette slid off the woman's lap and jumped to the ground. She started to run toward the stableyard, but just before she was out of sight, she turned and waved. The woman was still there. Watching.

CHAPTER 20

Nicolette stood on tiptoe in the closet and rested the side of her face against the wall to peer through the hole. As sweat dripped into her eyes, she blinked, but she didn't move. She could feel the lady's locket brushing her chest. She hadn't seen the lady in the carriage again, but the locket was still a secret. She had found a hiding place in her room, a missing chunk of plaster covered by peeling wallpaper. When she was forced to take a bath, or when she was wearing her nightgown, she hid the locket there.

Now it felt cool against her skin, but the rest of her was hotter than a summer afternoon. There was no air stirring in the small space where she stood, and the heavy folds of Florence's gowns were smothering her.

"See anything yet?" Fanny whispered.

"Shhh...." Nicolette squinted to bring the room next door into sharper focus. Most of the rooms at the Magnolia Palace had armoires. A closet, like the one in which she stood, was unusual, and therefore worthy of exploration. Fanny had been the first to find the peephole. She had been dusting Flo's room, and she had gone into the closet to put away a corset.

The hole was perfectly round, as if someone had put it there on purpose. It was high over their heads, but the girls had solved that problem by piling hatboxes one on top of the other until they could peek through the hole into Violet's room. Now they were taking turns.

There was a man with Violet. Nicolette could just see him. He wasn't short or tall. His hair wasn't dark or light, but somewhere in between. There wasn't anything interesting about him except the way he leaned back in an upholstered chair and watched while Violet took down her hair.

Nicolette knew that Violet always took her time for this particular man. The other women said that Violet could lure a man into her depths, then close like steel around him until she had wrung out every last drop of passion. All in sixty seconds or less. But this man was a regular, and Violet had told Nicolette that he paid her well *not* to hurry.

Nicolette didn't know exactly what any of the women meant, but she thought maybe she'd learn if she stayed on the hatboxes long enough.

Now she watched as Violet removed the last hairpin. Gold slid over her shoulders and hid her naked breasts from view. It spilled over her back and the sleek curve of her bottom, shimmering as she crossed the room. "Shall I leave my shoes on, Henri?"

"Can you see somethin'?" Fanny whispered again.

"Shh... Nothin' to see yet," Nicolette lied.

"Fanny..." The sound drifted into the closet, despite the fact that there were two closed doors and a staircase between them and its source.

Fanny muttered. "Shit. My mama's calling. She be coming to look for me, I don't git."

"Better go. She finds you in here, she'll beat you good."

Fanny cursed again. Nicolette was jealous of her vocabulary. "You caught, don't go tellin' anybody I was in here," Fanny warned. "Tell, and I'll git you."

"You don't go tellin' anybody where I am!"

There was a discreet swish of the closet door, and Fanny was gone.

Nicolette returned her attention to the man in Violet's room. She couldn't believe her good fortune. She could see everything, but nobody seemed to know she was watching. Fanny had searched for the hole on the other side when she dusted Violet's room. It was between two pictures hanging close together. Even though she knew it was on the wall somewhere, it had taken Fanny a long time to find it, because of the pattern in the wallpaper.

The man shoved his hand through Violet's hair and took her breast in his hand. She didn't flinch when he squeezed it. "Leave the garters on, too," he said.

"*Oui.*"

Violet wasn't French, but Nicky knew some of the men liked her to pretend that she was. For enough money, she would be anything they wanted. The duchess was familiar with all the girls in the Basin Street mansions, and she said that Violet, with her baby-doll blue eyes, golden hair and touch of colored blood, suited more customers than almost anyone in the district. The duchess claimed that the colored blood was for flavor. All her girls had a touch of color for flavor.

Clarence said that the duchess herself had more than a touch.

"Shall I take off your clothes, Henri?" Violet asked.

"Unless you want me to fuck you with them on."

"This will be better." She slid onto his lap and spread her legs around him. Then she began to undress him. Her hands slid against his skin, and his head slipped back.

More sweat dripped into Nicolette's eyes. The air in the closet, like the rest of Florence's room, smelled terrible, as bad as castor oil tasted. Fanny said the smell came from medicine the women used when they washed the men.

As Violet's hands fluttered over the man, he stared at the light bulb hanging from the ceiling.

"You smell like a whore," he said. "Like the man who had you last."

"I smell like violets, *m'sieu.*"

"Five-and-dime-store toilet water."

"Perhaps you'd like to give me expensive perfume to wear for you. You have no wife to spend your money on, Henri."

"That's about to change."

Violet's hands stilled for a moment. "Then you won't be coming to see Violet anymore?" Nicolette thought she sounded glad.

"I don't think that's what I said." He leaned forward so that she could slip off his shirt. His hands rested at her waist before they slid to her breasts. He cupped them and drew them close together into one hand.

Nicolette heard Violet take a quick, sharp breath.

"Such tiny breasts for a whore," he said. "I don't know why I bother with you, Vi."

"Because I give you pleasure," she said.

Nicolette frowned. Violet sounded funny. The man was tugging at her breasts.

"Do you like that?"

"Oh, oui." She whimpered, deep in her throat, and Nicolette thought she was lying. The man had hurt her.

"I like to hear you whimper. No woman should forget who controls her."

She unbuttoned his trousers and slid her hands inside. "Henri," she whispered. "Come to my bed."

"Aren't you forgetting something?" he asked.

"I'll wash you there."

He tugged her closer. "Tell me how bad you've been this week."

She whimpered louder. "Oh, I've been very, very bad."

He released her breasts, and she sighed. But before she could move away, his hands tangled in her hair, and he began to twist. "Tell me."

"I've...I've slept with other men, Henri."

"And did you like it when you did?"

Her eyes rose to meet his. "No. No, Henri."

"You're a liar." He jerked, and her head snapped back sharply. She cried out as he grazed her breasts with his teeth. "What else did you do?"

"I...I danced naked for money. I'm sorry!" She put her hands on his shoulders. "Please, I'm sorry!"

"Sorry enough?"

"Please..."

Nicolette wanted to run into Violet's room and make the man stop what he was doing, but she knew she wasn't big enough. Worse, she knew nobody else would stop him, either, because the man had paid to do this, and the duchess always said that the men should get what they paid for. No matter what it was.

More sweat poured down her forehead, and her stomach began to roll. She had thought it would be fun to watch Violet, more fun than it had been to listen through the door. But now she wished that Fanny had never found the peephole.

"Show me how sorry you are, Vi," Henri said. He yanked her hair again, then released it. Violet slipped off his lap, and he let her go. Nicolette felt a moment of hope; then he stood, and his trousers slid to the floor. He let Violet lead him to the bed.

Nicolette couldn't seem to stop watching, no matter how sick she felt. She knew what a man looked like. She had seen men in various states of undress in the halls. Once a naked man had run after her when she opened a parlor door early in the morning and found him on the floor with one of the maids.

But this man was different. His man-thing pointed straight at Violet, like one of the nightsticks the policemen who patrolled the district used to break up fights. Nicolette knew that his man-thing was a weapon, too, and that Henri was going to hurt Violet with it.

Violet washed him, and the smell of the disinfectant seeped through the peephole and nearly choked Nicolette. Violet took her time, murmuring in a voice so low that Nicolette couldn't hear her. When she was finished, she lay down beside him in her little-girl shoes, her stockings and garters. She didn't move toward him. She waited for him, wide-eyed and apprehensive.

He stretched out over her, pressing down on her shoulders so that she would remain still. "Don't play the whore for me," he said. "Don't move, and don't pretend. I plan to take as long as I want, and when I'm finished, I might start all over again. Do you understand?"

Violet nodded, gnawing nervously at her bottom lip.

"You're nothing," he said. "A vessel to catch my seed. You exist to give me pleasure, and not for any other reason."

But as Nicolette watched, she didn't think that the man really took any pleasure from what he was doing to Violet. He didn't smile, and he didn't make any noise. He moved up and down on top of her like he wanted to force all the breath out of her body. And when he was finished, he threaded her hair through his fingers so that she couldn't escape and fell asleep.

Violet, trapped by her own golden hair, lay quietly beside him and stared at the ceiling. Nicolette watched her for a while, just to make sure she was all right. Violet didn't cry. She just stared at the ceiling, like there was something there she wanted to see.

That evening, Nicolette bathed and struggled into her prettiest dress, then slipped the locket around her neck again. She wished Violet was around to help her with the buttons, but Violet still hadn't come downstairs. Her father was gone, and she guessed he wouldn't be coming back that night. If she had expected Mr. Rafe to return, the duchess wouldn't have told Nicolette that she could listen to Clarence play.

The duchess didn't like Nicolette, but she didn't mind having her in the parlor sometimes. She said the men behaved more like gentlemen when she was around, and some of them were particularly fond of little girls. Tonight she had promised Nicolette that she could serve wine and keep whatever coins the men gave her. In only a few months it would be Christmas, and Nicolette was saving to buy Clarence and Violet presents.

Clarence was playing the piano when she skipped into the dogwood parlor. It was a fine piano of lustrous dark wood, with almost all the ivory still on the keys. There was a mechanical piano in the azalea parlor. A man could feed it two bits if he wanted music. But the azalea parlor was where the newest girls entertained, and the men the duchess seated there didn't deserve a professor of their own. The duchess could tell by looking at a man which parlor he belonged in.

Clarence didn't approve of her being in the parlor when the gentlemen were there, so she said nothing to him, slinking past the piano as quickly as possible. Two men were seated on plush green chairs beside the stained-glass windows. Dora and Emma sat with them, and Maggie, who had just been moved up from the azalea parlor, was wandering the room, twitching her hips as she went from fireplace to window. Nicolette saw one of the men eyeing Maggie, and she knew he wouldn't be downstairs for long.

"Please, gen'lmen," she said, just the way Violet had taught her, "may I get you some wine? Or mebbe champagne?"

One of the men laughed. He was tall, with whiskers all over his face. "What have we here?" he asked. "A baby whore?"

"Hush." Auburn-haired Emma looked down her elegant nose at him. She was very good at looking down her nose at gentlemen—she claimed some of them came especially for that. "Come here, Nicolette, and meet our callers."

Nicolette moved closer. She wasn't sure about the man with the whiskers, but the other one looked nice. She was glad that neither of them was the man she had seen with Violet earlier. "We have Mumm's Extra Dry," she said. "Only the best."

Both men laughed, and the one without whiskers ordered a bottle. When she came back, Maggie took it and poured it into glasses on a table by the door. Nicolette brought the men their glasses first. She knew that what Maggie served the women would be mostly water.

The man with the whiskers held out a dollar when she handed him his glass. "Give me a kiss, sugar, and I'll give you this."

"You be careful with her," Emma warned.

"A kiss on the cheek," he said.

Nicolette thought that was a fair swap. She kissed his cheek. His whiskers were soft, but not unpleasant; then he turned his head before she could pull away and kissed her hard on the lips. She jumped back, and everyone roared with laughter.

Nicolette narrowed her eyes. "Two dollars," she said, holding out her hand. They laughed harder. "I mean it!" she said, stamping her foot. "Two dollars!"

The man reached in his pocket and pulled out another dollar bill. "You're worth the price, sugar," he said.

She decided she liked him. She took the money and stuffed it down her dress, like she'd seen the women in the house do. "I can sing. Do you wanna hear me sing?"

She heard a noise behind her. Clarence had been playing softly, but now he was clearing his throat louder than he was playing. She backed up, until she was even with the piano bench. "Please?" she asked, rolling her eyes at him. "Just one song?"

"Your papa's gonna take a stick to you, Nickel, he hears about this."

"He's not here." She rolled her eyes. "Please, Clarence?"

He was a large man who'd made his living hauling bales of cotton on the riverfront in the days before he could get jobs with his music. He was an uptown black man—not as fine a thing to be as a downtown Creole—who had taught himself to play the piano. He couldn't read a note, but play a song, any song, for Clarence, and he could play it right back, the same or better.

Tonight he was dressed in gray, shades lighter than his skin. He had a gray and white striped vest, and a jeweled stickpin in his stock-tie that showered rainbow flecks against the creamy wallpaper. He sighed, but when he ran his nimble fingers over the keyboard, the sound was almost too joyful for the room to contain.

Nicolette folded her hands in front of her and let Clarence finish the introduction to "Alexander's Ragtime Band." Sophie Tucker herself had sung the song in New Orleans. Nicolette had been too young to hear her, but the way Clarence told the story, the song was one of Miss Tucker's favorites.

She stepped forward and began. The gentlemen were talking, and at first they didn't pay her any attention. But a few lines into the song, the whiskered man held up his hand to quiet his friend and turned to watch her.

She liked having an audience. It was the one time she could be absolutely sure she was noticed. She sang louder and clapped her hands with the rhythm. When she got to the part about "the Swanee River," she waved her hands in the air, the way she had seen a singer with a brass band do it. The men laughed and applauded, along with the women.

She was flushed with success when the music ended. She curtsied as Clarence began another song. This one was a dance, "Swipsey's Cakewalk," that Clarence had learned on a riverboat a long time before she was born, from a man named Joplin. She'd seen the sheet music once, and the little boy on the cover looked like Tony Pete. It was one of her favorite songs, but there weren't any words, and she guessed that might be why Clarence was playing it now. She fooled him and began to dance instead.

The men threw coins at her feet, and she stooped to get them all. When she straightened, the duchess was in the doorway, and her father was just behind her.

Nicolette knew better than to look to the duchess for support. She would deny telling Nicolette she could come into the parlor. Nicolette considered disappearing out the opposite door, but she knew Mr. Rafe would find her eventually.

Holding the coins tightly in her fists, she started forward. The duchess was wearing her best satin dress, a rich purple adorned with dark red lace. Her dark hair was piled on top of her head in sausage curls that made her nose look longer. She had ears that looked better when they were covered by hair, and they weren't covered tonight— which was the only thing Nicolette could find to be glad about.

The duchess stepped aside, sweeping her skirts against the wall as Nicolette passed. Nicolette knew her father wouldn't speak to her here. He clamped his hand on her shoulder and led her through the twisting passageway, toward her room near the kitchen. He towered over her, and his fingers burned through her dress.

"What were you doing in there?" he demanded, when they were far enough away from the parlor not to be heard.

"Singing." She didn't tell him about serving the champagne, and she certainly didn't tell him about the kiss.

"Who told you you could go in there?"

"Nobody."

His fingers tightened. "Who?"

She decided to risk a look. "Duchess," she said.

"Don't lie to me."

She clamped her lips together. She could see no way out of this except lying, and although she didn't mind lying, she couldn't think of anybody except the duchess that she wanted to get into trouble.

"Somebody dressed you up and sent you in there. Who was it? Violet?"

"No!" This time she stared into his eyes, temporarily forgetting she was scared. "Violet's been 'taining upstairs."

"I'll see about that."

"I was just singing!" She stuck out her lower lip, but she didn't cry. The thought that Violet might get in trouble for something she hadn't even done made her suddenly brave. "I sing good!"

He shook her, and she wasn't prepared for it. She went limp, like the cherished rag doll Clarence had given her. She forgot about the money she had stuffed down her dress until it fell to the floor at her feet. As suddenly as the shaking had begun, it ended. She moved to grab the bills, and the coins spilled from her hands. Her father gathered it all.

"Is there more?" he asked.

She shook her head.

"Why do I bother asking? Turn around and let me unbutton your dress. I'll see if there's more."

There wasn't any more, and she tried to tell him, but he ignored her. He spun her around. She could feel the air against her back as he slid her dress forward over her arms.

There was no money, but there was a small gold locket gleaming against her slip. She felt it tighten around her neck in the moments before he lifted it over her head. When he released her, she shrugged the dress back into place.

She didn't look at him.

"Who gave you this?"

She searched for an answer, but none occurred to her.

"Someone in the house?"

She knew if she said yes he would ask that person and find out the truth. She shook her head.

"Did you steal it, Nicolette?" His voice was quieter.

She was afraid now. He was very still, like the stable cat, Barney, right before he jumped on a mouse. "I never stole nothing."

"Did one of the men give it to you?"

She started to say yes. Then she realized that if she did, her father would know she had been to the parlor before. She shook her head again. There was something about his expression that scared her more than his soft voice or the way he held himself. She didn't know what to call the way his eyes narrowed, or the way he grew paler. She only knew she had to tell him the truth, because he was thinking of something worse.

"A lady gave it to me," she said softly.

"What lady? Where?"

"A lady in a carriage."

"When?"

She didn't know how to measure days or weeks. Sometimes it was hotter, sometimes colder. It had been hot then, too, that was all she knew. She started to tell him that, then she brightened. She had a better answer after all. "On my birthday. She said it was a secret."

He had been still before. Now he seemed carved of marble. "Go to your room and stay there," he said at last.

"The lady said I could keep the necklace." She held out her hand.

"Go to your room!"

She continued to hold out her hand. "Please?"

"If you go to the parlor again, I'll send you away, Nicolette. Do you understand?"

Her hand fell to her side.

"If you talk to any of the men who come here—" he paused, and his eyes grew colder "—or if you ever again speak to the lady who gave you this, I'll send you away. Is that clear?"

"Away from Clarence and Violet?"

He stared at her. She thought he probably hated her. No one had ever stared at her that way before. Not even the duchess. Her eyes blurred, and she looked away from him. She thought she saw the gentleman who had spent the evening in Violet's room standing in the kitchen doorway.

When she blinked, the gentleman was gone, and her father was walking away.

CHAPTER 21

Belinda lay stretched out beside Phillip, her thin cotton gown taut in sleep against her thighs. She never touched him as they slept, as if that were an unacceptable act of possession. She gave generously of herself, but she demanded nothing in return.

Phillip had never thought to offer anything, either, at least nothing of lasting value. He brought her gifts, bought all the groceries when he came to stay, took her out as often as she'd go. But he had viewed their relationship as he viewed the others in his life. They were together until they decided not to be. He would understand if another, more devoted, man claimed his place in her life. And she would understand if his work kept him away so long that by the time he returned they were strangers.

Now he lay with his hands folded behind his head and stared at her bedroom ceiling. The room was painted the dark red of garnets, and the ceiling was a deep brown. Morning sunshine filtered through sheer curtains, but the windows were narrow, and the light barely pierced the darkness.

Belinda's home was her sanctuary, a place where she could retreat from a world that had never cared much about her. She had grown up in poverty, in a house where children slept three to a mattress and the oldest learned early how to cook and clean and mind the others. Her mother had died after the birth of the sixth baby, given up and died, Belinda had told Phillip once, because she couldn't stand to open her eyes every morning and see the world she'd brought her kids into.

There had been four more brothers and sisters by her daddy's second wife, and then her daddy had died, too, and the kids had been parceled out to family members who already had too many kids of their own. Belinda had been luckier than most of them. As one of the oldest, she had gone to live with her father's aunt, an old woman, childless and nearly blind, who needed her help.

The remainder of her childhood and adolescence had been lean, with one dress for school, one dress for church and nothing different on the Sunday dinner table than on any other day. But the aunt had been kind, and after her death it had become clear why she had been so careful with her tiny pension. She had died with her life savings intact, and she had left it all to Belinda to use for college.

Nowadays, Belinda's brothers and sisters were scattered all over. One brother hoed corn on an Arkansas prison farm. Another made a good living repairing television sets. Two of her sisters were married, with children of their own, and another had been found dead last year beside a Mississippi railroad track. The rest were gone, blown by the four winds to the far corners of the country. Every so often Belinda got a lead on one of them. Every so often it proved to be false.

Her past explained why she expected so little of Phillip. She had been given one gift in her entire life, and she had used it well. She did not expect another. She did not expect Phillip to love her or to stay with her, or even to care about her in any significant way. People had come and people had gone, and eventually she expected him to be one of the latter.

"What are you thinking so hard about?"

The question was a welcome interruption. He turned so that he could see her face. Belinda came awake as she did everything else. She didn't move. She didn't make a sound. She lay perfectly still, as if she didn't expect the world to adjust itself in any way just because she was back in it.

"You," he said.

"Really?" She gave a sleepy morning smile. "Now there's a way to start a morning."

"What do you want from me, Belinda?"

She didn't look surprised. Very little surprised her. "A cup of coffee would be nice. You know where the percolator is."

"And after that?"

"Seems to me you're leading up to something here."

"Not sex, if that's what you mean."

"Could be a lot worse."

"What do you think I'm leading up to?" he asked.

"Not a bacon-and-egg breakfast, that's for sure."

"You don't expect anything from me, do you?"

She looked up at him through her lashes, not coyly, but as if she wanted to screen her thoughts. "No, I don't. If you're trying to tell me you're leaving again, I expected it. Your suitcase is still packed, just like it always is. Did you get a call this morning?"

She was right about the suitcase. When Phillip lived with her, he never unpacked. He wore his clothes, washed them and put them back inside, neatly folded. He bought clothes with an eye to how well they suited that routine.

"You've never made room in your closet for me," he said.

"This about closet space, Phillip? You want space, there's space."

He didn't know what the conversation was about. He just felt dissatisfied, like a child who has always gotten what he asks for and doesn't know what to ask for next. "I'm not leaving. Unless you want me to go."

"Did I say so?"

"You like your privacy."

"You're an easy man to be private with."

"What about being personal with? Am I an easy man for that, too?"

She thought about it. For once, he could almost see her thoughts. "No," she said at last. "Because it scares you."

"And how about you? Does it scare you, too?"

"I don't know."

He knew she wasn't hedging. She didn't know, because intimacy had happened rarely, if at all, in her life. He was slapped by such a wave of tenderness for her that for a moment he couldn't speak. He rested his palm against her cheek and burrowed his fingertips in her hair. "I never spent any time thinking about who I was or what I wanted. Now, I don't think about much else."

"It's that woman."

"Aurore Gerritsen?"

"You can't sit there day after day listening to her and not think about your own life. You get to be that old, all you can do is wish you'd done things different. But you're not that old. You're young enough to know you still can."

"What if I like what I see when I look at my life?"

"Then you keep on doing what you always do."

"What about you? What do you see when you look at where you are? Where you're going?"

"Maybe I'm a lot like this Mrs. Gerritsen. Maybe I just do what I have to and figure that's good enough. I don't know."

He wanted to ask her where *they* were going. But he was afraid she would turn the question around, and then what would he say?

She scooted a little closer and threw her arm over his shoulders. He could feel her long fingers against the back of his neck. He didn't even know he'd been tense until he began to relax.

Aurore hadn't slept most of the night. When she was a young woman, a sleepless night hadn't completely depleted her. She'd spent many sleepless nights lying beside her husband, and she'd gotten up the next morning anyway and done what needed to be done.

This morning she could barely dress herself, but she struggled through it. She supposed the time would come soon when she would have to ask for help. Her fingers would stiffen, or tremble too hard; her legs would give way when she tried to stand. But until that definitive moment, she would not give in.

She was waiting in the library for Phillip when he arrived. There was no fire today, since the weather had taken a warm turn, as it so often did in February. Sunlight poured in through the French doors and caressed the leather-bound volumes that her oldest son, Hugh, had so loved.

She was leafing through one when Phillip walked in. She held it up. "You've heard that you can't judge a book by its cover?"

"I've heard it."

She closed the book. "Well, that's what my husband did. He went to a book dealer on Royal Street and bought everything you see on these shelves, without ever reading a page. He bought the entire contents of a philosophy professor's library, just because he liked the color of the leather."

"A man who lived for appearances?"

"Henry Gerritsen was many things." She replaced that volume and removed another. "As it turned out, this was one of the better things he did. Henry was not an intellectual, but our son Hugh devoured these books, along with every other piece of reading material he could get his hands on."

"Was your other son a voracious reader, too?"

She didn't look at him. "Ferris hadn't the patience, still doesn't, although he's every bit as intelligent as his brother was."

"I've thought from the beginning that the difference between your two sons might be the reason you invited me here. That perhaps you were trying to side with Hugh, somehow, by asking a black man to write your story."

She was surprised that he hadn't figured out the real truth yet. But the fact that he hadn't said everything about secrets in his own life. "Taking sides was never my intention."

"But you don't seem surprised I might think so."

"There is very little someone of my age finds surprising."

"Until I met you, I thought I was particularly good at turning questions and comments to suit my purposes. Now I think I'm a novice."

"A story unfolds as it's meant to, and in no other way." She put the second volume back, as well, and moved to the sofa. While she seated herself, Phillip set up the recorder. Then he settled himself on the love seat and took out his notebook.

"I wasn't at all certain you'd come back today," she said, when he was ready.

"I said I would."

"What I told you yesterday must be very distasteful to you."

"Because I'm a Negro and so was your daughter?"

"Because you're a human being and what I did goes against everything we believe about ourselves. We believe that we'll fight to the death for our children, protect them at all costs. Then we discover that it's not always true."

"Did you ever see your daughter again?"

She settled back against the cushions. "Yes, I did. It took me some time to find her. Étienne changed her name, as I knew he would. But he changed his own, as well. From the moment that he came and took my daughter, I looked for her. But she was nearly six before I found her again."

"Will you tell me what he named her?"

She nodded. She wondered what the name would tell him and how much he would understand immediately. She was certain that by the end of their time together today he would understand most of it.

"Nicolette," she said. "He called her Nicolette. And, as you might expect, he took back his own name. He called himself Rafe. Rafe Cantrelle."

CHAPTER 22

Aurore lived on Frenchmen Street in the Faubourg Marigny. The one-and-a-half-story Creole cottage was the property of a former associate of Lucien's. Her rent was minimal; the house, although in serious disrepair, was worth more. But when she tried to make a more equitable payment, the money was always returned with a note explaining that, once again, she had miscalculated.

She had allowed herself only one week to recover from the loss of her child, to bind her breasts and dry her tears. Then she had left the convent behind and returned to New Orleans to claim what was left of her inheritance.

Few helping hands had been extended to her when she arrived back in the city. What had seemed great tragedies at first had become mysteries with her absence. The near destruction of Gulf Coast Steamship had left many of Lucien's creditors deeply in debt. There was a rumor that he had committed suicide because he had allowed Gulf Coast's insurance to lapse, and another that he had tried to save money on premiums after profligate spending to ready the *Dowager*.

The stories hadn't stopped with Lucien. Claire was remembered, Claire who had been locked away for years in an institution for the insane. What madness had come to roost in the Le Danois family, and what of the daughter, who had disappeared after her father's death? What could one say about a young woman who wouldn't stay to see the family estate sold, piece by elegant piece, and the family business dismantled? Aurore had left New Orleans as the only survivor of a proud Creole name. She had returned to find that name tarnished beyond recognition.

A few friends had remained true. Tim Gilhooley had stayed on to salvage what was left of Gulf Coast. Not a brilliant manager, but a fair and honest one, Tim had retained what little he could—a rat-infested office far downriver from the fine new office building that had gone up in smoke, barges and tugs that were worth only a little more than what they would have brought in scrap, a few contracts, fewer promises.

Sylvain Winslow, Aurore's landlord, had continued to invite her to social functions organized by his wife. Several friends who had come out with her stalwartly continued to involve her in the periphery of their lives and intrigues.

Most important of all, Ti' Boo had moved to New Orleans. Another flood had devastated the family's life on the bayou. When Jules was offered an opportunity to work in a weighing and gauging business in the Vieux Carré, they had left Lafourche and moved to the city; though each year during the sugarcane harvest they traveled back to visit with friends and family.

Ti' Boo seemed to thrive on her new life. Pelichere had been joined by a little brother, Lionel—called Ti' Lee from the moment of his birth. She was busy raising four children and making a home for them in a small shotgun house off Bayou Saint John, with neat little rooms lined up one behind the other. She grew vegetables and herbs in tidy beds and took the children crabbing along the bayou. When Aurore visited, the house always smelled of freshly baked bread and simmering sauces.

Aurore had needed support in the years after Nicolette's birth. Every morning she awoke to a life she didn't recognize. Gone were sumptuous meals and creature comforts. Roaches nested in cracks in the old cottage walls, and heat and cold punished her. A fetid ditch separated her house from the street, and she tried not to see what floated past during heavy rainstorms.

She had retained Fantome and Cleo, neither of whom would have been employable if she had let them go. Fantome was too old, and Cleo too inclined to do exactly as she pleased. Both had been loyal beyond duty after Lucien's death. They had stayed on to take care of the Esplanade house until it was sold; then they had moved to Frenchmen and attempted to make a home for Aurore with what was left of the Le Danois and Friloux heirlooms. Fantome lived in rooms above the carriage house, and Cleo had made a place for herself in the half-story attic.

Despite their efforts, many of the daily chores fell to Aurore. She did what marketing she could afford, and a portion of the cleaning. Fantome tended the yard, the carriage and the horse, but secretly she clipped and weeded to lighten his burdens.

Once, her standards had been those of her ancestors. A life well lived had been everything to the Creoles. Now she contended with poverty and ostracism from all that her family had held dear. No one had prepared her for her new status.

Nor had anyone prepared her to work in the family company. Every morning at eight she went to work with Tim at the new office on Tchoupitoulas. Gulf Coast Steamship was no more. The limited-liability corporation founded by her grandfather and expertly tended by Lucien had been dissolved, and Gulf Coast Shipping had risen from the ashes. Tim had advised her to sell what was left and invest the money so that she would have a small income for life. She had refused.

The new century had not been kind to river shipping. The proliferation of railroads had been the worst blow, but the condition of the river itself added to the problem. Over the years, channels had not been improved or even maintained. Now the Mississippi, once a colorful Mardi Gras parade of steamboats, tugs and barges, looked like the lifeless streets of New Orleans on Ash Wednesday.

There had been no room for mistakes when Aurore assumed control of Gulf Coast. Decisive leadership had been needed, a restoration of confidence in the Le Danois name, a demonstration that, although she was a woman, she had either Antoine Friloux's sound judgment or the young Lucien Le Danois's brilliance.

She had evidenced neither. Confused and unsure of herself she had taken Tim's advice in all but selling the company. Tim, whose days in the boxing ring had taught him the wisdom of caution, was reluctant to gamble. He missed important opportunities and stuck with more than one sure thing that failed to turn a profit. As the years passed and Tim aged, his decisions grew steadily more guarded.

Aurore lived in a house that was collapsing and spent each day trying to salvage a business that was collapsing, as well. On the rare occasions when she was part of a social gathering, she was a pariah. As a spinster of twenty-five, only the husbands of the women who had once been her friends looked at her with interest.

Pregnancy had ripened her figure and left its mark in other ways. Her hair had a new luster, her skin more color, as if her body had feasted on the nutrients it had stored to nourish her child. She was attractive to men—those looking for a mistress made that abundantly clear. But men searching for wives no longer looked in her direction.

One month after the all-too-brief reunion with her daughter in the yard of the Magnolia Palace, Aurore stood in her room and regarded the clothes hanging in her armoire. Sylvain and his wife, Vera, had invited her to a picnic supper at their cottage in Milneburg. The tiny lakeside community was a popular place to spend Sunday afternoons, with picnic pavilions, dances and restaurants. The Winslows' cottage, shrimp pink and dripping with gingerbread trim, stood high on pilings in the water and commanded an extraordinary view.

She wanted to decline. The past month had been a cruel one. She had felt little except the imprint of her daughter's small body against her own, seen little except the tiny hand waving goodbye.

Étienne Terrebonne called himself Rafe Cantrelle now, although the reason was a mystery to her. Perhaps he had needed a new name to go with his identity as the owner of a brothel. But now that so much time had passed, Aurore thought of him as Rafe, too. Étienne Terrebonne, the man she had loved, had never really existed.

He had threatened to return to New Orleans with their daughter, but even then Aurore hadn't imagined he would torture her by bringing the child he called Nicolette to the district, to raise her in the company of prostitutes, pimps and drunks.

Aurore had watched Nicolette from a distance for months before her birthday, with never the courage or opportunity to get close. But that day—Lord God, that day of all days—when she had heard children's voices from the stableyard, she had ordered Fantome to drive up beside the house. She had known Rafe was gone, she had seen him leave, and at that moment she hadn't cared who else discovered her. Nicolette had been so close. So very close.

She had feasted hungrily on her daughter's face. From a distance, she had seen that Nicolette was beautiful. Up close, that judgment had been confirmed. Her hair—didn't anyone ever brush it, tie it back with ribbons, smooth it with loving hands?— was dark and curling. Her skin was darker than Aurore's, nearly as dark as Rafe's, with a tawny, golden tinge that made her hazel eyes seem even brighter and more exotic. Could Nicolette have passed for white? Could this child have been smuggled into white society after all? Were her features narrow enough not to reveal her African heritage? Could Aurore have kept her daughter, nurtured her, somehow forgiven her for having Rafe's blood? She didn't know. She just didn't know.

She still didn't.

She had thought of nothing else since that day. She had gone through the motions of living, and despite her lethargy, today she would go through them again. Sylvain Winslow was Gulf Coast's only sure path back into the New Orleans business community. As a coffee broker and director of the board of trade, Sylvain had access to everyone in the city who could either foster or snuff out the life of Gulf Coast. He had given Aurore what business he could and recommended Gulf Coast to others, but his greatest assistance had been in introductions. At parties or balls, picnics or evenings at the Opera House, he and Vera never failed to seat her near someone who might patronize Gulf Coast.

By displaying confidence, Sylvain and Vera had kept Aurore from social isolation and Gulf Coast from bankruptcy. She could not afford to ignore their invitation, even if the trip out to the lake drained what little was left of her spirit.

Since she seldom socialized, she had little need for an extensive wardrobe. But Cleo, an accomplished seamstress, had freshened and updated an old summer dress of pale blue linen. It was not quite the style of the moment, but neither was it as severe as the clothes she wore to the office. With chamois gloves and a wide-brimmed hat the same creamy white as the lace bodice and collar, she thought it might pass. She wound her hair behind her head to accommodate the hat, and packed a small valise.

Smoky Mary, the Pontchartrain Railroad's line to the lake—which began at Elysian Fields, not far from her house—was late, and the terminal was crowded. Even her hat, tied around her chin with yards of pink chiffon, was no protection from the sun. She stood on the platform waiting for the train and listened to the good-natured musical war between two bands of Negroes with shiny brass instruments.

She remembered her conversation with Nicolette, and the child's obvious love of music. She wished her daughter was with her. At the lake, she could teach Nicolette to swim, as Ti' Boo had taught her. She thought of the locket, which had been hers as a child. She had worn it next to her heart for weeks to infuse it with her love. A small, meaningless trinket for her only child.

"Miss Le Danois?"

She heard the deep voice over the honky-tonk bleating of trumpets. She turned and saw Henry Gerritsen, a friend of Sylvain's. "Mr. Gerritsen." She held out her gloved hand. He took it in his and held it for just a moment longer than etiquette dictated.

"Are you by chance heading out to the Winslows' camp?" he asked.

She regained possession of her hand. "You, too?"

He inclined his head. "I always look forward to their parties. Their cook's one of the finest in the city."

She noted the way he was watching her. She had never thought Henry Gerritsen a handsome man, although there were women who clearly did. This was the first time she had seen him alone. Usually there was a smitten debutante hanging on his arm, a young woman firmly on the path toward marriage—to somebody else.

Henry was not well-connected or well-bred enough for serious consideration by the best New Orleans families, but even if the daughters of Comus, Momus and Proteus ultimately rejected him, his prospects were still excellent. The social world of New Orleans was like the *dobos tortes* the Hungarians had brought to the city. There were layers of lavish dessert under the brittle golden glaze. Aurore knew, from her own experience, just how superficial—and fleeting—were the pleasures at the top.

Smoky Mary blew her whistle, two sharp blasts that signaled boarding. The bands crowded into a car at the back, but not the last one. That one, Aurore knew, would be left empty, a rolling jail for anyone who disturbed the peace on the lakefront.

"Why don't we sit together," Henry suggested, "and get to know each other better?"

She had no ready excuse for wanting to sit alone. And if she was honest, she had to admit that a distraction from thoughts of Nicolette would be appreciated. The trip was short, but long enough for her to dwell on her own unhappiness.

She stepped on board and felt him close behind her. He wasn't a tall man, although he was half a head taller than the crown of her hat, but he was broad-shouldered and muscular. In the August heat she felt smothered by his bulk, overtaken, somehow, as if she had run a race, only to give ground just before the finish line.

He seated himself beside her, and the feeling deepened. Even if he wasn't handsome, he had a presence, an unmistakable magnetism, that some women found engaging. His hair was a coppery brown, and his wild, thick brows were a darker shade of the same. The Louisiana sun had freckled and warmed his pale skin.

His eyes were candid and unshadowed, but nothing Aurore knew about Henry Gerritsen convinced her the man was the same. He owned a business that was in direct competition with Gulf Coast. Gerritsen Barge Lines had the most up-to-date tugboat fleet in the port, and Henry himself was said to be the reason for the business's success. He seemed to have a sixth sense about trends, investing capital when other lines were holding firm, cutting losses before they were felt elsewhere. More than once, Gerritsen Barge Lines had taken contracts from Gulf Coast because of Henry's ingenious maneuvers. Aurore had no reason to like the man, but she had often envied his business savvy.

"Do you get out to the lake often?" he asked, after the train had moved out of the station.

She removed her hat and set it across her knees. "Not often enough."

"Then you enjoy the beach?"

"It's a nice change from the river levees."

"I won't go in the water myself. I never learned to swim."

"No? What if you fall off one of your own barges?"

"I sign enough pay vouchers that one of my employees would be sure to rescue me."

"Not if you're as hard to work for as they say."

He laughed a very male, very appreciative, laugh. She was struck by it, suddenly aware of how little laughter she had shared in during the years since her father's death.

"Maybe I shouldn't be telling you my secrets," he said. "One of your faithful followers might get ideas the next time I steal one of your contracts."

"Faithful followers?"

"Don't pretend you don't understand."

"I don't, Mr. Gerritsen."

"Please. Henry. You have a reputation for engendering amazing loyalty in the men who work for you. I've offered some of them more pay if they'll come and work for me. Nearly every time they've refused."

"Nearly?"

"I'm still working on one of your men, but I won't say who."

"As long as it's not Tim."

"You should pay me to take Tim off your hands."

She was silent. Loyalty demanded that she protest; common sense demanded that she listen.

"Gilhooley's not doing you any favors with his hemming and hawing," Henry said. "But I think you already know that."

She considered his words. "Tell me about yourself," she said, when the city was behind them and the summer heat was rising in waves from the palmetto scrub marsh outside the train window.

"I've probably already told you everything you'll ever need to know."

"Shall I tell you what I've learned?"

He sat back and folded his arms, turning so that they were even closer. "I'd enjoy that."

She didn't move away, although she imagined he had expected it. "You're brash, and prone to shortcuts. You can be ruthless and charming at the same time, which probably explains why you've come so far in New Orleans, despite being from nowhere. For some reason I can't fathom, you've decided I'm worth cultivating. But I'll tell you right now that Gulf Coast Shipping isn't for sale."

His smile was wide and appreciative. There was something possessive about his gaze, something that sharpened all her senses. "And neither am I," she added.

"Shall I tell you what I've learned about you?"

"I live in a man's world these days. I suppose I have to take the consequences."

"Your eyes turn a darker blue when you're angry, and anything that threatens Gulf Coast angers you. You're every bit as loyal to the men you employ as they are to you, even to the detriment of the company you love. You have nothing else in your life, but you've discovered you can't feed on the past without endangering the future. And you want and need a future."

She stared at him. "You don't look like a voodoo priest."

"You're a very complex woman, but underneath, don't all women want the same thing?"

"And men?"

"Men want power. Women want love."

"Then perhaps women and men should stay with their own kind."

"On the contrary. There's room for power and love in a marriage."

"And if that's true, why haven't you married?" she asked boldly. The entire conversation was so far outside polite boundaries that nothing seemed too shocking to ask.

"Until now, I hadn't found the woman who could give me the power I crave."

"May I ask who this paragon could be?"

"You, my dear."

It was much too late to rebuke him. Instead, she gave a throaty chuckle. "You make me laugh, Mr. Gerritsen. I wasn't certain I still could."

"We both know I'm perfectly serious."

"But this is the first conversation we've ever had."

"I know everything about you."

For a moment, she was pricked by fear. Then reason asserted itself. He couldn't know everything. She and Tim had gone to the greatest lengths to be sure that her past stayed hidden. "Noticing that my eyes turn a darker blue and my loyalties can be foolish is hardly everything."

"You want what *I* want, Rory."

She frowned at both the nickname and the sentiment.

"No, I don't see the Creole belle when I look at you," he said. "Oh, Aurore Le Danois has her attractions. A name, a home in New Orleans society, a history to guarantee my daughters a place in the best carnival courts and my sons access to the best families, despite the temporary blemishes. But it's Rory who attracts me. A woman thought to be unfeminine by the men in her social circle because she works like a man every day. A woman thought to be headstrong and difficult, perhaps just a touch wild. A woman with a past that doesn't bear close scrutiny—"

"I think you've said enough."

"You disappeared for seven months, Rory, after your father's death. Do you know what they say about you?"

She turned back to the window. Now the landscape was cypress trees and ribbons of swamp. The fact that a train track had ever been laid through this watery wilderness seemed a miracle. "What do they say?"

"That you went a little mad. Like your mother."

She closed her eyes in gratitude. "Would any sane man want to marry a madwoman?"

"Would a woman of your breeding want to marry a man whose great-grandfather came downriver from Kentucky on a flatboat and met his wife in a floating whorehouse?"

She didn't answer.

"Haven't you learned that in business it's best to have leverage?" he asked. "Most workable contracts are negotiated by two parties with completely different strengths...and weaknesses."

"And to you, marriage is a contract to negotiate?"

"Has it ever been otherwise?"

She watched the flight of a heron, its wings spread wide as it sailed to the shade of a large tree. Then she turned back to him. "You've told me what you might gain. You neglected to say what I might."

"A merger with Gerritsen Barge Lines." He held up a hand to stop the words rising to her lips. "To be called Gulf Coast Shipping. I can see the advantage of an old, trusted name. Perhaps if you hadn't been so determined to pay off your father's debts, that might not be true. But you gained respect for Gulf Coast by playing fair."

"Only that? A larger company? More problems?"

He smiled. She noted that his eyes remained the same clear green, whatever his expression. "Fewer problems, because I would manage the company and leave you to manage our home."

"No."

"No?"

"Gulf Coast is mine."

"Gulf Coast would be ours. That wouldn't be negotiable. Your place in it might be."

"My place in it would *not* be negotiable. I'd share in all decisions. All of them. That would be enforced by a legal document signed before marriage."

"Very good. You've learned a few things about business, haven't you?"

"What else would you offer?"

"My knowledge and experience, and enough funds to set Gulf Coast firmly back on its feet. A house of your own design in the Garden District—I already own a choice lot on Prytania. Respectability, because even if I'm not of your class, marriage to me will stop the rumors about you." His eyes focused on her lips, then trailed to the lace at her neck and below. "Children. You want children, don't you, Rory? And a man to warm your bed?"

The steam whistle shrieked a final blast that made it impossible for her to answer. They were reaching the end of the line. She knew Sylvain would be waiting for them in his newest toy, a pearl gray Stanley Steamer. She wondered if Henry had discussed her with Sylvain before issuing his unorthodox proposal.

She could feel heat rising to her cheeks as Henry continued his frank perusal. "What does Sylvain say about this?" she asked.

"That you'll continue to lose ground without me. That I can't hope to do better than you."

"We're so much merchandise to be sorted and priced according to quality."

"I think I'll enjoy marriage with you. I think I can make it tolerable for you."

She could feel his gaze roaming her body, a physical, visceral sensation. The heat rising to her cheeks was more than embarrassment. She could imagine his hands caressing the same places, Henry's hands, a man's hands, marking her forever, the way Rafe's hands had marked her.

Through the years she hadn't allowed herself to think of the moments of euphoria that she had experienced in Rafe's arms. With those memories came the bitterness of betrayal. She had hoped never to think of them again. Now, she could think of nothing else.

"You're a woman who needs a man in her bed," Henry said. "And I'll fulfill that part of our contract with the greatest pleasure."

She turned away, but she could still feel his gaze. Outside her window she could glimpse the blue of the lake. She felt his hand on hers, felt his fingers glide along the skin above her glove.

She did not pull away.

CHAPTER 23

By society standards, the wedding wasn't large, but the guests were important. At first Aurore hadn't realized the extent of Henry's contacts in the city. Now, five months after their ride out to Milneburg, she knew she was about to wed a man who had spun a web of influence that drew together a variety of political and business interests.

Mayor Behrman was present, along with other officials of the city government. Men who daily feuded over power and how it should be distributed stood shoulder to shoulder as she started up the aisle of the Church of the Immaculate Conception. With her head held high, she walked slowly toward the imposing golden altar, savoring the moment. She was wearing her mother's wedding dress, carefully preserved with vetiver and fragrant herbs.

She was superstitious enough to wish she could have worn a new dress. She was not marrying for love, yet she had hopes for this marriage that didn't include the experiences of her mother. But Henry had paid for the wedding; she couldn't allow him to buy her dress, too. Instead, she and Cleo had lowered the modest neckline and added rows and rows of tiny satin and pearl blossoms salvaged from the dress in which she had made her debut. Her hair and face were covered by a gossamer lace veil that trailed the floor behind her, and she carried a long spray of gardenias, orange blossoms and tiny cream-colored roses that Henry had sent to her house that morning.

The mixture of heady scents was as brash, as individual, as the man who had sent them. He stood at the altar now, under a dome as high as heaven, watching every step she took. Sylvain walked beside her, visibly giving his blessing to this union, but Henry's eyes were on her alone.

His eyes remained on her during the reception at Sylvain's Garden District home. Men and women who had given her only the barest nods of recognition since Lucien's death now beamed with smiles. An Italian Renaissance table by the parlor window groaned under the weight of gifts, and the newest crop of debutantes hoped out loud that their own weddings would be as stirring.

Aurore saw the young women gazing at her new husband, wondering, perhaps, about the wedding night to come. But Henry only had eyes for her. He stayed close by her side, taking her arm whenever appropriate, touching her waist, her hand. Once, when no one seemed to be watching, he kissed her; it was a hard, possessive kiss that plucked a nerve inside her until she vibrated with apprehension.

She knew what was to come. All too well she remembered the stolen moments in Rafe's arms, the intimacies, the emotions. She had thought of Rafe during the ceremony, not the man who had destroyed her world, but the one who had offered her love, the man who had touched her, warmed her, taught her the mysteries and pleasures of her body and his. It had been the first time she had thought of him without hatred since the night of the fire. Perhaps, while the priest droned the familiar litany of the mass, hatred hadn't dared to intrude.

Whatever the reason, she had been shaken. As the priest bound her irrevocably to Henry, another man had filled her mind. She didn't believe in omens, but what good could come from disloyalty? Henry offered her everything that Rafe had taken, yet as she gazed at him through the delicate clouds of her veil, she saw him more clearly than at any time in the months he had courted her. He offered her everything she craved, but she was suddenly afraid he would give her nothing she really needed.

The disquieting thoughts continued throughout the afternoon. She told herself they were to be expected. She broached her fears with Ti' Boo as her friend helped her prepare for the trip out to Milneburg, where she and Henry would stay in the Winslows' cottage for a week. Ti' Boo, growing round with her third child, said only what was expected. Aurore had married Henry in the eyes of God and the church, and in the even more judgmental eyes of New Orleans society. She must give him her loyalty and trust, and work, from that day forward, to be the wife he deserved.

Ti' Boo said this without emotion. "What do you really think?" Aurore asked, gripping Ti' Boo's lace-trimmed sleeve until she stopped bustling around the room. "Don't just say what you're supposed to say, Ti' Boo."

Ti' Boo fell to the bed beside her. "Why do you ask me now, when for months I hoped to tell you my thoughts?"

Aurore considered her friend's question. She hadn't asked because she hadn't wanted to hear any criticism of Henry. She had seen him as her last opportunity to set her life back on its intended path, a chance to have children to replace Nicolette, a chance to infuse Gulf Coast with cash, a chance to take her place in the community again. Marriage to Henry had offered all these things, and that had been enough.

She stood and straightened the skirt of her dress. "He'll have my loyalty until the day he doesn't deserve it, but he'll never have my trust. I'll never trust a man again."

Ti' Boo didn't try to change her mind. She rose and took Aurore's cape and draped it around her friend's shoulders. Aurore and Henry would make the trip out to the lake in Henry's new Packard, and there was a chill wind blowing from the north. "I wish you the greatest happiness," Ti' Boo said wistfully. "The happiness I've had with Jules."

Aurore suspected that same kind of warm acceptance wasn't within her reach, but she didn't spoil the moment. She hugged Ti'

Boo, and the two women stood together for a long time. Then she pulled away and went to begin her life as Mrs. Henry Gerritsen.

When the Winslows went out to Milneburg, they took remnants of their household staff, but Aurore and Henry had decided to spend their time here alone. A local woman would come in to clean for them each morning and leave them something for dinner, but no one else would disturb them. February was not the fashionable season to enjoy the peaceful vistas of the lake; the city was firmly in the grip of carnival.

The woman, Doris, was waiting to unpack their trunks when they arrived. Aurore went outside on the gallery jutting over the water while Doris worked. The gallery was nearly as wide as a steamboat's deck, and the view as spectacular as the most colorful river bend. The sun was setting, and purple faded into a thousand subtler shades.

She leaned against the railing, entranced. Geese flew across the sky in a perfect wedge. She had never seen the lake so calm. No sailboats broke the glassy surface of the water; no fish leaped into the air.

"After the wind we had this afternoon, I'm surprised it's so still now."

She hadn't realized Henry had come to stand beside her. It disconcerted her that he could move so quietly. "It's a beautiful sunset, isn't it?"

"It's cold, and far too quiet."

She turned to him and smiled. "It's beautiful, Henry. Enjoy it."

"I wonder, will you spend the rest of your days trying to convince me to think as you do?"

For the first time, she felt the cold, too. "I hope I'll spend them more productively than that."

He was watching her, not the spectacle of the sun's disappearance. "Your eyes are the color of the lake this time of year, just as cool and still. I can almost believe what I see. No passions, no secrets. Nothing to stir the surface."

She had never told him anything about the events that had

scarred her, and she didn't now. "I'm no different than anyone. I have passions and secrets, but none grand enough to worry you."

"No?"

She turned her back to the rail and faced him. "No. But you must know that. You're not a man who'd marry a woman he didn't understand."

"I understand you."

"Well, not completely, I hope. There should be a little mystery, don't you think?"

"None." He fingered a strand of her hair that had come loose from the fashionable high knot that Ti' Boo had arranged. "Tell me exactly why you married me, Rory."

She sensed he would settle for nothing but the truth. "Because you can give me everything I want. And I think I can do the same for you."

"What do I want?"

"Beyond what you told me that first day we talked?" She considered. "You don't want peace, you're not a peaceful man. I don't think the pleasures of hearth and home appeal to you." She considered again. "I think you want a challenge. And I can promise you that."

"A challenge?"

"You would never be happy with a woman who tried to make your life comfortable or simple. You don't want an equal partner, but you don't want a servant."

The image that came to her mind as she spoke was of a gymnasium that Tim had once described. Tim's boxing days were long since over, but he still got into the ring from time to time, just to prove he could. There were men at the gym who made their income fighting others. They weren't content to be pummeled indiscriminately. They were good enough boxers to give back some of what they took, but only some, and then only so that the men who paid them could hone their own skills.

"You want a sparring partner." She hoped he would deny it.

He laughed. "And what do you know of such things, Rory?"

"Enough to see the similarity."

"Right now I just want the woman."

She shivered. The sun was gone now, and Doris must be, too. The house was theirs, and since the reception had been sumptuous, there was no need to eat a meal before they retired.

She sensed that this was no time to act the shy maiden. Henry would relish signs of weakness, and the results would not bode well for the rest of their marriage. Her gaze didn't waver. "The woman is yours."

"I think not. But she soon will be." He stepped closer. His fingers were warm against the back of her neck, and unyielding. She didn't close her eyes when he kissed her, and he didn't close his. She rested her hands on his shoulders, but she didn't push him away. She let him kiss her, let him take greater intimacies with his tongue, without a murmur of protest. Only when she tried to ease her position and found he wouldn't allow it did she feel the first flicker of fear.

Relief filled her when the kiss ended. He put his arm around her waist and guided her toward the house. From a great distance she could hear the honking of geese, but she and Henry were so very alone.

Inside, the lamps had been lit. There was no electricity here, and the softer glow should have been romantic. Instead, it seemed only to blur boundaries, as if nothing in the house were defined. As undefined, perhaps, as what was about to occur.

He left her alone in the guest room to dress for bed. The covers had been turned down, eyelet-trimmed sheets over a sprigged muslin comforter. A small coal fire burned in a decorative corner stove, but the room was still chilly. She undressed hurriedly, slipping into a gown and robe of handkerchief linen she had embroidered herself. She took her hair down at a table by the window. She was brushing it when Henry came into the room.

He stood near the doorway, watching her. He was wearing dark pajamas and half a smile. She turned so that she could see him as she finished. He stood with his weight on his front foot, as if he were ready to spring. She returned his smile, half for half, as she laid her brush on the table. When she separated her hair to braid it, he spoke. "Don't."

She nodded. "All right." She stood and shook it back over her shoulders. He seemed larger, somehow, and completely a stranger. Without the stiffness of a corset encasing her, she felt far too pliable and tempting, like a rag doll at the mercy of a spoiled child.

"Come here, Rory."

She wanted him to come to her, but even more vital, she didn't want him to be angry. She moved toward him, her eyes focused on his. She could read nothing there, neither desire nor a lack of it. He waited, as still as the water outside their window. Then she was in his arms, and no part of him was still.

Only later, when she was naked against him, her hair twisted tightly in his hands to keep her close as he slept, her body bruised and plundered, did she close her eyes and weep.

He had never lied to her. He had told her that he sought power, and she had foolishly accepted it as part of his masculinity. She had believed her own power was great enough to resist him. In the early hours of the morning, Aurore knew she was a fool.

Henry had taken her joylessly twice more in the night, both times just as she had finally relaxed into a restless sleep. He seemed to savor catching her defenseless, sinking into her before she could prepare for the onslaught, pinning her beneath him so that she couldn't adjust for what was to come.

He had poured out obscenities about her lack of virginity, and she had known better than to deny them. She had felt like a virgin, as if this humiliation were the real deflowering and the foolish joy she had felt in Rafe's arms a childhood dream.

She had stared at him in the darkness, willing herself not to cry or cry out. She had made no attempts to refuse him her body, had not even pleaded with him to be gentle. She had borne his abuse with silence and the shreds of her tattered dignity, and just before dawn, when his lust was finally satisfied and he slept, exhausted, she lay quietly beside him and considered what to do next.

Henry knew that she had once had a lover, and when he awoke again, she was certain she would be forced to answer questions.

The truth was a great temptation. Henry would investigate and discover who and what Rafe was. He might even be furious enough to take revenge against him.

Aurore's heart quickened at the thought. As sunrise lightened the sky, she realized that today she hated Rafe more than ever. She felt none of the wistful warmth she had felt at the altar. Rafe had taught her love, made her believe in its mystical possibilities, so that a night in Henry's arms seemed even more of a blasphemy. The desire for revenge was a knot inside her that tightened until she could barely draw a breath. If Henry punished Rafe, then some good would have come of the night.

But if Henry punished Rafe, then Nicolette might be punished, too. Aurore couldn't let that happen. Her child's life was precarious enough. She could only imagine what Nicolette was exposed to in that house, that despicable house on Basin Street. If Rafe wasn't there to offer his protection, what might happen? The day he took Nicolette, he had warned her that if she tried to harm him, she might harm their daughter instead. Now she could see how neatly the trap protected him.

She couldn't be honest with Henry, no matter how much she craved revenge. She had to tell him a lie he might believe, one he could neither prove nor disprove. She had considered this before, but not in depth. She had hoped that Henry wouldn't notice or care that she wasn't a virgin. She was older than the average bride. Surely he had considered the fact that, at twenty-five, she might not be pure.

She still wasn't sure that he cared, but he had noticed. His denouncement might well be a way of gaining control over her, but even so, she still had to answer to him.

She decided to tell him that her lover had been a business acquaintance of her father's, an older man, a European perhaps, and that when she went to him, after Lucien's death, she had discovered that he was already married. Heartbroken by everything that had happened, she had sought solace in travel until her heart was healed enough to allow her to return to New Orleans—which would also explain her long absence.

She would beg for forgiveness, assure Henry that she had only been young and foolish, and that the man had taken advantage of her innocence. She would refuse to give his name, claiming that he was rich and powerful and could create great trouble for Henry if he tried to expose him. She sensed that Henry would like knowing that his wife had once been the mistress of a powerful European, that in Henry's eyes her sins would be at least partially absolved by her good taste.

What to do about the rest of her life was much less clear. She was married to a ruthless man who wanted nothing more than to dominate her completely. She had shut her eyes to the worst truths about Henry, believing that she was strong enough to stand up to him. Now she doubted her strength. He had not won everything he sought last night, but he had already made inroads into her soul. She had to prevent him from destroying her.

She felt him stir beside her, felt his grip tighten on her hair. She turned on her side to stare at him, careful not to let her feelings show. "My wife," he said.

"I would say, my husband, but the words would stick in my throat."

"Don't tell me last night wasn't to your liking?" He smiled; it was a placid, friendly smile. "Were your other lovers better, Rory?"

"There was only one."

"And why should I believe that?"

"Because it's the truth." She didn't shrink away as he slid closer. She made herself return his stare. "I'll tell you about him, if you prefer it that way. Then, perhaps, we can be done with this."

"By all means, tell me."

With no embellishments, she repeated the story she had created. "I was young," she finished. "And ignorant. I made a terrible mistake, but now I ask you to put it behind us. I was wrong not to tell you before we married."

"I would imagine you hadn't yet thought of a story." He released her hair, and his hand traveled to her breast. This morning his fingers were gentle against her bruised skin. "When did this one occur to you? This morning, while I slept?"

She felt him gather her breast in his hand, and then pain streaked through her. "I'm smaller and weaker than you are," she whispered through a haze of tears, "but if you continue to hurt me this way, I'll find a way to hurt you. So help me God."

"Will you? That could be interesting." He didn't release her, but he didn't hurt her again.

"I've told you the truth. Now let me go."

He flattened her against the bed so quickly that she couldn't defend herself. "You've forgotten the truth," he said. "I'm sure that's all. You wouldn't be foolish enough to lie to me, would you, Rory?"

She turned her head and refused to answer.

"I'll tell you why," he continued. "Lies only work if the truth isn't known. And I always know the truth, because I make it my business. Do you see how simple it is?"

She waited for him to violate her. They were married, but what he intended was a violation. And, despite everything, she couldn't dredge up any hatred for him. She had lied to him, and she could never tell him the truth. Which of them was the more despicable?

When he entered her, she was surprised by the absence of pain. He moved slowly, carefully, as if protecting a precious possession. His thumb traced the path of her tears, caressing her cheek with a feather-light touch. She steeled herself for the return of his brutality, but he seduced her with gentleness, murmuring endearments and soothing words. He didn't trap her against him; when she moved, he accommodated himself to her. When she tried to push him away, he took her hands and kissed them.

She was more shocked by his gentleness than she had been by his violence, and more frightened. She was exhausted and distraught, and her thoughts were no longer clear. She felt herself responding to him, like a beaten dog who comes back to lick the hand of its master. She tried to steel herself against this new, deceitful tenderness, but the feel of his body healing what he had hurt was so welcome, she could only relax into gratitude.

He kissed her cheeks, her lips, her earlobes. He whispered apologies and gathered her close, as if true intimacy were his only wish. Her eyelids closed. She could almost believe him, almost convince herself that he'd had a right to his anger and that she had deserved the abuse of last night. When his rhythm quickened, the first tendrils of desire warmed her. Her body, taught to respond by a man she now hated, was responding to another. Her eyes flew open, and she gasped in confusion; she saw victory in his. She tried again to push him away, but her hands only fluttered uselessly against his chest.

She cried out once, surrendering in pleasure what she had refused him in pain.

Afterward he pulled her into his arms and held her close. His body was slick with sweat, and she wanted to move away. Instead, she forced herself to settle against him. She was confused and appalled by her own response, but she knew better than to let him see it. She had not found release, but she had given him far too much.

"I have something for you."

She sighed, fighting back tears. "Do you?"

"A gift. A trinket, really."

"Why should you give me anything? Haven't you already gotten what you wanted?"

"Consider it a reward of sorts." He moved away, and she felt only gratitude. She watched him stride to the armoire where Doris had hung his clothes. He took something from the pocket of his coat before he returned. She sat up, searching for the gown he had stripped away the night before, but he turned back the covers, burying it somewhere beneath them. She was icy-cold. The fire had gone out, and the sun hadn't yet warmed the room, but when she reached for the covers he blocked her.

He held out his hand. "For you."

She was trembling—whether from exposure or from the accumulation of emotions, she wasn't sure. She held out her hand in response and watched it waver.

He unclasped his fingers until his hand was flat in front of her. A locket lay against his palm.

She drew her hand back sharply.

"Don't you want it, Rory? I thought you might."

She raised her eyes to his and saw that there was no use in lying. "How did you get it?"

"Stories are better if they start with 'Once upon a time,' but I *will* tell you that a certain madam in the district is easily bribed."

She wondered if he knew everything, or if he was making guesses, hoping she would confirm them. "Just tell me you didn't hurt her." She pleaded with her eyes. "Tell me she's all right."

"Who, Rory?"

She spoke her daughter's name through a lump in her throat.

"Nicolette," he murmured, as if savoring the word. "She's a sassy little thing. She's allowed in the whorehouse parlor sometimes, I understand, to entertain the gentlemen."

"Bastard!"

"You've aimed your little insult at the wrong target, haven't you? Your daughter is the bastard—a light-skinned nigger bastard, at that. And her father's the same."

"If you hurt her..."

"Finish the sentence." He stroked her cheek. "I think you've forgotten which of us is vulnerable."

She didn't flinch. "Why did you marry me if you knew?"

"I married you *because* I knew."

She understood then just how far-reaching his quest for power was. He had chosen her because she had a secret he could expose if she fought his control. Her secret, as much as her name and her bloodline, had made her the perfect choice as his wife.

She had only one chance to turn this around, to make the rest of her life tolerable instead of the hell her mother had endured. One terrible chance, and if she waited, it would be over. "There's one thing you didn't understand."

"Enlighten me."

"You've badly overestimated what you can do to me."

"Have I? I can expose you for what you are. I know at first I might be tainted, too. But when the gossip dies down, I'll be the martyr and you'll be the outcast. I might lose a little respect, but you'll lose everything."

"You still don't understand." She lifted her head higher. "I have nothing to lose."

"You have Gulf Coast. Do you think you could stay in the city and continue to run it? You would be banned from every social and business gathering. No one would help you. No one would patronize you. In a matter of months, Gulf Coast would be gone."

"I see that." She forced herself to appear calm. "And maybe that would be best."

"There is nowhere you could go, Rory, where your secret wouldn't follow. Be sure of that."

"There are places where my secret would only make me more attractive. Places like Paris, places far away from you and your bed, Henry. And if I'm not in your bed, how will you get the sons you want so badly? This is a Catholic city, and even if your interest in the church is political, you have to respect its laws. You can't divorce me, no matter what I've done, and I don't believe my past is good enough reason for annulment."

He smiled. "I knew you had courage. I didn't realize the full extent. But you've forgotten. I know where your daughter lives. I know who your lover was. And I can affect their lives."

She suppressed a shudder. "Why should I care if you affect Rafe Cantrelle's life?"

She waited one heartbeat, two. There was no change in his expression, but she thought her words had given him pause. "When you were delving into my past, did you discover how much I hate him?" she asked.

He inclined his head, as if to see her from a different perspective.

"I would like to see him punished for what he did to me, but Nicolette is innocent, and I don't believe in hurting children."

"You love her."

"No. I have feelings for her. She's my child. But if I loved her, don't you think I would have kept her? I could have found a way. So make no mistakes when you measure the lengths you would have to go to hurt me. Nicolette is a weapon you have at your disposal, but not of the magnitude you hoped for. And if you harm her, I'll retaliate."

He laughed.

She lowered her voice. "On the blood of my unborn children, I swear to you that whatever you do to my daughter, I will do to a son of yours."

"You're insane."

"Like my mother before me." She smiled, though she felt sick. "There are things I want from you, Henry. If you give them to me, I'll stay with you of my own free will and be a model wife and mother. I want Gulf Coast rebuilt. I want children, and whatever kind of life we can make together. But if you harm my daughter or try to ruin me, you'll find you've married a demon!"

He stared at her, as if gauging her performance. Her own words swirled in her head until she didn't know which were true and which were lies. She only knew she was fighting for what was left of her life, just as she would have to fight him every day of the rest of it.

Finally he reached for her hand and put the locket in it, closing her fingers around it. "We'll see."

"Yes. We will." She saw that his eyes were the same untroubled green, but she thought she saw admiration there. Of course, like everything else about him, it could be a lie, or only a portion of the truth.

CHAPTER 24

Aurore looked down at the sleeping child in the Silver Cross perambulator Henry had ordered from England. Hugh's hair spread like silk tassels against the linen cover. His hair was a lighter brown than her own, but when his eyes were open, they were the same pale blue. There was nothing of his father in his face, as if Henry hadn't even been present at her son's conception. She spoke to the woman beside her. "Do you have anything to tell me today?"

"A thing or two."

Aurore reached into her handbag and pulled out a folded bill. She laid it on Hugh's cover. Since her marriage, she was no longer as concerned about money. The merger of Gulf Coast with Gerritsen Barge Lines had been a success, even if her merger with Henry had been a failure.

Lettie Sue stepped forward as if to admire the white woman's baby and slipped the money inside her dress. "Business's down. Ain't half so many men coming, and two of the whores got sent packin'. They's a couple streets over in a parlor house now."

"Why? Do you know?"

Lettie Sue shrugged. Her shoulders and arms were as substantial as cypress trees from years of scrubbing floors and washing clothes. In contrast, her neck was long and graceful, and the shape of her head under the colorful *tignon* that hid her hair was majestic. "Don't know. Mebbe the men are gettin' tired of payin' for what they can git for free if they's just nicer to their women."

"Or if they threaten or hurt them badly enough." Aurore stared at her son.

"Ma'am?"

"What else have you noticed, Lettie Sue?"

"You wanna hear about Mr. Rafe?"

Aurore leaned forward to straighten Hugh's covers. He smiled in his sleep, but she didn't smile back. "Yes."

"He's not there much. Girls say that's just as well. Mr. Rafe keeps things quiet, and the girls don't like that. Girl gets sick or goes a little crazy, Mr. Rafe sends her off."

"Where does he go?"

"Don't know. Comes back most nights, though. Didn't used to, but now he does. Little girl of his, she's a sassy child."

Aurore pondered what Lettie Sue had told her. Henry didn't know that Aurore kept track of Rafe's activities. But even though she had a new house and a baby, Nicolette was constantly on her mind. She had found Lettie Sue, who kept house at the Magnolia Palace, and she paid her well to bring back information about everything that went on there.

Lettie Sue was desperately poor, and much too astute to be a perfect source. Aurore knew she couldn't show more than a passing interest in news about Nicolette, or Lettie Sue might deduce why she cared.

She risked a question now. "Trouble? What do you mean?"

"Does what she wants. Goes here. Goes there. Found her hiding under a tablecloth in the parlor last week, just so she could listen to Professor Clarence play his music. Mr. Rafe's locked her in her room every night since."

Aurore didn't dare reply. She stared at Hugh, willing herself not to show any emotion. "Anything else of interest?"

"What you want to know all this for, Miss Gerritsen?"

In the months that Lettie Sue had been reporting to her, Aurore had waited for this question. Lettie Sue wasn't looking directly at her, since any white woman would consider that insubordinate, but there had been a challenge in her tone.

"I won't lie," Aurore said. "I want the district closed down, and so do a lot of other women in New Orleans. It will close. It's just a matter of time. You might as well make as much money answering questions as you can now."

"What's finding out about Mr. Rafe got to do with closing down the district?"

"The more we know about what happens inside the houses, the sooner we'll get our wish."

"Mr. Rafe wouldn't like it, he knew you was asking questions."

Aurore understood Lettie Sue, and wished she could tell her so. She knew what it was like to have to measure every step toward security and every mile away from it. "No. And he'd like it less if he knew you'd answered my questions. I'll be sure he knows it was you, Lettie Sue, if it ever comes to that."

"Nic'lette don't have a mama. I tell you that?"

"You did. Some time ago."

"Always wondered what happened to her mama."

Aurore's voice didn't waver. "You have to ask? A woman's lucky to survive a year in a house like that."

"You close down the district, I ain't got no place to work."

"I'll find you work when that happens, but I don't help anybody I can't trust."

"You can trust me."

Aurore's friends, the young New Orleans matrons who served on committees with her and chattered gaily in the call-out sections of the best carnival balls, would have said that Lettie Sue was like all blacks who didn't have a large enough dose of civilizing white blood, that her Christian exterior barely hid the African heart of a voodoo priestess. But Aurore understood what made Lettie Sue the woman she was, and she knew how closely she was bound to her. Under their thin veneers, they were sisters.

"You'd better go now. We've talked long enough." Aurore grasped the carriage and began to push. "If you have anything to tell me again, you know how to reach me."

"Yes'm."

Aurore pushed the carriage down the path that wandered through Audubon Park. She came here often. The park, once the site of a sugar plantation, had always served the city well, and it served Aurore better. Under the massive live oaks dripping with Spanish moss, she could escape the scrutiny of her husband and the servants he paid to keep watch over her.

She had nearly reached the lagoon where she would rest before she dared a look behind her. Lettie Sue had vanished.

While Hugh slept on, she spread a quilt in the dappled sunshine beside the lagoon. Ducks filed past, and a crow just as large cawed to her from the low-hanging branch of a tree before it flew away. Far in the distance, from the direction of the zoo, she thought she could hear the trumpeting of an elephant. Henry disapproved of her taking Hugh there, but she had, twice, and would continue to. She wanted her son to learn everything about the world except what sadness it could hold.

She stripped off her gloves. The April sun was warm against her bare arms, and she removed her hat to let it warm her face. She sat on the blanket, covering her white-stockinged legs with her skirts, and thought about everything Lettie Sue had said.

She hadn't seen her daughter, not even from a distance, since her marriage to Henry. She was carefully watched, and going to Basin Street would enrage him. Despite her threats, Aurore knew that if Henry thought her sins were serious enough, he would punish her by hurting Nicolette. She had to content herself with Lettie Sue's information, as scant as it was. At least she knew that Nicolette was alive and still in New Orleans.

It wasn't enough. Everything that Lettie Sue had reported churned through her mind. Nicolette was a troublesome child, so much trouble that her father had to return home each night to supervise her.

Aurore could imagine the lively, spirited child she had so briefly held on her lap alone in a locked room. Nicolette's spirit could be destroyed by isolation, if it hadn't already been destroyed by proximity to the evils of Basin Street. Which was worse, her daughter alone and frightened, or her daughter in the clutches of the men who frequented the Magnolia Palace? Men like Aurore's own husband.

Alone in the sunshine, she gave in to the tears that Henry never saw her cry. She had thought the birth of another child would fill the empty space inside her. How could she have fooled herself? How could she not have realized that having Hugh would only expand the wound? That watching him grow, watching every sweet, indescribably perfect thing her son did, would remind her that she had lost these years with her daughter and would lose all the years to come?

Her cheeks were still wet when he awoke. He didn't fuss. He always announced he was awake with laughter. He was only five months old, and he had probably been conceived during the horror of her wedding night. But she was closer to him than she had ever been to another human being. When he was out of her sight, she felt as if part of her were missing.

She lifted him from the pram and smiled through her tears. "Mama's dearest," she said softly. "Did you have a good nap?"

He cooed at the sight of her, batting his hands against her nose and mouth as if he were asking her to smile. Already he could make noises that sounded as if he were calling her.

She had refused to find a wet nurse for him. She wanted her son to be nourished on her milk, and although Henry had threatened her, she had stood firm. She had agreed to let Cleo watch over him when she couldn't be there. But she, and she alone, fed him. Surprisingly, Henry had given in, although he delighted in keeping her from Hugh when it was feeding time. He was not pleased with their son. Hugh's good nature seemed to prove that the child had none of the spunk a son should evidence.

Aurore changed him, then settled back on the quilt to nurse him. No one was about, except a Negro nurse with two small children several hundred yards away. She was well hidden by trees and shrubbery, and she threw a shawl over her shoulders and wrapped Hugh in its folds for modesty. As his tiny lips began to pull at her breast, she shut her eyes and willed herself to believe that, someday, loving this child would grow to be enough.

Somewhere in the distance, Rafe heard the trumpeting of an elephant. He took two dollars from his pocket. "Don't bother coming to work tomorrow. Duchess doesn't want spies working for her." He handed the money to Lettie Sue. "That's what you're owed. And don't look for a job anywhere else on Basin Street. You won't find one."

"I never told that lady nothing that mattered," Lettie Sue said. She didn't look down. She stared straight in his eyes. "I was just makin' a little money. Don't get paid enough for what I do. I can't feed my children meat no more, just beans and rice. And they git tired of beans."

"You should have come to me if you needed more money."

Lettie Sue gave a harsh laugh. "Why? So's you could work me twice as hard and give me half as much? You think you're something, Mr. Rafe. Struttin' 'round this town like you owned it. But you're the same as me, not one drop better, even if your skin's whiter. You don't remember what it's like to be poor. Somebody oughta beat you good and make you remember!"

He started around her, but she grabbed his arm. "No, you're not the same as me," she said. "You're not half so good. I take care of my children, give 'em whatever I can. I take 'em to church and send 'em to school, and at night, Mr. Rafe, I put them in bed and listen to their prayers. You treat that little girl of yours like she was the devil. Well, she ain't no devil. She's a little girl, same as mine, and someday, when my children remember me and feel sad 'cause I'm dead, Nic'lette won't feel nothing about you. She won't even remember what you looked like!" She dropped his arm, then she wiped her fingers on her apron.

He walked on, but he heard her spit on the path behind him.

He had followed Lettie Sue to the park. This morning she had gone to the duchess with one more in a long series of trumped-up excuses to leave the house, and he had become suspicious. Aurore had not come near the Magnolia Palace in the past year, at least, not to his knowledge. But he doubted she had given up watching over the daughter she hadn't wanted to keep. Now he knew for sure that Aurore had been using Lettie Sue to gather information. Aurore was here, in this park with her new baby, a child whose skin was white enough to suit her.

He hadn't come to confront her. He did that in his dreams, angry, violent dreams in which he forced her to listen as he detailed Lucien's sins. Revenge was a strange thing. He had thought that seeing the Gulf Coast empire burn would give him victory over his hatred of Lucien. Then he had thought that taking Nicolette would give him victory over Aurore. Instead, in his dreams he raged and swore, and for what? Understanding? Did it still matter that Aurore learn why he had acted as he had?

Aurore was married now, to a man despised by all those Gulf Coast employed. Rafe had heard stories about Henry Gerritsen, both from men he had known when he worked on the river and from the women who worked at Magnolia Palace. The duchess claimed that when Henry Gerritsen visited he paid well, but not a woman wanted him in her bed. He was cruel, but never quite cruel enough to bar from the house. He was too powerful to trifle with, and a friend to those who were even more so.

Aurore had chosen to marry someone like her father, more transparent perhaps, but with the same soulless disregard for others. If Rafe had forced her into this marriage, then his revenge had been even more complete.

And yet still he dreamed of her.

He walked in the direction he had seen her go. He wanted her to know that she had no listening ear at the Magnolia Palace now, that Nicolette no longer wore her locket or even remembered that one had been given to her. He yearned to see Aurore in defeat one more time. Perhaps then the dreams would stop.

He found her in a sheltered grotto where she sat on a blanket, holding her baby in her arms. She was the very picture of young motherhood, dressed in the softest lilac, with lace ribbons woven into her collar. The intervening years seemed to have left no mark; if anything, she was more beautiful. He stood silently and watched her for a long time before she looked up.

He saw her cheeks flush with color. She didn't hurry to cover herself more thoroughly with the shawl; she didn't straighten her dress to hide her ankles. She stared at him, and her gaze never wavered. "So," she said finally. "You know."

"Lettie Sue no longer works at the Palace."

"There are better jobs than keeping house for thieves and whores."

"I suppose she'll find out if that's true."

"I'll find her a place with one of my friends."

"A legitimate whore? A useless creature who gets on her back for her husband twice a week and does her Catholic duty?"

"The word is *wife*—one you're probably not familiar with."

He leaned against a tree and folded his arms. "My daughter no longer has your little gift."

She looked down at her son. "I know."

"Do you? Do you know she has no memory of you, or of it, either? What had you hoped to accomplish, Aurore? Had you thought to make her love you a little? How could she love the woman who abandoned her at birth?"

He got the reaction he'd hoped for. She flinched and grew paler. "You haven't told her that?"

"Haven't I?"

She put her son over her shoulder and began to pat him. She looked at Rafe again. The defiance in her eyes had waned a little. "You hate her so much that you'd hurt her that way?"

He wanted to tell her that he hated Nicolette's mother that much, but something inside him refused. He didn't answer.

"She has so little. You've given her almost nothing. Not a mother to love her, not a home where she can be safe and secure. Nothing of yourself. Isn't there anything inside you to give our daughter?"

"How can you ask? Don't you remember who I am and what I've done?"

"She's beautiful. You know I saw her. Do you know I held her on my lap? Just for a moment." Her voice caught. She looked over his shoulder, as if she couldn't meet his gaze. "She looks like you. But there's a little of me in her, too."

"Inconvenient for you. That might make it harder to deny her again, if the opportunity arises."

"If I had the opportunity, I would take her and run away!"

"You had that opportunity."

"And I'll pay forever...for not having done it."

"She's dead to you. Don't try to see her anymore, and don't pay anyone else to answer your questions. If you don't want Nicolette to know that her mother gave her away because she wasn't good enough to keep, then stay away from her."

She squeezed her eyes shut. "How can you? No matter how much you hate me, how can you think of hurting her that way?"

"It's the truth."

"A part of it, and I hate myself for it." She opened her eyes, and they were filled with tears. "You're all she has now. Can't you stop trying to hurt me? What's to become of our daughter? I know as much about her as you do. I've spied and lied to find out about her, but she lives with you, and you know nothing!"

"I know she's too much like her mother."

She gasped. "No! She's a wonderful little girl, full of spirit and laughter and music, and you lock her in her room like an animal! Do you know her dreams? Do you care that she's living in the most depraved area of the city? That she's growing up to think that whores and the men who frequent them are normal?"

He pushed himself away from the tree and turned. He had said everything. He started back the way he had come, but her words followed him. "How soon before she sells herself, too, Rafe? And why wouldn't she? There's no one who loves her! She doesn't know what it's like to have a mother or father touch her in love! She'll look for it from the first man who smiles at her, just like I did! She deserves better!"

He could hear her sobbing now. The baby began to cry, too, upset by his mother's distress. "How can you hate her so?" she sobbed. "How can you?"

He still heard her questions when he was nearly a mile away. Although he walked faster, ignoring the streetcar that thundered past, her questions kept pace.

He didn't hate Nicolette, although he hated her mother. He made sure his daughter had enough to eat and a warm place to sleep. He isolated her from the worst depravities of the Magnolia Palace, and as landlord there he made certain that the Palace was as clean and safe a house as any on Basin Street. He had done more for her than her mother had been willing to do. At least he did not pretend she was someone else's child.

But he did not give anything of himself to her, and he never had. Aurore's final words haunted him. The picture of his daughter searching for love in the arms of a stranger haunted him.

The afternoon sun was high overhead by the time he reached Basin Street. He was assaulted by the fragrance of sweet olive and the tinkling of an out-of-tune piano at the end of the block. He passed a house with three yawning residents in dressing gowns on the front stoop, and one of the women called to him.

At the Magnolia Palace he heard children's voices behind the house. He moved quietly toward the back, avoiding the crunch of oyster shells under his shoes. Beside the back gallery, in the shade of a magnolia, he watched his daughter at play.

Her middy dress flapped against her bare knees as she ran, screaming with laughter, from tree to tree. Violet, skirts hitched above her ankles, chased her, and Tony Pete, busy weeding the garden, made the occasional pretend grab as she passed. Nicolette's curls flew in disarray, and she was smudged with dirt.

She darted not more than twenty feet from the tree where he stood. Only when she was well past did she stop and turn to look at him. He watched her laughter die and the sparkle in her eyes disappear. He saw fear take its place.

He remembered fear in the eyes of a child so much like this one. Angelle had been frightened in the boat. He remembered the way she had clung to his mother until she could cling no longer. He shut his eyes, but he could see Nicolette still. Nicolette, who looked so much like his adored sister.

"I'm sorry, Mr. Rafe."

He opened his eyes and saw Violet standing in front of him. She was not pretending to be a little girl today. She *was* a little girl, far too young to be working in a whorehouse. Far too young to have discovered how casual and cruel the world could be. "Go inside and pack," he said.

"But we were only playing. No one complained about the noise."

"Pack and wait for me in the azalea parlor. I have a better job for you."

She tilted her head. For the first time he saw how beautiful she really was. He wondered which would weigh heavi- est against her in the years to come, her beauty, her years at the Palace, or the drop of Negro blood that made her less than human in the eyes of white society.

She seemed to think better of questioning him. She sought out Nicolette with her eyes; then she started toward the house. Nicolette approached him slowly. She scuffed her toe along the ground when she was just in front of him. "Please don't make Violet go away," she said. "I'll stay in my room all the time if you just don't make her go."

"Look at me."

She did, and he could see it was a great act of courage. Defi- ance shone in her eyes, the final defiance of a cornered animal.

He squatted in front of her so that they were face-to-face. The world looked very different from this angle. For the first time in many years, he remembered how it had looked as a boy.

"You can't live here anymore, Nicolette. It's not proper. I have a house below Canal Street where I'm going to take you. I'm going to ask Violet if she'll come and take care of you there. Would you like that?"

Her face puckered in a frown. Already she was looking for the trap behind anything that was said to her. "Violet can come?"

"Yes. If she wants to."

"Will the men visit her there?"

"No men will visit."

"What kind of house?"

"A small, pretty house." He couldn't think of anything else to say. He didn't know how to talk to her.

"Just Violet and me?"

"No. I'll live there, too."

Her eyes narrowed. "And the duchess?"

"No."

"Clarence, too?"

He shook his head. "Clarence can visit."

"Then we'll need a piano." She moved a little closer.

"We'll buy a piano. It's time you started lessons."

"Lessons?"

"Yes. Music lessons. And you'll need a tutor, too. You have to learn to read, don't you?"

"I already read. I'd rather go to school."

"Maybe."

She looked down at her feet. "I'll be very good."

"No, you won't. You'll run and scream and do everything you want as soon as my back is turned."

"Only sometimes."

He laughed softly. He didn't know where the sound had come from. He thought all the laughter inside him had withered years before. He stretched out his hand and touched her cheek with the backs of his fingers. She flinched.

He stroked carefully until she relaxed a little. She had not backed away, but only because she was filled with courage. His daughter, a valiant, rowdy brat-child who was his only tie to a world he had given up on.

He stood and turned his back on her, but having gained ground, she wouldn't retreat so easily. "What about Tony Pete?"

"You'll make new friends."

"I want Tony Pete to come, too."

He turned his head. She looked down at the ground again.

For the barest part of a second he saw Aurore in her, the woman at the lagoon, impotent, but never truly defeated. "There might be something for Tony Pete to do there," he agreed.

He left before she could ask anything else, but he didn't know who he was really trying to escape—his daughter, or his daughter's mother.

CHAPTER 25

"Rafe moved Nicolette away from Storyville after our encounter. She was still very young. As she grew up, I don't know what she remembered about those days. But she was a resilient child...."

Aurore watched Phillip, who very soon into their session had abandoned the love seat for the window. He was staring at the garden beyond. He didn't speak.

"There's more to the story," she said. "I suppose you think that you know everything you were meant to. But you don't. Not yet."

He faced her, his arms crossed in front of him. He was so much like his grandfather, but she would not tell him so. Telling him was a gift he wouldn't appreciate. Not yet.

"Your reasons for wanting me to write your story never rang true." He didn't move toward her. Aurore thought that perhaps he was afraid to be too close, as if he couldn't trust himself. "I knew there was more to this than you were telling me. I thought something interesting might come of it."

"But you never expected this."

"Why?"

There were a thousand whys, and a thousand answers. She didn't know which question he had asked, so she chose the only one she wanted to answer now.

"If I had called you and told you I was your grandmother, would you have agreed to come and talk to me?"

He stiffened when she said the words, as if he had hoped, wildly, foolishly, that his conclusions had been wrong. "I don't know."

"Neither did I. This was the only way I could be sure you would." She held up her hand to silence him as he started to speak. "But I never lied to you about wanting this story told. There are things you still don't understand. More than I can tell in a day, or a week. You are not my only grandchild. I have another. And someday, with your help, Dawn will understand it all, too."

His eyes blazed with anger. "What makes you think I want to help you? Blood ties? Do you think you've told me anything I'd want to repeat? Do you think I feel honored being part of your family or your race? That I feel more human somehow?"

"And what about your mother, Phillip?"

"What about her? Shall I tell her that her mother didn't die at her birth after all? That she's a rich white lady who's sorrier than she can say that she didn't love her enough to be a mother to her? Did you imagine that I'd intercede for you? That I'd help you plan a reunion?"

"Nothing like that." Her hands were folded in her lap. She resisted twisting them.

"What, then?"

"If I was certain that knowing this would be good for Nicolette—"

"Don't call her that. Her name's Nicky. It's been Nicky for decades. Nicky Valentine."

"And once it was Clarissa."

"You didn't have the right to name her!"

She wasn't surprised that pain could lie dormant for half a century, only to torture her again. The voice was Rafe's, and so was the sentiment.

"If I was certain knowing this would be good for your mother,

I would have told her myself. But I'm not sure of anything, except that *you* must hear the rest."

"You're doing this to ease your conscience, aren't you? Confession is good for the soul? Well, maybe it's good for yours, but it's not good for mine." He scooped his recorder off the table, jerking the plug from the wall as he did. He was nearly to the door when she made her final plea.

"And if you do tell your mother someday, Phillip, what will you tell her? Part of a story? Will that satisfy her, do you think? Or will she want to know it all?"

"If she wants to hear more, she can come to you herself."

"I won't be here. I'm dying, Phillip. The doctors say I may have six months. I may not. And at the end, there are no guarantees that I'll be able to think clearly or express my thoughts."

"So this is a deathbed confession, or nearly?"

"It's not a confession. I'm not trying to purify my soul before I die. If an afterlife exists, I'll gladly take my punishment. But I see no reason to punish those who've come after me. I know things that can change the lives of my children and my grandchildren. I've been a terrible coward all my life, but this is my last attempt at courage."

He didn't turn, but he paused, as if considering her words. She supposed it was the most she could expect.

"Please come back. When you're ready," she added after a moment.

The room had been empty for some time when she rose and went to the window. She stared, as Phillip had, at the view. Crepe-myrtle limbs rustled in the breeze, and a delivery truck passed on the side street.

It was the small things that made dying so hard. The way sunshine dappled the grass under the thick canopy of live oaks. Blue jays screeching from telephone wires. Air as lush, as soft, as velvet.

Phillip would return. He was a man who lived his life for answers. That passion, that drive for the truth would not desert him now. She thought of Rafe, a man as intelligent, as gifted, as his grandson. She wished with all her heart that Phillip had known him.

She was a woman who could study Eastern religion on the same day she attended mass and never see a conflict. Years ago she had become entranced by the idea of reincarnation. She had imagined herself born again into another body. She had imagined finding Rafe again, marrying him, proudly bearing his children, no matter what the obstacles.

Then she had learned that those who believed in reincarnation also believed that people were reborn with all their faults—as well as their strengths—intact. She could be a coward into eternity.

The dream of reincarnation had died, but not the vision of her own cowardice. She could not resurrect Rafe. She could not start anew with him, no matter how much she wished it. But she could act, in what was left of this life, to right the wrongs she had done.

That much she could do for Rafe, and for herself, no matter who or what awaited her when her eyes closed for the last time.

Belinda wore red, a red so vivid and pure that her skin glowed in response. The dress was just tight enough, the neckline just low enough, to dispel all images of Miss Beauclaire, the kindergarten teacher. Her long legs were clad in dark, textured stockings, and rhinestones flashed in her earlobes.

Phillip wore the same clothes he had worn since that morning. After leaving Aurore Gerritsen's house, he had walked through the streets of New Orleans for hours. He had walked through neighborhoods where his very presence was suspicious, and others where the color of his skin was the only passport he needed.

"You don't look like a man who wants to go out this evening," Belinda said.

Phillip suddenly remembered that he had asked Belinda to go to Club Valentine tonight. Now he had no desire to face the crowds or his mother. He wondered if Mrs. Gerritsen realized that from this moment on, every time he looked at Nicky, he would remember what he knew of her past and wonder what he should do about it.

"You sit on the sofa. Now." Belinda pointed to the corner. "I'll be back."

He took the offered seat, sank down in the cushions and rested his head against the back. The dark sapphire walls were as comforting as a womb, and the faint fragrance of incense as familiar as his own heartbeat. He had stayed away for hours, walked through streets he had never lived on, just to find some small measure of peace.

All he'd had to do was come back to Belinda's.

"Here."

He opened his eyes. Belinda was holding out a drink. He took it gratefully, knocking back half of it before he even registered the flavor of good bourbon.

"Have you had anything to eat since breakfast?"

"You've been taking care of people all your life. You don't have to take care of me."

"It gets to be a habit." She left again. When she returned, she had cold boiled shrimp and the sections of a fresh orange.

She set the plate on the table beside him and joined him on the sofa. "Do you want me to change and make dinner here?"

"No. I'll be okay in a few minutes."

"Hard day?"

He'd had a thousand hard days. He'd been in Philadelphia, Mississippi, when the bodies of the three slain civil rights workers were found, and at Arlington Cemetery when Jack Kennedy was buried. He'd been denied service in a Virginia restaurant on the evening of Martin Luther King's speech at the Lincoln Memorial, and jailed, briefly, in Birmingham. Never, at any point along the way, had he expected anyone to make him feel better.

Sometimes a man got more than he asked for.

He set down his glass and pulled her close. Her perfume had the same spicy notes as the incense she burned. He was reminded of Asian and African markets, and exotic, veiled women.

"This town needs a revolution," he said.

"You know a town that doesn't?"

"You've lived here all your life. Do you really see the way things are? I walked down streets today where the guard dogs are specifically trained to attack Negroes. An old man I passed told me that. It was meant to be a warning."

"Had a neighbor once who trained her Doberman to bark at white people, just for spite. Little kids on the street could pet it, dog would wag his stump of a tail and slobber for affection. White man passed by, he'd snap and strain against that chain, hoping for a white-man steak for dinner." She kissed his hair. "You want to tell me what's got you planning battles in the streets?"

"I feel impotent."

"Now, I can say a word or two about that."

He smiled, despite his heavy heart. "Why did you stay here, Belinda? Why didn't you move out and on? You got a good education. You could have gone north or west."

"To the promised land?" She clucked her tongue in disbelief. "Never believed that, and I still don't. Can you really tell me it's better anywhere than it is here? That when you're in New York or San Francisco, people look at you and see a man first? I understand what's happening here. I don't have to get used to a whole new kind of racism. And when I teach my little boys and girls who they are, what they have to do to be proud, I know exactly what I've got to say."

"And that's why you stayed?"

"This is my home. Nobody's chasing me out. This town belongs to me as much as it does to anyone. And I can make a difference here."

The words were an echo of something Nicky had said to Phillip years before. He had questioned her decision to live in New Orleans, and she had replied that she didn't know a place that needed her more. Her music could open doors.

It had, too. Club Valentine had been open to Negro and white from the moment the sign went up, even though that kind of racial mixing wasn't strictly legal. Whites had stayed away at first, but they had begun to trickle in when the lure of Nicky's artistry became too potent. One small building on Basin Street had been integrated before the public schools, the swimming pools and the lunch counters.

He realized that he wanted to see Nicky tonight, after all. He wanted to see her standing on that Basin Street stage, the object of praise and outright devotion. He wanted to watch her there and know that nothing Aurore Gerritsen had done to her had dimmed his mother's bright spirit.

He wanted to figure out what to do from here.

"I suppose you think I'm crazy," Belinda said.

"No. I think you've already figured out things I've never even thought about."

"Glad to share my wisdom."

"You share more than that. You share everything. Why?"

"You haven't figured that out yet, either?"

"You don't get much in the bargain."

"I get you. Sometimes. So far, that's been good enough." She stood. "I can make that dinner."

"No, let me change, and we'll go."

"Before you go looking for your things, I made room in my closet and hung your clothes next to mine. You can fold them and put them back in your suitcase if you want. It's up to you."

He watched every step Belinda took as she left the room. His mother moved with the same proud grace. Phillip had never expected to meet a woman who held her head as high as Nicky held hers. But this woman did.

And so, despite everything she'd confessed today, did an old woman on Prytania Street.

Club Valentine was already crowded when they arrived. The fragrances of red beans and boiling crawfish debated the fine points of Creole cuisine. They were seated at a table near the stage before Jake found them. He kissed Belinda, then ordered some of everything for them before they could protest.

"Stuffed artichokes are particularly good," Jake said, flopping down beside Belinda. "And the crab came out of some bayou south of here just this morning."

"Where's Nicky?" Phillip asked. He called her by her first name as often as he called her anything else. Neither of them knew exactly how it had happened. It had always been that way.

"She doesn't like to come out before she sings. Too many requests. But I'll tell her you're here."

"Might as well let us surprise her."

"She'll be glad you're here. Last night she's headlining for a while. We've got a group from Savannah coming in tomorrow. She's ready for a break before Mardi Gras. Place will really be hopping then."

Nicky's upcoming break made it a perfect time to tell her that Aurore Gerritsen was her mother, of course. She would have some time to assimilate it, to decide what, if anything, to do about seeing Mrs. Gerritsen. But Phillip couldn't imagine passing on that bit of news to her. Not until he knew more.

He was going to have to go back and hear the rest.

"Phillip?"

He looked at Belinda and saw that Jake was gone.

"What's going on? You were staring off into space, and I know it's not that woman over there in the purple dress that's got your attention."

"How do you know?"

Her laugh was deep and rich, café brûlot on a steamy honeysuckle night. "Because you're with me." She rested her hand on his. "How about some company to get your mind off your troubles?"

"You're sitting there, aren't you?"

"Some friends of mine just walked in, and we've got room. We can share some of that food Jake ordered." At his nod, she stood up and caught the attention of two couples waiting near the doorway that led into the bar. Phillip stood when they reached the table. None of them were familiar, and it occurred to him how little he knew about Belinda's life when he was away from her.

Introductions were made, and everyone was seated. Sam and Vivian were a striking couple in their early thirties, and from the conversation, it was clear this was a rare night away from their two children. Sam was a junior high school principal, and Viv designed and sewed costumes for carnival floats, something she could do while their children were in school.

Debby and Jackson weren't married. Debby, who looked like a

teenager, taught sixth-graders at Belinda's school, and Jackson worked in a bank. They were an unlikely couple, Jackson with a bulky, powerful physique suited for a Mississippi River long-shoreman, and tiny Debby, who didn't weigh as much as a bale of cotton. But from the way Jackson hovered over her, it was clear that he intended to make their relationship permanent.

"We've heard about you," Sam said. "Belinda's told us about your work, and I read your interview with Martin Luther King last fall. Very impressive."

Phillip was used to hearing that his work was impressive. He wasn't used to hearing that Belinda had told anyone about him. He wondered how the subject had come up, and exactly how she had characterized their relationship.

The food arrived with a round of drinks for everyone, and the talk was as satisfying as the crawfish. Phillip hadn't really been in the mood for company. He had met most of the local people who were active in civil rights, and some of those who were vehemently opposed, as well. But he'd never had a desire to make friends in New Orleans or to involve himself in any way in daily life here. As the evening progressed, however, he found himself warming up to the two couples. He had rarely experienced this instant camaraderie.

Watching Belinda with people who obviously cared about her gave him new insight, too. She blossomed under their attention, like a flower preening in the sunshine. He hadn't even noticed how quiet she was tonight until she wasn't quiet anymore. As he watched her, he realized how much he had come to depend on her understanding, and how little understanding she demanded of him. She was a complex woman, but her complexity was part of her charm. He could live with her forever, delve into her mind and soul for a hundred years, and there would still be uncharted depths.

Nicky's band played for most of an hour before she finally appeared. The club, always crowded, was busier tonight than Phillip had ever seen it. Mardi Gras was still weeks away, but the carnival season was in full swing. By the time Nicky came out onstage, the celebration was at a high pitch.

Nicky, dressed in an emerald satin sheath, took the mike off the stand. "Now all you good people got to simmer down just a bit so you can hear what I've got to tell you."

The room went wild. It was always this way. Phillip had seen his mother perform beneath the harsh glare of a bare light bulb, as well as the diamond light of a dozen crystal chandeliers. Always, sometime during the evening, when the crowd realized the immensity of her talent, there would be a tribute like this one.

This crowd knew exactly what they would be getting. Nicky was theirs. She belonged to them, a child of Storyville, a child of their beloved city. It was the New Orleans in her voice that had made her famous, and the New Orleans in her voice that made them love her.

She launched into a song, her own rendition of "Heatwave," obviously aware that they wouldn't quiet down until she did.

There was an edge to the excitement tonight, an electricity that crackled through the crowd. In the past, Phillip had always avoided the carnival season in New Orleans, but now he felt its effects. Carnival was a primal, emotional celebration, and that spirit infused the room tonight. Everyone was reaching for something, for a brief taste of joy, for a connection, for sustenance. Lent was learning to live without, but carnival was asking and receiving. And tonight the patrons of Club Valentine were asking Nicky to fill the holes in their lives with her talent and her presence.

"She's the best," Viv said, during the applause. "And the best thing that ever happened to this city. Why did she come back here, Phillip, when she could have lived anywhere in the world?"

He thought about everything he'd learned. "I don't know. Maybe it was in her blood."

"She came back because she knew we would love her like nobody else ever had." Belinda was looking straight at Phillip, and she wasn't smiling. "She looked around one day and knew it was time to go home. And that's what she did."

He thought about Belinda's words during the remainder of Nicky's set. Belinda's own life had been an eternal Lent, forty days of deprivation, then forty more, until she had learned to expect nothing else. She had been deprived of most of the things people needed to grow strong and emotionally secure, yet she had. With very little help, and very little reassurance.

But what about now? Belinda didn't expect anything of him. That had always been perfectly clear. But in the spirit of carnival, was she reaching out to him? Was she telling him that it was time for him to come home, and that home was right here, with her?

The room seemed to grow smaller and more crowded. His mother's voice soared above the whispers, the clatter of silverware. The beat grew steadily faster; the volume rose higher and higher. His head began to pound, and he closed his eyes for a moment against the smoke of a dozen cigarettes.

He missed seeing the man leap up to the stage.

Belinda put her hand on his arm. "Phillip..."

He opened his eyes and saw a fat middle-aged man who had clearly had too much to drink, swaying just yards from his mother. No one from the band had reacted yet, it had happened so quickly. Phillip sat forward, ready to spring if necessary.

"She's got it under control," Belinda said, holding him back.

Nicky had her hands on her hips, and she was shaking her head at the man like a tolerant schoolmarm. She had stopped singing, but they were close enough to hear her tell him to get down and stop making a fool of himself. It was the same voice she had used on the rare occasions when Phillip got into trouble as a child.

The man swayed, as if he planned to obey if he could just remember how. The sax player, who rivaled Jackson for size, started toward the man to help him off the stage, and from the corner of his eye, Phillip could see Jake heading their way. That would have been the end of it, and should have been. Except for the cops.

Phillip wasn't sure where the two policemen came from. They were white, which put them in a distinct minority tonight, and they were young enough to be new academy graduates. The cop with the blond crew cut looked uncomfortable, as if he knew that there was no reason to interfere. The other, dark-haired and flat-featured, was obviously in his element. He pushed his way past people who didn't need to be pushed, shoving tables as he made his way up front. He had his nightstick in his hand, and he thumped it against his thigh as he walked.

Phillip could see the next few seconds as clearly as he could see the dark-haired cop stomping his way to the stage. Club Valentine was a neutral zone in the conflict between the races. A truce had been declared here, led by his mother and defended by everyone, black or white, who walked through the front door. But the cop, this cocky, reckless representative of the outside world, could undo all that. If he dragged the drunk off the stage and roughed him up in full view of everyone there, all hell would break loose. It was carnival season and tolerance was a Lenten virtue.

Phillip was on his feet and blocking the cop's progress before he'd even made a conscious decision to interfere. "Officer." He stood his ground, and he didn't smile. "There's nothing to worry about. We've got this under control." He had his back to the stage, but he knew that behind him, the drunk was being hustled away.

"Get out of my way!"

Phillip moved closer and lowered his voice, holding out his hands to make sure that the cop knew he wasn't a threat. "I'm Phillip Benedict. My mother and stepfather own this club. We appreciate your concern, and we're glad you've got the courage you need to do this job. Because it takes courage. If you lift a hand to that man, all these people are going to come down on you like gravy on rice."

The cop put his palm against Phillip's shoulder and shoved, but Phillip was prepared. He didn't budge. "Look," he said, just loud enough for the cop, and no one else, to hear. "You push me again and I go down, you're going to be at the bottom of a pile of bodies six feet deep. And I know what the mayor would say if you caused that kind of problem here. Nicky Valentine draws people to this city, especially this time of year. You want to be known as the man who started trouble at her place?"

For a moment Phillip thought the cop wasn't going to listen. He wanted a fight, and he wanted to be the one to spark it. Worse, he wanted a fight here, in a place renowned for tolerance. That was why he was in this room, to prove something to himself and every-one else like him. To prove that black and white could not enjoy themselves together without an explosion.

"You see your people stay in line," he said. "We don't want nig—"

"I wouldn't use that word right here and now," Phillip said smoothly. "Or my people, as you put it, might stand in line to have first chance at *you*."

The cop with the crew cut came up behind his partner. "Come on. There's no problem now. Let's go." He shook his head once for Phillip's benefit. It was almost imperceptible, but more than Phillip had expected. This cop knew what his partner was, and he didn't approve.

"I'll sing you out, gentlemen," Nicky said from the stage behind them. As if it had been planned, she swung into "The Times They Are A-changin'," a Bob Dylan song that Phillip had never heard her perform, but which she performed tonight with feeling. The cops were gone by the second verse, and Phillip took his seat.

The crowd whistled and stomped their approval at the song's conclusion, even after Nicky had left the room. Sam leaned across the table, his face serious. "You ever thought about going into pol-itics?" he asked Phillip.

"Last time I looked I was still black."

"The times *are* changing. It won't be long before we'll need men like you to run for office here. This city's about to bust wide open."

"If I'm not mistaken, I'd have trouble voting in New Orleans, much less making a bid for mayor."

"Sam's right," Jackson said. "We need you here. We're looking for men who don't back down and don't kiss up. Educated men who can stand tall."

"Not my city, and not my home." The words came as naturally to Phillip's lips as any he'd ever spoken. The episode with the cop was symbolic of everything he despised about the South. He had been forced to become involved, something a good journalist never did. And now he felt a connection he didn't want to feel.

He had taken stands every day of his career, but they had been impersonal and rational, and his stomach hadn't churned afterward with emotions he didn't want to recognize.

"It *could* be your home," Sam said.

"No. I don't think it ever could." Phillip looked at Belinda and saw his answer written in her eyes. Her expression didn't change, but he knew that something had changed between them.

And that, too, stirred up emotions that he didn't want to recognize.

When he arose the next morning, Belinda was gone. She always left early for school, but this morning she had probably left the house just after dawn. The sun was barely over the horizon, and only the call of a mockingbird broke the neighborhood's stillness.

They hadn't fought after they returned home last night. Phillip had tried once to explain what he'd said to Sam, but he hadn't been able to explain what was behind it. He hadn't been able to tell Belinda about Aurore Gerritsen and the prejudices that had caused her to abandon his mother. He hadn't been able to tell her about his own revulsion at being descended from a man like Lucien Le Danois, who would murder his own child rather than admit to her existence.

What had he learned about his Louisiana roots that would make him want to stay?

He found coffee brewing, but no note. He drank a cup over the morning paper, but by the time he went to the closet to get clean clothes, he was no closer to knowing what he should do that day than he had been upon waking.

He opened the door and stared at his suitcase, lying prominently on the closet floor. It was fully packed, although last night his clothes had been hanging beside Belinda's.

He had only to snap it shut and he could be on his way again.

CHAPTER 26

There were azaleas blooming at the end of the garden path. Azaleas in February, but only because the new gardener had mistakenly planted them on the south side of Aurore's garden. Now the crimson blossoms lifted their glorious faces to the New Orleans winter sun, like bathing beauties on the French Riviera, but by August the shrubs would have shriveled and died.

The warm afternoon had drawn Aurore outside to spend an hour on a stone bench beside her goldfish pond. She had brought a book to read, but instead she had stared at the fish and the fat brown toad who drowsed in the cool shadow of a rock and dreamed of mosquitoes.

She heard Phillip's footsteps before she saw him. When she looked up, he was standing several yards away, his arms folded across his chest.

He had left town several weeks ago, the day after he learned the truth about who she was. She knew he had been to New York and California chasing stories. There was little that went on in New Orleans that was a secret, and little Aurore couldn't find out if she asked the right people. She hadn't been surprised. She had expected Phillip to go away. She had also expected him to return.

"What made you come back?" she asked. "A journalist's curiosity? A duty to your mother?" She didn't add her final guess out loud. Had he been influenced by a young woman named Belinda Beauclaire, who was simply too perfect to leave behind?

"You won. Just like you knew you would."

She patted the bench beside her. He moved forward and sat reluctantly. "At my age, and in my condition, I'm allowed a fault or two. Forgive me for being smug."

"Are you really dying? Or was that a way to assure my presence here?"

Aurore didn't answer directly. She pointed to the azaleas with the tip of her cane. "I really should have those moved. They need protection in summer, but I wanted so badly to see them flower."

"You said you probably had six months."

"I would like to live until summer," she said.

"Most people would prefer to die rather than face the heat and humidity here."

"I'll miss breathing steam." She smiled. "I suppose I'll miss breathing in general."

"Are you in pain?"

"Blessedly, very little. But I can feel death settle over me. I sleep less, eat less. When I move, I feel the way I did as a little girl when I walked out into the Gulf and the water sucked at every step."

"None of that means that death is just around the corner."

"When I do sleep, I'm visited by those who've already died. I dream of them, and when I wake up, they're still with me."

"Your husband?"

She shook her head. "Never Henry."

"From what you've told me, I suppose you're grateful."

She smiled again, this time sadly. "Perhaps Henry went to a place with no visiting hours."

"The marriage never got better?"

"You're beginning to sound like a journalist again, Phillip. Does this mean you'll hear me out?"

"When I write up your memoirs, I'll say that you were an old woman who always got what she wanted, no matter who she had to manipulate, no matter what she had to do."

She was silent for a moment, considering his words and somehow liking the sound of them. "And will you also say that I was an old woman who did what I thought was best, even when it might have been easier to spend my last days watching goldfish and toads?"

"I don't know."

She used her cane to stand. She was increasingly unsteady on her feet, and more disgusted daily that her body could fail her so completely. "Walk with me, Phillip."

He had already gotten to his feet. "I don't have my tape recorder with me now."

"Oh, I think you'll remember what I tell you."

"I already know there's no happy ending to look forward to."

"Perhaps not for me, not in the way you mean. But there are compensations for almost everything that happens in life."

"Are there?"

She held out her hand. "May I lean on you?"

He hesitated. She could see him struggle; then he shrugged. He moved closer. She rested her hand on his arm.

As she thought about how to begin, she stared at the azaleas at the end of the garden path. They were blooming now, but in a month, when their blossoms had faded, she would have the gardener dig them up and plant them in the proper spot. Perhaps she would not be alive next spring to see them bloom again, but she would know that they bloomed for those who came after her.

"Let me tell you about my garden," she said. "And about the ways my life changed in the years when this garden first began to grow."

CHAPTER 27

After careful analysis, Aurore had been certain that the United States would eventually enter the Great War. Henry hadn't agreed at first, but eventually he had recognized the wisdom of her position, and together they had sunk every surplus penny into reconditioning their old stern-wheel towboats and wooden barges. They had even scraped together a loan to add to their fleet.

Now, just as she had predicted, the railroads couldn't handle the huge loads of foodstuffs, armaments, machinery and military supplies heading south. The river was speckled with barges again. Soon it would be blanketed. Their investments had already begun to pay off, and if the war lasted a while, they would come out winners, no matter the eventual fate of the doughboys.

At thirty-three, Henry was too old for the new selective service law, but young enough to have a long life ahead of him. He had made it clear to Aurore that he planned to live it as a rich man. He also planned to live it with his wife firmly at heel beside him.

Henry had wanted a home to showcase his ascendancy in New Orleans society. Aurore had wanted one of quiet good taste. A home like the one she had envisioned could be built for four thousand dollars, with elaborate plumbing and enameled bathtubs, tiled hearths, hardwood mantels and enough rooms to keep a small household staff employed.

Henry had insisted they spend several times that amount and engage one of the most popular architects of the day, Thomas Sully, who had designed numerous homes along Saint Charles Avenue and Carrollton. The result of their warring taste was an elegant Greek Revival mansion. She had insisted on floor-to-ceiling windows and a double gallery with iron lace railings that mimicked those of her childhood home. Henry had insisted on high Victorian touches of beveled and etched glass and an asymmetrical wing for the library.

Henry had obtained prime property on Prytania, owing his good fortune to the previous owner's bad. A fire had destroyed the home formerly occupying their lot. Live oaks and magnolias had survived, but most of the beautiful plantings that were important features of every Garden District home had been destroyed.

Aurore had found the design and construction of the house taxing, but work on the gardens had been her delight. Henry had little interest in shrubbery and a great deal in fences. He had demanded cast iron and geometric spikes, which she had promptly softened with masses of camellias, azaleas and sweet olive, in the Creole style. Against the house she had planted myrtle, jasmine and althaea, and in the yard, fig, orange and oleander. A rose garden bloomed under the bedroom windows.

As she consulted with landscapers, she had envisioned her children playing there. The house might be imposing, but she wanted the gardens to beckon merrily. Her children would live in the house, but they would thrive in the gardens.

Hugh did thrive there. A quiet child who seemed to be cataloging the experiences of childhood, Hugh loved the roses best of all. Aurore never chose flowers to bring indoors without Hugh at her side. He was sweetly serious about his mission, weighing the pros and cons of his choices with the intensity of a theologian considering original sin. He pointed; she cut and stripped off the thorns and gave them to him to place in his straw basket. Inside the house, he was always beside her to help when she arranged them.

In the hottest part of summer and fall, few flowers bloomed, and Hugh had little interest in them. Late on an October morning, he played under the shade of the magnolias instead, tossing a ball to the spaniel Aurore had bought him the day she realized he might never have a brother or sister to play with.

She wanted more children. Her menstrual periods were as regular as the waxing and waning of the moon, and despite the suspicions Henry often voiced, she had not tried to prevent another pregnancy. But, despite Henry's frequent attentions, she remained barren.

Nicolette was ten now, so completely lost to Aurore that sometimes it seemed as if her daughter's birth had been a dream. Hugh was the joy of her life. She couldn't replace one child with another, but Aurore knew that she had more love to give than one child should have to absorb. Already she could see how hard it would be for Hugh to separate from her when the time came. As poor a father as Henry was, he was right when he criticized her for protecting their son so strenuously. Hugh had to grow up, and she had to allow it.

"*Mamete.*" Quickly bored, Hugh flung himself into her lap.

She held him close. "Are you tired of Floppsy already?"

"I want to draw."

Even though the sky was clear, an earlier rainstorm still seemed to hang in the hot air. She understood his desire to go inside. She signaled his nurse, Marta, a stocky, silver-haired widow whose husband had piloted barges for Gulf Coast. Aurore had chosen Marta after Cleo went to live with a sister. Marta had endless patience, and although her standards were high, her expectations were reasonable.

She watched Marta lead Hugh away. Marta never spoke to him as if he were a child. She was teaching him German—despite the nation's wholesale rejection of all things Germanic—and Aurore often spoke French in his presence. Hugh learned languages effortlessly, just as he had learned not to speak anything except English to his father, who ridiculed his abilities.

"Ro-Ro."

She turned at the unexpected sound of Ti' Boo's voice and crossed the yard to greet her. Ti' Boo had her youngest child in tow, Val, who was only a year older than Hugh, but who already looked exactly like his father. Val galloped after Hugh and Marta and left the women alone in the garden.

"I'm so glad you brought him today. Hugh needs a friend. Join me for coffee?" Aurore ushered Ti' Boo to a table under the trees. "I'll get a fresh pot."

"No. Sit. Me, I've had three cups today already, and it just makes the morning hotter."

Ti' Boo had grown plumper through the years, but this morning she looked as fresh as a new day, in a white dress with striped trim. The skills she had learned in her childhood served her well now that the country was at war. Meatless days weren't strong enough conservation measures. Everyone with land was expected to grow and preserve his own food, so Ti' Boo taught vegetable gardening and canning to city women who had never grown more than a flower or two. At her insistence, Aurore had even dug up a large section of her prized lawn to plant vegetables.

"I brought you seeds," Ti' Boo said. "Cabbage and mustard and onion sets."

"Good. I still have room along the back fence. Hugh can help me plant them this evening, when it's cooler."

"Is he well now?"

"He's fine. It was only a mild fever." Aurore thought of her frantic telephone call to Ti' Boo the week before. Hugh had always been healthy, but at his first normal childhood illness she had become panic-stricken. The days when epidemics of yellow fever and cholera were commonplace had ended, thanks to a new emphasis on sanitation and pest control. But there were other diseases that could strike down children. Aurore had felt Hugh's flushed cheeks and listened to his labored breathing, and she had been certain he was going to die.

"Every day I expect him to be taken from me," Aurore said.

"We all feel that way."

"I love him too much."

"You need another."

"I have another."

Ti' Boo reached for her hand. "Have you learned anything new about Nicolette?"

Aurore knew that her daughter no longer lived at the Magnolia Palace. Several years ago, Rafe had moved her to a small house on a quiet street below Canal, in what was commonly called the Creole Quarter. Most of its residents were Creoles of color. Rafe couldn't have chosen a more foreign environment for a child who had been raised in the honky-tonk swirl of the district. Family ties, breeding and gracious manners were all-important to the colored Creoles. But although Nicolette might never be a real part of the community, she would blend in there. She could go to school and church, perhaps even make friends. Aurore was grateful, so grateful, that Rafe had listened to her.

But had he? At their encounter in Audubon Park, Rafe had been cold and mocking. Had he really heard her pleas and acted on them? Had she really changed his mind, or had he only moved their daughter to keep her farther from Aurore's reach?

"You haven't seen her?" Ti' Boo asked.

"I've never found a way." Aurore took Ti' Boo's hand and squeezed it. "Have you heard that the district is going to close? It's official now. There's been too much trouble lately, and sailors have been injured. The navy insisted. The city council voted for it last night."

"How such a place could exist!"

"Rafe has investments there besides the Magnolia Palace, Ti' Boo."

"How can you know so much?"

Aurore didn't know how to explain. She had learned to listen, to ask the right questions and bribe the right people. She wasn't proud of her skills, but without them she would have no control of her life. "Sometimes it's easier to be a woman. No one ever thinks we're listening. The men gather to talk at dinner parties, and they say things as if we women had no ears."

"These men talk about Rafe Cantrelle?"

"It's very possible to hear things that aren't said out loud. But it doesn't matter how I know. I just do."

"And what will happen to Rafe when the district closes? Have you heard that, too?"

"No. But I can guess." Aurore rose to get the ball for Floppsy, who lay at her feet staring forlornly toward the house, where she was never invited. She threw the ball and watched the grateful spaniel retrieve it. "Rafe Cantrelle will survive this. He's survived worse. I wouldn't even be surprised if he prospers."

"I think you admire him."

Aurore turned, surprised. "How can you say that?"

"It's not what *I* say that's important."

"I don't admire him. I hate him!"

"I no longer think so."

"He killed my father. He stole my baby."

"I think, perhaps, he did neither." Ti' Boo stood, too. "I've asked myself again and again why Rafe did the things he did. But for every time I've asked, you must have asked a million, yes? And until you know, you'll never have peace."

"Peace?" Aurore threw the ball again, hard enough to send it through a hedge of sweet olive. "I wasn't born for peace."

"Were you born for revenge?"

"I'm not seeking revenge anymore. I don't want my daughter hurt."

"Is that the reason, Ro-Ro, or is it that you can see more clearly now? You must honor your father, the church tells us that. But must you also believe lies about him? Lucien Le Danois was not a good man. And Rafe never stole your daughter. You put Nicolette into his arms yourself."

Aurore faced her. "How can you say these things to me?"

Ti' Boo looked suddenly tired. "Because I'm getting older, and you never say them to yourself."

"I've lived my life the only way I knew."

"Again, what I think isn't important, but I'll tell you anyway. I've watched you since your father died and since your marriage, and I've seen you change. You're like the crab who grows a shell so rigid that one day he must abandon it and grow another. On the bayou, we wait for these crabs to leave their shells, but it's not the shells we wait for, no. It's the crabs themselves, because in those hours when they have no shells, they're the most delicious. If you continue to grow a shell of lies and secrets around you, Ro-Ro, you will have to leave it for another one day. And you, too, will be *très vulnérable.*"

Aurore was stunned. Ti' Boo had never criticized her before. "Why say this to me now? Is it because of everything I have and you don't? Has it finally separated us?"

"I pray to God that I never have what you have, Ro-Ro." Ti' Boo touched Aurore's arm lightly in farewell before she crossed to the house to get Val.

In the summer of 1918, Claire Friloux Le Danois died. Through the years she had grown less aware of her surroundings, until one morning she was gone. Against all advice, Aurore had often visited her mother. Aurore had hoped that her continued presence would ignite any spark that remained. But there had never been the faintest flicker.

Claire was buried in the Friloux family tomb in Saint Louis Cemetery Number 2. Burial was nearly impossible in a city below sea level. Vaults resembling the outdoor ovens of an earlier time were used instead. The Friloux vault had room for only one body. After disintegration, Claire's remains would be deposited in a lower vault, to mingle with the remains of generations. That seemed kinder to Aurore than a solitary grave. In death, at least, her mother wouldn't be alone.

The war and a new century had softened the city's mourning customs. There had been too many gold-starred telegrams from the War Department and too little time to honor those who had fallen. No crepe adorned their doors; no mirrors were covered or clocks stopped. The trip to the cemetery was silent, with no brass band to celebrate a life that had really ended long ago. The wake was dignified and blessedly short.

After the funeral, Aurore was haunted by the specter of her own death. Laid out in a dress of Aurore's choosing, Claire had seemed as withered and drained of life as an Egyptian mummy. Aurore was just thirty, but she felt the weight of Claire's death when she counted the years that separated them. She, too, might die young. And what would happen to her son?

What would happen to her daughter?

Gulf Coast was thriving. The Merchant Marine Act of 1916 had projected a program for the expansion of American-flag shipping. With the profits from their new and successful expansion, Henry and Aurore had purchased their first ocean freighter. Her dreams of rebuilding Gulf Coast to its past glories were coming true.

Although every day with Henry was a duel for power, the new surge in business often kept him away from home. She arranged to be at the office when he wasn't, and she accepted social engagements for the times they had to spend together. But through their years of marriage, he had learned to keep her off-balance. Weeks went by when he was coldly polite, even distant. Then, as she relaxed into acceptance, he swooped down and attacked. Her bedroom was the dueling ground, his body the favored weapon. He slept with her hair twisted in his hands.

Aurore found herself sinking deeper into melancholy, and Claire's death continued to haunt her. Given the choice between discussing her concerns with a priest and consulting an attorney, she chose a stranger named Spencer St. Amant.

On a cloudy morning, she crossed Canal Street near Maison Blanche and climbed two flights of stairs. She arrived early. Spencer was not Gulf Coast's counsel; nor was he a friend of Henry's. His name was an old one in New Orleans, but although the St. Amants had mixed in all the correct circles, they had remained on the periphery. Despite their heritage, the St. Amants were suspect, because they sometimes championed unpopular causes.

That reputation for tolerance had brought Aurore to Spencer. She was secure in the knowledge that whatever she told him would not be repeated. Still, as she waited, she paced the short length of the reception area, debating whether she should have come.

She continued that debate when she was sitting across from him. She twisted the beads at her neck as he welcomed her, and she tried to read his character. She guessed he was several years younger than she, and rather shy. He was slight, with hair so dark and skin so white that despite the fact that he was clean-shaven, the slight shadow of a beard was evident. His eyes were a brilliant blue, and they seemed to be assessing her, even as his hesitant smile promised no assessment at all.

"I believe our fathers were acquainted," he said. "I'm told they competed for your mother's hand in marriage."

"Are you aware she died several weeks ago?"

"You have my sympathy."

"There's no reason to be sad." She found herself telling Claire's story, leaving nothing out. "So you see, she might have done better to have chosen your father," she concluded.

He sat back, drumming his fingers on his desk. "I don't envy your childhood."

"The saddest part is that I didn't learn anything from it."

He waited, as if the rest of the day was at her disposal. She was touched by his patience, and heartened. "I've made some terrible mistakes," she began.

Much later, he leaned forward. "What is it you want me to do?"

She felt as if all the pustulant hatred that had swelled inside her for more than a decade had been lanced. She knew that anger would swell again and fill her, but for the moment, she was free. "If I die, I want Nicolette to be taken care of."

"From what you've told me, her father is a wealthy man. Why are you worried, Aurore?"

She noted the use of her first name, and everything it implied. By her confession, she had asked for more than legal advice. She had asked for an undeserved acceptance, and now he had given it. "Rafe Cantrelle can't be trusted. I don't know what he'll do when Nicolette's older. I want to be sure she's provided for, so she can be her own woman."

"But only if you die?"

"I don't know what I can do for her while I'm still alive."

"Do you expect to die?"

She grew cold. "It's always possible."

He leaned closer. "Do you expect to die at your husband's hand?"

She shuddered. "No, of course not."

"You could divorce him," Spencer said.

"No! He would trumpet my past, take my son. I can never leave him."

His eyes were kind, but behind that kindness was strength. "Does Mr. Gerritsen know you're here?"

She shook her head.

"I think you should tell him."

"I can't imagine what he'd do if he knew I had told someone the truth about my past."

"It might make him think."

"Why?"

"Because from this moment on, I'll be sure that if anything happens to you, the authorities look beyond the easy answers."

"Henry's a powerful man, and he's growing more powerful. No one would listen to you."

"In this city, a man can be powerful one day and friendless the next. I can be patient. I can wait. Tell him that." He stood. "We'll begin your will next time, but I want you to think carefully about how you'd like it worded. Only you know how much you want to reveal about your relationship with Nicolette. You have Hugh to think of, too."

"I want to leave Hugh a letter. When my mother died, I wished there had been something from her, a letter, a few sentences in a will. Anything."

"Was there a will?"

"No. She had nothing to give away. I paid for her care myself."

"Have you thought of a memorial?"

She gathered her gloves. "It seems a sacrilege to memorialize such a sad life."

"Were there happy times?"

She thought of fleeting, lazy days in the sunshine. "One summer at Grand Isle, although even that ended tragically."

"You know they've built a church there, don't you? I'm sure they'd welcome a donation in your mother's name."

"Do you think it's important?"

He came around his desk to sit on the edge, just in front of her. "In the years to come, you'll remember her, no matter how much you try not to. Go to the dedication of the church. Then the memories will be better."

She thought of a woman's arms protecting her from the terrors of a hurricane. Her mother had twice given her life. Years had passed since she had thought of that woman, battling the beginning of madness but still courageous enough to act on her own judgment, despite Grandpère Antoine's demands. Despite Claire's own fragility. Tears rose to her eyes, tears she hadn't cried during the recitation of her own sins.

"Yes," she said. "Thank you."

He held out his hand to help her rise. He continued to hold it for seconds after she was standing. "Your secrets will be safe here."

She knew he was telling the truth.

For the entire journey down to Grand Isle, Aurore worried about Hugh. For days she had considered Spencer's advice, but only when she discovered that Henry would be out of town during the dedication did she make plans. The final incentive had been a letter from Father Grimaud. Father Grimaud served a parish in Carenàlro now, but someone had mentioned Aurore's contribution to Our Lady of the Isle. He planned to be at the dedication, and he had something he wanted to give her.

She was curious. She had never met Father Grimaud, but she knew how he had stood at the presbytery window with a lantern to guide his flock to safety during the hurricane. Her own father had been the only one to reach him. The story brought back memories of howling winds and trembling walls. What could the priest have for her, except a memento of that night?

On the island, she settled into a small, rustic guest house. The hurricane had destroyed more than homes and lives; it had destroyed an entire industry. Few people, if any, summered on Grand Isle now. The hotels were gone, and the Krantz Place was a memory. An attempt a decade before to build a railway from Gretna had failed, and hopes of resurrecting the health and pleasure resort reputation of the island had died with it. Aurore had been lucky to find accommodations at all.

After a brief rest, she found her way down to the beach. She remembered the walk as a long one, fraught with magic and expectation. Now she reached the beach in minutes and stood looking out on the waves nibbling at the shoreline. Hundreds of yards away, men in straw hats were hauling in nets filled with glistening, wriggling fish, but there were no sailboats lazily skirting the horizon and no parties of bathers enjoying the water. Sea gulls circled the fishermen, and porpoises leaped not far from shore, but the colorful, pleasure-filled days of her childhood were gone.

She sat at the edge of a sand dune and stared at the water. The sun was the same sun she remembered, nipping her cheeks and the back of her neck when she didn't immediately raise her parasol. The sand had the same sugar texture; the water was the blue-gray of her mother's eyes.

Something close to peace filled her as the sun warmed more than her cheeks. Hopes and fears locked deep inside her began to thaw. Away from the responsibilities and restrictions of her marriage, she could almost remember the little girl who had loved the waves and the oleander-scented breeze. From that child had come the woman who sat on the sand today. That woman had become a creature of lies and secrets.

Ti' Boo was right.

The sun was almost perched on the horizon when she rose and began to stroll. She started toward the island's central ridge to find the cottage that had sheltered her during the storm. Ti' Boo had told her that Nonc Clebert had passed on years before. Now the cottage was the property of a son who lived in Thibodaux.

The sky was nearly dark before she found it. The house sat by itself, protected from prying eyes by a dense stand of oaks and denser underbrush. A padlock barred the door, and lavishly twisted vines testified that no one had tried it recently. She remembered the safety of its walls, the hospitality of its cozy rooms. Someone had covered her with quilts; someone had brought her soup and tea. Someone had murmured stories in soft Acadian French as the storm raged outside.

Now the house was silent and alone, its days of usefulness so obviously at an end. She imagined it was a matter of time before someone tore it down and replaced it with a structure that would collapse in the first wind.

That night, she slept fitfully. The island had gently convinced her to lower her guard. Now images crept through her dreams, lapping at her consciousness. For the first time, she wondered if her life could be more than a battleground. She couldn't dissolve her marriage, because she would surely lose her son. Hugh and Gulf Coast were everything to her, and she couldn't hand them to Henry to destroy. But perhaps there were other ways to reclaim her humanity. Somewhere inside her dwelled the child who had laughed and run at the Krantz Place, the child who had believed that happiness was possible.

By the next afternoon, she was ready for the dedication. The church had been built on donated land on the central ridge, no more than half a mile from Nonc Clebert's house. Archbishop Shaw and other dignitaries had arrived for the event, and bright-eyed children crowded the yard in anticipation of a special confirmation ceremony. The church was white frame, with soaring arched windows and a belfry of graceful Moorish curves.

In their days at the Krantz Place, her mother had yearned for a church here. Now, at her death, that wish had come true.

"Do you know about the bell?" A woman clad in an ill-fitting blue print dress joined Aurore in the yard, staring up at the building.

Aurore was glad to break her own silence. "No."

"It's the pirate's bell from the chénière."

"Pirate's bell?"

"*Oui, chère*. Made of doubloons and pirate's treasure. Don't you know about it?" The woman's eyes brightened at the chance to tell a story. When Aurore shook her head, she continued. "There was a big storm in '93." She spread her arms wide.

Aurore warmed to her immediately. The woman's Acadian accent reminded her of Ti' Boo. "I was here."

The woman clucked in sympathy. "Me, I was living up the bayou. It flooded so high, we lived on a lugger for two weeks, till the water went down. But we were the lucky ones, us. The people on Chénière Caminada, well, most of 'em died. And while they did, this bell rang and rang."

"The same bell?"

"It's been buried for years. After the storm, someone found the bell in the sand. There was a struggle over who it belonged to. Nobody could agree. The church was gone, so some thought they'd move the bell to a church far away. But before they could, the bell just disappeared." She snapped her fingers.

"Where was it?"

"Some people who survived the storm, they took it and buried it in a cemetery in Westwego. And it would be there still if this church hadn't been built. But when it was time, the people on the island, they asked the right men if they would bring it back, and they agreed. It's our history, don't you see? Nobody else's. And when it rings now, it rings for our sister the chénière, too, even though nobody lives there except the ghosts."

At that moment, the bell began to ring, signaling the solemn beginning of the services. Surprised, Aurore found her eyes filling with tears. She didn't move as she listened to the same resonant summons that had called so many to their death.

She remembered that Lucien had never been able to tolerate the sound of a bell, that he had built his office like a fortress, far from the river and its sounds.

The woman beside her gave a small cry and covered her mouth. Aurore followed her gaze to a priest with a long white beard who had just entered the churchyard, not far from where they stood. As she watched, he covered his ears at the sound of the bell and fell to his knees.

"Ma cloche! Le même son!" he cried.

"The same sound," Aurore whispered.

Father Grimaud continued to kneel in the churchyard and weep.

Rafe didn't know why Aurore was at the dedication. He wasn't even sure why he was. He had read a small notice about Our Lady of the Isle in a New Orleans newspaper, and memories of struggling toward a white frame church had overtaken him. The memories had made it difficult to concentrate, to walk the narrow line that made his existence in New Orleans tolerable.

He possessed no sentimentality, but in the days after he read the notice, his life had no longer seemed his. He made arrangements to travel to Grand Isle. He'd made arrangements with Violet to care for Nicolette during his absence, and arrangements with his attorney to put all business affairs on hold.

Since his attorney always acted as go-between, no one in the city realized just how much Rafe was worth or how excellent his instincts were. Even the change in Storyville's status hadn't affected him. He had begun to sell his holdings there well before business in the district dropped off. He had become disgusted with his role as landlord for a house of prostitution. Rationalizations that worse men, men with no principles at all, would succeed him, had no longer rung true for him. He had found that he was a better man than he had wanted to be.

By the time the navy stepped in with its demands, the Palace—now a second-rate rooming house—was already somebody else's problem. He owned property in the business district for immediate income, and vast tracts of swamp at the city's edge, because he knew that with technology's advances, the swamps would be drained and the city would expand. He was wealthy enough to live a comfortable life, or as comfortable a life as a man of color could lead.

Rafe didn't know exactly when he had accepted himself as he was. Perhaps it had been at the moment of Aurore's rejection. But soon afterward he had realized that he couldn't deny the father he had never known, any more than he could deny his mother and the life she had been forced to lead. Juan had said his father was a good man. Rafe knew his mother had been a good woman. The blood of two races ran through his veins. The heritage his parents had bequeathed him was one of which he could be proud.

But pride was a lonely place, and he guarded it well. He kept to himself and conducted much of his business through his attorney and accountant. He gave no explanations about his bloodlines, but he lived among the *gens de couleur* of the city, and, by association, he was damned. He didn't look for acceptance; acceptance had always been denied him. He didn't look for respect or friendship. He woke up each morning with the sole goal of surviving the day with his pride intact.

So why had he come to Grand Isle? And why had Aurore come, an Aurore a decade older than the girl he had loved? As the service progressed, he could watch her undetected. She sat near the front of the church, her head covered with a floppy-brimmed hat that served the function of blinders. He could see the proud set of her shoulders, the grace with which she knelt and stood, the narrow curve of her waist. Although she hadn't seen him, he had caught a glimpse of her face as she entered the church. The years had whittled away her youthful innocence and left in its place a wiser, colder woman. But she was no less beautiful.

When the service ended, he left the building quickly, but he lingered in the churchyard. Grand Isle, indolent Louisiana stepchild, had only rarely had an event of this magnitude to celebrate. Islanders and visitors crowded the yard as the little girls in white veils and the boys in dark suits endured family greetings and congratulations. He thought he recognized a face or two from his years on Bayou Lafourche, but he made no attempt to announce himself. Those days seemed to belong to someone else entirely, Étienne Terrebonne, the boy he had never been. Here he felt closer to the child Raphael.

Aurore came out of the church, and he watched her move through the crowd toward Father Grimaud. Seeing the old priest again had been nearly as surprising as seeing her. Rafe felt certain that Father Grimaud would remember him. He had been kind during those lonely years, one of the few people who accepted Raphael as a child, simply one of God's children.

Aurore spoke to the priest, and as Father Grimaud bent his head, his long white beard dusted the front of his cassock. He straightened. Even from a distance, Rafe could see warmth in his expression, as if he were greeting an old friend.

Rafe was intrigued by this conversation he couldn't hear. Aurore had been too young to have known Father Grimaud. Rafe watched the priest beckon a young boy to his side and whisper something in his ear. Then the child started toward the church.

Aurore stepped aside, and others came to speak to the priest, but Aurore didn't retreat until the child returned, carrying what looked like a thin stack of papers tied with a ribbon. He gave it to the priest and received a pat on the head. Then Father Grimaud turned to Aurore and spoke before handing her the papers.

Rafe watched her leaf through them before she looked back at the priest. Father Grimaud touched her shoulder. She nodded; then she started across the yard.

Rafe didn't move. He had no wish to confront her here. Through the years, he had made a measure of peace with himself, and he had come to the island for more. But no one could make him hide; there was no battle he would surrender.

The bell rang again in celebration. With the first peal, Aurore's gaze found his. She stared at him until the bell was silent. Then, without a word, she continued past.

CHAPTER 28

Dusk stole over the island while Aurore read the letters. The evening was quiet except for the screeching of sea gulls. She rose once to light a lamp, once more to fill the enameled coffeepot with boiling water. When she finished the letters, written over a period of years, she rearranged and read them again. Nothing leaped from the pages. Instead, one embroidered on the other to tell the story of the night of the hurricane.

Father Grimaud's responses had been kind and priestly, absolving her father of all guilt. But her father had continued the correspondence, as if absolution were still withheld.

That afternoon, Father Grimaud had asked her whether Lucien had found forgiveness before he died. She had been puzzled by the question. Her father hadn't been a man who concerned himself with spiritual things. Why would he care whether the God he ignored forgave or condemned him?

But the picture that emerged from the letters was one of a different man. Lucien had been tormented. On the night of the storm, he had struggled toward the presbytery, towing a small skiff occupied by a pregnant woman and two small children. Nearly to safety, he had been overtaken by a wall of water and forced to release the rope or die. He had saved himself, but the others had been lost.

The woman's name had been Marcelite. Her children had been Raphael and Angelle.

Could Raphael be Rafe?

Rafe had changed his name after Nicolette's birth. By doing so, had he taken back his real identity? Had Raphael come back to haunt Lucien?

Aurore pictured the man who had watched her in the churchyard. His stance had been that of the youth she had met on Bayou Lafourche, proud, cautious, ready—if necessary—to attack. The years had heightened his masculinity; he was someone men wouldn't easily challenge or women easily forget. Since seeing him that afternoon, she had thought of little else. Rafe and her father's letters were now entwined.

And what of her father's letters? Discrepancies proved that Lucien had been trying to hide important pieces of a puzzle. Sometimes he referred to Marcelite as a stranger; at other times he wrote as if she were someone he had been long acquainted with. In one letter he was poetic about the little girl, Angelle, how sweet she had been, how healthy and full of life. He had eloquently captured the warmth of a child's chubby arms around his neck, the feel of her childish kisses.

One letter dated 1894, not quite a year after the storm, was more garbled than the others. He rambled at length about his father-in-law, Antoine, and demands he had made. But as the letters continued, Antoine was never mentioned again. Near the end of his life—and bemoaning his poor health—her father had seemed only to care that his acts not be held against him.

There were mysteries still, but the mystery she had lived with for so long might be explained. If Rafe was Raphael, perhaps he had blamed Lucien for his mother's and sister's death, and set out to avenge them.

But why had he chosen her as a vehicle? Had she simply been the easiest avenue to Lucien? Had he believed that her father loved her so much that her shame would finish his destruction?

She paced the cottage with a full cup of cold coffee clutched in her hands. Rafe had come for the dedication. Had he followed her? Did he want her to suffer more punishment?

The house seemed unbearable. She went outside to the gallery, where a warm breeze ruffled her hair. As she stared into the darkness, she realized that if he had wanted to punish her again, a million opportunities had probably passed. Perhaps he had simply come to make peace with his memories, just as she had.

Peace. Could a man like Rafe really hope for such a thing? Even as she told herself it was impossible, the picture of a small boy in a storm-battered skiff crowded her mind. When the lantern came into view in the presbytery window, it must have seemed like a beacon from heaven. Then Lucien, the boy's only chance for survival, had abandoned the tow rope, and the skiff had rushed toward certain death. If Rafe was Raphael, as much as she hated him, how could she believe that he needed peace less than she?

There were so many unanswered questions. She was halfway to the beach before she realized where she was going. She couldn't endure the cottage any more than she could endure her own thoughts. She didn't want to think of Rafe as a frightened child; she didn't want to think of her father as a coward. Most of all, she didn't want to forgive Rafe Cantrelle for what he had done to her.

The waves were almost calm. A nearly full moon hung low in the darkening sky and silvered the water. She had been wrong to come. Tonight there would be no memories of childhood days. Despite the placid surf, she saw waves as tall as the island oaks and heard the screams of children. She covered her face, but the picture grew more horrifying.

A man's voice spoke from the shadows of a sand dune. "My sister was the first to die, but my mother followed quickly. I wanted to dive after them, but I was too frightened to let go of the skiff. I clung until my fingers were so cramped that I couldn't."

She dropped her hands and stared as Rafe stepped away from the dune. "Who are you?" She moved toward him until she was only a few feet away. "Who are you?"

"I'm a ghost. At least, that's what your father thought ten years ago, when I told him I'd come back from the dead."

"Then you *are* Raphael?"

He lifted a brow. "I was."

"Did you follow me here?"

"I came for my own reasons."

"What were they?"

"Why should I tell you?" He turned and began to walk.

"No!" She ran after him and grabbed his arm. "I know what my father did. Today, in the churchyard, Father Grimaud gave me letters that he and my father exchanged."

He stopped. She could feel the muscles tense in his arm. "Letters," he said. "Filled with the truth, I suppose."

"He said he was towing a boat with three passengers. He said he let go of the rope before he reached the presbytery."

In the moonlight, his expression was inscrutable. "Did he tell you who the passengers were?"

"He gave names."

Without warning, he grasped her shoulders. "Did he tell you who we were? *What* we were to him?"

She tried to move away, but his grip tightened. "Let me go, Rafe."

"What, or you'll scream? Do it. End it all right here. Scream, and if anyone hears you, tell them a man of color dared to touch you. You'll have your revenge right here and now!"

"What were you to him?" she shouted.

"I was an abomination! But my mother was his mistress, and my sister was his child. Angelle was my sister—and yours!"

She went limp. "No. You're lying."

"Am I? Do you think I wasted my youth hating a man who simply wasn't brave enough to haul our boat to safety? Am I that stupid?" He thrust her backward, turned and walked away.

"You're lying!"

He continued to walk.

She was torn between running back to the cottage and running after him. She was at his side again before the decision was fully formed. "Why are you saying these things?"

"I would have said them years ago, if you would have listened."

"Why should I believe you?"

He stopped. "Your father gave my mother gifts in return for her affection. I don't think she loved him, but she adored her children. She saw Lucien as a path out of the poverty and shame that my birth had doomed her to. I think she believed he'd take us away from the chénière someday."

"And the child she was carrying? It was my father's child?"

He faced her. "What child are you talking about?"

She watched the truth settle over him. She hadn't really believed his story until that moment. But for an instant sorrow gleamed in his eyes, and she knew. She knew.

"No!" She looked away, her fist to her mouth.

"I never knew she was pregnant. She hid it from me, but apparently not from him."

"Even if this is true, how could you blame my father for what he did? He would have died if he hadn't released the tow rope. Can you blame him for trying to save his own life when everything else was hopeless?"

He gave a harsh laugh. "Is that what his letters said?"

"Then what's the truth?"

He grasped her chin and turned her head until they were eye to eye. "Do you really want to know, Aurore? Or do you want to go on thinking I had no reason for what I did? The last is easier. You've already settled into it nicely."

She pushed his hand away, but she didn't flinch. "What should I believe?"

"That your father cut the tow rope and doomed us to death because we had become an inconvenience."

"No! How can you know that?"

"Because I remember everything that was said that night. My mother had begun to make demands on him, and he'd finally realized what I was. We were nearly at the presbytery door when he took an ax to the rope. We were in easy reach of safety. Easy reach for all of us! Your father killed my mother. He killed his own daughter and his unborn child. And he tried to kill me!"

She wanted to refute his words, but she couldn't. All the pages of Lucien's letters fell into place; the fact that he'd written them was proof.

"But what did my grandfather have to do with this?" Even as she asked, the answer became clear. Somehow Antoine had discovered Lucien's love nest and insisted that Lucien end his connections there or face the consequences. She remembered that Antoine had come to Grand Isle unexpectedly, and that because he had, he had died in the hurricane.

He shook her off. "I don't know anything about your grandfather. But can anything about your family be hard to believe? You know what kind of man your father was."

"You were young. Can you be sure?"

"By the time I was found in the marsh, I was older than you'll ever be. And now we're both sure, aren't we?"

"You plotted revenge all those years? And when I came along, you knew you'd found a way to reach my father?"

"Exactly."

Anger blotted out shame. "You destroyed my life! I had nothing to do with this. I was Lucien's victim, too, and you knew it! You saw the way he treated me. He never loved me. Wasn't destroying the *Dowager* enough for you?"

"Nothing could have been enough."

"So you used me, lied to me, got me with child, then took my baby, all because of my father's sins? What kind of man are you?"

"A satisfied one."

She slapped him, but it wasn't enough. Her hands balled into fists, and she began to beat against his chest. She was sobbing. She didn't care if he killed her in return; she only wanted to inflict a small measure of the pain he had caused her.

He grabbed her hands and held them still, but she kicked at his legs. "Bastard!" She choked on the word. "Bastard!"

"Don't forget the rest of it!" He shoved her away. "Don't forget what kind of a bastard I am. My father was a mulatto, with his master's blood running through his veins. My mother loved him, but he was murdered because of his race. And here I am, their child, raised white, living black, neither and both!"

She covered her ears, but she could still hear him.

"Remember exactly what kind of a bastard I am! The kind you wouldn't listen to when I tried to explain. I didn't take our baby. You gave her to me. And if I hadn't taken her, you would have given her to a stranger! You're no different from Lucien. You sacrificed your own daughter so your life would be easier!"

"I'm not like my father!"

"No, you're worse. Lucien knew what he was, even if he didn't care. You think you're a good woman who's been terribly wronged. But look at yourself closely. What do you see?"

"I had nothing to do with my father's sin. Our daughter had nothing to do with it. And still you've destroyed us both!"

"You've destroyed yourself. You gave away your child, married a monster—and why?" He laughed; it was a twisted, tortured sound. "Because you were afraid of contamination."

She saw his torture, his shattered pride and rage. Shame and denial warred inside her. "No! You never loved me. You used me for revenge! That's why I hated you! That's why I couldn't keep Nicolette! I couldn't bear to see your face every time I looked at her."

He stared at her. "You're lying, and you're wrong. I loved you."

Everything she had built her life on began to crumble. "No."

"Not at first. I'd forgotten how. But a little at a time. I looked for Lucien in you, and didn't find him. I tried to tell myself you'd hate me if you discovered why I had come into your life, but I didn't listen to my own warnings. Then I started to believe I could have it all. Revenge, love..." He shrugged. "When you told me you were carrying our child, I wanted us to go away together and start a new life."

Her voice trembled. "You sabotaged the *Dowager.*"

"I told you. I wanted it all."

"And what did you think when you watched my father's ship go down in flames? What did you think when he lay on the floor at your feet? For those few minutes, did you finally have it all?"

"Yes."

"No." She moved closer. She could see his eyes. His gaze was steady, but he couldn't hide what he felt. "No, you didn't. You knew you'd lost everything, didn't you?" When he started to turn away, she grabbed his arm. "You knew you'd become like him, and you knew you'd never have me."

His expression grew cold. "No, I knew I'd never have you when Lucien told you what I was. I saw the horror in your eyes, and I knew there wasn't any hope, that nothing I could say could ever overcome that, not a confession, not a plea for forgiveness. I was branded by my father's blood, and so was our child."

She wanted to deny it, to tell him that she had been horrified by his acts, not his heritage. But she couldn't, because it wasn't completely true.

The hate that had filled her for ten long years vanished as if it had never been. Turmoil filled her instead, a rising tide of emotions, and images of the man she had once loved above everything else.

"How did it come to this?" she whispered. "Are we as helpless as the people killed by the storm that night? Don't we have a say over our lives, or do we spin from one tragedy to the next, causing more tragedy for our children? What about them? You're right, I married a monster because of you and what you did to me. And now my son pays every day because of my choice of a father for him. Where does it end? Where?"

She dropped her hand. She was sobbing again. He moved closer. "Do you even have to ask? We'll pay forever. Both of us. I've despised you for ten years, but I still have dreams about you. I remember you the way you were. I dream that we've gone away together, that I wake up in the morning and you're beside me, and when you look at me, you see a man. Not a black one, not a white one." He touched his chest. "A man."

"No!"

"Do you dream of me? Of what we could have had? Or did your father destroy that, too?"

"Don't, Rafe."

"Answer me."

The dreams had been so deeply hidden that she hadn't admitted to them. Now she knew they had been with her since the night of the fire. Once she had believed in love and in herself. She had dared to reach for happiness, and still did, when she slept. But in her waking hours she had reached for little but revenge. She had struggled to regain everything she had lost, everything except the one thing she really wanted.

She couldn't tell him; she would never be free if she said the words out loud. "Now I know everything. Be content with that." She tried to turn away, but he clamped his hand on her shoulder.

"Content? Can you imagine I feel anything like contentment? I don't care if you understand me. I want you to look at me and see exactly what I am. I'm a better man than the one you married, a better man than your father. I'm the man who could have made you happy."

"You killed my father!"

"No! Greed killed him. And he took you down with him, Aurore. There's nothing left of the woman I loved. Nothing!"

Her cheeks were wet with tears. "How could it have come to this? Love's a poor word for what I felt for you. You were all the things I'd never even dared to hope for. When you betrayed me, all those things died. If there's nothing left of the woman you loved, that's why."

He touched her cheek. Not gently, but as if he needed a test to see if her tears were real. She thought his hands trembled. "Don't shut your eyes. Look at me. What do you see? The man you loved? Or the man who betrayed you? A man, or a man whose blood is tainted?"

"Can it matter?"

"It matters!"

"I see Rafe Cantrelle, a man I've loved and a man I've hated. A man who is what he is despite and because of his heritage. A man."

"Do you see a man who still wants you?"

She saw desire in his eyes then, desire as new as this night and as old as their first meeting. An answering flicker stirred within her; she turned away to hide it. "No."

He put his hand on her shoulder. "I see a woman who's learned to lie."

She could feel each of his fingers through her blouse, drawing her toward him. "I'm going back now. Let me go."

"I don't think so."

"You won't force me."

"If you see that much, then try looking into yourself. Tell me what's there."

"Nothing! You left me nothing!"

"I left you my heart."

She faced him. She saw that he meant it, and that he hated himself for it. She saw how he had tried to protect himself and how he had failed. She saw ten years of hell, but, most terrible of all, she couldn't tell if the hell was his, or a reflection of her own. "No..."

He dropped his hand. "Our lives have led us here. If you're strong enough to challenge fate, run away now."

She couldn't run away. In despair, she realized that she couldn't move.

He cradled her face in his hands and held it still. His lips were warm and searching, and as he drank her tears she knew there would be no force. She wouldn't run; she wouldn't submit. She would consent; she would rejoice, as if ten years and terrible betrayal had never separated them.

His taste, his scent, the texture of his skin, all were unbearably familiar. He moved his fingers through her hair, not to possess or punish, but to savor the feel of it. She was exhausted from struggle; there was nothing left inside her to summon a voice of reason. The only realities were his lips on hers, his fingers releasing the buttons on her dress, his hands against her skin, her heart beating faster.

The years faded away, and she was a young woman in her beloved's arms. Rafe had taught her what little she knew of love, and she had never forgotten it. Everything that had happened since seemed a blasphemy, and his body was redemption. There was no

cruelty in his hands, no punishment in his lips. As he took, he returned pleasure until she was heavy with it.

"This will change your life," he whispered.

She remembered their night on the *Dowager,* and her response.
"Dear God, I hope so." And it was true. She wanted nothing so
much as change. She wanted to be the woman who had believed
in love. She wanted to forget the lies, the deceptions, the secrets,
of the past ten years. She wanted him. She wanted to be reborn.

His flesh was warm, and the breeze from the Gulf was cool against
her naked skin. He pulled her into a hidden place beside a dune, where
the sand was as soft as clouds against her back. In a voice hoarse with
emotion, he told her that he loved her, and she knew it was true, just
as she knew that he hated himself because it was a weakness.

There was nothing to say in return. Her body warmed to his as
if it had been frozen in time. As he entered her, she knew that she
had never stopped loving him, and that she never would. They were
doomed to love each other.

They were doomed.

"Look at me. Be sure you know who I am."

At the height of passion she opened her eyes and stared into his.
She knew who he was. She saw his torment, his struggles, the boy,
the man. The man who would haunt her dreams forever. "I know."
She wrapped her arms and legs around him. She wanted to swal-
low him, to keep him inside her forever, to never relinquish a moment of their coming together. "I know!"

He spilled his seed inside her as she found her own pleasure.

Afterward, they lay without touching. Shadows moved between
them, visions of moments that had passed and moments still to
come. Tears choked her, and she didn't know which of them she
wanted to cry for first.

"Will you tell me about Nicolette?" she asked at last. "Or will
you still punish me?"

He turned to her. "Nicolette is her mother's daughter. In the end, it
was impossible to resist loving her, no matter how dangerous it was."

She gave a small, choked cry. He gathered her close and held her tightly against him. "You gave her to me when she was an infant, but the day I saw you in Audubon Park was the day you made her mine."

"Then you're a real father to her?"

"I try."

"Tell me about her. Please?"

He told her the little things, and the big. She listened avidly.

In too short a time, he had finished. "She'd rather sing than talk, and usually does. She exasperated every music teacher I found until Clarence Valentine took her under his wing. She knows the words to any song after she's heard it once. She sings for me every night before she goes to bed. Sometimes, hours later, when I go upstairs to my room, I still hear her humming."

She couldn't speak. This was what she had wanted for her daughter, but the picture tortured her. She had sacrificed this: contented evenings, the warm arms of the only man she had ever loved, a daughter she could never replace.

"She asks about her mother more often now," he said. "Next time I'll tell her that her mother loved her. That she wanted her very much and watches over her still."

"Please."

He stroked her hair. "We haven't been given a second chance."

"This...tonight...will only make things harder for us."

He turned so that she could see his face. "I'm going to leave New Orleans."

"No..."

"I'm going to take Nicolette and go. I'll start a new life, and so will you."

"Rafe, you can't leave. Not now."

"Especially now."

Even as she protested again, she knew he was right. Their lives were so terribly entwined that disaster was inevitable. She couldn't leave Hugh; she couldn't live openly with Rafe. There was no place where together they could keep Nicolette safe from hatred and prejudice, no place safe from Henry's reach.

"Will I know where you are?"

"No. Your husband's a dangerous man. What would he do to you if he discovered you no longer hate me?"

"I just need to know where you'll be. I just need to be able to picture you there."

"Don't picture me. Forget I exist. We've nearly destroyed each other already. You have to be completely free of me or I will destroy you, and you me."

"Why did it have to come to this?"

"Because neither one of us was pure enough to challenge fate and win." He brushed her hair off her cheek. "Have you forgiven me for everything I've done?"

"Have you forgiven me?"

They stared into each other's eyes and knew that neither would ever really forget the pain endured at the other's hands. It was as much their legacy as the love that had brought them to this place and time.

"You'll be gone, but you'll still be in my life." She kissed him, but her lips trembled. "I'll always wonder where you are. I'll think about Nicolette until the day my heart stops beating. I've always prayed I'd catch another glimpse of her. Every time I turn a corner, I hope that by some chance she'll be there. Now I'll never see her again." Her voice caught.

"It would just be harder for you if you did."

"No! I'd have a memory of her, a real memory. Rafe, can I see her before you go? Talk to her? Hear her sing? Just once?"

"It's too dangerous."

"We could be careful. Please! It's all I'll ask."

"I don't know."

She knew she had to be content with that. She touched his face, memorizing all the planes and angles, the textures of his skin. "Remember I loved you. Wherever you go, remember that. I can give you that to keep."

He kissed her, and no more words were exchanged. Their

bodies said what their lips could not. When he was gone, she dressed in the shadows. It was almost morning before she returned to the cottage and packed to go home.

CHAPTER 29

She was not to tell Nicolette who she really was.

Aurore folded the letter from Rafe and gazed around the room, searching for a hiding place. After the letter arrived that morning, she had slipped it under her mattress. Her bedroom was decorated sparingly with cypress furniture made by Louisiana artisans of the early nineteenth century. But none of the sleek inlaid armoires or cabinets was a safe place for secrets.

A small fire burned on the hearth to steal the chill from the November air. As the United States celebrated the end of the war, the deadly Spanish influenza had arrived. Aurore kept the house warm, just as she diligently kept Hugh out of crowds and away from Henry, who went to the riverfront every day. Epidemics of old had often arrived on foreign ships; Aurore was frightened that the flu might, too.

Silently she repeated the contents of the letter. On Friday, Rafe and Nicolette would wait for her in an apartment above a shop he owned in the Vieux Carré. The old woman to whom he rented it would be away, and she had agreed to let Rafe use it. Aurore was not to tell Nicolette who she was.

How could Rafe believe that she would ever have the courage?

She went to the fireplace, where she had known since receiving the letter that she would have to consign it. She didn't want to burn it. Even now she could see Rafe's handwriting, a bold scrawl that was so like the man. They had created a child together, yet she had nothing of him.

Nothing was left but ashes on the hearth when she heard the door open behind her. Without turning, she recognized the footsteps crossing the room. She rubbed her hands together as if she had been warming them. "We left supper for you, Henry. Sally roasted a hen, and there are potato croquettes and turnip tops, I think."

She turned before he could reach her. She could protect herself best if she knew what to expect. "I'm sorry I ate without you. Would you like me to come sit with you?"

"Such an accommodating woman."

"I try to be." She smiled the cool, inscrutable smile she saved just for him. She saw that he had been drinking, though it might not have been apparent to anyone else. He had a large capacity for whiskey, which usually seemed to intensify his mood. But she had never blamed any of Henry's failings on alcohol.

"Who else do you accommodate, Rory?"

"What do you mean?"

"Who else?"

She searched for an answer. "I try to please Hugh, but not spoil him. I try to be as pleasant as possible in business dealings...."

"And Rafe Cantrelle? Do you accommodate him, too?"

She was careful not to show her alarm. She lowered her voice. "Please. That was a long time ago...before we were married. Are you going to punish me forever for something that happened before we met?"

He moved so swiftly she didn't have time to retreat. He wrapped his fingers around her neck, the heel of his hand pressed tightly against her throat. "Then let's talk about Grand Isle."

She tried to get away but couldn't. He held her while she struggled. "Let go of me!" she gasped.

He pressed his hand against her throat until she could barely breathe. She struggled more, but the harder she tried to get away from him, the harder he pressed. Finally she made herself go limp, and he relaxed his hand until air rushed back into her lungs.

"Tell me about Grand Isle."

She took a deep breath, then another. The room spun. "There's nothing to tell. I went there for the dedication of the church. I...I gave a donation in my mother's name after she died. As a memorial. That's all."

"You didn't tell me."

"I didn't want you to be angry. It was my money, but I thought you might disapprove."

He stepped away and dropped his hands, as if he were satisfied. She knew better.

"And where did you stay?"

"Someone on the fund-raising committee had a cottage."

"You stayed there alone?"

She rubbed her throat. The skin felt raw. "Of course."

"Tell me about the ceremony."

"I was moved. My mother would be happy there's a church on the island now."

"Your mother was a slobbering lunatic committed for most of her miserable life to an asylum."

"I'm sorry. I should have told you, but it was something I needed to do, and I was afraid you'd make it difficult."

"What else would you like to tell me?"

She went very still. "What else would you like to know?"

He struck her so swiftly, and with such force, that only when she was lying on the floor did she realize what he'd done. She had just enough time to cover her head before he fell on top of her and rained more blows over her shoulders and arms. When she tried to get away, he hit her harder.

The attack ended as swiftly as it had begun. He got back to his feet. "Get up."

When she didn't move quickly enough to suit him, he kicked her ribs. But the kick was just a warning. She rose with her hands out in front of her to ward off more blows. He lifted a brow, as if to ask why she thought she needed to defend herself.

"What else would you like to tell me, Rory?"

"Have you gone crazy?"

"Tell me about Rafe Cantrelle."

"He was there. I admit it. But I didn't know he was going to attend. How could I have known?"

This time, when he hit her, she was ready. She braced herself so that she only stumbled backward. "Tell me what happened," he demanded. "All of it. Because I'll know if you leave anything out."

"Nothing happened, except that we talked for a few minutes!" She was dizzy and nauseated, but fear eclipsed both. She could feel something, probably blood, trickling down her chin. "He told me he was leaving New Orleans and taking Nicolette. I told him I was glad, because I've spent too much of my life hating him. Now I never have to think about either of them again." She held out her hands, pleading. "It's over, Henry. Completely over!"

He smiled and moved toward her again.

Nothing was over until the door finally closed behind him. Aurore lay in front of the fireplace, by the ashes of her lover's letter, too bruised and aching to rise.

At the end, she had done nothing to defend herself. She had allowed Henry to beat her, because he had earned that right. Not because he was her husband, but because she had deserved his abuse. She was everything he suspected and more.

From the attic room of the house in the Vieux Carré, Nicolette stared out at roofs that looked like waves in a storm-tossed sea. Rain had fallen recently, and the old slate and tile glistened. Behind her, Rafe paced back and forth. The room seemed too small for him, the ceiling too low. He was a giant in a child's dollhouse adorned with lace and faded flowers.

The door had been left ajar, but neither Nicolette nor her father realized that Aurore was standing on the other side of it, or that she could hear them. Nicolette tugged at the hem of her dress. Aurore wondered if Rafe had bought it for her just for today. The dress was blue, with red-and-white trim. She wore matching red bows in her hair, and soft white stockings. She was the most beautiful little girl Aurore had ever seen.

"Where's the lady who lives here?" Nicolette asked.

"I told you. She's gone away for a while."

"I'm tired of waiting."

"It shouldn't be much longer."

Nicolette closed her eyes as Rafe stepped forward and smoothed her hair back from her face. She leaned against him, as if it were the most natural thing in the world, and he wrapped his arms around her. "You look very pretty today," he said.

"Will the lady who's coming think so?"

"If she has eyes."

"Tell me about her."

"I told you, Nicolette. She was a friend of your mother. She wants to see you before we leave."

"But why do we have to meet here? Why can't she come to our house?"

"She's white. And we're not."

"My skin's white. Almost."

"But you're a Negro. Like me."

"Your skin is white, too."

"Do you want to be white?"

She appeared to think it over. "I could sit at the front of the streetcar," she said.

"Yes, you could."

"If I was white, I could go to any school I wanted."

"Except the ones that only have colored children."

"I'd miss Anne Marie and Mignon."

"A good reason not to be white."

She moved away to search his face. "Why was my mother friends with a white woman?"

"You can ask her."

"Violet married a white man."

"Violet will have to spend the rest of her life pretending she is what she isn't," Rafe said.

"I don't understand why."

"You never will."

Aurore couldn't bear to stand in the hallway any longer. She couldn't bear any more barriers between them. She knocked on the door and stepped inside. She stopped, afraid to move forward. Nicolette gave a little curtsy, as if she had been tutored in advance. "Hello."

Aurore still didn't move. She turned her eyes to Rafe, because looking at her daughter, so close and yet a million miles away, was painfully bittersweet. "Rafe?"

"Come in, Mrs. Friloux, and meet Nicolette."

Aurore forced herself to move forward. Slowly, so that the room suddenly seemed much longer than it was. She stopped just in front of Nicolette. "Do you remember me?" she asked.

Nicolette appeared to search her memory. "I don't think so."

"I met you a long time ago. When you were only six. You got into my carriage, and I gave you a locket."

"Oh." She looked up at her father, as if she dimly remembered that he had taken it from her. "I don't have it anymore."

"I know."

Aurore addressed Rafe. "May we sit?"

"I'm going to leave you alone," he said.

"Alone?"

"Yes. I think it's best." He put his arm around Nicolette's shoulder. "I'll be back in a little while."

Aurore wished with all her heart that Rafe would stay. For a moment she thought he might, because he didn't move. They stared at each other, the way people did when they wanted to speak but didn't know what to say. Then he left the room.

Emilie Richards

Nicolette stood quietly, waiting for her to speak. Aurore found her voice. "Shall we sit?"

"I guess."

There was a bench across the room, padded with faded velvet-and-satin cushions. They sat together, and Nicolette stroked her hand against the velvet.

Where should she start? Aurore knew she had only a brief time to ask the questions of a lifetime, minutes to absorb the sweetness of this child, her child, who she would never see again. "Nicolette, what did your father tell you about me?"

"He said you knew my mother. He said you wanted to see me before we go away."

"Yes."

Nicolette looked up, interested. "Well, did you know her?"

Aurore looked away. "Yes. I knew her well."

"Did she want a little girl, do you think?"

"Absolutely. She very much wanted a daughter. She would have been proud of you. She would have loved you, Nicolette."

"Do you think so?"

"I'm absolutely sure."

Nicolette scuffed her toe against the carpet. "Did she work for you?"

"No. We were...friends."

"Is that why you wanted to see me? To see if I look like her?"

"I've thought about you since she died. I just wanted to be sure you were happy." Aurore tried to smile. "And well."

"Oh, I never get sick." Nicolette obviously couldn't sit still a moment longer. She began to cross her ankles, first one way, then another. It became a dance.

"Are you happy you're moving?"

"Oh, yeah. Yes, I mean. I can ride the streetcar in Chicago. And I can sit anywhere I want."

"Chicago?"

"That's where we're going." Nicolette frowned. "I don't know if I'm supposed to tell you that. Papa said I shouldn't tell anyone where we're going, but I don't know if he meant you."

"What will you do there?"

"I have to go to school, but I can have music lessons again. Do you like music?"

"Oh, yes."

"My friend Clarence lives there now, and he'll give me lessons. Clarence plays the piano. He's better than anybody, even Jelly Roll or Tony Jackson. Least, that's what everybody says. I never got to hear them." She frowned. "Maybe I will someday. Think so?"

"I hope so. Your father says you like to sing."

"I sing all the time. Sometimes he has to tell me not to." She leaned closer, frowning as she gazed at Aurore's face. Aurore knew too well what the child saw. "Did you fall and hurt yourself?"

"I can be very clumsy."

"Me too. Papa says I'll have to learn to be still someday."

"I can't imagine why."

"Because I'm annoying. I have the worst manners at my school, and my French is worse than anybody's."

"You're beautiful and intelligent and altogether wonderful."

"Would my mother have liked me, do you think?"

"She...would have adored you."

"What did she look like?"

Aurore hesitated. "How do you imagine her?"

"Tall. Bea—ut—iful. With one of those smiles like the ladies in the moving pictures. You know, like this?" She stretched her mouth wide. "Like the Gish sisters."

Aurore smiled, too. "That's a very good description."

"I don't know if I want to be in the movies or just sing."

"Will you sing for me now?"

Rafe had told Aurore that Nicolette never hesitated to sing when asked. Music was her greatest joy, as comforting as his arms. But now she seemed suddenly shy.

"Please?" Aurore asked.

Nicolette stood reluctantly. "I sing the blues sometimes. Do you like the blues?"

"They make me cry."

"Well, if you cry, that means I sang them right."

"Then go ahead."

"I know some funny songs that make people laugh. Maybe I should sing one of those."

Aurore realized that the child had sensed her sadness. "Sing what you want to. Anything that seems right to you," she said softly, touching Nicolette's hand.

"I wish Clarence was here. When he plays for me, I don't even have to think about the words." Nicolette closed her eyes and started into one of Aurore's own favorites, "Saint Louis Blues." As she gathered confidence, she sang a little louder.

By the time Nicolette opened her eyes, Aurore was crying and Rafe had returned.

"Oh, Nicolette." Aurore wiped her eyes.

"I guess I sang it right."

Aurore held out her arms, and Nicolette went into them shyly. Aurore inhaled the scent of talcum powder. She wanted to hold Nicolette this way forever, to cushion and protect her. She would have fought a hundred battles to keep Nicolette against her. Nicolette put her arms around her neck and hugged her back.

Rafe spoke. "Mrs. Friloux has to go now, Nicolette."

Aurore made a sound of protest, but she felt Nicolette stir against her. In a moment she would be gone.

"Thank you for coming to see me," Nicolette said. "I'm glad you liked my song."

Aurore put her hands on Nicolette's shoulders and held her away so that she could see her. "I brought you a gift, but your father has to agree to let you have it."

"Of course," Rafe said.

Sadness was like a fog in the room. It seemed to surround and yet separate them all. Rafe's face was lined with tension, and Nicolette looked as if she wanted to go home.

Aurore pulled a small box from a soft leather bag that was the same pale gray as the dress she was wearing. "Will you open it now?"

Nicolette nodded, glad, perhaps, to have something to do. Inside the box was a gold locket. She held it up and swung it slowly back and forth. "You took it away from me," she said, turning again to her father. "I remember."

"I was wrong to take it."

"May I have it now, then?"

"Yes."

"Open it," the lady said.

Nicolette didn't struggle. She pressed the clasp and stared with interest as the two halves parted. Inside, cut to fit, was a small photograph of Aurore.

"To remember me," Aurore said.

"Thank you." Nicolette appeared to be thinking about what to say next. "I'll keep it always," she added with a grin, as if she were delighted that, for once, her manners hadn't failed her. She slipped the locket over her head. It fell to the middle of her chest.

"I'll walk you downstairs," Rafe told Aurore. "Nicolette, stay here."

"Do I have to?" Nicolette glanced up at him again and changed her mind when she saw his expression. "Okay."

Aurore kissed her on the cheek. Nicolette hesitated; then she returned the kiss. Aurore stood and touched Nicolette one last time. Just a light pat on the shoulder. Then she crossed the room, and without another look she went out the door with Rafe just behind her.

Aurore stopped at the bottom of the stairs. "When will you leave?"

Rafe watched her. She hadn't looked at him as she spoke, and she hadn't said anything about her visit with their daughter. Rafe wanted more, and knew he should have had less. "In the next day or two."

"It was easier not knowing how perfect she really is." Her voice caught. "It was easier hating you."

"Neither of us was born for easier."

"You could write me through my attorney, Spencer St. Amant."

"I won't."

Her sigh became a moan, a downward spiral of misery. "Rafe."

He had promised himself that he wouldn't touch her again. Their lives were already so hideously intertwined. He pulled her into his arms, despite everything he had vowed. They would pay for this as they would pay for everything else.

She locked her arms behind his head and returned his kiss with the same desperation that rushed through him. There were noises from the street and from the shop she had entered to reach the apartment. He pressed her harder against him, as if he could absorb her into his soul and take her with him.

He was the one who finally broke free. He stared at her in the dim light and saw what he had missed before. "Gerritsen beat you."

She was crying. "No. I fell."

"What does he know?"

"Nothing. I'm fine. Please, don't worry."

He tilted her chin and stared at her. She looked away. "It's come to this, hasn't it? I can't protect you. My very existence is a threat to you."

"He only knows we met on the isle, Rafe, but I told him you were leaving town. I told him we would never see each other again. I think he believed me."

"Does he know—?"

"No. I'm sure he doesn't suspect we were lovers."

"He suspects."

"It doesn't matter. You're leaving. We'll both be safe."

He was filled with rage. He had never felt less like a man. Now he knew exactly how he had been branded by his father's blood. Men like his father had died for so much less than loving and protecting their women.

"I'll be with you wherever you go," she said. She touched his cheeks. She was still crying. "I love you. I'll never love anyone else."

He couldn't speak. He turned away; then he turned back. He pulled an envelope from the pocket of his coat. She took it without a word. Inside was his favorite photograph of Nicolette. It captured everything their daughter was.

She held the photograph to her chest. He stared at her and saw the whole woman, her intolerance, her cowardice, as well as all the things he had loved too well. He knew he would remember her this way. He would never forget.

When he reached the top of the stairs, he didn't look back. He went into the apartment to take his daughter home.

CHAPTER 30

"Henry worked late that night, just as he did almost every night after the Armistice. His life at that time was a precarious balance of city politics and Gulf Coast. When his efforts to become a real part of the city's political machine stole too much time from his work, he had to make it up when he could."

Phillip helped Aurore up several steps and through the door into the morning room. He had remained silent as she spoke. From their first meeting, he hadn't wanted to feel anything for this woman and her struggles. Then, after he discovered her identity, he had been coldly furious. Now, despite himself, he felt compassion. Fifty years had passed, but she still suffered for decisions she had made. That suffering was in her voice.

She continued. "We still weren't certain how the war's end would affect Gulf Coast. The purchase of a freighter had been so successful that we'd bought another. I believed there would be a market for almost any commodity we could import. The war had been a time of deprivation. With the world safe for democracy, I believed that thoughts would turn to a higher standard of living. Prices would soar, and Gulf Coast would prosper.

"Henry half believed me. I'd shown an instinct for trends. Although I didn't frequent the office as much as I once had, I stayed up-to-date. There was little he could do that I wasn't aware of, and despite my successes, my meddling infuriated him."

Aurore sank to a seat in the morning room. Phillip leaned against the wall, his arms crossed against his chest.

"But then, much about me infuriated Henry," she said. "He'd thought I would be easy to manipulate, but in every way I frustrated him. I escaped his control. I traveled to Grand Isle without his knowledge, and only a passing remark by someone who had seen me there alerted him."

"So that's how he knew."

She rested her head against the back of her seat and closed her eyes. "That night was particularly dark and quiet. The new Gulf Coast offices were in the middle of a poorly lit section of the riverfront. Usually there were others on the street, men like Henry, who stayed late to squeeze every ounce of profit from the day's successes. But by the time Henry left, even the most die-hard had gone home, and the street was empty. He had driven himself to work. He hurried toward the corner where he had parked, but not quickly enough. A man stepped out of the shadows."

She opened her eyes and turned to Phillip. "In later years, when Henry was at his worst, I tried to imagine that beating as a small compensation. I could imagine the night growing darker. The quiet suddenly shattered by the impact of a fist against his flesh. I'm sure he defended himself, hands up, feinting, darting from side to side, but he was no match for the attacker he couldn't see."

"Rafe?"

She didn't answer directly. "Henry's attacker was a phantom. He struck again and again, with lightning speed. Eventually Henry fell to the banquette. He curled into a ball and protected himself as best he could while the phantom kicked him. When the blows finally ceased, he fainted where he had fallen. He was found there much later that night. His recovery took weeks."

Phillip was silent as he thought about everything she had told him. He had felt compassion for Aurore, but he felt none for her husband.

"I never saw Rafe again." Her eyes didn't waver. She continued to watch him.

"What happened to him?"

"Have you ever asked your mother about her life in Chicago?"

"My mother prefers not to talk about her past. She never even told me her real surname."

"Ask her about Chicago, Phillip."

"And if she pretends that she can't remember?"

"Ask her again. Because only she can tell you."

By anyone's standards, Nicky was a success. She'd had an enviable career, first in Europe, then, in later years, in the United States. She had toured with some of the world's finest bands, rubbed shoulders with jazz greats and rhythm-and-blues idols. Her earliest recordings were classics now, in honored positions on the shelves of musicologists and collectors. Her newest recordings sold well enough to prove that she still had an audience apart from the one that crowded Club Valentine. She had avoided the addictions that often went with her profession, and after years of searching she had found a man who cherished and respected her.

There had been sorrows along the way. She had loved two men before Jake, and those love affairs had nearly destroyed her. She had struggled alone to raise Phillip in the midst of a war so vast and terrible that at times she had lost all hope of surviving it.

And she had watched her beloved father die at the hands of a madman.

It was the last that had haunted her since the day Phillip had asked about his roots. It was no surprise to Nicky that her son wanted to know who he was. She had been a good mother; she had no regrets about the decisions she had made and the love she had showered on him. She couldn't look at Phillip without being proud—or without wishing that she and Jake had been blessed with children together.

But she had failed her son in one important way. She had not told him about the man he so resembled. And she hadn't told him, because so many years later, the memory of her father's death still had the power to claw at her, to wound her in new and different ways each time she remembered it. She hadn't wanted Phillip to suffer, too.

Now she knew that she had been wrong.

"I have reasons for asking," Phillip said. He sat across from her in the apartment above Club Valentine that served as an office, as well as guest quarters for out-of-town performers.

Nicky thought she knew his reasons for wanting to know more about who he was. Phillip had always known exactly what he wanted to do with his life. Even adolescence hadn't shaken him. He had come through those troubling years with self-assurance. He was a man who looked forward, not inward. But Phillip had reached a turning point.

"Have you seen Belinda since you got back?" she asked.

"No." He bit off the word as if it hurt to say it.

"I haven't seen her since the night she was here with you. Maybe she's using the Mardi Gras break to visit family out of town."

Phillip stood and began to pace the narrow strip of carpet in front of the sofa. "We didn't part on the best of terms."

"That could be fixed."

"What have I got to offer her?" He stopped in front of her, hands shoved deep in the pockets of his dark slacks. "The world's going up in smoke, and I don't know where it's going to end. Somebody killed Malcolm X last week. We're bombing North Vietnam now, and that war's only going to get worse. There's going to be a civil rights march next week starting in Selma, and already people are talking about what to do when it gets violent. Not if, *Mère,* but when. What kind of world is this? Am I supposed to settle down and make a life with Belinda in the middle of chaos?"

"You're not supposed to do anything except what you know is right for you. But don't wait for the world to be safe and comfortable, Phillip, before you make your choices. Because it never will be."

"Look at yourself. You can't even talk about your childhood. Your memories are so painful you've locked them away. What kind of world were you brought into? What kind of world would a child of mine be born into?"

"Yes, look at me." She stood, too. "What do you see? Someone who suffered? Welcome to the human race. Someone who'd rather not dredge it up? Welcome to the human race. But how about someone who persevered and led a good life in spite of everything?"

He didn't smile. "Welcome to the chosen few."

"I've been wrong not to tell you more about my childhood. Some wounds bleed no matter how old the scars that cover them. Even at my age, it's easier not to remember some things."

"I'm sorry. I shouldn't have asked."

"Come sit with me." She settled back on the sofa and patted the space beside her, as she had when he was a little boy. "Because I've been thinking about this since the last time we talked about it. And I want to tell you about your grandfather. I always planned to, but I told myself the time was never right. Well, it's past right. Way past it. You can be proud of the people you've come from, even if you're not proud of the world that they lived in."

He took her hand and squeezed it. "I've always been proud of you."

"Someday I'll tell you what little I remember about my years here. But not now. You asked about Chicago." She took a deep breath, as if she might not have the chance again. "We left New Orleans for Chicago when I was eleven. When I say we, I mean my father and me. I loved my father. And you know how I adored Clarence. When Papa and I got on that train to Chicago, all I could think about was that I was going to see Clarence again. He wasn't really my grandfather, Phillip. My father's name was Cantrelle, Rafe Cantrelle, and Clarence was just a good friend. Clarence had gone north a year before, because the money was better. Seemed like New Orleans jazz just packed its suitcase and started toward Chicago about the time of the first World War."

She waited for Phillip to question her about that, but he seemed willing to let her warm up slowly.

"It was a different world. I don't even know how to tell you. My father had money, from investments in New Orleans, I suppose. We bought a house in a neighborhood on the South Side, outside the Black Belt. Negroes were just starting to move in. There'd been trouble about it, I think. I remember talk of bombings. But by the time we got there, things were quiet, and if we weren't welcomed, at least nobody burned a cross in our yard. There weren't many other places to live. Black people were living ten to an apartment. The only way to change that was to spread into white neighborhoods. Clarence refused to. He didn't mind the crowding. He grew up in the worst New Orleans slums. The Black Belt felt just like home."

She slipped her hand from his and folded her hands. "I don't know how to tell you what I felt. The air was different there, and I'm not talking about the weather. In New Orleans, Papa and I kept to ourselves. I wasn't white, and I wasn't black. I wasn't even a colored Creole. I didn't fit anywhere except with Papa."

"And suddenly you belonged?"

"Belonged? I don't know about that. But Chicago was like a light coming on. There was energy there, a different kind of energy. In New Orleans our energy was all in our music. We knew we were going no place fast, and we sang about it, blew our frustration into pawnshop coronets and banged it on the keys of barroom pianos. But up north there was hope. I sat anywhere I wanted on the streetcars and trains, went to school with white kids, said hello over the back fence to white neighbors. I'm not saying it was perfect. But it felt like a place to start. Do you understand what I mean?"

"It's still just a place to start."

"My father got involved in the community right away. There weren't any Jim Crow laws to make it hard for him to do business. He bought into a real estate company, made investments. I don't know how many, but we lived well, and we were accepted in a way we never had been before. I can't tell you what my father felt, but I can tell you what I saw. He got quieter in those first months away from New Orleans, and he turned into someone else. It was like he decided he needed to change the world."

"He was right."

"Problem is, I think he began to believe he could. Then it turned into summer. Everything changed, all right. And he was caught in the middle of it." She stopped, stopped talking, even stopped breathing for a moment.

Then she faced Phillip and touched his cheek. "That's when he was killed—saving my life." .

Nicolette was an avid reader, and she was aware of some of the worst effects of racism. In 1917, resentment over Negro employment in East Saint Louis erupted into violence, and when the fury spent itself, forty-seven people, mostly Negroes, lay dead.

Racial hatred continued to simmer wherever Negroes moved into jobs vacated by the whites who had gone to fight. But not all Negro men stayed behind. At the war's end, the return of proud black doughboys, men who had served their country and risked their lives, fanned the flames of prejudice. In Georgia, a Negro soldier was beaten to death for wearing his uniform home from the train station. By the summer of 1919, race riots had broken out in the North and the South alike.

Nicolette read about lynchings and riots in the *Defender,* one of Chicago's Negro newspapers, but they were horror stories from far away. She preferred to study what musician was playing what music where. Names like Keppard and Oliver, Ory and Armstrong, sent songs trilling through her head, and she dreamed of nights at the Royal Gardens or the Lincoln Gardens Café.

Clarence was playing with a band at the Dreamland, and she had been there once to see him, but only before the night really began for everyone else. A singer—not much older than she was, and not nearly as good—had come to their table to wiggle her hips and serenade them, and when the song ended, Nicolette had wanted to follow her right around the room, collecting her own tips.

Her father always insisted that he understood what music meant to her—just before he reminded her that school was more important. She liked school, and she haunted the library because she loved to read. But music was different. It throbbed inside her, building until it had to escape. She breathed it in with every breath, tasted and touched and saw it in bursts of radiant color. Sometimes the voices of her teachers became songs; sometimes the words on a page changed to notes, and she could chart the rise and fall of a story like the wailing of the blues.

As the temperature soared in July, her father spent more time away from home. She didn't know exactly where he went, except that his meetings had to do with improvements for Negroes. People listened to him when he spoke, even though he hadn't lived in Chicago long. But a lot of people hadn't lived there long, and sometimes it seemed like most of them had come from Louisiana.

The lazy summer days ended abruptly on a Sunday afternoon in July. Nicolette had gone to spend the day with a new friend who lived nearby, because her father was away on business. The temperature had hit a record high, and she and her friend Dolly were too hot to do more than sit under the shade of a tree in a nearby park and complain because no one could be coaxed to take them swimming at the lake.

By late afternoon, it was clear that something was wrong. Groups of people passed, chattering excitedly, and from somewhere in the distance whistles shrieked. But only after Dolly's mother, Etta, came to fetch them did they learn what had happened.

Etta Slater had short legs and no visible neck, as if at birth someone had compressed her like the squeeze box of an accordion. She didn't greet them with her usual smile, but she was obviously relieved when she spotted them. "We're going home. Right now."

"Why, Mama?" Dolly whined. It was too hot to move, and certainly too hot to hurry. Nicolette would have whined, too, if Etta had been her mother.

"Don't talk back. Just come. You, too, Nicolette. Right now."

The girls got to their feet, but they were still moving slowly. Etta grabbed Dolly and shook her. "I said come on! Don't think I don't mean it!"

Both girls moved faster. Etta took each of them by one arm and dragged them across the park. She looked both ways as she went, and when she spotted a group of white men approaching, she pulled them behind a clump of trees. "Be quiet," she mouthed.

By now both girls knew something was terribly wrong. They waited in silence as the men passed. Then they stumbled along with Etta, stopping once more to make themselves inconspicuous behind shrubbery as another group of men went by.

Nicolette heard snatches of the men's conversation, but none of it made sense until they were safely inside Dolly's house and Etta had closed and locked the windows—despite the heat.

"Boy was killed up at the lake a while ago, a colored boy," Etta said as she worked. "Some white boys threw stones at him 'cause he drifted into their part of the water. Like water would know or care who was in it! Some people say a stone hit him, others say he fell off his raft and drowned 'cause he was afraid to go in to shore. I don't know, but I do know there's gonna be trouble. Already is, if I'm hearing right."

"Are the white boys in jail?" Nicolette believed she was in the Promised Land, or a rough equivalent. Surely here murdering Negroes was a crime, even if it wasn't a crime in the South.

Etta made a sound like the wind dying. "You think they're gonna arrest a white boy for killing a colored one? They arrested a colored man for telling them they was doing wrong!"

Nicolette wished her father were there. The way Etta had dragged them home frightened her.

"It's hot in here, Mama," Dolly said. "Why do we have to close all the windows?"

"Listen up, and listen good. Whenever there's trouble like this, we get blamed." She punctuated her words with the slam of another window. "Don't matter whose fault it is. We get blamed. We got to stay out of the way of white people till they get tired of blaming us. I know what I'm talking about. This is gonna be the worst place for trouble right here, 'cause there ain't a lot of us around. If there were, whites'd be scared. But like it is, there's more whites than colored, so they know they can do what they want and nobody going to be around to stop them."

"Why would they want to hurt us?"

"'Cause we're colored. Only reason they need."

"I'm not very colored," Nicolette said. She held out her hand beside Dolly's. Dolly was many shades darker.

"You think that's gonna matter? You any colored at all, that's good enough," Etta said. But the sting had gone from her voice. She almost sounded as if she wanted to cry.

"Will they hurt Daddy?" Dolly asked. Her father was across town for the day, visiting his mother.

"Your daddy's smart. He'll stay out of the way till he can get home."

"I hope my papa's smart," Nicolette said.

"I hope so, too," Etta said. "I hope he don't think 'cause he's living in Chicago he's invisible."

Nicolette hoped not, too. But as the day wore on, then the evening, and Rafe didn't return, she worried more and more.

She stayed with the Slaters that night, although no arrangements had been made. The Slaters had no telephone, so Rafe couldn't have called, even if he was able. They heard gunshots sometime after dark, gunshots so close that she and Dolly hid under an upstairs bed and Nicky taught Dolly to say the Hail Mary until they both fell asleep from exhaustion.

Just before dawn, Mr. Slater came home. Etta left the lights off as he told them what he'd seen. Men, Negro men mostly, had been beaten on the streets. He'd heard that several had been killed right in this neighborhood.

Nicolette was forbidden to wait by the window for Rafe. The shades were all drawn, anyway. All she could do was pray he would come and get her.

She worried about Clarence, too. She wondered where he had been when the riot broke out. He loved the lakeshore because it reminded him of the West End in New Orleans. What if he had been there when the boy was killed? The boy had a name now. Mr. Slater said he was called Eugene Williams and that he hadn't known how to swim very well. That made it worse somehow.

By the time the sun came up, the streets were quiet. Peeking out a window, Etta reported that people were on their way to work. Over his wife's protests, Mr. Slater got ready for his job at the stockyards. From the second story, Nicolette and his wife and daughter watched as he ventured outside, but the streets remained quiet. No one said a word to him as he walked toward the park and the streetcar stop on the other side.

Half an hour later, Rafe arrived. Nicolette threw herself into his arms and sobbed with relief. He made no pretense of trying to reassure her. He thanked Etta and explained that he and some others had spent the night trying to organize a constructive solution to the violence. By the time it became apparent nothing could be done except take cover, it had been too late and too dangerous for him to travel home.

Nicolette clung to him. He was haggard and preoccupied, but undeniably alive. It had never been clearer to her that her father and Clarence were all she had in the world.

On the way home, he held her hand tightly. Only when they were inside did he explain what he intended to do. He sat her down in a soft armchair and squatted in front of her so that they were eye-to-eye. His eyes were like the coals that burned through the night on their fireplace hearth. He hadn't slept, and he hadn't eaten, but his eyes still glowed with outrage.

"There's bound to be more trouble, Nicolette."

"But Mr. Slater went to work."

"Because he was afraid he'd lose his job. But there'll be trouble tonight, if not before. This area was the worst in town last night. I'm just glad you were with Etta. She's got a level head. When I couldn't get home, I knew you'd be safe with her."

"But you'll be home tonight, won't you?"

He shook his head. "We're trying to pressure the mayor to call in the militia. The more businessmen who pressure him, the better our chances. I have to do what I can."

In front of her was a man with her father's face, but his thoughts were somewhere else. "Can't you just stay here? I'll be afraid by myself." Her lip trembled.

"You won't be by yourself." He twisted one of her curls around his finger. "I'm taking you to Clarence's apartment. I don't think any white man is so stupid that he'll penetrate that far inside the Black Belt. If there's trouble, it'll be in places where the whites aren't afraid to go."

"We could stay inside and lock the doors and windows, just like Etta did last night."

"I can't, Nicolette." He smiled, but he'd never looked sadder. "I have to do what I can. I've spent most of my life running from what I am. But what I am is a man, and a man doesn't run. He stands, and he fights."

"But I don't want you to fight!" She threw herself into his arms.

"I'm fighting for you," he said, wrapping his arms around her so that he could stroke her back. He had comforting hands, strong and broad, with long fingers, like her own. "You're all I've got. How can I stay home when I've got a chance to make your life better? Clarence will take good care of you, and maybe when I come back the riot will be over."

"But it's all over now!"

"If you're right, then there won't be anything to worry about, will there?"

She clung to him anyway, and she clung to him again later that afternoon, when he dropped her off at Clarence's apartment. The streets were strangely quiet there, just as they had been at home. Usually there were gangs of children darting between buildings and fighting imaginary wars in the vacant lots. Now the streets were nearly empty.

Nicolette continued to cling to her father even after Rafe straightened. She only moved away when Clarence put his arms around her neck. "Your papa'll be back, Nickel girl. Let him go now so you and me can make some music."

She found a smile, one forlorn farewell smile. Rafe kissed her; then he was gone.

The afternoon wore on into evening. Even her beloved Clarence couldn't make her forget her father's absence. She couldn't concentrate on the words to the new songs Clarence tried to teach her, and she barely touched the red beans and rice that he'd simmered all day especially for her.

In the evening, she heard the first gunshots. An automobile sped through the street outside the front window. She heard the squealing of tires, the gunning of an engine, then the staccato pop of bullets. She'd fallen to the floor and covered her head before Clarence could reach her. The automobile roared past, and the street was silent for a few minutes. Then doors slammed and angry shouts began.

"Young fools!" Clarence helped her up, then peeked between the curtains. "What call they got coming here and shooting at us?"

"My papa said no white man would come this far, that they'd be afraid!"

"Your papa's got sense. Them fools ain't got nothing inside them 'cept hate." He guided her away from the window. "Now there'll be trouble, all right. They think colored people ain't got the sense to defend themselves, but they's wrong. Men on this street killed a hundred Huns between 'em. Lots of 'em armed and itchin' to pull the trigger in a white man's face. We gotta get into a back room and stay there. Wish I had that apartment upstairs."

She let him guide her to a back bedroom. "What if Papa comes? Who'll let him in?"

"He won't come now, not till it's safe. I told you, your papa's got sense."

"But what if he doesn't know what's happening?"

"Nickel girl, he told me to take care of you, and that's just what I'm doin'."

She couldn't argue with Clarence. There was a comfortable bed in the room he deemed safest, and despite her fears she fell asleep quickly.

It was still dark when she awoke. She had heard noises through the night, the distant whine of bullets, and men shouting. But she had drifted back into sleep each time when the noises faded away. This time the streets were quiet, but despite the calm, she sat up and gazed around the room. She was alone.

She got up and went to look for Clarence. He was standing in the front room with a dearly familiar figure. She ran into her father's arms and started to cry.

"Hush, Nicolette." He held her close. "I'm fine. We're all fine."

"I want to go home." She tried to bury her head against his chest. "Or I want you to stay here!"

"I'm not going to leave you. We'll wait a few minutes, and if it's still calm, we'll go."

"You're taking her back home?" Clarence asked.

"No. I was just there, and it's not safe, either. A streetcar strike started at midnight, and tomorrow there's going to be hell to pay when Negroes start walking to work through white neighborhoods. But the mayor still won't call for the militia. I've done what little I can. I've got Nicolette to think about now. We're leaving town."

"Until this is over?"

"No, for good."

Nicolette pulled at his sleeve. "But I don't want to go for good. I want to stay here in Chicago, with Clarence."

"Nicolette, you have to trust me."

"But what about Dolly? What about Clarence?"

"I'm going to take you somewhere we can finally be happy." He squatted so that they were eye-to-eye. "You have to trust me to do what's best for you," he murmured in French, the language they had sometimes spoken at home in New Orleans but never in Chicago. Speaking the words in French strengthened them somehow, and she knew they were final. He touched her hair before he stood and whispered, *"Je t'aime."*

On his feet again, he turned to Clarence. "You could come with us," he said in English. "At least until things are safe here."

"Nah. I guess I'll just stay and watch a while longer. Never saw colored men fighting back before. Never thought I'd live to see the day when we could. If I die watchin'?" Clarence grinned. "It'll be a fine day to die."

"Suit yourself. Just watch from inside." Rafe extended his hand.

"You're a good friend. I'll write and let you know where we are once we get settled."

Clarence shook his hand. "Nickel girl's the grandbaby I never had. I'd do anything for her." Clarence ruffled her hair. "Now don't go getting your papa's shirt all wet. You two get out of here while it's still quiet."

"I'll go out first to be sure. Nicolette, stay here and wait until I motion you to come."

She didn't want her father to leave her behind, but she had no choice. She stood with Clarence's hands on her shoulders and watched as Rafe opened the door and slid into the darkness. She watched through the crack as he descended the steps. The night was still quiet when he got to the gate and eased it open. She could hardly see him as he surveyed the street. Their new Ford was parked half a block down from Clarence's apartment, under the drooping limbs of a giant elm. Rafe started toward it, stopped, then turned and motioned for her to join him.

"'Bye." She kissed Clarence's cheek. "You be care- ful."

She followed her father's path as quietly as she could. Halfway to the gate, she heard a noise and stopped to listen. It was the quiet hum of a motor. She looked to her father for guidance, but he motioned her on. At the gate, she stumbled in the darkness, but caught herself before she fell. When she straightened, she saw a shape moving slowly down the street. It took her precious seconds to realize that it was an automobile with its headlights off. It took her more seconds to realize that her father was waving her back toward the house.

Just as she turned to flee, the automobile gunned its engine. The sudden flare of headlights lit the street. The automobile roared toward them. She saw her father caught in the beam, and she heard a shout.

"This one's for you, Cantrelle!" A gunshot punctuated the words.

She stood, horrified, as her father fell. The automobile slowed as it passed him, and another shot rang out. Then it roared away. Terrified, she ran toward him. "Papa!"

He raised his head. "Go back! Get in the house!"

She couldn't abandon him. The auto was gone, and she was sure her father had been shot. He managed to get to his feet and start toward the elm for cover. She kept running until she had covered half the distance. Only then did she realize that the auto had turned into a side street and was coming toward them again.

She stopped, confusion and horror blocking all thought. The headlights pinned her to the spot. She saw a leering smile, and the outline of a man's hat.

She couldn't move. She was afraid to run, and too confused to seek cover. "You, too, you little yellow bastard!" A bullet whined as it plowed into the ground at her feet.

"No!" Rafe reached her before the automobile did, and she fell under the weight of his body. She heard more gunfire, louder than she had ever known it could be. She felt her father stiffen, then go limp. There was a loud explosion, then another. She screamed and clawed, trying to free herself so that she could help him, but he was too heavy to move.

"Papa!" She tugged at his shoulders.

Rafe's weight was lifted from her, and Clarence knelt by her head. "Are you hit?"

"Papa!"

"Nickel, were you hit?" He touched her face, as if he expected to find blood. But the only blood on her was Rafe's. She pushed Clarence's hands away and sat up. Her father lay beside her, lit by the glare of flames. His eyes were closed.

"They torched the house," Clarence said. "The neighbors', too. We got to get out of here now."

She looked around wildly. Clarence's porch was already in flames. People were pouring into the street. There were screams from the apartment above Clarence's as the residents scrambled to escape.

"Papa!" She bent over her father. "Papa!"

"He's gone, Nickel. He was hit bad, and he wouldn't want you to stay here and die with him."

She fought off Clarence's hands. "No, he's not dead! He's not!" She shook her father's shoulders.

"He's dead!" Clarence tried to pull her away. "Come on, now. We got to get out of here."

"But he wasn't dead," Nicky told Phillip. "Not yet. I bent over him and put my face right up next to his."

Tears slid down her cheeks. For a moment, she couldn't go on. She felt Phillip take her hand and squeeze it. They linked fingers, just as she often had when she walked with her father.

"He opened his eyes." She looked up at her son. "He wasn't surprised he was going to die, Phillip. I could see that, even then. It was like he had always known life was going to end like that for him. He looked at me, and he said..." She turned her head and stared out the window. "He said, 'You are the best of us both.'"

Phillip squeezed her hand and went on squeezing it until she could speak again.

Finally she nodded. "Then he died."

CHAPTER 31

There were children on Belinda's front porch, children dressed as clowns in simple homemade costumes of purple and gold. At first Phillip thought they were just some of the little girls who frequented her life, until an older woman with tired eyes and badly processed hair joined them.

"Is Belinda home?" Phillip started up the stairs. He had never met any of Belinda's family, but he thought this might be one of her married sisters.

"No one by that name here." The woman looked suspicious, but Phillip had gotten suspicious looks since leaving Nicky and Jake's house that morning. He hadn't seen another man in town wearing a sport coat. Had he been dressed as Satan himself, no one would have given him a second look.

He had chosen Mardi Gras day to see Belinda again—a decision that had appealed to him, because he still wasn't sure what he would say to her. Immersed in the noise and confusion of the day, he thought he might be able to feel his way through their reunion. He was a journalist, a man so intimately familiar with words that he ought to have a thesaurus stored inside him. But he still didn't know how to tell her what he was feeling. About her. About his life and who he was. About their future—or even if they had one together.

He paused on the top step, because the woman was moving swiftly toward him, as if to head him off.

"Belinda Beauclaire," he said. "This is her house."

"Uh-uh. This is *my* house." She barred his progress with wide hips.

It had been only weeks since Phillip had seen Belinda and lived right here with her. For a moment, he was as suspicious as the woman's eyes. "How long have you been here?"

"I don't see why I got to tell you."

"Look, a friend of mine, Belinda Beauclaire, lived right here just a few weeks ago. I need to find her."

"I live here now."

Frustration filled him. "Did you just move in?"

The woman shrugged.

"Miss Beauclaire done moved away," one of the little girls said.

The woman waved her hand to shush her. "You better get on," she told Phillip. "Ain't none of our concern."

"Look, I'm not going anywhere until you tell me where she is. I've got to find her."

The woman pursed her lips and folded her arms.

It had never occurred to Phillip that Belinda wouldn't be right here waiting for him to return. For the first time since he'd seen the children on the porch, he realized that he might not find her at all. He could wait until the holiday was over and go to her school, but what if she'd left town? What if her destination was confidential? Few people here knew him or knew about their relationship. Who would he go to for information?

Belinda had always been there for him.

Now she wasn't.

His feelings must have shown in his eyes, or maybe the woman had just gotten tired of him standing there. Her sigh was appropriately world weary. "She be down on Claiborne today."

"Claiborne?"

"You not from here, are you?"

"My mother is Nicky Valentine. I visit here a lot." He was ashamed to use Nicky this way, but only a little. If anyone could open doors, it would be Nicky.

"Belinda's staying with a friend. Don't know where, exactly. You ask down on Claiborne, you find her soon enough." She pointed to the left.

"Thanks. I really appreciate it."

"You wait there." The woman went inside and returned a few moments later carrying a handful of gaudy glass beads. "Put these on."

He took them reluctantly.

"Put 'em on," she ordered. "You Nicky Valentine's boy, you got to look like you part of things."

From the moment he went out into the streets that morning, Phillip hadn't wanted to be part of things. Mardi Gras had always seemed a colossal waste of time to him. He had never been sure that there was anything to celebrate here. Everywhere he looked, he saw walls that all the Joshuas in the world couldn't tumble. Even the parades were segregated, with Rex and other krewes representing the white elite, and Zulu, a Negro krewe in satirical blackface, slyly spoofing the pomposity of Rex.

He strung the beads around his neck anyway and unbuttoned the top two buttons of his shirt. At the car he ditched his sport coat, then locked the doors. Claiborne was a fair hike, but walking seemed easier than driving through the crowds. The trip to Belinda's—or what had once been Belinda's—had been just short of suicidal.

Why had she given up her house? By most standards, it wasn't much, half of a double, with small rooms and no hall. But it was hers, paid for with a job she loved, decorated in colors that would always make him think of her, firmly rooted in a neighborhood where she was loved and respected. There she had taught her heritage classes, watched over the children who played on her street, sat on her porch in the spring when the jasmine was a cascade of fragrant yellow stars.

And why hadn't she gotten word to him that she had decided to move? Surely, despite the way they had parted, she knew he would be back.

He needed her today in a way that he'd never let himself need anyone. He needed to tell her what he'd learned about his family. She was the only one who would understand his confusion. Belinda would feel what he had felt upon learning the way that his grandfather had died. He could count on that. He could count on her.

A day hadn't passed since he'd seen her last that he hadn't wanted to pick up the telephone and tell her that and more. He had spent months away from her in the past, but after their relationship had become established he had believed deep in his heart that he could always come back to New Orleans and take up where they had left off. Now he no longer knew that, and there was a large empty space inside him where that certainty, that foolish, arrogant certainty, had been.

He stopped on a corner to get his bearings. The houses bordering the intersection were southern-shabby, weathered by tropical sun and overgrown with foliage that appeared to snake and twine around doors and windows as he looked on. There were people everywhere, and a low, constant thrumming that seemed to come directly from the earth under his feet.

Something not quite music, more like a litany, poured from a run-down bar in the middle of the next block, a bar like so many throughout the city. The building was compact and, from all visible evidence, jammed beyond capacity. Sound spilled out of the windows, and on the sidewalk in front of the bar, groups of men took up the cadence.

Phillip wanted to find Belinda; he didn't want to stop and see what was happening. He had no interest in local celebrations, or in the fights that would most likely ensue from the lethal mixture of alcohol and testosterone. But the sound coming from the bar was so compelling, he found himself standing still to listen.

There were drums beating, drums like those he'd heard in small African villages. Men's voices chanted words he couldn't understand, and the sound filled the street. Children strutted to its beat or clanged soda bottles together in support. Mothers with babies in their arms clapped their hands and stomped their feet.

The chanting grew louder, the words still foreign to him, nonsense syllables strung together with an odd, raw intensity. He didn't know how long the chanting had been going on. It built subtly but steadily, and he suspected it had been building that way for hours. He found himself swaying to the beat; then he found himself moving closer.

He lost track of time as the chanting and the music continued to crescendo. He was caught in something that went beyond a day or even a season. The cadence was as old as Adam's heart-beat, as sensuous as Eve and as tempting as forbidden fruit. Then the bar door was flung open, and a man in the beaded and feathered costume of an Indian emerged.

The crowd that had gathered outside the bar parted respectfully to give him plenty of room. There was loud appreciation for the exquisite beauty of the costume, which was a brilliant burst of scarlet and turquoise. The man wearing it stood tall and silent; then he started forward, dramatically scanning the area.

"He the spy boy."

Phillip turned and looked at the young man who had come up to stand beside him. He was a teenager, lithe and athletic, whose only attempt at a costume was a satin bandit's mask riding high on his forehead. "Spy boy?"

"Yeah. He the spy boy for the Creole Wild West."

"What's that?"

"You not from here?"

For the second time that morning, Phillip owned up to it.

"They an Indian tribe. Mardi Gras Indians."

Phillip remembered having heard something about the Mardi Gras Indians, but he hadn't understood it, and he hadn't cared. "What's that, exactly?"

"Just one of the tribes. We got lots of 'em."

There was another burst of appreciation, and another man in costume stepped out of the door. His costume was not as elaborate, but he carried a staff, decorated top and bottom with feathers of the same scarlet and turquoise.

"He the flag boy." The young man danced from side to side with the beat of the chanting, which still echoed from inside the bar. "He carry the flag all day. The spy boy watches to be sure no other tribes around. You keep watching. You learn what's what." He went off to join other boys his age on the corner.

The costumes grew steadily more elaborate, until at last, with a huge burst of sound, the last man of fewer than a dozen stepped out. The crowd roared their approval. The costume and matching headdress were spectacular, but the man wearing them was more so. Phillip calculated what the suit and the headdress must weigh, and how much strength the man needed just to walk. But he didn't walk. He glided. He strutted. He was as regal as any European monarch.

The Indians began to sing as they moved off down the street. The others, not in costume, followed at a respectful distance, but as the Indians sang and chanted, the crowd joined in on the chorus.

The young man who had instructed Phillip passed by to catch up with the foot parade following the Indians. He grinned at Phillip. "You like that suit? That's the chief. He got a heart of steel."

"Who makes the costumes?"

"Suits. They make 'em. Every stitch. Every year's different, too."

The Indians disappeared around the corner, but the beat continued. Music spilled from windows and in front of houses where impromptu brass bands blew one-of-a-kind refrains. Phillip walked up a street the Indians hadn't taken, dodging wrestling children and scolding mamas. Crowds overflowed from doorways, and parties flourished on porches and driveways.

The crowd grew larger as he neared Claiborne, and the beat intensified. It was still early, but the heat had intensified, too. He was part of a great surge of people, but he was aware of how alone he really was. All around him people were celebrating together. Masked friends greeted each other in the melee, and grandmothers, aunts and uncles corraled and carried children to share the burden. He was apart from it all, yet he was being swept into the very center of it.

He had come to find Belinda because he thought he wanted solace. Now he realized it was something more he required. He wanted her. The whole woman. The companion. The lover. He wanted to share the strange exuberance of the day, a day that was slowly seeping over him—despite his own melancholy—like a bath of warm honey. He wanted to tuck her securely beside him while they drank in this unique outpouring of culture. The word *lonely* had never existed in any significant way for him, but it did now.

On Claiborne he was swept along by the crowd as he crossed to the neutral ground, the local term for the wide strip of land between the traffic lanes. It was heavily forested with live oaks, and overnight it had developed into a settlement of blankets and picnic tables. Transistor radios countered the steady rhythm of shouts and laughter, and battered horns and saxophones reinforced the din.

He was beginning to feel like a fool for coming. There were thousands of people crowding the streets, and he could have walked right by Belinda and never seen her. He pushed on anyway, glad he had when another Indian tribe, this time in gold and green, came around a corner. He watched the crowd surge around them.

A small contingent of men dressed as skeletons loped by, shaking bones at passing children. An old woman gathered up a wailing child and turned him so that he couldn't see, while three small boys, shaking sticks, took off after the skeletons. The children brushed past him, and one stumbled at Phillip's feet. Phillip lifted him off the ground, and the boy was off like a shot again.

"What'd you do to Percy?"

Phillip turned around to find a little girl glaring at him.

She slapped her hands on her hips. "I said what'd you do?"

The child was familiar, but it took Phillip a moment to place her. "He tripped over my foot. I just helped him up. You're Amy, aren't you? I'm Phillip, Belinda's friend."

The glare faded slowly.

"Hi, Amy." He put out his hand.

She took it with poise, then released it.

"Amy, have you seen Miss Belinda? I'm looking for her."

Amy shrugged. "Ain't seen her."

"Oh."

"She live over there now." Amy pointed to the block just past the one where they stood.

"Do you know which house?"

She shook back her braids. "'Course I do."

He tried again. "Will you tell me which one?"

"White one on the corner."

"Thanks. Maybe I'll find her there."

Amy took off after Percy, and Phillip took off after Belinda. He wound his way through family groups and friends. He interrupted a game of catch and skirted a large group of men playing cards. A vendor tried to sell him peanuts while two older boys in raggedy devil costumes jabbed forked spears at him. As he stepped into the road, an old lady in a flour-sack apron offered him the drumstick off a chicken she was expertly carving up.

The music got louder the closer he got to Belinda's. Someone had hooked up a hi-fi in an upstairs window, and rhythm and blues poured out of large speakers. In front of the house four particularly pretty teenaged girls with arms around each other's waists were dancing in step, moving back and forth along an invisible line, like Radio City Rockettes.

The house, white stucco and well cared for, sprawled over every allowable inch of space on the lot. He estimated it had six bedrooms, at least, and a porch large enough to sleep a dozen. Right now the porch held a party in progress, but Belinda wasn't among the partiers.

On the porch he stopped a young woman and shouted Belinda's name questioningly, but she frowned and shook her head. The second woman he asked cupped her hand behind her ear to hear him better, but he wasn't sure she ever did. He made his way into the house, where the din was muted, and found two men in their early thirties loading up plates from a dining room table groaning with food. Three women carrying casseroles appeared and disappeared, leaving their bounty behind.

"Get you a plate," a broad-shouldered man in a madras shirt and Bermuda shorts said.

"I'm just here to find Belinda Beauclaire. Somebody told me she's living here now?"

"She is."

"Do you know where she is right now?"

"She's off seeing Zulu." The man seemed absolutely sure. As much as Phillip wanted the information, he would have been happier if the man was a little less sure of himself. And of Belinda.

"Do you have any idea how I might find her?"

"It's hard to tell where Zulu will be about now. Why don't you just eat and wait? She'll come back when she gets tired."

"I think I'll go look for her. I'll come back here later if I don't find her."

"Want me to tell her who was here?" The man gave Phillip the once-over with narrowing eyes. He didn't look as friendly as he had at the beginning of the conversation.

"That's okay. I'll be back."

"Try Jackson Avenue," the other man said. He waved a bottle of beer in the general direction.

Out on the street again, Phillip wound his way toward Jackson. He was halfway there, skirting a rugged-looking crowd of pirates, when he saw Belinda. She was coming toward him across the street on the neutral ground, dressed in stark white. A tight white skirt cupped her perfect bottom, and a gauzy blouse flowed over the curves of her torso. A white satin mask with two gracefully drooping feathers covered the top half of her face.

"Belinda!" There was nothing much in the way of traffic to dodge. He avoided pedestrians and made his way into the madness again.

She stopped and stood very still.

He lifted her mask and searched her eyes. She had never looked more beautiful or desirable to him. He wanted to kiss her, but one look told him what a bad idea that would be. She was a woman capable of great emotion, a woman who could melt with passion and ignite a man in the process. But the Belinda staring back at him was a woman who had hidden her feelings well.

"I've had a hell of a time finding you," he said.

"No one asked you to look."

"I wanted to." A crowd of shoving adolescents knocked him closer to her. He took her arm to steady them both. She didn't shake him off, but she looked as if she wanted to. "I was just at your new place. Why did you move?"

"I moved in with a friend."

He pictured the man in the madras shirt and the narrowing eyes. "Why didn't you tell me where you were?"

"How would I have done that?"

"You could have left a message with Nicky."

"Could have." She nodded.

"Why didn't you?"

She pulled her arm from his grasp and started across the street. He stopped her. "No, you don't. Don't go off like that. I want to talk this through, right here and now."

"You made your wishes known, Phillip. You always do. I didn't see any reason to leave you messages." She shook off his hand once more, and this time she made it across.

"Belinda." He took her arm gently this time. "We need to talk. Will you talk to me?"

"I've got nothing to say. I've got a new life now, and you've got the life you always had. The one you want."

"What do you mean, a new life?" When she didn't answer, he made his worst fears a guess. "I met a man at your house who seemed to know you pretty well. Is he part of that new life?"

Before she could answer, a woman came up beside them. "Belinda?"

For a moment, Phillip didn't recognize her, then he realized it was Debby, the teacher he'd met at Club Valentine on the last night he and Belinda were together. She wore a dress of leopard spots and a black half mask that turned her pert face into something feline and mysterious.

"What are you doing here, Phillip?" she asked.

"Just looking for Belinda." He dropped Belinda's arm. "And I guess I found what I was looking for."

"How'd you find her? She just moved in with us."

"Us?"

"Us. Vicki and me and my family."

"Vicki?"

"My baby. You haven't seen her yet? My brother's bringing her up to see Zulu. Jackson's on a float, but the parade's late. I'm going to see if I can find them." With a wave, she crossed the street and headed in the direction of her house.

"It's Debby you moved in with?"

Belinda didn't confirm or deny it.

Phillip had a list of questions a mile long, and he knew she wasn't going to answer them. He had hurt her, and she wasn't going to let herself be hurt again. He didn't understand why or how, not exactly, but she had left him as surely as she had left the house she loved.

"Belinda." He touched her cheek. Her expression didn't change. He dropped his hand. "Let's go see Zulu. Maybe we can talk along the way."

"I'm going home."

"May I walk with you?"

She started toward the house, and he fell in step beside her. He had just blocks to tell her what he was feeling, and he couldn't find the first word. In the midst of the biggest party he'd ever witnessed, he was dead sober, and mute besides.

He cast around for something to say. "I didn't know Debby had a daughter. How old is she?"

"Three."

"Is Jackson the father?"

"Plans to be."

"He's a good man." He reached down and took her hand. She didn't resist, but her hand was limp and unwelcoming. "You loved your house and your privacy, Belinda. I can't imagine you living in that house with all those people. They're not your family."

"They're good people."

"I'm sure they are. I just want to understand what's happening here."

"Why does it matter?"

He stopped and pulled her to a halt beside him. "It matters because you matter to me."

She studied his face. Clearly she didn't think his answer was enough. "I wanted to save money."

"If things were that tight you should have let me know."

"Why?" She started back down the sidewalk.

He tried to understand her responses. She wasn't hostile or disinterested, although with a different inflection, most of her answers might have sounded that way. Instead, she seemed merely intent on getting through this conversation, focused so completely on what she was saying that there was no room for emotion in her voice.

They came to a corner, and he heard a familiar chanting. "Come on this way." He pulled her off Claiborne and toward the sound.

"I have to get back."

"Come with me, Belinda. I've already seen two of the tribes this morning, and I'd like to see this one."

"What would you know about the Indians?"

"I don't know about them. I've just seen them for the first time today."

"Why are you interested?"

He detected skepticism. "I don't know." He honestly didn't. He was a journalist, not a sociologist, and he knew there wasn't a tremendous market for articles on the cultural life of black people.

"Do you think it's silly?"

"Silly? No." He pulled her along. The chanting was getting louder. "I think it's incredible. I don't understand it. Why do they dress that way?"

"They've been doing it for a long time. This is our Mardi Gras you're seeing. Not the white Mardi Gras everyone knows about. Indians and black people have a lot in common. The Indians hid slaves after they escaped, hid them in the swamps and protected them, because they knew what it was like to be hunted. Some people think that's how the Mardi Gras tribes began, as a mark of respect. But it doesn't even matter. Because this is us. This is who we are. This is that culture you don't understand and don't want to be a part of."

"You're angry at me."

"No."

"That night at the club, when I said this wasn't my home, I wasn't saying that I didn't want you."

She faced him and pulled her hand from his. Her eyes were unwavering. "You don't want me, Phillip. You want what you thought we had. You want me to be there waiting when you need a place to come back to for a while."

"I have to travel. I have to be where the news is. In fact, I've got to leave for Alabama the day after tomorrow, so I wanted to settle things with you before I left."

"This isn't about your job, and you know it."

"Then what is it about?"

"It's about being part of something. And you don't know how to do that. Maybe you never will."

"I thought you and I were part of something together." But even as he said the words, he realized it was the first time he'd ever said any like them.

She shook her head. "You stand off by yourself, and you watch. That's what you'll do in Alabama, too, whatever happens there. First time something starts to tug at you, you get on a bus or a plane. You do that too many times, you stop feeling anything. I think maybe that's already happened."

As he was searching for the right response, she carefully skirted him and disappeared into the crowd that was surging forward to see the Indian tribe just turning the corner. He tried to follow, but he was cut off immediately.

Against his will, he was carried along by the enthusiastic crowd. The beat, the steady insistent beat that had drummed all morning, seemed to swell in intensity. Now it was a primal roar, the throbbing of hundreds of hearts and voices. He was immersed in it, and he couldn't fight his way out to find Belinda again, no matter how hard he tried. He could feel the heat and soft give of flesh, smell sweat and beer and woodsy perfume. He was carried forward, stumbling once, then righting himself easily, because there was no room to fall.

The crowd was chanting words he didn't understand. The sound rumbled in his chest until he wanted to chant with them, chant past the strange lump in his throat, chant his own pain. But he couldn't follow the voices of those around him. He was still a stranger here, and his pain was his own. The words, the ritual celebration, were theirs.

The crowd began to fan out and thin as they neared the Indians. People were moving to the sides in respect. He was thrown against a small female body clutching a little girl in her arms. He grabbed them both to stop them from pitching forward, and realized it was Debby.

"Hey, are you all right?"

She laughed. "Sure."

"Let me take her. She'll be safer." He reached for the child, and she went to him willingly. She was tiny, a beautiful little girl with a head of soft dark curls and pale brown skin. She clutched a rag doll in her arms. "Is this Vicki?"

Debby said something, but he couldn't hear her over the chanting. She nodded.

They moved toward the edge of the crowd. The Indians, this time costumed in orange and blue, were surrounded, and only flashes of them were discernible. As Phillip and Debby moved away from the center of the action, the noise lessened.

Phillip lowered his head. He felt required to say something to the child. "I like your doll."

She held it up for him to examine. The doll was handmade. Dark-skinned, like the child holding it. Someone had wanted her to have a toy that resembled her, instead of the white baby dolls that were the only commercial ones available.

They were far enough away from the heart of the noise that Phillip could be sure Vicki heard him. "What do you call her?"

"B'linda."

"Did Belinda give you this?" It would be just like Belinda to be sure that Vicki had a doll she could identify with.

She nodded, and her curls bounced against her cheeks.

He smiled. "She's beautiful, and so are you."

"I gotta learn to hold a baby."

"Do you?"

"B'linda's going to have a baby."

For a moment he didn't understand. "What do you mean?"

"B'linda's got a baby inside her. I gotta learn to hold a baby so I can help when her baby's borned."

Debby snaked her way to their side and held up her arms for her daughter. Phillip held Vicki tightly against him. He couldn't seem to relinquish her. He didn't know what Debby saw in his face, but her arms dropped to her sides. She pushed her mask back and waited warily for him to speak.

"Why did Belinda move in with you?" he asked.

"That's for her to tell you."

"Vicki says she's pregnant."

Debby held out her arms again, and this time he swung the little girl into them. Debby tried to move past him, but he put his hand on her shoulder. "Debby, please."

She lifted her chin. "There's nobody more careful than Belinda."

He knew how true that was. They had never made love without birth control. "I know that accidents happen."

She looked relieved, as if she had been afraid he would think Belinda had gotten pregnant on purpose. "You want to talk about this, you talk to her."

But he and Belinda had already talked about it, only Phillip hadn't known it at the time. They had talked casually about children, about making a home together, about commitment and responsibility. She had carefully, subtly, led him into those conversations and listened to his answers. And then she had gone away.

Because none of his answers had been the right ones.

Debby disappeared with Vicki, and the chanting swelled again. The Indians would move on, but they would leave honor and a fierce, stunning pride in their wake. The lump in Phillip's throat threatened his breath.

From the moment he left Nicky's house, he had been a bystander, an observer. He had thought himself above the ragtag mobs in the street, but now he saw the celebration for what it was. Nothing had kept these people, *his* people, down. Not slavery, not Jim Crow, not the prejudices that would probably rule the city for decades to come. These descendants of the slaves who had defiantly danced in Congo Square, who had developed their own patois, their own religion, their own traditions, had turned their backs on the Mardi Gras that the world knew and made their own. It was a life-affirming celebration, rich in satire, spirit and courage.

He thought of Aurore Gerritsen, who had lost her daughter because of her own prejudice and fears. He thought of Rafe Cantrelle, the man he supposedly resembled, who had nearly lost his daughter because he had been too afraid to love her.

He had not been raised at the knees of his grandparents. They had not been childhood heroes or role models. He had never known them, but still they had bequeathed him a legacy of uncertainty. Like them, he was afraid to love, to hold Belinda safely beside him and make a home despite the mess the world was in. He had never found a place where a black man could truly live free, and so he had never lived anywhere. He had existed on the sidelines, moving, noting, reporting, then moving again. Like his grandparents, he had never taken the largest risks or reaped the largest gains.

Like his grandparents, he had been afraid.

But there was more to Aurore's story than cowardice, revenge and betrayal. Now, at the end of her life, she was struggling to set things right, no matter how agonizing that was. And Rafe had died fighting for his daughter, for Nicky's future and, at the very end, for her life.

His grandparents had bequeathed him uncertainty, but they had bequeathed him more, as well. For the first time, Phillip realized what their story meant, and why Aurore's revelations had been so painful to hear—and so powerful.

Aurore and Rafe had been doomed by their love.

But they had bequeathed their grandson a second chance.

CHAPTER 32

Finding men to clear the trash and debris from the abandoned house and yard in Belinda's old neighborhood had been the least of Phillip's worries. There was serious termite damage to the upper gallery, and vandals had destroyed more than half the windows. The iron lace that defined both galleries—and had so enchanted Belinda—was rusted, but not destroyed. Phillip cleaned it himself, gently sanding off the rust with fine steel wool until it was ready for multiple coats of black paint.

The day after he closed on the house, painters came to sand and prime the old barge board siding, and carpenters tore holes as wide as Lake Pontchartrain in the gallery floors before nailing new boards in place. Replacing the windows took most of a week, because the sashes, sills and ancient louvered shutters had to be carefully repaired, as well.

The inside of the house had fared slightly better. The cypress floors and most of the woodwork were still intact, and a thorough cleaning and waxing restored them to their original luster. Plasterers patched walls and ceilings, and electricians came along behind them to wreak havoc with the fresh plaster. There was no hope for the kitchen, and Phillip had it gutted, replumbed and rewired. But he bought no appliances. That could wait. _The yard, even after its liberation from years of trash, was an eyesore. On his darkest days he was tempted to hack the tangled jungle to the ground with a machete and start all over again. But there was a magnolia tree as tall as the house on one side, and a centuries-old live oak dripping Spanish moss in the back. There was jasmine spilling over the fence, and a row of gardenias that, despite years of neglect, were loaded with buds. He brought in Jake—who could hardly contain his delight—for a lesson in landscaping. Together they tamed the worst of the wilderness, and even Nicky, who had shown great talent as a window washer, agreed that the two men had made a good start.

He chose a warm spring evening after most of the work was done to park in front of the white stucco house on Claiborne. He had carefully timed his visit. It was too late for dinner, too early for Belinda to be immersed in lesson plans. A brief call to Debby had assured him that Belinda was home.

She was sitting alone on the front gallery when he walked up the steps, almost as if she had been waiting for him. But she hadn't been waiting, because in the instant when she first realized who was there, her eyes grew wary and her back stiffened.

"Hi." He moved closer slowly, leaving a carefully calculated distance between them. He leaned against the gallery and rested his fingertips on the railing. "How have you been?"

"I'm not complaining."

"Of course not. That's not your way."

She got up, as if she were going inside. He gripped the railing to keep himself from lunging at her. "Don't go."

"I don't see any point in staying."

"I'd like it very much if you would."

She lowered herself back to the chair. His gaze darted down, just low enough to see if his son or daughter was making its presence known. Belinda was still slender, but, to his educated eye, her shape had grown lusher and more womanly. For a moment he imagined a better look. He had missed everything about Belinda, but the sweet glide of his hands over her warm flesh had been somewhere near the top of his list.

"I heard you were back in town," she said.

He riveted his gaze back on her face. "Did you?"

"I heard you got knocked around pretty bad in Selma."

He had gotten a chestful of tear gas and a crack on the skull that would have been deadly if one of the white marchers hadn't thrown himself in the policeman's path just before the club made contact. "Not as bad as some."

"Did you make it all the way to Montgomery?"

It had been the longest walk of Phillip's life. "I made it. But I didn't come here to talk about that. I have something I'd like you to see."

"I have to do plans for tomorrow. You know my evenings are busy."

"I know lots of things about you, Belinda. More than almost anyone, wouldn't you say?"

She had never been a woman who spent time on verbal games. "Debby told me that you know about the baby."

He nodded slowly. "I do."

"I don't want anything from you. You didn't want this to happen, and you don't have to do anything now that it has. I'll manage just fine."

"I have no doubt you will. You're resilient to a fault."

She stood again. He pushed himself away from the rail. "I think, under the circumstances, you can spare me a few minutes. Don't you?"

"What for?"

"I told you. I've got something to show you."

Her back was still straight, but she seemed less sure of herself. "Did you come here with some idea that you could buy me off?"

He frowned. "What?"

"I don't want your money, Phillip. I don't want it for myself, and I don't want it for my child. I take care of what's mine. I don't need your help, and I don't want you messing with us."

"Don't you?" He moved closer, cutting her off so that she would have to push past him to get to the front door. "What exactly is it that you don't want me messing with? You don't want me to be a father to my own kid?"

"Do you think that any father is better than none?"

Anger flared. "I'm not just any father. Who do you think I am? Some no-account bastard who doesn't live up to his responsibilities?"

"No!" She folded her arms. "You'll live up to them, all right, if I let you. But there won't be any joy in it. Don't you think this baby will know that? I was raised like that. My mama was so tired and so poor that every kid she had was just one more burden. She fed us what she could and made sure we had a place to sleep, but she never once looked at any of us with love! Most of us didn't come out of that family in one solid piece. And I won't have that for my baby. I won't!"

"Belinda..." He took a deep breath. He had understood the depth of her pride. He just hadn't understood the depth of her sorrow. "Sweet girl, come with me. Let me just show you something. Just this. Then you decide. I won't crowd you. But you have to come with me."

"I don't have to do anything!"

"Yes. You have to do this." He towered over her. She was not a woman to feel menaced by anyone, but she seemed to wilt. Not from his words or his proximity, but, he suspected, from her own revealing display of emotion.

"Then will you leave me alone?"

"There is no way I'm going to desert you or this baby. No matter what you do or say. But I'll help you work out a way to make my presence less painful, if that's what you want."

She considered. He thought she would refuse again, but she nodded at last. "What do you want to show me?"

"Come with me. It's a short drive. My car's out front."

They made the trip in silence. She gazed out her window, and he couldn't even see her profile. The drive was a chance to castigate himself over and over again for all the mistakes he had made—and to wonder if he was making another by bringing her here.

He parked in front of her old shotgun. "Let's take a walk."

"What for?"

"Because we're here, and that's what we came for." He got out and rounded the car to open her door. He held out his hand to help her from the car. She took it reluctantly and dropped it as soon as she was standing.

"Have you been back here since you moved?" he asked.

"No."

He took her arm and steered her to the sidewalk. "I've missed living in the neighborhood with you."

She didn't respond.

"I wake up in the mornings sometimes, and I hear the mockingbirds singing outside my window. I turn over, and I put out my arms to find you, but you're somewhere else."

"Don't."

"I'm just telling you what I'm thinking."

"Where are we going?"

He might have done a million things wrong in this life. He had certainly done a million things wrong with this woman. But he had done one thing right. He had picked exactly the right moment to show her the house. The sun was just setting, and the remaining light was saturated with color, a brash Mardi Gras display of violet and bronze. The house was painted white now, waiting for its final coat of color, but the light had transformed it into a shifting rainbow. The iron lace, black and glistening, stood out in sharp relief.

He faced Belinda and put his hands on her shoulders; then he turned her to face the house. "This is my house." He dropped his hands and waited.

She stared at the house, taking all of it in. It would never be one of the city's finest architectural gems. It wasn't a large house, or even an unusual one in a city where whimsy and artistic vision had constructed entire blocks worthy of their own fairy tales. It sat on a street that tourists would never visit, on a lot that was surrounded by plainer, shabbier homes. But tonight, it was a masterpiece of hope restored.

She turned back to him. "Your house?"

"Yes. Do you like what I've done with it so far?"

She didn't answer.

"Come see the inside."

"No."

"You said you'd come with me. You're not a woman who goes back on her word."

"Damn you."

The words were whispered. He felt them all the way to the bone, but he steeled himself. "Are you coming or not?"

She was coming. He saw it in her eyes. He turned and walked to the gate, and she followed. He pointed out everything he had done in a voice that didn't even sound like his. At the front door, he inserted his key and stepped inside. She stepped in behind him.

"Where's your furniture?"

"I don't have much yet." He took her through rooms, turning on floor lamps that he'd borrowed from Nicky and Jake for the nights when he worked late.

"There are three bedrooms up here," he said, when they were standing in the second floor hallway. He opened the closest door. "This is the smallest." He ushered her inside, but he leaned against the doorjamb to block an immediate retreat.

It was the only room where he'd had the painters do more than prime the walls. It was painted a soft buttercup yellow, and yellow-and-green curtains hung in the windows. A crib sat between them.

"I come here every night before I leave the house, and I imagine our baby in this crib. Light streams in through these windows in the morning. I can see the baby standing here, trying to catch sunbeams in a tiny little hand."

She crossed the room and stood by the crib; then she stroked one finger along the top railing. "What did you do this for, Phillip? Did you think it would change anything? That I'd think you had a change of heart?"

"You'll have to decide what to believe."

She came to stand in front of him. He didn't move. "I told you I didn't want anything. I don't want this house."

"I'm not offering it."

She lifted one regal brow in question.

"It's my house," he said. "I'm not giving it away. Not even to you. This is my home, and now that I've finally got a home, I plan to enjoy it for a lot of years."

She gave a humorless laugh. "Not your home, and not your city. Remember?"

"Not when I said that, maybe. But it's both now."

"Why? Guilt? You made a baby with me, and now you're trapped?"

"I made a baby with you, and now I'm a father. And it's not guilt I feel." He cupped her cheek with his hand. She turned her head, but his hand followed right along. "I love you, Belinda. I was just way too big a fool to understand what I was feeling. But I've loved you for a long, long time. I won't give you this house, but if you'll come and live here with me, I'll gladly share it."

She made a sound low in her throat.

He pulled her slowly forward. She resisted, and he gently urged. "Belinda..." He turned her head slowly toward his. "My clothes are hanging in that closet across the hall. I'd like to hang your clothes right next to mine. If you don't say yes, I'm going over to Claiborne and steal them, hangers and all."

"What makes you think I love you? What makes you think I want to live here and raise our child together?"

"Some things a man's just got to take on faith." He lowered his lips to hers and pulled her closer. It took her forever to yield. She came to him one inch at a time, proud and determined and everything he had ever needed in a woman.

She was as warm as he remembered, as generous with her body as she had always been with her heart. In all the weeks he had spent preparing for this moment, all the weeks when he had wondered if they still had a chance, he hadn't dared to recall exactly what it was like to hold her in his arms. Now he knew he had never forgotten.

He pulled her against him and backed into the hall. He reached behind him to turn a doorknob and pull her into their bedroom.

"Welcome home," he murmured against her lips. "You can furnish the rest of the house. But I furnished this."

She spared the room one quick look. The bed was wide and soft, and there was nothing else to see.

She turned back to him. A slow smile lit her face. "It'll do."

It was dark before they spoke again. She lay across his chest, her head perfectly molded to the hollow under his shoulder. The faint mound of her belly pressed against his hip. "I've got a story to tell you," he said.

"About Selma?"

"I'll tell you about the march later. All about it. This is something else."

"I'm listening," she said sleepily.

"It's about me. About who I am."

Much later, she stirred. Phillip had been silent for a while. She lifted her head so that he could see her face in the moonlight. Her eyes told him that she understood much more than he'd been able to put into words. "Are you going to tell your mother?"

"I think so. When the time is right."

"How are you going to know?"

"I won't know by myself. I thought maybe you'd help me decide."

She continued to stare at him. "Okay," she said at last. She nestled her head against his shoulder again and splayed her fingers over his chest. "You know I'll help if I can."

He thought that this was what marriage was going to be like. Bodies entwined and secrets shared. And a whole wide world to be part of together.

He stroked her hair until both of them fell asleep.

CHAPTER 33

"Rafe was thinking of you when he died," Phillip told Aurore.

She was noticeably more frail than when he had last seen her. She had remained perfectly still as he briefly related the story of Rafe's last hours to her. Her eyes were fixed on some point so distant that Phillip knew that it couldn't be inside the room.

"He told Nicky that she was the best of you both. And she is," he added.

"And she went to Paris from there." It wasn't really a question. Phillip guessed that Aurore knew the next part of the story in detail. But he outlined it anyway.

"After that night, Clarence Valentine hid her with friends for nearly a month, then he got her out of the country. He'd been offered a job at a club in Paris. Jazz was hot there, and so were American Negroes. He claimed Nicky was his granddaughter, and since most colored people were still born at home back then and didn't have birth certificates, it wasn't hard to get the authorities to believe him. Nicky says that Clarence was convinced her life was in danger because she had seen the men who killed her father. She took his name and lived the lie."

"Clarence must have been a good man."

"Nicky loved him like a grandfather."

Aurore turned to him. Her eyes glistened. "I thought your mother was dead, Phillip. It was so many years later when I discovered that she was still alive. I believed she was killed in the fire that was started that night."

"Had you been following her life in Chicago? Did you have someone watching her? Is that how you knew about the fire?"

"In a way." She took his hand. He didn't resist, but he was sharply aware of the contrasts. "My attorney located Rafe for me. You see, I had decided to join him there."

He stared at her.

"Yes." She nodded. "I had thought that when Rafe took Nicolette and left New Orleans, everything would end between us. But I was still connected to them. I woke every morning and thought only of what I'd lost. My life with Henry was a blasphemy. I tried to go on with it, but I couldn't, not while I knew there was something more waiting for me if I just had the courage to reach for it. So I wrote Rafe and asked him if he would have me. I was going to take Hugh and disappear, leave everything except my son behind. Gulf Coast. My marriage and the church. Everything. And once I made it safely to Chicago, I wanted Rafe to take us to France. We both spoke French fluently. I thought we could start over there as a family, that if we didn't find acceptance, we might find tolerance. I wrote him, and I begged him shamelessly to let me come. Then I waited."

"Did you ever receive an answer?"

She shook her head. "I don't know if he never received my letter, or if he just couldn't bring himself to tell me no. Not knowing has haunted me all my life. Spencer came to me two weeks after I mailed the letter, and he told me that Rafe had died in the riot. Spencer investigated thoroughly and discovered that your mother was never seen again after the fire that devastated the entire city block. There were bodies in the ruins that couldn't be identified...."

So many years later, and the tears were still in her voice.

Phillip sat holding Aurore's hand tightly. He wanted to comfort her, this woman who had made so many terrible mistakes. This woman. His grandmother.

"Wait..." He gripped her hand a little harder. "Mrs. Gerritsen..."

"You'll never find it in your heart to call me Aurore, will you?"

"My grandfather—" the title came easily to his lips now "—got your letter. I'm sure of it. And he was making plans to have you join him."

"What do you mean?"

Phillip thought carefully about Nicky's story. Her last encounter with her father had been so clear to her. She had held on to it the way that Rafe himself had held on to his memory of Marcelite and Angelle and the way they had died. And when Nicky had told him about the day of Rafe's death, she had told the story in detail.

"The night that my grandfather died, he told my mother that they were leaving Chicago for good, for a place where they could finally be happy. Then he asked her if she would trust him to do what was best for her. But he asked her in French. She told me that. It stood out for her, and she remembered it all those years, because after they left New Orleans they had only spoken English at home. I think my grandfather was preparing her for the trip to France. With you."

Her hand trembled. She looked away.

"And when he died, he told my mother that she was the best of both of you. He was thinking of you then, and what the two of you had created together."

They sat in silence. Finally, much later, she sighed; it was a long, broken sound. "I've had a long life."

"Yes, you have."

"Will you stay here in the city for a while longer, Phillip? Will you hear about the rest of it?"

"You haven't told me everything you want me to know?"

She turned to look at him. Her pale blue eyes glistened, but there were no tears on her cheeks. "I would like you to know everything. I would like to leave you that much."

"I'll be staying in the city."

She inclined her head. "Will you?"

"I'm getting married. By late summer I'll be a father."

She squeezed his hand. "We made a bargain, you and I. Will you honor it?"

He smiled. "You're some old lady, you know that?"

She smiled, too, and for a moment, he saw the young woman his grandfather had fallen in love with. "Rafe would have been proud of you," she whispered.

He leaned over and kissed her cheek. It was cool and soft against his lips. "I hope so, Aurore."

Turn the page for an excerpt from

RISING TIDES

by

Emilie Richards

the sequel to IRON LACE
Available January 2002

CHAPTER 1

September 1965

The young man Dawn Gerritsen picked up just outside New Orleans looked like a bum, but so did a lot of the students hitchhiking the world that summer. His hair wasn't clean, his clothes a marriage of beat poet and circus performer. To his credit he had neither the pasty complexion of a Beatles-mad Liverpudlian nor the California tan of a Beach Boy surfer. In the past year she had seen more than enough of both types making the grand tour of rock bands and European waves.

The hitchhiker's skin was freckled, and his eyes were pure Tupelo honey. Biloxi and Gulfport oozed from his throat, and the first time he had called her ma'am, she'd wanted to drag him to a sun-dappled levee and make him moan the word over and over until she knew, really knew, that she was back in the Deep South again.

She hadn't dragged him anywhere. She didn't even remember his name. She was too preoccupied for sex, and she wasn't looking for intimacy. After three formative years in Berkeley, California, she had given up on love, right along with patriotism, religion and happily-ever-afters. Her virginity had been an early casualty, a prize oddly devalued in California, like an ancient currency exchanged exclusively by collectors.

Luckily her hitchhiker didn't seem to be looking for intimacy, either. He seemed more interested in the food in her glove compartment and the needle on her speedometer. After her initial rush of sentiment, she almost forgot he was in the car until she arrived in Cut Off. Then she made the mistake of reaching past him to turn up the radio. It was twenty-five till the hour, and the news was just going over.

"And in other developments today, State Senator Ferris Lee Gerritsen, spokesman for Gulf Coast Shipping, an international company based in New Orleans, announced that the company will turn over a portion of its land holdings along the river to the city so that a park can be developed as a memorial to his parents, Henry and Aurore Gerritsen. Mrs. Gerritsen, granddaughter of the founder of Gulf Coast Shipping, passed away last week. Senator Gerritsen is the only living child of the couple. His brother, Father Hugh Gerritsen, was killed in a civil rights incident last year in Bonne Chance. It's widely believed the senator will run for governor in 1968."

Dawn retrieved her sunglasses from the dashboard and slipped them on, blowing her heavy bangs out of her eyes first. As she settled back against her seat she felt the warmth of a hand against her bare thigh. One quick glance and she saw that her hitchhiker was assessing her with the same look he had, until that moment, saved for her Moon Pies and Twinkies. Dawn knew what he saw. A long-limbed woman with artfully outlined blue eyes and an expression that refuted every refined feature that went with them. Also a possible fortune.

He smiled, and his hand inched higher. "Your name's Gerritsen, didn't you say? You related to him?"

"You're wasting your time," she said.

"I'm not busy doing anything else."

She pulled over to the side of the road. There was a light rain falling and a harder rain forecast, but that didn't change her mind. "Time to stick out your thumb again."

"Hey, come on. I can make the rest of the trip more fun than you can imagine."

"Sorry, but my imagination's bigger than anything you've got to offer."

Drawling curses, he reclaimed his hand and took his duffel bag out of the back. She pulled back on the road after the door slammed shut behind him.

She was no lonelier than she had been before, but after the news, and without the distraction of another person in the next seat, Dawn found herself thinking of her grandmother, exactly the thing she had tried to avoid by picking up the hitchhiker in the first place. This trip to Grand Isle had nothing to do with pleasure and everything to do with Aurore Le Danois Gerritsen. On her deathbed Aurore had decreed that her last will and testament be read at a gathering at the family summer cottage.

And the reading of the will was a command perfor- mance.

The last time Dawn had driven the route between New Orleans and Grand Isle, she'd only had her license for a year. South Louisiana was a constant negotiation between water and earth, and sometimes the final decision wasn't clear.

It had been clear to her that day. She had flown over the land and crawled over the water. Her grandmother had sat beside her, never once pointing out that one of the myriad drawbridges might flip them into murky Bayou Lafourche, or that some of the tiny towns along the way fed their coffers by catching the unwary in speed traps. She had chatted of this and that, and only later, when Aurore limped up the walk to the cottage, had Dawn realized that her right leg was stiff from flooring nonexistent gas and brake pedals.

The memory brought an unexpected lump to her throat. The news of her grandmother's death hadn't surprised her, but neither had she truly been prepared. How could she have known that a large chunk of her own identity would disappear when Aurore died? There were parts of Dawn's life that Aurore Gerritsen had held in her hands and sculpted with the genius of a Donatello. Now that she was gone, those parts no longer seemed to exist.

Some part of Dawn had disappeared at her uncle's death, too. Two deaths in less than two years. The only Gerritsens who had ever understood her were gone now. And who was left? Who would love her simply because she was Dawn, without judgment or emotional bribery?

There was too much to think about, and none of it good. She turned up the radio again and forced herself to sing along with Smokey Robinson and the Miracles.

An hour later she crossed the final bridge. Time ticked fifty seconds to the minute on the Gulf Coast. Grand Isle looked much as it had that day seven years before when she had temporarily crippled her grandmother. Little changed on the island unless forced by the hand of Mother Nature. The surf devoured and regurgitated the shoreline, winds uprooted trees and sent roofs spinning, but the people and their way of life stayed much the same.

Today there was wind, and the surf was angry, although that hadn't discouraged the hardcore anglers strung along the shoreline. A hurricane with the friendly name of Betsy was hovering off Florida, and although nobody really expected her to turn toward this part of Louisiana, if she did, the island residents would protect their homes, pack their cars and choose their retreats before the announcement to evacuate had ended.

Halfway across the length of Grand Isle she turned away from the Gulf. A new load of oyster shells had been dumped on the road to the Gerritsen cottage, but the road still showed fresh tire tracks. The cottage itself was like the island. Over the years Mother Nature had subtly altered it, but the changes only intensified its basic nature. Built of weathered cypress in the traditional Creole style and surrounded by tangles of oleander, jasmine and myrtle, it was as much a part of the landscape as the gnarled water oaks encircling it. Even the addition, designed by her grandmother, seemed to have been there forever.

Dawn wondered if her parents had already arrived. She hadn't called them from London or the New Orleans airport, sure that if she did, they would expect her to travel to Grand Isle with them. She had wanted this time to readjust slowly to Louisiana. She was twenty-three now, too old to be swallowed by her parents and everything they stood for, but she had needed these extra hours to fortify herself.

As she pulled up in front of the house she saw that a car was parked under one of the trees, a tan Karmann Ghia with a California license plate. She wondered who had come so far for the reading of her grandmother's will. Was there a Gerritsen, a Le Danois three times removed, who had always waited in the wings? It would be just like her grandmother to arrange surprises for this, the last event she had orchestrated.

Dawn parked her rented Pontiac under an oak beside the little convertible and pulled on her vinyl slicker and John Lennon brimmed cap to investigate. The top was up, but she peered through one of the rain-fogged windows. The car belonged to a man. The sunglasses on the dashboard looked like an aviator's goggles, and a wide-figured tie was draped over a briefcase in the back.

She clutched her slicker tighter around her. Mary Quant had designed it as protection against London's soft, cool rain. Now it trapped the Louisiana summer heat and melted against Dawn's thighs, but she didn't care. Her gaze had moved beyond the car, beyond the oleander and jasmine, to the wide front gallery. A man she had never expected to see again was leaning against a square pillar and watching her.

She was aware of rain splashing against the brim of her hat and running in streams across her boots, but she didn't move. She stood silently and wondered if she had ever really known her grandmother.

Ben Townsend stepped off the porch. He had no protection against the weather, Carnaby mod or otherwise. The rain dampened his Oxford cloth shirt and dark slacks, and turned his sunstreaked hair the color of antique brass. His clothes clung to a body that hadn't changed in the past year. Her eyes measured the span of his shoulders, the width of his waist and hips, the long stretch of his legs. Her expression didn't change as he approached. Repressing emotion was a skill she had cultivated since she'd seen him last. She called it survival.

"I guess you didn't expect me." He stopped a short distance from her, as if he had calculated to the inch exactly how close she would allow him to come.

"A masterpiece of understatement."

"I got a letter after your grandmother's death asking me to hear her will. That's why I'm here." He shoved his hands in his pockets. Dawn had seen him stand that way so many times, shoulders hunched, palms turned out, heels set firmly into the ground. The stance made him real, not a shadow from her memories.

"I'm surprised that you bothered." She rocked back on her heels, too, as if she were comfortable enough to stand under the dripping oak forever. "Expecting to find a story here?"

"I'm an editor now. I buy what other people write."

Dawn knew that, for the past year, Ben had worked for *Mother Lode,* a celebrated new magazine carving out its niche among California's liberal elite. She had read just one issue. *Mother Lode* obviously prized creativity, intellect and West Coast self-righteousness. She wasn't surprised Ben had moved quickly up its career ladder.

"Well, you always were good at pronouncing judgment," she said.

He hunched his shoulder another inch. "And you seem to have gotten better at it."

"I've gotten better at lots of things, but apparently not at understanding *Grandmère.* I can't figure out whether inviting you here was an attempt to force a lovers' reunion, or if she just had a twisted sense of humor."

"Do you really think your grandmother asked me here to hurt you?"

"You have another explanation?"

"Maybe it has something to do with Father Hugh."

As always, her uncle's name brought back a host of memories for Dawn. Some of them were like memories of Ben, too painful to probe, too painful to forget. Some of them were warm and wonderful, which made them painful, too. She had loved Hugh Gerritsen. She had loved him far more than Ben had ever believed.

She tossed back her hair. "I don't know why it should. Uncle Hugh's been dead a year."

"I know when he died, Dawn. I was there."

"That's right. And I wasn't. I think that was the subject of our last conversation."

That conversation had taken place a year before, too, but she remembered it as if Ben's words were still carving catacombs under her feet. She had been standing beside Ben's hospital bed, hours after her uncle's death. A nurse had come at the sound of raised voices, then scurried away without saying a word. Dawn could still remember the smell of lilies from an arrangement on a side table, the tasteless Martian green of gladiola sprays. A pleasant voice on a hallway intercom announced the end of visiting hours while Ben shouted questions and waited for answers that had never come.

"Did you know, Dawn? Did you know that your uncle was going to be gunned down like a common criminal? Did you know that a mob was on its way to that church to turn a good man into a saint and a martyr?"

"We didn't have a conversation," Ben said. "I did the talking. You ran without defending yourself."

She stood a little straighter. "I didn't have to prove anything to you then, and I still don't."

"Look, I'm staying," Ben said. "I don't know why I was invited, but I'm going to stay long enough to get some answers. Can we be civil to each other?"

"You're a Louisiana boy. You know hospitality's a tradition in this part of the world. I'll do my part to live up to it."

Dawn studied him for another moment. His hair was longer than it had been a year ago, as if he had made the psychological transition from Boston, where he had worked on the *Globe,* to San Francisco. He wore glasses now, wire-framed and self-important. He no longer looked too young to have answers to all the world's problems. He looked his full twenty-seven years, like a man who had found his place in the world and never intended to relinquish it.

Her father was also a man who radiated confidence and purpose. Dawn wondered what would happen when Ferris Lee Gerritsen discovered that Ben Townsend had received an invitation to Grand Isle.

Ben waited until her gaze drifted back to his. "I'm not going to push myself on you."

"Oh, don't worry about me. Nobody pushes anything on me these days. And nobody puts anything over. Stay if you want. But don't stay because you want to finish old conversations."

"Maybe there'll be some new conversations worth finishing."

"I don't know about what."

"I'm guessing your grandmother did," he said.

She shrugged, then turned back to her car for her luggage, making a point of dismissing him. By the time she straightened, Ben was no longer beside her. She watched as he walked down the oyster shell drive, glad she didn't have to pretend to be casual for even a moment longer.

In the distance, thunder exploded with renewed vigor, and the ground at Dawn's feet seemed to ripple in response. The sultry island air was charged with the familiar smells of ozone and decay, and, for her, they were the nostalgic smells of childhood.

The summers here had been a time to bask in her grandmother's love, and there had been no expectations. The sun had been too hot, the occasional breeze too enticing. She had done nothing of consequence on this island except grow up. But Aurore's pride in her had been the solid ground upon which Dawn had built the best part of herself.

How proud had Aurore been before she died, and exactly what had she known? Had she known that Dawn still loved her? That despite Dawn's flight after Hugh Gerritsen's death, she had still mourned the loss of her family?

That falling in love with the man who had just turned his back on her had not been the same as declaring sides in a war Dawn had never understood anyway?

Most important of all, had *Grandmère* understood that even though Dawn had crossed an ocean to escape, she had never really been able to break free of any of the people that she loved?